RANGE OF GHOSTS

RANGE
OF
GHOSTS

ELIZABETH BEAR

A Tom Doherty Associates Book

NEW YORK

RANGE OF GHOSTS

Copyright © 2012 by Elizabeth Bear

Map by Ellisa Mitchell

A Tor Book
Published by Tom Doherty Associates, LLC
175 Fifth Avenue
New York, NY 10010

www.tor-forge.com

Tor® is a registered trademark of Tom Doherty Associates, LLC.

Library of Congress Cataloging-in-Publication Data

Bear, Elizabeth.
    Range of ghosts / Elizabeth Bear.—1st ed.
        p. cm.
    ISBN 978-0-7653-2754-3
    1. Civil war—Fiction.   2. Alliances—Fiction.   3. Magic—
Fiction.   I. Title.
    PS3602.E2475R36 2012
    813'.6—dc23

                                                    2011025171

First Edition: March 2012

Printed in the United States of America

0 9 8 7 6 5 4 3 2 1

This book is for Sunil Robert and
Naveen Alexander Srinivasan Shipman,
great-great-great-(. . .)grandsons of Genghis Khan.

ACKNOWLEDGMENTS

Thank you to Celia Marsh, who names horses after pastry; Robert Couture and Teresa Nielsen Hayden, my *harissa*-pushing friends; my own great-grandfather the Cossack, whom I never met but through whom I inherited the steppes history I borrowed from so liberally— and some of whose family myth I have lifted for Temur (There's a Russian saying: Поскобли немножко русского и скажется та-тарин—"Scratch a Russian and you'll find a Tatar"); my father, Steve Wishnevsky, my source for that legend; my amazing editor, Beth Meacham, to whom I owe everything that's right about horses in this book; my equally amazing agent, Jennifer Jackson, who continues to believe in me; a person in Kazakhstan who prefers to remain nameless, who read of my book-writing adventures on the Internet and volunteered with beautiful photos and descriptions of the local landscape; and to Sarah Monette, Michael Curry, Amanda Downum, Kat Tanaka Okopnik, and Jodi Meadows, all of whom read this manuscript in draft.

STEPPES

KHAGANATE

°QARASH

ther River

RANGE   OF   GHOSTS

°QESHQER
(KASHE)

RED
STONE   SKY
ALT   RIVER

ESERT   The   island-in-the-mists

COLD FIRE   TSAREPHETH

°

Steles   TSARETHI

of   RASAN
EMPIRE   SONG

RASA   °

Range of Ghosts

1

RAGGED VULTURES SPIRALED UP A CHERRY SKY. THEIR SOOTY WINGS SO thick against the sunset could have been the column of ash from a volcano, the pall of smoke from a tremendous fire. Except the fire was a day's hard ride east—away over the flats of the steppe, a broad smudge fading into blue twilight as the sun descended in the west.

Beyond the horizon, a city lay burning.

Having once turned his back on smoke and sunset alike, Temur kept walking. Or lurching. His bowlegged gait bore witness to more hours of his life spent astride than afoot, but no lean, long-necked pony bore him now. His good dun mare, with her coat that gleamed like gold-backed mirrors in the sun, had been cut from under him. The steppe was scattered in all directions with the corpses of others, duns and bays and blacks and grays. He had not found a living horse that he could catch or convince to carry him.

He walked because he could not bear to fall. Not here, not on this red earth. Not here among so many he had fought with and fought against—clansmen, tribesmen, hereditary enemies.

He had delighted in this. He had thought it glorious.

There was no glory in it when the men you killed were the

husbands of your sisters, the sons of your uncles. There was nothing to be won when you fought against those with whom you should have shared a shield and a fireside. He could not find the fire of battle fever within himself. The ember had burned to a husk, and Temur was cold, and weary, and the lonely sorrow ran down his bones with an ache like cold.

Perhaps he was a ghost. For weren't ghosts cold and hungry? Didn't they crave the warmth and blood of the quick? The wound that gaped across Temur's throat *should* have been his death. When it felled him, he'd had no doubt he was dying. Because of it—so obviously fatal, except that he had not died of it—nobody had thrust a second blade between his ribs or paunched him like a rabbit to make sure.

He had been left to lie among the others, all the others—his brother Qulan's men and the men of his uncle Qori Buqa: the defenders of one man's claim on Qarash and the partisans of the one who had come to dispute it—on the hard late-winter ground, bait for vultures who could not be bothered to hop from their feasts when he staggered close.

One vulture extended a char-colored head and hissed, wings broad as a pony blanket mantled over a crusting expanse of liver. The soot-black birds were foul and sacred. Tangled winter-crisp grass pulling at his ankles, Temur staggered wide.

But if Temur was a ghost, where were all the others? He should have been surrounded by an army of the dead, all waiting for the hallowed kindness of the carrion crows and of the vultures. *Please. Just let me get away from all these dead men.*

His long quilted coat was rust-stained with blood—much of it his own, from that temporary dying. It slid stickily against the thick, tight-woven silk of his undershirt, which in turn slid stickily against his skin. The fingers of his left hand cramped where they pinched flesh together along the edges of the long, perfect slice stretching from his ear to his collarbone.

The wound that had saved his life still oozed. As the sun lowered in the sky and the cold came on, blood froze across his knuckles. He stumbled between bodies still.

The fingers of his right hand were cramped also, clutching a bow. One of the bow's laminated limbs was sword-notched to uselessness. The whole thing curled back on itself, its horsehair string cut. Temur used it as a walking stick, feeling it bend and spring under his weight with each step. He was beyond suffering shame for misusing a weapon.

The Old Khagan—the Khan of Khans, Temur's uncle Mongke, son of the Great Khagan Temusan, whose enemies called him Terrible—was dead. This war was waged by Mongke's would-be heirs, Qulan and Qori Buqa. Soon one of them would rise to take Mongke Khagan's place—as Mongke Khagan had at the death of his own father—or the Khaganate would fall.

Temur, still stumbling through a battlefield sown heavy with dead mares and dead men after half a day walking, did not know if either his brother or his uncle had survived the day. Perhaps the Khaganate had fallen already.

Walk. Keep walking.

But it was not possible. His numb legs failed him. His knees buckled. He sagged to the ground as the sun sagged behind the horizon.

The charnel field had to end somewhere, though with darkness falling it seemed to stretch as vast as the steppe itself. Perhaps in the morning he would find the end of the dead. In the morning, he would have the strength to keep walking.

If he did not die in the night.

The smell of blood turned chill and thin in the cold. He hoped for a nearby corpse with unpillaged food and blankets and water. And perhaps a bow that would shoot. The sheer quantity of the dead was in his favor, for who could rob so many? These thoughts came to him hazily, disconnected. Without desire. They were merely the instincts of survival.

More than anything, he wanted to keep walking.

In the morning, he promised himself, he would turn south. South lay the mountains. He had ridden that far every summer of his young life that had not been spent campaigning. The wars in the borderlands of his grandfather's empire had sometimes kept him from joining those driving the herds to his people's summer ranges—where wet narrow valleys twisted among the stark gray slopes of the Steles of the Sky, where spring-shorn sheep grazed on rich pasturage across the green curves of foothills. But he had done it often enough.

He would go south, away from the grasslands, perhaps even through the mountains called the Range of Ghosts to the Celadon Highway city of Qeshqer. Away from the dead.

Qeshqer had been a Rasan city before Temur's grandfather Temusan conquered it. Temur might find work there as a guard or mercenary. He might find sanctuary.

He was not dead. He might not die. When his throat scabbed he could capture some horses, some cattle. Something to live on.

There would be others alive, and they too would be walking south. Some of them might be Temur's kinsmen, but that could not be helped. He'd deal with that when it happened. If he could find horses, Temur could make the journey of nine hundred *yart* in eight hands of days. On foot, he did not care to think how long he might be walking.

If Qulan was dead, if Qori Buqa could not consolidate his claim, the Khaganate was broken—and if he could, it held no refuge for Temur now. Qarash with its walled marketplaces, its caravanserais, its surrounding encampments of white-houses—the round, felt-walled dwellings Temur's people moved from camp to camp throughout the year—had fallen. Temur was bereft of brothers, of stock, of allies.

To the south lay survival, or at least the hope of it.

TEMUR DID NOT TRUST HIS WOUND TO HOLD ITS SCAB IF HE LAY FLAT, and given its location, there was a limit to how tightly he could bind it. But once the long twilight failed, he knew he must rest. And he must have warmth. Here on the border between winter and spring, the nights could still grow killing cold. Blowing snow snaked over trampled grass, drifting against the windward sides of dead men and dead horses.

Temur would take his rest sitting. He propped the coil of his broken bow in the lee of the corpse of a horse, not yet bloating because of the cold. Tottering, muddy-headed with exhaustion, he scavenged until he could bolster himself with salvaged bedrolls, sheepskins, and blankets rolled tightly in leather straps.

He should build a fire to hold off the cold and the scavengers, but the world wobbled around him. Maybe the wild cats, wolves, and foxes would be satisfied with the already-dead. There was prey that would not fight back. And if any of the great steppe cats, big as horses, came in the night—well, there was little he could do. He had not the strength to draw a bow, even if he had a good one.

No hunger moved him, but Temur slit the belly of a war-butchered mare and dug with blood-soaked hands in still-warm offal until he found the liver. Reddened anew to the shoulders, he carved soft meat in strips and slurped them one by one, hand pressed over his wound with each wary swallow. Blood to replace blood.

He would need it.

There was no preserving the meat to carry. He ate until his belly spasmed and threw the rest as far away as he could. He couldn't do anything about the reek of blood, but as he'd already been covered in his own, it seemed insignificant.

Crammed to sickness, Temur folded a sweat-and-blood-stiff saddle blanket double and used it as a pad, then leaned back. The dead horse was a chill, stiff hulk against his spine, more a boulder than an animal. The crusted blanket was not much comfort, but at least it was still too cold for insects. He couldn't sleep and brush flies from his wound. If maggots got in it, well, they would keep the poison of rot from his blood, but a quick death might be better.

He heard snarls in the last indigo glow of evening, when stars had begun to gleam, one by one, in the southern sky. Having been right about the scavengers made it no easier to listen to their quarrels, for he knew what they quarreled over. There was some meat the sacred vultures would not claim.

He knew it was unworthy. It was a dishonor to his family duty to his uncle. But somewhere in the darkness, he hoped a wolf gnawed the corpse of Qori Buqa.

TEMUR WAITED FOR MOONRISE. THE DARKNESS AFTER SUNSET WAS THE bleakest he had known, but what the eventual, silvery light revealed was worse. Not just the brutal shadows slipping from one corpse to the next, gorging on rich organ meats, but the sources of the light.

He tried not to count the moons as they rose but could not help himself. No bigger than Temur's smallest fingernail, each floated up the night like a reflection on dark water. One, two. A dozen. Fifteen. Thirty. Thirty-one. A scatter of hammered sequins in the veil the Eternal Sky drew across himself to become Mother Night.

Among them, no matter how he strained his eyes, he did not find the moon he most wished to see—the Roan Moon of his elder brother Qulan, with its dappled pattern of steel and silver.

Temur should have died.

He had not been sworn to die with Qulan, like his brother's oath-band had—as Qulan's heir, that would have been a foolish vow to take—but he knew his own battle fury, and the only reason he lived was because his wounds had incapacitated him.

If he never saw blood again . . . he would be happy to claim he did not mind it.

Before the death of Mongke Khagan, there had been over a hundred moons. One for Mongke Khagan himself and one for each son and each grandson of his loins, and every living son and grandson and great-grandson of the Great Khagan Temusan as well—at least those born while the Great Khagan lived and reigned.

Every night since the war began, Temur had meant to keep himself from counting. And every night since, he had failed, and there had been fewer moons than the night before. Temur had not even the comfort of Qori Buqa's death, for there gleamed his uncle's Ghost Moon, pale and unblemished as the hide of a ghost-bay mare, shimmering brighter among the others.

And there was Temur's as well, a steely shadow against the indigo sky. The Iron Moon matched his name, rust and pale streaks marking its flanks. Anyone who had prayed his death—as he had prayed Qori Buqa's—would know those prayers come to naught. At least his mother, Ashra, would have the comfort of knowing he lived . . . if she did.

Which was unlikely, unless she had made it out of Qarash before Qori Buqa's men made it in. If Qori Buqa lived, Temur's enemies lived. Wherever Temur walked, if his clan and name were known, he might bring death—death on those who helped him, and death on himself.

This—this was how empires ended. With the flitting of wild dogs in the dark and a caravan of moons going dark one by one.

Temur laid his knife upon his thigh. He drew blankets and a fleece over himself and gingerly let his head rest against the dead horse's flank. The stretching ache of his belly made a welcome distraction from the throb of his wound.

He closed his eyes. Between the snarls of scavengers, he dozed.

The skies broke about the gray stones of high Ala-Din. The ancient fortress breached them as a headland breaches sea, rising above a battered desert landscape on an angled promontory of wind-eroded sandstone.

Ala-Din meant "the Rock." Its age was such that it did not need a complicated name. Its back was guarded by a gravel slope overhung by the face of the escarpment. On the front, the cliff face swept up three hundred feet to its summit, there crowned by crenellated battlements and a cluster of five towers like the fingers of a sharply bent hand.

Mukhtar ai-Idoj, al-Sepehr of the Rock, crouched atop the lowest and broadest of them, his back to the familiar east-setting sun of the Uthman Caliphate. Farther east, he knew, the strange pale sun of the Qersnyk tribes was long fallen, their queer hermaphroditic godling undergoing some mystic transformation to rise again as the face of the night. Farther east, heathen men were dying in useful legions, soaking the earth with their unshriven blood.

And that concerned him. But not as much as the immediate blood in which he bathed his own hands now.

Twin girls no older than his youngest daughter lay on the table before him, bound face to face, their throats slit with one blow. It was their blood that flowed down the gutter in the table to fall across his hands and over the sawn halves of a quartz geode he cupped together, reddening them even more than the sun reddened his sand-colored robes.

He stayed there, hands outstretched, trembling slightly with the effort of a strenuous pose, until the blood dripped to a halt. He straightened with the stiffness of a man who feels his years in his knees and spine, and with sure hands broke the geode apart. Strings of half-clotted blood stretched between its parts.

He was not alone on the roof. Behind him, a slender man waited, hands thrust inside the sleeves of his loose desert robe. Two blades, one greater and one lesser, were thrust through his indigo sash beside a pair of chased matchlock pistols. The powder horn hung beside his water skin. An indigo veil wound about his face matched the sash. Only his eyes and the leathery squint lines that framed them showed, but the color of his irises was too striking to be mistaken for many others—a dark ring around variegated hazel, chips of green and brown, a single dark spot at the bottom of the left one.

Al-Sepehr had only seen one other set of eyes like them. They were the eyes of this man's sister.

"Shahruz," he said, and held out one half of the stone.

Shahruz drew a naked hand from his sleeve and accepted the gory thing with no evidence of squeamishness. It was not yet dry. "How long will it last?"

"A little while," he said. "Perhaps ten uses. Perhaps fifteen. It all

depends on the strength of the vessels." The girls, their bodies too
warmed by the stone and the sun to be cooling yet. "When you use
it, remember what was sacrificed."

"I will," said Shahruz. He made the stone vanish into his sleeve,
then bowed three times to al-Sepehr. The obeisance was in honor of
Sepehr and the Scholar-God, not the office of al-Sepehr, but al-
Sepehr accepted it in their stead.

Shahruz nodded in the direction of the dead girls. "Was that
necessary? Saadet——"

"I cannot be with your sister always." Al-Sepehr let himself
smile, feeling the desert wind dry his lips. "My wives would not like
it. And I will not send you into the den of a Qersnyk pretender
without a means of contacting me directly. All I ask is that you be
sparing of it, because we will need it as well as a conduit for magic."

Shahruz hesitated, the movement of his grimace visible beneath
his veil. "Are we dogs, al-Sepehr," he asked finally, reluctantly, "to
hunt at the command of a pagan Qersnyk?"

Al-Sepehr cut the air impatiently. "We are jackals, to turn the
wars of others to our own advantage. If Qori Buqa wants to wage war
on his cousins, then why should we not benefit? When we are done,
not a kingdom, caliphate, or principality from Song to Messaline will
be at peace—until we put *our* peace upon them. Go now. Ride the
wind as far as the borderlands, then send it home to me once you
have procured horses and men."

"Master," Shahruz said, and turned crisply on the ball of his
foot before striding away.

When his footsteps had descended the stair, al-Sepehr turned
away. He set his half of the stone aside and bathed his hands in sun-
hot water, scrubbing under the nails with a brush and laving them
with soap to the elbow. When he was done, no trace of blood could
be seen and the sky was cooling.

He reached into his own sleeve and drew forth a silk pouch, white
except where rust-brown speckled it. From its depths, he shook out

another hollow stone. The patina of blood on this one was thin; sparkles of citrine yellow showed through where it had flaked away from crystal faces.

Al-Sepehr cupped his hands around it and regarded it steadily until the air above it shimmered and a long, eastern face with a fierce narrow moustache and drooping eyes regarded him.

"Khan," al-Sepehr said.

"Al-Sepehr," the Qersnyk replied.

The stone cooled against al-Sepehr's palm. "I send you one of my finest killers. You will make use of him to secure your throne. Then all will call you Khagan, Qori Buqa."

"Thank you." The son of the Old Khagan smiled, his moustache quivering. "There is a moon I would yet see out of the sky. Re Temur escaped the fall of Qarash."

"No trouble," al-Sepehr said, as the beat of mighty wings filled the evening air. "We will see to it. For your glory, Khan."

2

THE *WHUFF* OF SOFT BREATH ACROSS TEMUR'S CHEEK AWAKENED HIM. HIS hand clenched on the knife hilt; he nearly drove the forged blade into his own belly before he realized that what stood over him, filthy in the morning light, was a liver-bay mare whose sparse mane was still braided down between her eyes with red war ribbons.

She *whuff*ed again, not startled by his sudden movement, and resumed lipping the fleece that Temur huddled under. She was sucking up the frost from his breath, which hoared his blankets. When Temur pushed himself out of their warmth, cold water ran down his back—melted by the residual heat seeping from the bulk of the dead horse. Every movement ripped pain through the tight muscles of his neck and along his spine. The edges of his wound were hot and thick, stiff as unstretched leather. He pressed his left hand over the cloth he'd used to cover it and felt the wetness of lymph and blood, but there was no reek of pus. The wound was still seeping.

The mare must have been numb to the smell of blood by then. As Temur rose, she ambled a few steps off and paused, head hanging, cropping winter-dry grasses where she could find a patch untrampled. Her tack was complete, though her reins had been broken and her quilted chest armor swung from a tangle of straps, whacking her brown-and-black-striped forelegs with each step. Temur could see the dings and abrasions on her knees and cannons where the furniture had struck her.

That was why she was still here, among all the dead. She was effectively hobbled.

The knife was in his hand. He dragged a worn whetstone from the slash pocket in his quilted trousers and scoured the blade to hone it. The barding had to come off, and he didn't think the mare would stand still long enough for him to release the knots and buckles— assuming his hands were strong enough for the work. And assuming she didn't knock him over.

She stood steady as the gray morning when he came up to her, humming low in his throat. *I'm here*, the noise said. *I'm not sneaking. I'm a friend.*

When he got close enough, he just stood beside her for a moment, speaking nonsense. He told her she was pretty and asked her name. Her ears flicked, but she didn't lift her nose from the grass. He didn't recognize the pattern of triangular nicks cut from their edges— without a shaman-rememberer, there was no way for him to know to whom she might have belonged. She had a good look about her, though—a short straight back, sharp angles, and dense muscles under the hide. She was thin and long-boned after the manner of steppe ponies, not fat with muscle and thick-necked like Song horses.

Gently, Temur slipped the blade beneath a tangle of her harness, edge out, and began to saw the leather. It parted well enough: In a few breaths he had the strap severed. She stood for it, nonchalant, and the next as well. After that, he could slide what remained down her skinny neck one-handed, saving the injured side, and let her shake it off her own ears.

She didn't like that, snorting and backing away precipitously until her hind hooves thumped on a dead man's outflung arm and she startled forward again. Temur opened his arms gently and tried to reach her with his voice. "Hush, now, dumpling, little brave one. It's all right. Everything's going to be fine now."

It was a good thing everything on the steppe smelled like blood, because she didn't shy from the reek all over him when she picked her way forward. She shoved her nose into his chest, not too hard. Her unchipped hooves, planted stubbornly in the grass, were banded tawny and black. Her eyes were large and clear. Temur felt tears spring up in his own as she pushed him again and whickered.

"I haven't got any," he said. "If I had, I would have eaten it."

She still looked at him expectantly, turning her head aside the better to see him out of one egg-sized eye. He scowled, then when she would not stop staring, he glanced around at the dead. "What am I saying? We can find you all the sweets you want, dumpling, can't we?"

SWEETS—SEEDS POUNDED WITH HONEY AND MUTTON FAT—REINS, A saddlebag's worth of clothing that wasn't soaked in blood or piss: All this and more—food, a cooking pot, spare bowstrings, and fresh arrows, though their weights and shaft lengths varied, so he hoped he would not be shooting for prizes before he had a chance to learn the peculiarities of each. He also found a hoof pick and a brush, a bow that wasn't notched to uselessness, and an iron hatchet. He kept the blankets and fleeces he'd salvaged the night before, rolling them as tightly as he could one-handed. He improvised a sling for the left arm, because the weight of it dragged at his wound and pulled the edges open. Better to go easy and be one-handed for a while than to compound his injury, he thought, though it was harder to apply the wisdom to himself than it would have been to a mount.

He kept calling the mare "Dumpling"—*Bansh*—and soon it became obvious that she had accepted it as her name. She pricked her ears every time he said it. She had wounds, too, which he found when he brushed the blood and grime from her sides. A long shallow slash across her ribs was the worst of it. The blow could have split her open, and Temur flinched in retroactive sympathy as he cleaned it. Her girth or her master's leg was all that had saved her.

She let him tend it, though, and begged for more mutton-fat sweets when he was done. She pushed her soft, mottled nose into his pockets and licked his quilted trousers while he worked, and he hadn't the heart to shove her head away. He sang to her—the clean-healing song and the sound-feet song—and she pricked her ears and huffed sweet breath across his mouth.

They might have been the only two things living for a hundred *yart*, except the carrion beasts.

When Bansh was clean, Temur picketed her in the least devastated grass he could find and went to butcher another horse. The livers were no good now, after a night and a day and a half, but in the cold the meat hadn't turned yet, and he took as much of a haunch as he could eat before it went bad. He wrapped it well in oiled hides so the smell wouldn't bother the mare, then he tied it on behind her saddle.

Mounting one-handed, weak as he was, was no mean feat, and Temur considered himself lucky that Bansh stood for him as sturdily as a practice block. He was glad his grandfather Temusan couldn't see him as he hauled himself into one iron stirrup, belly down across the saddle. With sharp agony pulling at his neck and shoulder, he struggled upright, stepped through the gap between the pommel and cantle, and found the other stirrup before the mare moved off.

She stayed to a walk, picking her way among the stinking bodies, ears moving unhappily as her head swung from one side to another. It was just as well, Temur thought; he wasn't sure he could sit a trot without falling, and if he fell he was sure to reopen his wound. While many a Qersnyk warrior died in a tumble from horseback— the Great Khagan himself had been killed so, leading an army at the age of eighty-two—Temur couldn't bear the irony of doing it now.

So he let the mare have her head, guiding her only in that he kept them pointed toward the south, where the Range of Ghosts was not yet even a smoky purple smudge on the horizon.

✳   ✳   ✳

ANOTHER NIGHT PASSED BEFORE THEY LEFT THE DEAD BEHIND, AND BY then they had begun to overtake the living. Temur had not been alone in his determination to reach the mountains. A straggling, numb, war-shocked column of refugees struggled south, moving like migrating birds—each individual but all of one goal, so the whole assembly gave the illusion of unity. In numbers, at least, there was some semblance of safety from the predators that stalked their margins—wolves and the massive steppe lion—waiting for twilight when the archers of the defenders would have to seek their targets half blind.

At first he feared he might be recognized—by warriors or by the women and children hauling their salvaged goods in carts. But either they did not know him or they were too focused on the business of survival to care, or perhaps some were of the faction that would have preferred his brother Qulan to Qori Buqa. So he and Bansh moved among them untroubled.

The vultures stayed with them. Most of the refugees were wounded or exhausted, and when they fell, the sacred birds would dine on their flesh and carry their spirits into the Eternal Sky.

Temur mourned his brother and lost track of the days. He should have fought on in Qulan's stead. He should have rallied the men. . . .

Except that was foolish. He might have spent half his life in army camps, but he was barely a man, and Qulan had been older and experienced. Qulan, Temur thought, would have known what to do. Temur could just get more people killed.

Temur had no sense of time passing, except in watching the slow attrition of the moons, the heavier darkness each night as the Eternal Sky noted the passing of another of his uncles or cousins. The days passed in hands with little variation, except that food became scarcer and scantier. Short rations impeded his healing, but eventually his wound scabbed and granulated, though he could tell from touching it that it would remain terrible to the sight for as long as he lived. The scar stiffened, making it difficult to turn his head to the right.

Each day he and Bansh moved until they could move no longer, and each evening he slept while she grazed, until moonrise brightened the night and they could move again. They rested again between moonset and morning. In summer, they would have conserved water by sleeping away the high heat of the day, but in winter the refugees kept moving—which meant less sleep and less rest for everyone.

The steppe stretched away on every side, trackless and unfeatured, spotted with the shapes of walking or riding men, of women with oxen pulling their carts, of boys and girls with no more than four summers riding scout.

His people. The Khaganate might have fallen, or Qori Buqa might be gathering his scattered allies and consolidating power. News was fragmentary and not easy to come by. But the Qersnyk people endured, as they always had. As they would whether there was to be a succession or whether the empire would crumble back into the scattered tribes and clans it had been before the Great Khagan conquered the world in every direction as far as a horse could run.

Whatever became of them, Temur thought, they were his people. His brothers and sisters. And he owed to them any hope of survival he could find.

The army of refugees swelled around him. After a few nights, there were songs by the dry-dung fires—and ceremonies to commend the inevitable dead to the Eternal Sky. After a hand of days or so, Temur took up his new bow to bring food back to those fires—marmots, mostly, and the odd *zeren* gazelle, because he could not range widely enough or draw the bow strongly enough to bring down larger game. But whatever he brought was accepted gratefully, and in return the others shared with him what they had—dumplings, clarified mutton fat, salted butter, *airag*—fermented mare's milk—from the bags that hung over the flanks of the cattle when the herds were on the move.

Those sheep and horses, the goats and oxen among the refugees were too precious to slaughter for food. They would be the foundation of the herds that meant next winter's survival.

Temur was welcomed there, and he was relieved that when he

failed to provide his clan name, no one inquired as to his family. That kind of reticence would have been a rare thing among his people before the fall of Qarash, for the steppe folk navigated their world through a complex and comforting system of clan and family allegiances.

But in the refugee caravan, no one spoke uninvited of clan or family outside—or the allegiances that had brought them all here. The potential that a new friend should prove an old enemy was more than anyone could bear.

THE DAYS WARMED, WHICH WAS BOTH GOOD—THE GREENING GRASS would help feed hungry livestock—and bad, in that one could no longer sweep up snow to boil for water, but must ration one's self between the shallow lakes that dotted the steppe. One morning four hands of days after the fall of Qarash, Temur roused himself in the long gray gloaming. He stood out of dew-damp bedclothes and pulled on the boots he'd tucked under a corner of the horsehide to keep them dry. Bansh cropped grass nearby. She'd grown leaner, as had Temur.

He offered her dried slices of persimmon as a bribe to slip the bit between her teeth; she lipped them up, whiskers brushing his palm, and stood patiently while he tacked her and rolled up his bedding. He was securing the bedroll behind his saddle when the *shush* and *thump* of hooves across steppe grass drew his attention.

He might have reached for his knife, but whoever rode toward him was making no attempt at stealth.

He looked up to see a girl about his own age, seventeen or eighteen winters behind her, seated astride a rangy rose-gray filly with the long ears and sparse mane of steppe blood. The young horse curvetted, snorting—showing off—and Bansh flicked her own ears as if to show herself unimpressed by the strenuous affectations of youth. The girl's nervousness, Temur judged, was communicating itself to her mount.

She was old to be unmarried and still riding astride rather than proudly in possession of her own cart and household. But not every married woman gave up horses, especially not when there was a need for swift travel.

"Hail," the girl said. "Are you Temur?" Long black hair, braided into ropes, protruded from under the wings of her hood. She was plump under her quilted breeches despite the rigors of travel, sloe-eyed, small-nosed between broad sweeps of cheek. Pretty.

Temur put a hand on Bansh's shoulder and felt the liver-bay mare lean into it. He thought of the moons falling out of the sky every few days. He could be in Bansh's saddle in an instant if he must. But it was just a girl, and she had not asked his clan. Just his given name.

He opened his mouth to answer and was struck by a sudden wave of grief. He was alone. Whatever family he had left might as cheerfully kill him as welcome him. And if his mother was dead, there was no one alive to speak his true name when he died, no one to whisper it to his wife when he married, no one to speak it in the ears of his mares so they might find him anywhere.

He was alone. He swallowed and said, "I am."

"I'm Tsareg Edene." *She* gave up her clan name without a thought. It was a good name, old and honorable, of a clan not prone to getting into other people's fights. She looked down, pressing a palm flat against one of the broad cheeks that might have been inflamed with embarrassment.

Temur strove to make it easier on her. He kept his gaze down, on her mare's fine-tipped silver ears rather than on the girl herself. The young horse was striking; she would eventually fade to the blistering, iridescent silver that gray steppe horses obtained, but for now she was the color of snow underneath and up the sides of her body, her head the color of new-hammered silver, her flanks and shoulders bright copper decorated with scalloped dapples of reddish silver.

The horse returned his examination boldly. The girl might not be accustomed to talking to strangers, but she was too stubborn to let modesty silence her. "My grandmother's mother, Tsareg Altantsetseg, wishes to know if you will eat with us. She boiled a lamb overnight."

Temur hesitated. Breakfasting on lamb in this time of need was near unto an offer of adoption, and he knew what brought it on—men of fighting and marrying age were scarce among the refugees. He'd heard of Tsareg Altantsetseg: She was a good part of the reason for her clan's reputation for reserve and good sense. If she was seeking his favor in order to protect her daughters—well, it did not mean she knew his former family. It meant only that he'd made a good display of himself among the refugee band, and she knew he was a strong provider.

And she'd sent a pretty, marriageable girl to make the offer, which was a coded message as well. Or would be, until he had to tell her that there was no one to share his true name with her, or with any potential wife.

Bansh nudged him impatiently.

"I will come," he said, and swung into the saddle, seating both feet in the iron stirrups. He let the reins hang casually and chirruped to Bansh as Edene swung her own mare around.

It was a brief ride, brief enough so Temur understood that Edene had only ridden for the confidence of speaking from horseback. When she showed him where to dismount and picket Bansh, he held his tongue. There was no good in pointing out to someone that you had noticed their insecurities. Instead, he gave his mare an extra rub across the poll and followed Edene toward the fire.

Most of the refugees had lost their clans and families, though a surprising number reunited on the road, and this seemed to be one of them. The clan hadn't set up a white-house, but there were two or three skin tents in evidence and more than one cart. A fire licked across coals in the center of the little grouping, and the same light breeze blew skeins of a late snow through tramped grass. A woman sat bundled in skins before the fire, surrounded by younger women and a few boys. Edene led Temur directly toward her.

Tsareg Altantsetseg was diminutive with age, her face like an apple doll's. The horsehides and sheepskins that wrapped her made her seem even more doll-like, while the crabbed hands that stirred the fire or ladled broth from the cauldron over it could have been dry black sticks.

Sticks were never so deft, though. As Temur and Edene approached, she first dished out bowls of milky tea and *airag*, the lightly fermented mare's milk that would not make your bowels sick, as fresh mare's milk was wont. By the time they had made an obeisance—deeper in Edene's case than Temur's—the tea was joined by bowls of broth.

Temur took up the tea in both hands and bowed once more over it to the matriarch of the Tsareg clan. "I am grateful."

"It's nothing," she demurred, in a voice stronger than her cracked appearance would have hinted. She pushed a platter of boiled, fatty lamb across the cleared ground toward them. It had been picked over, Temur could see, but there was quite a bit of meat and fat left.

The tea was salty. He sipped it, then drank down the broth and the *airag*. With chopsticks from his belt, he worried loose morsels of lamb, dipped them in the tea, and ate. Sparingly, despite his hunger, for there were not that many more lambs where this one had come from—perhaps it had been stillborn, so early in the year?—and the Tsareg had a lot of women and boys to feed.

Beside him, Edene ate with similar reserve. The Tsareg watched them closely, all polite attention, and Temur found it difficult to chew and swallow under the regard of so many friendly eyes. After a few bites, though, Altantsetseg *humph*ed her satisfaction and turned back to partitioning out food among her horde of descendants and collateral relatives. As the edge came off his hunger, Temur enjoyed the leisure to watch others. Two of the youngest who were old enough to feed themselves—a boy and girl who might have been twins—argued over the remains of a plate of hard-baked dumplings that must have been wrapped in leather and buried in the ashes the night before.

Temur sipped his tea, eyes half closed, and allowed himself the luxury of imagining himself in his mother's white-house, watching younger siblings or nieces and nephews quarrel. True, there was no white-house here—the Eternal Sky stretched overhead, and there was little point in setting up a white-house every night only to pull it down again, when simple hide tents would do—but that seemed like a quibble. This was more comfort than he'd known since Mongke Khagan died the previous summer—so much more comfort than the rough fire circles of a military campaign, if there was less food to be had.

The comfort and the companionship settled some deep craving in him. Something he hadn't even been truly aware of until now, except as a sort of disembodied longing.

He set the *airag* down and picked up the broth, which had been replenished. There was no sense in letting it make him maudlin. What was gone was gone, and the future that unrolled before him was a mystery road whose destination only the Eternal Sky knew.

He glanced over at Edene and caught her looking at him over the top of her tea bowl. She ducked her head again, spilling tea, and whatever he had been about to say was sanded from his mind by sudden squealing, as the girl twin piled onto her teasing brother, yanking his long, ink-black ponytail.

Temur sighed and shook his head. Altantsetseg was grinning at him toothlessly. He raised his eyebrows in a question he wasn't sure how to put into words.

She shrugged and tossed a lamb bone to one of the massive, lion-maned mastiffs that lay comfortably far from the fire. The Bankhar dogs were still in their winter coats, their black sides and enormous red-gold feet almost invisible under puffs of undercoat plate-matted like that of musk oxen. Bankhar were called the "four-eyed dogs" for the gold spots marking their eyebrows, said to be able to keep evil spirits at bay, and now the eyes and eyespots of every dog around the fire were trained on Altantsetseg.

Temur, amused, watched as she prised loose another bone for the pack. Dogs were not livestock; they were honored as near-brothers. No clan or tribe could long survive without its dogs—mastiffs to guard and shepherds to tend—and both breeds served as loyal hunting companions.

A good dog was sky-buried with as much honor as a good horse.

She gave the bone to Temur, and Temur—aware that this, too, was a test—offered it to the nearest mastiff, a great-headed dog whose yellowed teeth showed alongside a lolling tongue. Even a third of an *ayl* from the fire, he was too hot in his winter coat.

Gravely, the big dog stood and came to Temur, softly placing feet as big as a lion's paws. Gravely, he accepted the bone.

Despite the heat of the fire, he lay down beside Temur to dispatch with it.

Over the splintering bone, Temur heard Altantsetseg say, "You have a good eye for a dog. That is Sube, the 'Needle's-Eye.' He's the best get of my old ruddy bitch."

Temur looked up and smiled. "He was closest," he said.

"He's Edene's dog, you know." She picked shreds of meat from the bones with her fingertips and tucked them between teeth still strong if worn. "Maybe the way to her heart is through wooing him."

"*Grandmother*," Edene said. But she covered her mouth with her hand and looked down as if her face were burning.

Temur looked from one to the other. "I know better than to war with women."

Edene looked at him directly, her eyebrows lifting. "As if you have a choice," she said archly, "when women would war over you."

THE OPEN AIR BURNED COLD AND WIDE, BLUE-WHITE WITH WINTER, around the wings of Shahruz's mount. The wind of her passage cut through the heavy weave of his trousers, plastering the cloth to his legs. It seared his knuckles in his gloves and struck tears from his eyes, until he remembered the wood-framed, wool-padded goggles that hung on their braided cord around his neck. Even with those, and several wraps of his veil protecting his face, his cheeks and lips chapped and peeled.

The rukh's body rose and fell between her wings as wide as sails, her crested head on its long neck stretched out before her. Shahruz straddled that neck just before her shoulders, legs bound to the saddle with an assortment of straps, and pretended the reins were anything but a suggestion. The wind served al-Sepehr because it feared his retribution, not because she was in any way tame or trained.

Lesser rukhs—the young of the mother bird, some no greater than falcons—flocked around them, sometimes landing to rest on their parent's back and shoulders. The rukh herself was tireless, sky spanning. She never hesitated nor varied the clockwork of her wings.

And so they beat east, into the setting sun of the Uthman Caliphate, until they crossed the broad but bounded waters of the White Sea, and the sun was abruptly behind them, setting in the west. As they flew over the sprawl of Asmaracanda at the mouth of the Mother River, they entered Qersnyk-held lands, and the sky reflected it.

The rukh brought Shahruz so close to the sky he thought he could almost touch it, raise a hand to rip through its folds and catch a glimpse of whatever wonders lay beyond. But of course that was illusion: Not even a rukh—perhaps not even a dragon—could fly so high as to touch the tent of the heavens where it draped the Shattered Pillars and the Steles of the Sky.

From here, though, Shahruz could see both mountain ranges before they widened away to the north and southeast and were lost to blue distance. In the throat of the funnel they formed, the Mother River ran down to Asmaracanda, and beyond Asmaracanda the level steppe stretched to where haze concealed its reaches.

The rukh flew on through nightfall, and Shahruz dozed on her back. He never quite slept—far behind, in Ala-Din, his sister Saadet slept for him. He could feel her there, the warmth of her dreams as she gave him her rest and took his tiredness into herself. She asked no questions, though she must have felt the wind tangling his veils and the cold cutting his bones. She just warmed him and ate for him and gave him her womanly strength without stint.

There were too many moons, scattered across the sky like empty plates. When the sun rose, it shone into Shahruz's eyes.

Not too long after, he spotted the distant smudge of a caravanserai. Perhaps a half day's walk; not bad at all, and from the way the rukh's head turned toward it with interest, he knew it was not deserted. Her keen eyesight told her there were animals within—animals big enough to be worth eating.

Perhaps there would be men there worth hiring, as well. At least worth hiring for as long as they lasted.

It was a sad truth, Shahruz reflected, that the nature of war was such that not everyone could survive it.

 3

When word of the fall of Qarash first reached Tsarepheth, the Once-Princess Samarkar did not hear of it. On that cold spring day, Tsarepheth shone bright with prayer banners strung between its granite towers. Its walls hummed loud with mills that turned relentlessly under the force of waterwheels hung horizontally, borrowing the strength of the swift Tsarethi. Trade bustled through cobbled streets in the swinging belly of a crooked mountain valley.

Fourteen hundred *li* away, the center of creation shifted. The world's mightiest empire fell, along with the walls of a place Samarkar would barely have recognized as a city, with its dusty paths and felted walls—though the beauty of the treasures those walls girdled round would have moved even a Rasan princess.

When the news of the fall of Qarash reached Tsarepheth, the Once-Princess Samarkar did not even know that a woman in red and saffron robes sat alongside her, because on that day Samarkar lay drowsy with poppy among rugs and bolsters in her room high up in the Citadel of wizards. Silk wraps wadded absorbent lint against a seeping wound low in her abdomen. When she woke—*if* she woke—she would no longer be the Once-Princess Samarkar. She would be the wizard Samarkar, and her training would begin in truth.

She had chosen to trade barrenness and the risk of death for the chance of strength. Real strength, her own. Not the mirror-caught power her father, his widow, her half brothers, or her dead husband might have happened to shine her way.

It seemed but a small sacrifice.

SAMARKAR WAS NOT SURE HOW OFTEN SHE HAD OPENED HER EYES BE-fore the time she managed to keep them open. A woman still sat by her bedside, and she had a fuzzy sense that that woman—or one like her—had been there for some time. Samarkar's eyelids and lips stuck together; her tongue adhered to the roof of her mouth. Her belly cramped with emptiness and injury.

She peeled her mouth open to speak, but the only sound that emerged was a hiss of air. It must have been enough, because the woman turned. Samarkar saw now that it was Tsering-la, one of the teachers and mechanics and scholars—a wizard who was without magic of her own. Tsering's black hair hung oiled and glossy over her shoulders, unbraided in her leisure. She wore a wizard's high collar; it would be folly to let the uninitiated guess which sworn and neutered magician could defend herself with eldritch power and which could not.

No matter what, now Samarkar had earned that river-pearl-and-carved-jade collar. When she died, she would be buried in it. Whether the power blossomed in her empty belly or not.

Something of her own. Something she had bought with her own currency. Something that had not been given her.

"Don't speak," Tsering said. "I know what you need."

Effortlessly she knelt on the thick rugs beside Samarkar's mat. A tray of mahogany and gold held offering bowls and a pot. Into a round cup no bigger than the dish of her hand, Tsering poured fault-less water, either filtered through layers of silk or drawn from some way upstream, where the Tsarethi's tributaries crashed among the steep valleys of the mountains called the Steles of the Sky. Safe water, which would not transmit cholera.

Samarkar thoughtlessly reached out her left hand for the cup. If she could have made a sound, the stitch of pain in her abdomen would have had her cry aloud. Instead she gasped.

Tsering's free hand fell gently on Samarkar's shoulder, fingertips pressing her back against the bolsters. Samarkar had grown to womanhood scrambling up the slopes and across the ridges of the terraced fields, swimming the wild Tsarethi as befitted a princess of the Rasa dynasty. But even that slight pressure was more than she could resist.

"I will hold the water for you," Tsering said. "You need *some* but still should not have too much. And no food yet."

Samarkar nodded, grateful for even the small wetness on her lips, the three measured swallows she was now allowed. If the surgeon's knife had perforated her intestine, she would probably be dying already. But there was no sense in taking risks, and the poppy destroyed her appetite anyway.

"My passionate thanks," she said, when her tongue worked properly.

Tsering smiled and set the cup aside. She must have dipped a bit of felt in cool water, because now she bathed Samarkar's face and scrubbed the crusts from her lashes. Samarkar sagged back on silk and wool and let her do it. The touch soothed and cooled, telling her by contrast how fevered she was still.

Fevered but awake and clear-headed. She was recovering.

The surgery was worse physically for women and emotionally for men, she had been told. Men almost always survived it. There were many fewer female wizards. In olden days, only those set aside as barren and those widowed and too old to bear had been allowed to present themselves before the Citadel of Tsarepheth. Now the surgery made wizardry an option for young widows such as Samarkar as well.

An option. Not a safe one.

I'm alive. She tasted the words in her mouth without speaking them. There had been a good chance it would end otherwise.

Failed wizarding women were even more of a tragedy, in Samarkar's eyes, than failed wizarding men. To take such a risk, and earn no magic . . .

Too late now for second thoughts. Either she would show the gift or she wouldn't, and only experience would tell. And even if she did not manifest, there were opportunities. Harlot. Teacher. Regent or courtesan. Wizard-errant.

She was alive, and once-princess no longer.

"Your brother called for you." Tsering dropped the rag back into the water.

"Half brother," Samarkar corrected. "Which one?"

"Songtsan-tsa. He came as a supplicant and left his entourage in the road. The Old Master Yongten-la stopped him at the stair and explained that you were healing from your neutering. Yongten-la said to the crown prince that you are one of us now, and that when he met you again he must address you as *aphei*, Samarkar-la."

"Oh, I wish I could have seen that." Despite herself, Samarkar smiled. La, not tsa. Yes. And she could imagine the venerable, stick-straight Yongten-la, with his moustache that trailed down his chest like something out of a storybook, holding back the king-in-all-but-name of all Rasa with a raised finger, a stern look, and the authority of rightfulness.

Whether she grew magic or no, she was a wizarding woman now. She hoped she lived long enough to earn half of Yongten-la's authority.

WITH GOOD FOOD—WHEN SHE WAS FINALLY ALLOWED IT—AND REST, Samarkar mended quickly. Two days after she awoke from her poppy haze, she managed to spare herself the indignity of pans in bed by tottering across richly knotted carpets to squat over a pot in one bare corner. She relished the grate of cold stone beneath her naked feet, but it was all she could do to hold the skirts of her bed robe clear and not topple over in the process. She had to call Tsering to lead her back to bed and was astonished by the weakness of her own voice, how it almost got lost under the glassy chiming of the devil-bells guarding the open window.

Two days after that, however, the stitches came out of her wound. She knew the surgeon-wizards did their work with mirror and tweezers and long delicate tools, so they could operate through the smallest incision possible, but when Tsering brought her a mirror and showed her the red line of the scar, she was startled by how small it was: only the span of her hand, and no more.

A day later, when there was no additional bleeding, she was deemed well enough to be carried through the halls and down the stairwells of the Citadel, down to the steaming baths of mineral-rich water that flowed hot from the earth and was reheated over a coal-fired hypocaust. Because the kitchens and the baths also heated the Citadel, the halls themselves grew warmer as Samarkar descended with her litter-bearers—three novices from her own classes, would-be wizards as yet uncut and uncollared, and one newly elevated wizard younger than herself, still stiff in his pristine collar.

She knew the novices well; now, they pretended for her sake that they did not exist. She chose to believe it was a kindness, that they did not force her to think through their changed status and relationships yet.

In summer, the baths would be allowed to run from warm to tepid; the kitchens would go mostly cold. Now, with the nights still frosty, the water was kept steaming.

Samarkar had meant to protest that she could walk, but Tsering had been so efficient about bundling her into bed robes and cloaks and seating her among the cushions of the litter that by the time it occurred to Samarkar to resist, it would have been churlish.

Five minutes into the journey, she realized that these traditions had their sense. *Tsarepheth* meant "white and scarlet citadel," and the Citadel that was now her home was the source of that ancient name.

The Citadel was a palace and a fortress and a library and a college. It was the home and shelter of all the wizards of the Rasan Empire. Its ivory and gold and crimson walls had sheltered them for centuries—through the fall of empires, the rise of conquerors, and a civil war or two. It was vast—spanning a promontory at the top of the narrow valley Tsarepheth inhabited, built to the buttresses of the mountains that flanked on either side so that its outline was a broad, irregular, and shallow triangle with the blunt tip pointed down. It was the tallest building in Tsarepheth—the city named for it—as well as the most massive, but the thirteen stories of its height were dwarfed by the basalt and granite peaks abutting it on either side. The domed basalt mountain on the left was called the Cold Fire; the taller granite peak whose flank it half enveloped was the Island-in-the-Mists.

The wild Tsarethi flowed through its foundations in an arched tunnel; the hot springs heating its belly sprang from the quiescent volcano that guarded its left flank. A thousand steps climbed its face; there were no doors at ground level, and no windows for thirty spans above the ground. Trade goods had to be hauled up in a basket, and for that reason bannered winches stood along its battlements.

On winter nights, mist dragons might creep down from their lairs among the heights of the Steles and drape themselves over and around those battlements for warmth. Samarkar had even once seen one, a translucent, ghosty thing with blue eyes winking along its feldspar length.

From the city below, the Citadel had the aspect of a great stone dam, a massive thing wrought of white and red granite, and in time of need it could become one, walling the sacred Tsarethi behind steel gates that only waited a command to fall into place across its tunnels. The city itself lay just below, rising in ranks to the steep valley walls above the river. Farther downstream, where the slope of the river's descent lessened and the valley widened in response, brown fields and paddies that would soon hold rice and vegetables and oats lay tiered like ruffles on a gown.

Samarkar's rooms, as befitted a new wizard, were in the highest and winter-coldest corner of the place. Twenty flights of stairs lay between the room where she slept and healed and the ones where hot baths pooled in cisterns scoured from the black basalt of the Cold Fire.

She would not have made it on her own.

Even being carried exhausted her beyond words. The ceilings in the pale granite corridors were high, so her bearers could hold her level even as they descended, but she fought not to clench her fists on the rails. She had not ridden in a litter, she realized, since her ill-fated trip to her husband's court when she was fourteen.

When they set her down and the newly ranked wizard extended a hand, she took it gratefully. She had been trained from the age when she could stand by herself to move with the grace and dignity befitting a princess, but now it was all she could do to not lean too hard on the man's arm as the bath attendants came for her, extending their tongues to show respect.

Two young women led her into the heat of the bath chamber. They were clothed in sheer white gowns that fell straight from the shoulder. Their arms were scandalously bare. Each of them was careful to hold Samarkar upright while making the touches seem natural and solicitous.

A heavy curtain fell behind Samarkar, and the heat of the bath chamber rolled over her. One of the servants opened her bed gowns and stripped her cloaks away while the other steadied her. She soon stood naked. It was an effort to hold her hands wide while the smaller of the two—a moon-faced beauty who could almost have been Samarkar's daughter, if Samarkar had had a daughter swiftly upon her marriage—unwound the gauze and silk across her belly. Samarkar wanted to defend the wound, to hide it with her hands as if it shamed her. She forced herself to stand proud.

The young women conferred over her abdomen—shrunken now by her fasting and recovery, and the taller and perhaps older one nodded. "It is healing well," she said. "Shall I help you into the water?"

"Thank you," said Samarkar. "I shall walk. If I can."

The entrance to the pools was shallow, not stepped but slanted, and scattered thickly with white sand that lay in pleasing ripples against the black basalt. Samarkar walked in slowly, as if savoring the warmth rising across the arches of her feet and the bones of her ankles, but in truth she did not trust her stability if she walked fast. From the way the attendants hovered, they were as worried as she. For the sake of her pride, though, she stayed upright.

The descent grew easier as the water took her weight. As the gentle swirl of the current washed her thighs and belly free of sweat and the crusts of dried blood and strong wine, as they soothed her shoulders and her neck, as they lapped her until she stood on tiptoe in hot water to her chin and felt it untangling her oiled hair down her back, she sighed and let go of a breath she had not known she was holding.

She stepped deeper. The water lifted her off her feet. Her toes dipped to brush the sand when she exhaled; her breasts bobbed weightlessly when she inhaled. Warm water licked her collarbone, shading hotter as she stroked deeper into the pool.

Each time she drew her arms forward, each time she lightly kicked, she felt the pull through the cramped and damaged muscles of her abdomen. But still she swam, as she had swum all her life except for the three terrible years in Song. She swam. And soon she would swim strongly once more.

Samarkar would live. And she would grow to become something new. Whatever the future held for her.

She would live.

BECAUSE SHE WOULD LIVE, SHE KNEW SHE COULD NOT AVOID HER brother forever. But still she stalled, giving herself another hand of days to recover and build her blood up with apples studded with nails (the nails were pulled out before serving) and a rich broth made with bones and liver, with plenty of wolfberries and the sweet, hard roots called beets that came all the way from Kyiv along the Celadon Highway. Everything she ate was served with the soy that came from Song along the same ancient road. She dined on the steamed immature beans, hot and crunchy with a sprinkling of Tsarepheth's famous violet salt; the soft curd sweetened and served mixed with rice; the pressed curd fried crisp in toasted oil and sprinkled with crunchy seeds.

Yongten-la had explained that she must eat a great deal of soy now—soy with every meal, when she could—and a great deal of butter and yogurt and milk, or her bones would grow brittle as an old woman's, without the life force harbored in her stones to keep her strong. It wasn't an edict she found difficult to endure: Samarkar had always enjoyed her food.

She stalled too until she was permitted to return to her studies, which was several days before she faced Yongten-la on one of the great decked battlements of the Lower Citadel. Her brother and sister wizards and the novices gathered in every overlooking window and along the curves of the walls and the banks of white steps leading down to make a sort of auditorium, and she tried not to weep tears of joy and apprehension as the master bent her wizard's collar about her throat. Fireworks—one of the sacred and secret sciences of her order, which she might one day undertake as a profession if she proved unmagicked as well as unwomaned—whistled and cracked overhead, showering bright sparks in all the colors of dragonfire across the evening sky.

Down in the city, Samarkar knew, across the valley at the great black basalt palace that stood opposite the Citadel like its far-cast shadow, in the terraced mountain farms—in all of these places, men and women looked up from their work and knew that a wizard had been made. One of the thousands of dark sets of eyes reflecting these fiery blooms probably belonged to her elder half brother.

Samarkar flourished. And after the ceremony of her elevation, she could no longer easily find excuses to avoid her brother. She was a ranked wizard now and could do as she liked. But somehow each day passed without her summoning a sedan chair—or simply walking down the Thousand Steps—crossing through the bustling streets of Tsarepheth to find him.

The mountains that embraced the Citadel meant that morning

came late to its windows, and evening early—but Samarkar's room, high in its towers, received the first light of the sun over the shoulder of Island-in-the-Mists. Still, it was only gray and not yet light when she awakened one morning from a terrible dream, clutching the covers to her collarbone and breathing loudly in her terror.

Her stomach no longer hurt with each deep breath. But she still remembered the horror of the dream, in which she had been sent back to her brother in disgrace by Yongten-la, because her gift had never manifested itself.

It was foolish, she thought, soothing herself, to stall an immediate duty because you were waiting for something that might never materialize.

Today. Today I will go to the palace.

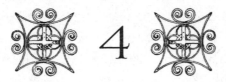

THE NEXT MORNING, TEMUR AGAIN RECEIVED AN INVITATION TO DINE with the Tsareg—this time on marmot cooked in its skin, and tea with noodles. Before long, Temur found himself attached to the household of old Altantsetseg and her tiers of children and grand-children.

Altantsetseg must have put her back to eighty winters, but she still rode upright on the shelf bench of her two-wheeled wagon, drawn by a pair of red oxen, the felt panels of her white-house and its long, precious wooden poles heaped up behind her. As evidenced on that first day, Altantsetseg's kin-band was mostly women and boys—like the rest of the refugee train—and they were happy to have Temur's companionship and protection. And Edene somehow managed to put herself in his way every day or two, a situation which he found more confusing than disagreeable.

You cannot have her, his rational mind argued. And yet another part answered, *Why not?*

After each break, Temur rode out before Altantsetseg's people, pushing Bansh on until he found a camping site that was both un-occupied and desirable. He'd turn the mare loose to graze, as the distance he could travel in one day was limited by his lack of a remount, and he would begin building a fire, hunting game, and carrying water, if there was water to be had. When Altantsetseg's granddaughters and grandsons arrived—the ones who had ponies ahead of the ones on foot, driving their few salvaged cattle, sheep, and goats with the help of a pack of scroungy dogs—they would set up the camp around him and take over the chores. At the very last came the adult women with the wagons and the heavy goods—the whitehouses, an anvil, iron cook pots, and so on.

Temur had seen Song refugees when he rode with his uncle Mongke south and east to war. The Song were a sedentary people, with their farms and fields of millet and rice, their oxen yoked to turn earth with plow blades rather than haul women's possessions in their carts. They had suffered greatly without their villages and their homes.

His own people were far more adapted to this life. They knew how to spread out, to make use of the land, to travel safely. Like tortoises, they carried their homes with them wherever they went. Indeed, if it had not been for the war, they would have been making this migration anyway. But now they were months early and moving in greater numbers than was their wont. And because of it, Temur worried for their food, come next winter.

Normally, at the end of the winter season, before moving up to their summer range, the Qersnyk would harrow under the last year's straw and plant grains and root vegetables in the fields to grow through summer so they could be harvested when the clans returned. This year, there had been no planting, and the ground that now grew green and soft underfoot had been frozen too hard to turn before they were driven from it—which meant famine, come autumn.

But they would worry about that when they were in the mountains alive. For now, the challenge was not dying on the high steppe, bereft of ten-elevenths of their animals and adequate food for the journey.

One sunrise in the second or third hand of days of Temur's travel with the Tsareg clan, Edene rode up to Temur on that leggy rose-gray filly of hers, the one whose mane was so sparse it did nothing to soften the long stark line of her neck.

"May I ride with you?" she asked, as he finished securing his gear around Bansh's saddle and tramping the last embers into the wet earth.

This time, she did not cup her hands across her cheeks in embarrassment. She kept her eyes down, demure, and he glanced away to show respect.

He knew he should say no. He should say, *I am a man of no clan.* He should say, *I have no name to give you.*

He should do those things, but he was not strong enough to send her away. He said, teasing, "Do you think you can keep up?"

She grinned, teeth flashing white, and had turned her mare and urged her into flight before he had his leg over Bansh's rump.

The rose-gray filly could run. Temur got a good look at her dappled flanks as she kicked off, her pale belly flashing between dark legs as she alternately dug in and stretched out. Bansh didn't need his urging to follow. Temur's off-side foot was barely in the stirrup when she lunged forward, stretching against the reins, her hooves drumming a sharp and aggressive tattoo. He'd never asked her for this before, and it was probably irresponsible to run her now, after forty days of toil and poor diet.

But once he got himself settled and thought about taking up the reins, she had fallen into her stride and shook her head irritably at his interference.

She meant to catch that filly.

Edene rode like a burr stuck in her mane. Like a fat-cheeked manul cat clinging to the back of its prey. Temur heard her shrieking laughter, saw the flicker of the rose-gray's silver ears as she listened to her rider and to Bansh's hoofbeats. The liver-bay dug down deep and found the speed to creep up, span by span. Thundering hooves showered clods of muddy grass on the earth behind. Bansh's head bobbed low, her great shoulders rolling as she surged along in the wake of the taller gray.

They passed sleepy flocks, just beginning to move out with their dogs and tenders for the morning. They passed carts in the process of loading, and a few bands of mares guarded by wary men. So few horses left; so few of the sixty-four sacred colors of horses represented. Temur hoped that most of the bands had scattered on the steppe or been collected by Qori Buqa's men, rather than being cut down in their blood. He would rather see the horses wild or in his enemy's hands than dead.

As if responding to his distress, Bansh threw herself forward with ever-greater speed. Temur felt her gather and extend, the rocking motion, the way her body swelled and shrank around each tremendous breath. She moved, and he moved with her, then they were beyond the edge of the refugee train and running, still running, while the grassland rolled away under them as endless as a tax assessor's scroll.

Slowly, Bansh ate up the rose-gray's lead. Slowly, she drew up beside her, her breath trailing in smoky plumes through the morning chill, her mottled nose reaching the rose-gray's flank, her cinch, her shoulder. As he came up on Edene, he saw her turn to check under her arm for his position. He saw her lips moving as she chanted to her mare—swiftness songs, or songs of soundness, he did not know.

He had nothing to say to Bansh. She was flying; she was giving everything to the race, and it would be unfair to ask for more. The world whipped by. Stride by stride, the rose-gray's lead failed her. Stride by stride, Bansh came on.

Edene's rose-gray was one of the best sprinters Temur had seen.

But Bansh, he began to realize, was an immortal.

At two *yart*—Temur estimated—the mares ran neck and neck. At two *yart* and forty *ayl*, their black-and-pink noses bobbed side-by-side.

Another forty *ayl*, and the rose-gray folded. She broke stride, snorted, tossed her head. Gamely, she surged forward again, but

Temur saw her rally only because he glanced back through his arm-pit to see her. To see her fighting the reins as Edene restrained her gently, turning her in a broad circle so she dropped into a canter, then a snorting, blowing trot, kicking out at tussocks and still pro-testing her rider's counsel.

Temur settled his weight back, and Bansh too dropped into a canter. He brought her around, aware of the spring in her gait, the lightness of her motion. Having beaten the rose-gray, she was will-ing to stop. But she wanted him to know she wasn't finished yet, if he still cared to run.

He stroked a hand down the sweaty length of her neck, brushing away the lather where it had collected beneath the reins. He shook her sweat from his fingers and wiped his palm on his trousers as Bansh brought him up beside the now-walking rose-gray.

"Is she all right?"

Edene nodded. Her face glowed with the wind and excitement, almost as bright as the iridescent shimmer of her mare. "Buldshak is of the line of the varnish-colored mare Temurbataar. She does not *get* beaten. What a horse that is! What is her line?"

"I don't know," Temur said, smoothing down her mane once more. "She found me on the battlefield. I don't know her line."

Bansh reached, teeth bared ostentatiously, for Buldshak's neck, and he leaned down to tap her cheek. She backed off, making a per-formance of shaking her head. "Clown," he called her.

She snorted and danced a step.

Edene was looking at him, hands folded on the pommel, eyes half lidded. When he returned the glance, she turned away and looked down. "Temur—"

He drew a breath. He had to say this now, before she made her-self embarrassed.

"Edene."

She met his gaze, eyes wide, and swallowed her words.

"I have no clan," he said. "I have no one to tell my name. If you want that of me—"

Her eyes widened with pity, which wasn't what he wanted. But then she schooled herself and grinned. Her voice was strained, but she made it come out light anyway. "I don't need to marry you," she said. "What if we were just friends?"

AL-SEPEHR RECLINED ACROSS CUSHIONS BEFORE THE SHADED WINDOWS of Ala-Din's stoutest tower, listening to his youngest wife read aloud from a book of histories purported to have been written by the hand of the ancient Sepehr al-Rachīd himself. The door to the hall had been left slightly ajar on purpose, and another of his wives—older and white-eyed with cataracts—sat beyond, her hands occupied with her stitching.

Al-Sepehr heard her stir as someone came up, and two women's voices speaking in low tones. He held up a hand for the youngest wife to cease reading and found his feet. A moment later, the door swung open and Saadet entered—as slender as her twin, but not so tall. Being a woman, she was not clad in the indigo sash and veil of the Nameless, and while she carried an unseemly long knife—in case she should need to use her brother's combat training—she did not go so far as to offend the Scholar-God by handling a sword.

"Al-Sepehr," she said, lowering herself to the floor.

"Stand," he said, extending his hand to her. His youngest wife snapped the book shut—al-Sepehr made a note to speak to her about respect for ancient objects—and exited the room hastily, tripping over the rug edge on her way.

Saadet rose without his assistance, holding the ivory silk of her veil across her nose and mouth with one hand. "My brother has reached Qori Buqa," she said. "He has with him a dozen mercenaries dressed in indigo, and Qori Buqa has made him welcome. He says to tell you that he will be among the pagan dead tomorrow."

"That is good," al-Sepehr said. "You may go, and tell Shahruz to contact me directly when he has reached the battlefield."

She bowed again, though this time not so floor-scrapingly, and retreated through the door. "Close it," al-Sepehr said.

She pulled it silently to behind her, before either of his wives could reenter the room. Al-Sepehr stood for a moment and watched the empty space before he allowed a frown to crease the corners of his mouth.

His chambers were simple for a man who claimed the title al-Sepehr. A bed, the cushions, a low couch or two. The shelves that held boxes, and books, and small trinkets—but not too many. He thought better if he kept his space and his head free of clutter.

But toward the rear of the chamber there was one thing that stood out. A heavy stone table hung suspended from the ceiling-beams on iron chains, insulated on every side by air. Al-Sepehr crossed to it, measuring his footsteps, and looked down at the single thing it supported.

A book. Or what could have been the ghost of a book, perhaps—its covers translucent gray, marked with letters white as bone; its binding rings silver; and every transparent page within etched with the gorgeous serpentine cursive letters and diamond-shaped accents of the dialect of ancient Erem.

The glass covers chimed softly as al-Sepehr drew on a kidskin glove and opened them with infinite care. Some of the page edges were chipped, and he was too well acquainted with the illness that followed when he let this dire old thing taste his blood. One by one, he turned the crystal leaves, watching as transparent letters cut in transparent pages caught the sunlight.

Every word twisted in his head and made his eyes ache and burn. He found the page he wanted and settled down to study the spell inscribed therein.

To raise the enemy's dead and bind them to your bidding, he read, in a book that had been ancient, a language that had been dead, when the founder of al-Sepehr's order—Sepehr al-Rachīd—first unearthed it from the tombs of a crumbled city and spoke its phrases aloud.

TEMUR WAS AWAKE STILL AT SUNSET, CHECKING HIS MARE'S LEGS, BRIB-ing her with the last of the mutton-fat sweets. He worried for her condition, on the spare diet of wintered-over hay and first spring shoots of grass, when they had so far to go. Bansh was steppe-bred, and now that she was properly groomed, even by starlight the bay hide stretched over her long muscles and prominent bones showed the characteristic pearly glow of her ancestry. The steppe horses were legendary for it; in sunlight, they gleamed like hammered metal, like jewels, like mirrors, in shades of silver or brass or pearl or steel no animal should reflect. There were legends of how they came by those colors, but Temur thought it was probably some trick of the shape of the hair shaft. Not all the steppe horses exhibited it, and it never endured in preserved hides.

Temur hobbled Bansh loosely while she lipped his shoulder, hoping for more sweets. The smell of honey, cinnamon, and grain clung about her breath, laced with the slightly rancid mutton fat. Temur's stomach grumbled; his marmot supper, stewed with coals inside a bag sewn of its own skin, had been long ago and fairly insubstantial once divided with Edene and her seven-year-old brother.

He had pitched his bedroll some distance from the Tsareg tents. Now he stood in the cool calm and the firelight, watching the stars prickle out across the darkening veil. They faded away in the still-lit west, their light the silver and pale gold of ghost-colored horses.

Slowly, methodically, Temur brushed Bansh's hide and combed out her mane and tail until she gleamed like a horn bow in the firelight. The long slice along her ribs had healed completely, with no sign of proud flesh—unlike the distended, livid scar that bulged across his own neck—but the new hair was coming in white across the scar.

He heard the footsteps behind him. And this time he did not reach for his knife, because he knew them well.

He tossed the brush and the wide-toothed wooden comb towards his saddlebags and turned. "Edene—"

She wore a long white shirt that closed up the front over trews of rough, undyed wool. Her hair was down over her shoulders, combed out and oiled smooth. In the firelight, it gleamed with almost the luster and depth of a steppe mare's. "Hush," she said. "I said we could still be friends."

She stepped up close, her face tucked into the curve of his shoulder, her warm breath bathing his neck. When she leaned forward, her hair made a drape all around her face and shoulders; she smelled of civet and sandalwood and vetiver, rare treasures from the reaches of the empire. The Tsareg clan had indeed come away from ruin with certain of their riches intact.

Her fingers slid under his coat and under his tunic, gliding over flesh that shivered at her touch as if her hands were the hands of the rain.

Temur closed his eyes. He placed his hands upon her hair. The warm curves of her ears filled his palms. He knew what to do, of course. He'd grown up surrounded by it. But knowing what to do and knowing how to go about it to her satisfaction were different things indeed.

His heart raced so loudly in his ears that he barely heard his own voice. "I haven't done this."

"You're no beardless boy," she said. She looked up at him, her eyes huge and black, and pressed a finger to his lower lip.

"I've been ten years in war camps," he said, and saw her doing the sums in her head. "I could have gone to camp followers or captive women. . . ." He shrugged. Some did, some didn't. But his own mother Ashra was a captive, one lucky enough to be taken as one of Otgonbayar Khanzadeh's wives, and every time he looked at the captive women, he'd seen her.

Edene's lips curved. "I like you more for what you've not done, then." Her one arm slipped around his waist—still under the tunic—and her other hand emerged to take his and slide it down across her face. She brushed his knuckles with her lips in passing. "Come on. I'll show you."

Temur's mother Ashra was the daughter of an Aezin prince, bartered in marriage for politics once already, before the Qersnyk

khans had claimed her from her Uthman husband. She had gone to
Otgonbayar Khanzadeh as his third wife, and she had borne him
only one son that lived—Temur, who had grown up surrounded
nevertheless by his father's other children, even after his father died.

Ashra had taught Temur all sorts of things. One was that she
thought herself lucky to have come to Qarash, for before that she had
been a captive in the women's quarters of an Uthman household,
and the women in the Uthman Caliphate went veiled and shrouded
and lived as the property of men, secreted away in female quarters
where they saw none but their husbands, their fathers, their brothers, their sons. This was done out of respect for them as living incarnations of the Uthman Scholar-God and Her Prophet, Ysmat of
the Beads, Ashra had said.

They could have professions—they could be scientists or physicians, historians or mathematicians, in honor of the Scholar-God
and Her Prophet. But learning did not free them to walk in the air.
Ashra herself had been raised to the Scholar-God's religion, but her
Aezin father practiced it differently. Ashra had chafed under veils.

And in the Qersnyk lands women rode free; they owned white-
houses and all the livestock (except horses—though women might
ride, horses belonged to men and men milked and maintained them,
unless there were no adult men in a family); they could divorce their
husbands; and no one cared in whose bed they lay until they married.
And sometimes not even then.

And so when Edene led Temur to his bed and drew him down
upon it, there was no one to say her nay. By the fires of her clan, an
ayl or so off, children cried and women sang; pots clattered; the
cracked voice of Altantsetseg rose above the din. Someone took up
a working song and other voices joined.

She slipped the toggles on his coat, opened his belt, and put it
aside. She unlaced the collar of his shirt and made him raise his arms
over his head so she could pull it off. She placed his knife neatly beside the bed, and she untied the wrap of his trousers and drew those,
also, down.

And then, as he reclined upon the scratchy wools and the fleeces, she knelt over him and slipped the knots from the loops that held her shirt closed. She let the wide sleeves slip down her arms and showed him her breasts. She hooked the trousers down, and the light of the rising moons silvered her belly and thighs and laid mysterious shadows across the alluvial fan of her sex. Those same shadows cupped her breasts, stroked her throat, and defined the line of her jaw. Temur wanted to reach in and trace them with his hands.

Temur's breath quickened, first, then became strong and deep. The night air cooled his flesh. When he reached out a hand and laid it against Edene's arm, he felt the tiny prickles as her skin tensed around fine hairs. She covered his hand with her own, calloused fingertips scraping, and drew it across her breast so his thumb grazed her nipple.

"It is permitted to touch," she said with a ghostly smile.

So he did.

Her hands drew swaths of warmth against him; her mouth, arcs of fire that burned then chilled. She pressed him against the blankets, her skin smooth against his chest. Wool scratched his shoulders pleasantly. She threw one round, soft thigh across his hips so he gasped aloud when the rough wetness of her sex brushed the underside of his. She reached between them and grasped his shaft, and he did more than gasp: He arched to the touch, bearing her weight up. From the Tsareg fire, there was a burst of conversation, but Temur couldn't care. What could they see, anyway, looking from the glow of embers into the dark?

"You are the stars," he said to her, words from an old tale to make her smile.

"You haven't seen anything yet," she said, and grinned as she lifted his sex in her hand and glided down to envelop it.

She smiled at the intake of his breath, long and ragged, and the soft moan that followed. She was . . .

She was honeyed silk and heat and horsewoman's strength as she rocked against him and rose up on the old-ivory pillars of her thighs

and brought herself down again. She was softness, lush dimpled softness of arms and flanks wrapped around strength, like a bent bow.
She was the fall of cool hair across his throat and his burning
face, like water to a man sick with sun. She was the smell of sweat
and pungent oils. She was the warmth of the night, and seventeen
moons rose over her shoulders while she rode him with the same
purpose and intensity with which she raced her mare.

Temur grasped those shoulders in both hands. She lifted her
breast to his mouth, the long nipple pointed and salty between
his lips. He suckled like a babe. She took his hand in hers and
pressed it between them, showed him where to touch and how.
Her head stretched back, her face a mask of concentration. Her
thighs slipped in the sweat of his body when she moved. He felt her
body tense in ripples. . . .

One moon in the sky behind her flared briefly white, brilliant
enough to wash the whole of the Veil of Night in blue, then flickered
dark as a mirror that reflected nothing. It was the Feather Moon of
his cousin Mongke, named after Mongke Khagan, the cousin's father—
and then it was gone.

A hole in the night, that was all.

Temur pulled her down to him and buried his face against her
shoulder, crying out something that could have been her name and
could have been release and could have been despair.

She slept in his arms, afterward, and Temur lay awake and
watched the night go by. The talk at the campfire lulled and surged
and caught and eventually drifted silent, except for one voice that
muttered on, low and plaintive, long after everyone else had either
dropped off or resorted to feigning sleep. Another night, Temur might
have called out a demand to shut up, people were sleeping. But tonight it was part of the music that surrounded him—the *shush* of wind
through the tent lines, the rip of mare's teeth cropping new grass, the
snores of women, the soft talk of young boys on the night watch, the
pop of a dying fire. Somewhere in the darkness he heard the cough

of a lion, but it was distant, and even the horses barely paused their evening meal to listen.

Sixteen moons drifted across the Veil of Night, towed in a pattern Temur, no shaman-rememberer, did not know how to read for portents. *So few of us left.* He watched them trail through the night, one outracing another, a third falling behind. His own Iron Moon was set apart from the others now, wandering off to the north of the sky. Temur wondered if Qori Buqa was somewhere with a shaman-rememberer, casting stems to find him, or if his uncle had decided to let him live in defeat and ignominy.

It would be smarter, of course, to have him sought and silenced. But Temur didn't know what resources Qori Buqa still commanded, or if they would extend to a hunt and assassination.

He turned on his side and curled against Edene's back, burying his face in her hair.

In the morning when they awoke, it seemed that the entire camp had picked up in the night and reintegrated itself around them. Cookfires blazed on three sides, and Temur—unearthing himself from Edene's hair—found Tsareg Altantsetseg cross-legged beside a cooking fire, a shaman-rememberer—third-sexed, like all those who spoke for Mother Night and the Eternal Sky—sitting beside her and rebinding the eight blue knots on his saddle. He smiled as Temur struggled into his trousers and came up. Altantsetseg just sniffed, and without looking at him, said pointedly, "This fire needs more dung if there's going to be enough tea for everyone."

"So it does," Temur said, as Edene rolled over and propped herself on an elbow. "I'll go fetch that, then."

Edene threw him his boots as he went past. He threw her a smile.

From then on, there was no question that Temur was part of the clan. As the hands of days passed, he even heard one or two people from other traveling alliances refer to him as "Tsareg Temur," and though he was careful to correct them, he began to wonder, with a little hope, if Altantsetseg did indeed intend to adopt him.

Edene came to his blankets every night, until Altantsetseg offered to give them a small tent of their own—with a show of bad grace and a complaint about scaring the horses. Edene refused: Her small sister and cousin needed the tent more.

Altantsetseg *humph*ed, but Temur caught the edge of her toothless grin and realized that she'd been teasing. That eased his heart more than anything. Old women teased and crabbed and picked—but only to their families.

He breathed in and breathed out and felt the war that much farther away and unmissed. When Edene came to him that night, he borrowed her comb and combed out her hair, the sort of office a man might perform for one of his women, if she liked him enough to permit it. And she sat with a small smile and allowed him.

TEMUR AWOKE AGAIN AFTER MOONSET, IN THE HOUR OF PHANTOMS, when the sky grayed and the mist rose and the cold found its way into every limb. Now, there was silence. Edene had curled in on herself, drawing up the blankets, and Temur lifted his head only reluctantly from the island of warmth they'd created to see Bansh standing over them, alert, ears pricked, her fine-boned head dark against the tarnished sky.

Something was wrong.

Temur shook Edene's shoulder, crouched, reached for his trousers, and pulled them on in haste. She rolled on her back, saw his face, and instantly sat up, pushing her hair behind her shoulders as she groped for her clothes. As she slipped her shirt on, he stuffed the long plait of his hair under his coat and cinched it on. The knife was still sheathed on his belt; he unhooked it and handed it to her.

She took it wordlessly and clenched it between her teeth as she tied her hair into a knot. Then she stood, stepping into her trousers, while Temur went to his pile of gear and lifted his quiver and bow.

A cold wind blew across the steppe. Bansh stamped a hoof, and across the breadth of the camp another mare answered. Temur saw heavy shadows moving against the grass around the perimeter; the Bankhar, awake and alert, scenting the darkness, their huge heads almost lost in the weight of their coats. In the mist, they looked like boulders shaggy with lichen, like molting bears, as they waited, silently, noses to the wind.

Bansh tossed her head once restively and stamped again. Edene put out a hand to the liver-bay's shoulder. Temur had just decided to risk slipping her bridle on when out in the grayness a mastiff began to bark.

First once, sharp and deep. A warning. Then savagely, heavily, a hard angry sound over a rumble like rolling thunder.

Temur knew that sound. Edene did too, by the look she shot him as she skinned the blade he'd given her. Then every dog in the camp was barking, shepherds and mastiffs both, horses stamping and circling, a stallion squealing threat and outrage.

There was no time to bridle the mare. He set an arrow to his string but did not draw, saving his strength for when he would need it. Around him, the camp was stirring to life, Edene's cousins and sisters and aunts rolling to their feet, finding weapons, checking on children or elders.

Temur saw two strong women he knew from the campfires start toward him, each shouldering a bow as they strode across the short soft grass, the mist that softened everything curling tenderly about their bodies. They never made it.

What came out of the mist seemed at first the mist itself—gray as a dove-colored dun, as immaterial and cohesive as smoke. But mist never went clothed in a warrior's quilted coat and trousers, and mist never showed the deep, unbleeding gashes of death wounds below the perfectly ordinary faces of staring dead men. Mist never wore helms bannered in the three-falls tiers of Qori Buqa, or the horsehair twist of the soldiers of Qulan.

Ghosts. The ghosts of the dead of the fall of Qarash. So many who had not had their remains commended to the carrion crows and the sacred vultures. So many who had not had anyone to speak their true names aloud to the wind, that they might pass to the embrace of the Eternal Sky.

So many doomed to haunt the steppe, hungry and lost and crying out for any scrap of warmth that might feed them a brief memory of what it had been to be living.

Temur heard Edene's sharp intake of breath as the ghosts closed around her cousins. He found himself searching the faces fruitlessly for ones he recognized, his heart savage behind his ribs. He took a step forward, then another, as the ghosts closed on the Tsareg women.

One woman nocked an arrow; the other drew a knife. They stood back-to-back, and Temur saw now that one had a baby on her shoulders, strapped into a cradleboard. They were Qersnyk women; they would fight any way they could.

There was no way to fight ghosts with a bow.

Temur watched in horror as a captain of Qori Buqa's army reached out his transparent hand and scraped it down the face of one of the Tsareg women. She was the one carrying the infant. She did not scream; she shouted, instead, and struck out, lashing around her with the knife. The child's outraged shriek joined the rising cacophony of fruitless battle.

"Salt!" Edene cried.

He looked at Edene. "Salt," he said, as the sense of her word penetrated his despair. Salt and iron. Iron alone couldn't harm a ghost. . . .

She was already scrabbling through his saddlebags, squeezing and discarding pouches until she found one that must have gritted between her fingers in the right way. She cut the knot with Temur's knife, then spat on the blade so grains would adhere when she plunged it into the gritty purple-black salt that came all the way from Tsarepheth.

Temur snatched a handful of arrows from his quiver and imitated her, then cast salt by the handful in arcs around Bansh and Edene to form a circle.

It might work. "Stay with Bansh," he said to Edene, not waiting to see if she nodded.

He snatched up the bag of salt, turned away, and hurdled over the protective circle. A pair of bounds took him almost to Edene's embattled cousins.

The woman with the bow loosed arrow after arrow futilely. Her clanswoman's face ran rivulets of blood where the ghosts had clawed her. The archer shouted, too, then she screamed like a peacock as one of the ghosts reached into the stuff of her face and dragged an eyeball down her cheek.

Temur, unthinking, planted his feet. At much too short range, he nocked, drew, and loosed.

The barbed arrowhead passed through three ghosts as if they had no substance at all, and he had the momentary satisfaction of watching their faces—the dead of Qori Buqa and the dead of Qulan, fighting as if they had served one army—as they shattered and drifted into shreds, like the mist they seemed to be.

The half-blinded woman sagged, her bow forgotten in one hand, palms on knees. The other struggled still, lashing out with a knife at four more mocking evil spirits that toyed with her, reaching around her to the child she struggled to protect.

"Salt!" he yelled, and threw a handful over her. It struck her like a scatter of small hail, grains bouncing here and there—but she and the infant were damp with mist, and some grains adhered.

Her dark eyes widened. She laughed a warrior laugh and stroked the side of her knife against her tongue, then her sleeve.

Now the ghosts drew back, wary. Temur dumped a handful of salt on his own head, shaking it down inside the collar of his coat. He advanced upon them, yelling, hoping someone else in the camp could hear him and take up the cry: *"Salt! Salt! Fight them with salt!"*

A snarl, and suddenly a dog tall as a young horse was at his hip, lips skinned back from teeth like yellow tusks, long matted hanks of undercoat swaying about it like an armor of quilted rags.

Sube, the Needle's-Eye, the best of Tsareg's great dogs, had come to defend his mistress. Temur upended the salt pouch over the dog's wide shoulders, throwing a handful into his jaws. Whether the dog understood his purpose or not, he never knew, but at the moment Sube lunged forward, ponderous and elemental in his fury, and sank his teeth into the misty fabric of the nearest ghost.

It opened its mouth as if to scream, but no sound emerged. Its mouth grew horribly to encompass and consume its whole head— and the head came apart in shreds. Temur fired a salted arrow through the next two, and Sube ripped the fourth to pieces before he could nock another shaft. Bansh screamed in a fury behind him, and he heard the thunder of her hooves as she whirled and kicked out; he did not have time to turn before another ghost came before him, rearing up suddenly, only to shrivel around the blade of the nearer Tsareg cousin's knife.

"Temur—" the cousin said, reaching over her shoulder to touch her child. It was still wailing, which Temur took to mean it was still all right. Behind her, the other Tsareg woman choked with pain but forced herself to stand. With fumbling fingers, she shoved her trailing eye back into the ravaged socket, swaying as she did so. She managed it, then she folded down, bloody hands on the earth, her bow forgotten behind her.

The woman with the knife crouched over her. "I'll see to Toragana. Get Edene—"

He turned, saw Edene lash out with her salted knife. The ghosts were piling up outside the salted circle like water behind a dam, and as Temur stepped forward, the pressure of the ones behind pushed the first ones over. They shredded, slipped apart, came to pieces and mist. But others rode that bank of mist up, up, towering until, like a snow cliff crumbling into avalanche, they washed into the circle.

Bansh whirled again, tearing up her picket, and kicked out with hooves that tore through the first rank of ghosts like hammers hurled against silk hangings. Edene must have salted her hooves, and Temur blessed smart women even as he leaped forward, Sube bristling and snapping at his side, into the midst of the wave of ghosts.

Edene lashed out, opening the belly of a ghost wearing the plumes of a private of Qulan's guard. Temur—too close now for bowshots— lifted an arrow to stab the next ghost, whose plumes were those of a ranking officer, through the eye as it turned to him.

He froze.

His brother's face was hewn from brow to jaw by the blow that had killed him, and in the bloodless bottom of the wound Temur could see brains, bone, the fibers of severed muscle, the fat of Qulan's cheeks. *He's dead and cursed,* Temur thought, and almost brought the arrow down. But then he remembered, as Qulan's one remaining mute eye stared at him, the tongue flopping through the ruined jaw.

He knew his brother's true name. "Go free, Re Sha-kharash Ar- slanjin, called Qulan. Go to the Eternal Sky now."

The ghost dissolved into mist. Behind it stood another, and this one—a one-armed, broken-backed soldier of Qori Buqa's army— was not Temur's kin. But now he had it in his heart what he was destroying, that these were the shades of men left unmourned on a battlefield, and some of them Temur might have left that way him- self. His battle rage was broken.

He thrust his arrow into the dead man's face, not in fury but in pity.

Sube began to bark, frantically, lunging in place like a dog bounc- ing on the end of a tether, and Temur turned. . . .

Edene reached for him through mist and morning, his knife in one hand and the other outstretched, her body pulled back as the ghosts surrounded and lifted her. She shouted—she didn't scream— and Temur lunged after her as they pulled her into a sky they van- ished against. His fingertips brushed hers. She twisted like a squirrel in a wolf's mouth, lashing out with the blade, hacking at the gray hands that dragged at her.

Bansh was there. Temur vaulted up her flank, dropping his bow, using her mane as a handle until he crouched on her shoulders.

He leaped.

This time he did not even touch Edene. The ground was a long way down. He landed, rolled, heaved himself into a crouch. Arrows fell around him, shaken from his quiver. His bow was there, just beside the circle of salt that glittered amethyst and obsidian on the grass. The mist was burning off, the sunlight starting to cut and sparkle as it shone through.

"Edene!"

She wailed, lifted higher, vanishing into the sky. Still fighting.

Temur snatched up his bow. He swept an arrow through the salty-wet grass, nocked, drew back.

Temur raised his left arm. Found the roughness of the serving with his right fingertips. Let the string pull back into his gathered strength, the bow's leathern grip settling into his palm. Spread the fingers of his left hand, reaching so his grip would not shake the bow. Raised the bow above his shoulders and waited until he felt it surround him, felt himself fall into the bow. Felt the pressure of the string at his thumbtip, unprotected by the flat horn ring he would have used to draw if he'd had time to find it.

The fall might kill her. But would that be worse than whatever the ghosts intended?

He bent his knees, tucked his tail, and the bow enfolded him. There was a moment when its balance encompassed his and the jouncing breasts of rising ghosts bounced up and down past the point of his arrow—or the point of his eye.

The arrow was the intention. There was no difference.

When Temur breathed, the bow breathed. When Temur waited, the bow waited.

When the fingers of Temur's right hand drifted open, the bow killed.

The arrow flew true. True and high, piercing the sky, piercing the ghosts that threw themselves into its path, shredding them, passing through them as if they were nothing.

But they were not nothing. There was something to them. Some presence. Some substance.

The arrow crested its arc an arm's breadth below the ghosts that held Edene, and began its long smooth descent back to earth.

Temur forced himself not to look down until he could not see her anymore, until Edene's cousins came to pry the bow from his stiff hands and tend the wounds and bruises he had not even noticed he'd acquired.

5

D<small>ESPITE WHAT HER OTHER BROTHER</small>, T<small>SANSONG</small>, <small>HAD SAID TO HER WHEN</small> she returned in disgrace from the nominally Song principality of Zhang Shung, Samarkar had striven all her years to be a dutiful daughter and a dutiful sister. She had even been a dutiful wife, in as many of her duties as her husband Ryi had permitted her to perform. And so she sent word ahead to the palace that Samarkar-la, *aphei*, would call after midday, and that she would be most pleased if her brothers would receive her.

She could have summoned a litter, but pride had something to say, even if pride was something a wizard should set aside. So instead she dressed herself with care in the clothing of her new office—the pearl and jade collar, the black trousers, the black coat—and pulled high-topped boots lined with the fleece of black sheep onto her feet. Winter might be ending, but rime and ice still lingered on the stone banks of the Tsarethi. She clothed her hands in gloves and was ready to walk the length of Tsarepheth.

It was a test for herself as much as anything, and she gritted her teeth until she could be sure no sudden weakness would overcome her.

A gorgeous day in early spring rewarded her. Though the air was crisp, the sun hung warm in the sky, and all the city's market streets bustled. Samarkar kept to the promenade along the river's west bank, following the flow of people—women with market baskets, herb girls selling what they had gathered in high meadows at the first light of morning, prostitutes sacred and profane.

Some of the whores were men, but not so many as the women. A few of both were maimed. One woman had had her nose and upper lip sliced away; she had probably been pretty before, and Samarkar imagined some powerful man had had her punished for refusing him. Now she could refuse no one with coin, if she wished not to starve. And who would pay much for a scarred prostitute?

Samarkar gave the whore alms, forcing herself to meet the woman's eyes. Better to be a neutered wizard than a woman.

A beggar with his right hand severed for some infraction caught her eye. She tossed him a coin, wondering what his crime had been. Once, she would have considered his punishment only what he deserved. But that was before she learned quite so much as she knew now of the ways of the world.

The city's white walls and red tile roofs rose on her right hand, and the river poured down smoothly on the left, filling its chasm and the whole of the valley with the sound of rushing water. The railings rustled with prayer flags; the eaves of houses rang with strings of prayer bells. Samarkar drew the air deep, delighted, for a moment setting the nagging thought of her task aside.

An hour or so of walking brought her to the Black Palace. She approached the towering black gate boldly, as if she belonged there still; it felt strange to come home to a place that was home no longer. The guards at the gate recognized her anyway, despite her black wizard's garb and her hair dressed plainly in two shining dark braids over the green and pearl collar.

Ushered inside the palace, she was greeted most formally by a chamberlain and a series of functionaries, all of whom she knew by name. One or two had been warm acquaintances when she was princess. But now, they treated her as an honored stranger—with absolutely correct dignity and deference, and not even the shade of a smile.

It should not have stung. She had made her choice to serve Rasa as a wizard and not as a princess—in some ways, a matter of preserving her own life and freedom, because as a wizard she could neither be sold off in another marriage to serve her brother's ambition (assuming he could find a man who would take her, after the last debacle) nor would she eventually find herself and any heirs murdered by a cousin to clear a line of succession.

It should not have stung. But Samarkar knew enough by now to understand that things were rarely as they *should be.*

"Will my brother see me?" she asked, as they swept her down the halls. Given the pace the functionaries set, she was glad she had waited to come here. Although the long strides and the wind of their passage made her wizard's black-on-black brocade coat and broad trousers—designed to set off the pearls and jade of her stiff high collar—flare out around her dramatically. She was adapting to the collar—not so different from court garb, after all—but despite her two years of novitiate, it felt strange to walk about bareheaded. Probably because now she was bareheaded in the *palace,* and she had not done that since she was old enough to toddle upright after her nursemaids.

As she asked the question, it occurred to her that she should have phrased it more positively, to make the functionaries work harder to deny her. Had all the learning of a lifetime of politics been snipped from her body with her stones?

"His Highness is unexpectedly detained," one of the functionaries—old Baryan—said, managing to walk sideways and backward like a river crab and still bow so low his headdress scraped the floor. "The princesses will entertain you while you wait, Samarkar-la."

Samarkar-la smiled and congratulated Songtsan silently. No one could claim he had not done her honor, and yet he could keep her waiting indefinitely to demonstrate his disappointment in her delays.

"Then we are going to the solar?"

"Yes, *aphei*."

"Never mind, then. I know the way."

The wizard's trousers allowed a person to move at a pace an old man reduced to scuttling in court robes could hardly be expected to keep up. Samarkar lengthened her stride, letting her bootheels hit the flagstones with a force she would not have dared when she whispered through this palace in narrow slippers that never kept her feet warm. She cruised down the hall like a great golden eagle, the wind of her passage filling her coat like dark wings, and the functionaries flocked behind, ineffectual and hurried as mobbing crows.

She had spent many hours in the women's solar. It took her two minutes to walk there, hustling up stairs two risers at a time, and even though her side caught a stitch in half-healed muscles partway up the final flight, she did not show it. When she paused in the doorway, she did put a hand out to the frame, but that could have been to show off her bare hands and bare fingertips as much as because she needed the support.

Because suddenly—she needed the support.

The doorway stood open, its curtains drawn wide, and sunlight streamed into the long room through windows glazed against the cold with oiled rice paper. At one end of the solar, heat rolled forth from a brazier beneath a hooded chimney. The face of the servant who crouched on a stool behind it, slowly lifting and lowering her fan, was dewed with sweat.

At the other end—the end closer to the doorway—fifteen women of various ages sat on thick rugs and cushions, their feet in horned slippers, their brocade robes falling about them in bright layers like the petals of so many variegated roses. Three of those women were princesses—Songtsan's and Tsansong's wives, Yangchen (with her babe at her breast), Tsechen, and Payma, who was barely fourteen. One of the women—Tseweng—was the Dowager Empress and Regent, accorded a stool in deference to her age and stiff joints and (Samarkar thought uncharitably) the skinniness of her ass.

It was to Tseweng-tsa that Samarkar bowed first, extending her tongue in a show of respect. "Honored Stepmother," she said, before turning to Yangchen—"Honored Sister"—and the other princesses in turn.

It was protocol. And it was easier to look at Payma's kind young face as it broke into a smile of delight at seeing Samarkar than it was to look at Yangchen gloating over her son.

In another life, that would have been Samarkar sitting where the light fell across her cushions, a baby chewing peacefully at her breast. It was she who would have read aloud in a bright room where her women sewed and spun. In another life, it would have eventually been Samarkar sitting where Tseweng sat, the entire empire hers to rule as she saw fit until her son turned twenty-five.

Samarkar flattered herself that in Tseweng's place, she would have lost less territory to the ceaseless gnawing of the Song and Qersnyk, and perhaps even gained a little. But she would never know that now.

"Samarkar-tsa," Tseweng said, extending her tongue as well. "What a delight! Are you well? Have you been refreshed? Will you sit?"

Her age precluded her rising, as the babe at Yangchen's breast precluded hers, but Payma and Tsechen and all the ladies started up, setting their embroidery hoops aside with a great rustling of silk and wool.

"Samarkar-la, Honored Stepmother," Samarkar reminded gently, allowing herself to be led to an unused cushion and seated. She squeezed Payma's hands before the girl got away, careful not to pinch the princess's fingers between the elaborate rings and finger-stalls she wore, careful too of Payma's long enameled fingernails. Samarkar remembered embroidering or serving tea with hands so decorated, and winced when Payma said, "Can I bring you tea, Honored Sister?"

But one didn't say no to tea. "I would be honored."

Samarkar settled the inky skirts of her coat around her, a silent reminder of her new honorific. Tseweng-tsa's plucked and stained eyebrows rose. Samarkar made a show of not noticing.

"Of course, Samarkar-*la*," the regent said. "How silly of me. How proceed your studies?"

"Very well, thank you." Samarkar took the celadon porcelain tea bowl Payma placed in her hands and bowed her head over it. She could see at a glance the two or three wilted, translucent flower petals that rolled in the depths of the clear greeny-amber fluid. Sweetened with rose jam, in just the idiosyncratic manner Samarkar preferred when it was not served as a meal. Someone had seen to it that the room was prepared for her visit, and she suspected it wasn't the regent.

If it had been—well, the odds of the jam being poisoned were lower than they had been when Samarkar still could have produced an heir.

"Can you make it rain?" Payma asked, her face alight below her elaborate headdress as she settled back onto her cushion.

Samarkar laughed gently. "Not yet." Roughness scratched her fingertips; she pulled them away from her collar self-consciously and forced them to return to her tea bowl, aware that the nervous gesture had already given away too much. "There's a weather-working tomorrow night, however. Perhaps I can arrange for you to be invited. I shall beg it of my masters."

The regent's sniff echoed. She disapproved of a member of the royal family acknowledging any mastery but hers. But a weather-working meant rockets, and rockets would please the princes' wives.

Here, too, Samarkar realized, she could hear the rush of the wild Tsarethi. It might run like a millstream through the city, channeled and mollified, but it was not the sort of river one could ever treat as tame. It would tumble on, down through the valleys that divided the Steles of the Sky, gaining tributaries as it fell. It would grow and grow, broad and calm now, until it fell into the sea fourteen hundred *li* away as one of the world's great rivers, bearing the fate of three empires, a dozen city-states, and countless crofts and farms on its broad grass-smoothed shoulders.

What was arrogance like the regent's before something like a river?

Now, said the sometimes-doubting voice in her head. *Now you are thinking like the wizard Samarkar.*

Samarkar reached across rugs and cushions to set her bowl on a small lacquer table. In so doing, though, she leaned across the great mirror set against the far wall—wizard-work, because no mere crafts-man's hand could forge that span of glass and silver.

She saw herself like a shadow among the jeweled and flowered ladies. She saw the black ropes of her hair and how they caught the filtered light behind her; she saw how that same light lay in oil-sheen gleams on the silk brocade of her coat. She saw herself—again—as a dark, predatory raptor, waiting in the midst of jeweled cage-birds.

She was surprised the comparison pleased her.

She addressed herself to Yangchen, bowing her head a little as in respect. If Samarkar was a once-princess, Yangchen was Empress-in-Waiting, and though Samarkar was older, their ranks were not so dissimilar than that. And of course now Samarkar was also a lowly newly elevated wizard, and if Yangchen could force her into that role, all hope of wresting some advantage from this situation would be lost.

"Honored Sister," she said. "Do you know why it is that your elder husband wished to speak with me? And so urgently that he came when I still lay in my sickbed after initiation?"

Yangchen looked down, too, seemingly consumed by the process of shifting her son the prince to the other breast. She might have de-manded wet nurses—Samarkar had been raised by a string of them—but a show of devotion to a firstborn son was considered womanly. Yangchen would never lose a chance to stroke the lute of her own regard.

And, Samarkar thought more charitably, nursing would likely keep her from conceiving again soon.

"I am sure I don't know, Honored Sister," Yangchen murmured. "But I am confident he will see you, if only you wait a while. As I am certain you know he is exceedingly busy."

Samarkar knew it very well. She'd been her father's only heir for seven long years before he or one of his brothers managed to get Songtsan on a different mother, and she remembered the endless preparations, the tutorials, the history and language and tactical lessons—in case he should not get a son. She smiled and picked her tea up again, cradling the bowl in her palm. "Then there is no remedy but patience," she said agreeably. "Were you reading?"

Gently, Yangchen lifted the rustling scroll from her lap. The two halves of the case were blue-enameled and weighted, so despite the baby, she could hold it open easily with a section of the case in one hand while the other rested in her lap. She said, "I was just about to read of the Carrion-King."

Of course you were, Samarkar thought patiently.

THIS IS THE TALE YANGCHEN TOLD:

There was a prince among the horse peoples in the west who learned sorcery at his mother's knee, for his mother had been stolen by her husband from a clan even farther west, where the people have blue eyes like devils and white skin like ghosts. And there in the outermost and foreign west, their magic is not like the good, homey magic of our wizards, who bring rain with black-powder rockets and knit poisoned wounds with silk thread and the soft blue-gray mold that grows in soy curd left too long.

The prince's mother did not teach him wizardry. Instead, what he learned at her knee was sorcery, the reddest sort.

He learned to cast the evil eye. He learned to curse with pennies and with oats. He learned spells to turn an enemy's ankle; to throw him from a horse; to make the wombs of his women and his cattle go dry. He learned spells of drought and downpour, spells of fire and flood. He grew into his manhood, and as well as a prince, he became a sorcerer, and eventually a king. He raised the dead up to do battle for him, and so some called him the Carrion-King.

Such was this Carrion-King's renown, both on the battlefield and in the ways of magic, that all his neighbors feared him. They believed no god could protect them from his wrath. They believed no blessing could avert his ill will.

His father's empire grew and grew, for this Carrion-King conquered every land he set his hand against. And the Carrion-King's power, too, grew and grew, until even his father and mother feared him a little. What would happen if he were not content to wait for the throne of his people? What would happen if he decided to overthrow his father's reign?

No one brought these whispers to the Carrion-King, for while he was feared, he was not loved in equal measure. And as his empire burgeoned, and his troops in their horse-hoof armor rode out to conquer every city of the Celadon Highway, the good people of Rasa heard the rumors of war in the wind and grew afraid.

As well they should, because although Rasa—girdled in its mighty pillars of stone, walled away from the wars of the world—was a mighty empire, it was also wealthy, and the Carrion-King craved gold. The emperor of the Rasani decreed that a Citadel be built, then, and wizards found from all over the empire to defeat the Carrion-King.

So it was written; so it was done. The wizards of Tsarepheth—for so they came to be called—researched and consulted. They experimented and delved. And finally they came back to the emperor and told him, "There is nothing we can do that will defeat the Carrion-King."

"That is unacceptable," said the emperor. "I will have you beheaded and your order disbanded."

"Wait!" said the head wizard. "We said we could not defeat him. We did not say we could not remove the threat he poses to Rasa."

The emperor sat back in his chair. "You have my attention," he said. "How do you remove him as a threat without defeating him?"

The head of the wizards leaned in to the emperor's ear and began to whisper. Slowly, the expression of puzzlement on the emperor's face began to change to amusement, then joy. When the wizard leaned back, the emperor smiled and nodded.

"I see," he said. "Make it so."

So one of the wizards, who was from far Asmaracanda, summoned a sort of devil indigenous to that place, called a djinn. This
djinn's power was concerned with the granting of wishes, and he was
constrained to answer three wishes for each master. The Asmaracandan wizard explained to the djinn that it was the wizard's will
that he be sealed into a ruby phial, and that the phial was to be sent
to the Carrion-King as tithe.

Because it was manufactured by the wizards, it was of incomparable
beauty of design, and of course the Carrion-King could not bear that
it be opened by any hand but his. "Such a treasure," he mused, weighing it in his hand, "must contain something even more precious."

So saying, he pried the stopper out. And a smoke flowed out, and
a mist flowed out, and the djinn said unto him, "Master, I am the
djinn of the bottle, and I must grant you three wishes. What is your
first wish?"

The Carrion-King was no fool. He said, "I wish first for eternal
youth and second for eternal health."

And so it was granted.

And the djinn said unto him, "Master, I am the djinn of the
bottle, and I must grant you one wish. What is your last wish?"

The Carrion-King was no fool. He said, "I wish third to rule the
world."

And so it was granted.

But in his immortality and invulnerability, you see, the Carrion-
King had ceased to be human. He was a god now, a god among gods
of many nations, and the other gods did not take kindly to him
usurping their territory. Now if he had wished to be undefeatable
instead of invulnerable, this might never have come to pass—so
perhaps the Carrion-King was just a little foolish after all. But what
happened was that the Warrior-God of the Messalines, he whom
they call Vajhir the Red, rode out to face the Carrion-King.

And Vajhir the Red's chariot was drawn by the sun, which in
their part of the world is an enormous lion with a golden mane, and
Vajhir the Red's javelins were lightning bolts, and Vajhir the Red

fought the Carrion-King until the steppe trembled and the mountains called the Buttresses of the World cracked and Vajhir the Red was wounded and grew tired. And those mountains are called now the Bitter Root, and they lie between Messaline and the Great Salt Desert, which was a green and lush land before Vajhir the Red fought the Carrion-King.

But when Vajhir the Red grew tired, there was the Scholar-God of the Uthmans. And *she* fought the Carrion-King with her globes of glass filled with tincture of vitriol, with her vast mirrors curved to throw the sun's flame a mile across bright water, with her tamed angels ranked ten deep and sporting spears that reached the breadth of the sky. And the God of the Uthmans, who has no name, fought the Carrion-King until the mountains called the Pillars of Heaven cracked and the span of the sky sagged at two corners.

And those mountains are called the Shattered Pillars now.

And then the Eternal Sky of the Qersnyk fought the Carrion King—and the Eternal Sky's weapons were arrows faster than thought, and he rode upon a pale stud horse of the steppe breed that looked more like skin stretched over a skeleton than the steed of a god. And the Carrion-King bellowed and beat his chest, but he had forgotten to wish from the djinn that he never grow tired, and after two and a half battles with the gods of the world, he was weary.

The Eternal Sky fought him almost to a standstill and might have defeated him, but time was passing. The Eternal Sky had to take up his veil so night could fall over the land and the Eternal Sky's hot face would not burn it sere.

In that battle, the mountains called the Range of Heroes were shattered, and the Heroes themselves were burned to ashes by the Eternal Sky before he thought to veil his face, and so that place is known now as the Range of Ghosts.

And that corner of the sky, too, sagged earthward.

So there was only one Warrior-God left, or so all the other gods of the world thought. They turned to Song, and from among the Holy Ancestors they cajoled the Old Master to stride forth, to stroke his white beard and pick up his staff and come and join the battle with the Carrion-King.

Wearily, the Old Master did. The Old Master and the Carrion-King fought each other up and down the sagging sky. They fought with staff and spear, and never could one get the better of the other, though one was ancient and one was new. But slowly, slowly, the Old Master wore the Carrion-King down, until it looked inevitable that the Old Master would win.

The people of Song and Rasa looked on with terrified fascination.

Until with one great sweeping motion of his spear, the Carrion-King, who had seemed almost defeated, knocked the Old Master's staff from his hands and the Old Master himself from the sky. The Old Master tumbled down, and when he fell, he fell among the mountains called the Steles of the Sky and broke them off jagged and fierce as dragon teeth.

The wizards of Rasa wailed, for they were sure this was the end, and the emperor made plans to have them all executed before the new city of Tsarepheth itself could be destroyed by the Old Master's struggles.

But that was not what happened.

Instead, as the Old Master heaved himself wearily up, pushing the collapsed sky above him with his staff, something came forth from the mist that collected around the broken pillars of the world.

It was the Mother Dragon, and she was angry, for the gods fighting in the skies overhead had awakened her.

First she went to confront the Old Master, but he pointed his staff to the Carrion-King, and the Mother Dragon, being a mother, could tell that he was not lying. So she flew up and took the Carrion-King in her talons, and she buried him deep in the rubble of the mountains he had shattered, and raked heaps of stone over him.

YANGCHEN LET THE SCROLL EASE CLOSED. THE WOMEN WERE SEWING, and Samarkar was staring into her tea. After a long gap, Payma said, "But I thought he wished to rule the world."

"He did," said Samarkar, when no one else answered. "But he did not ask to rule it forever. So now he waits under the mountains for his chance at vengeance, and the Mother Dragon guards him."

Slow applause sounded in the doorway. Samarkar turned, startled as the rest of the women, to find her half brother standing there snapping his fingers gently. "Well told, Honored Wife," he said, as she settled the baby against her chest and began to rise. He brushed her face. "You should have been a storyteller."

"I have all my stories here," she answered, and leaned her cheek against his hand. Samarkar swallowed a spike of envy. If Yangchen's affection was feigned or dutiful, she had never seen any sign of it.

Samarkar gathered her legs under her and rose, aware of the skirts of her coat falling around her legs like petals furling for the night. "Honored Brother," she said, bowing low and extending her tongue. "I understand you wished to see me?"

Songtsan bowed, too, more shallowly. When he stood, Samarkar stood with him. "Walk with me."

Samarkar bowed her farewell to the ladies, reminding herself that she was a wizard now and not a princess as she followed Songtsan from the room. He walked slowly at first, as if favoring a woman hobbled with impractical shoes—or perhaps in deference to her presumed infirmity. But when she kept stride easily, he soon lengthened his pace.

He spoke in low tones, in the Qersnyk language, and they moved and kept moving. Samarkar was not surprised; there was no true privacy in a palace, and they had spoken so many times before.

But never of such things as he said now.

"Samarkar-la, I need your counsel. Qarash has fallen. The Old Khagan is dead, and our sources report that his sons are at war over the remains of the Khaganate."

"Songtsan-tsa," she said, and hesitated. They had seen each other through many troubles, her brother and herself, and together found the means to wrest advantage from more than a few. But he had also used her shamelessly as a pawn of empire, and she had no illusions that he would not do so again. He had not approved of her choice to go to the wizards, but he had not quite gone so far as to forbid it. And from his words now, it seemed she still had his confidence—as much of his confidence as he extended to anyone. "When you say Qarash has fallen . . ."

"News from afar is only as reliable as the wings of the birds that bear it." He shrugged, the gold brocade on his shoulders exaggerating the gesture. "But you know we had agents in Qarash. One managed to get a pigeon away while the city was falling around her. It seems that Re Qori Buqa Khanzadeh, one of the brothers of Mongke Khagan, has claimed the succession—and that this claim is contested by some of his nephews and cousins. Most notably by Re Qulan Khanzadeh, who claimed primacy in that *his* father was named by the Great Khagan as heir before dying under somewhat mysterious circumstances. Qulan by rights should have inherited then, but he was ten years old, his heir a brother still on the cradleboard. And so, eighteen years ago, Mongke Khagan stepped into the void."

"And now Mongke Khagan is dead, and those brothers are adults?"

"The older, Qulan, would have been a man of twenty-eight winters, near enough. The younger is eighteen or nineteen, by my count. Which is adult as the steppe folk reckon things. He's accounted quite the warrior, having fought at Mongke's behest across half of Song." Songtsan spread his hands with a grimace. He was not yet twenty-five and still subject to the whims of his regent mother for a season—though of late, Samarkar knew, he had been concentrating more and more power in his own hands. It wasn't coming fast enough to keep the Song from chewing away at the border, though.

He continued: "Qulan, by all reports, is dead. When I say that Qarash fell, to answer your earlier question, I mean it was razed to the ground."

Samarkar nodded. She knew her face was impassive; she could feel how it hung slack across her bones, a mask over thinking she had learned well as a child. Right now, it kept her brother from knowing how she feared him.

As they swept side by side through long galleries and echoing halls, she said, "So it remains to be seen if Qori Buqa can consolidate power into his own hands and resurrect the Khaganate from its ashes."

"It is the drawback," Songtsan said, with a dry little smile, "of a political system whose basis is essentially, 'because I said so.'"

Samarkar laughed low, wondering why she had been dreading this meeting so. *Because his charm conceals not goodwill but a knife. Because there had never been anything in Songtsan's plans for me, except duty. Please. Please let me find my magic.* Her laughter chilled quickly when she let herself consider consequences. "If we act now, we stand a chance of liberating Kashe. And you can bet the Song rulers are thinking the same thing with regard to their cities—or will be as soon as the news reaches them."

"Qersnyk civil war is an advantage for us," Songtsan agreed. "But we have to be ready to grab it. Empires are not built and maintained without the taking of the odd city."

"And then there is the issue of the refugees. . . ."

"Yes," Songtsan agreed. "No doubt the Qersnyk herders will head for their summer ranges early. And when winter threatens and they know there is no grain on the steppe to feed them and their herds until summer—"

"—They will come to Kashe. Or Qeshqer, as they call it. By which I mean, they will come to us."

He nodded. "They will come to us. The steppe folk are falling. But as our father promised, we have outlasted them, and we will take back what they stole and more. Rasa is not finished as an empire yet."

He extended his hand and made it into a fist. But Samarkar saw how he glanced back the way they had come. A chill settled over her as she contemplated what, exactly, would have to take place before Songtsan could put his plans in motion—and what it would cost to all concerned.

SAADET CAME TO AL-SEPEHR WHILE HE STOOD IN PRAYER BEFORE THE altar of the Scholar-God, transcribing the God's sacred words from an ancient tome onto crisp, bound sheets of vellum. It was a meditation and a practice as well as a prayer, for the work had to be done mindfully, patiently, as perfectly as possible.

A devotee might spend years on the transcribing of one book, a lifetime on seven or eight. And in turn, each devotee himself became a copy of that perfect book—an imperfect copy, as flawed as human memory, but as close as one could approach to the divine.

Al-Sepehr's sect did not believe in the intermediation of prophets between the Scholar-God and the mortal world. Rather, they believed in study as the only sacrament.

So he finished the sentence he was scribing before he set his brush aside and—beckoning Saadet to follow—stepped out of the domed chapel into the light. There were five half stones in his pocket, each wrapped in its own silken pouch. The one he drew forth was still palled thickly in blood, only a few flakes missing despite all the use it had been put to a day or so before. Al-Sepehr still felt himself shaky and weak from the magic that had raised so many dead. It would be days before he found himself strong again.

The stone was cold, but Saadet nodded, making the sunlight flash in her striking eyes. "He does not need to speak with you directly now. I will speak for him."

"I listen, Shahruz," al-Sepehr said, returning the rock to his pocket.

Saadet straightened. Her posture changed, became that of a bold man, wide-stanced and cocky. "Your ghosts," she said. "They failed to bring Qori Buqa the death he craved?"

Al-Sepehr shrugged. It was as he had anticipated. For thirteen years, his Rahazeen believers had been at work fomenting rebellion, muddling dynastic succession, and unsettling regimes. That led to weak kings, and weak kings led to war. "They failed also to capture Re Temur for our uses," al-Sepehr said. "The surviving son of Otgonbayar is protected. He defeated them."

In his sister's form, Shahruz straightened. "Qori Buqa thinks he can bid you, and you will send your ghosts to do his murders."

"For now, he is right," al-Sepehr said, though he still swayed with exhaustion. He added wryly, "within the limits of my strength."

Qori Buqa could think what he liked, but al-Sepehr had raised the ghosts, and al-Sepehr's will alone dominated them. It was convenient to allow the would-be Khagan his illusions for a time, however.

Shahruz cleared his throat and said, "So whose arrival am I awaiting?"

"Not his," al-Sepehr said. "But we found his woman. With that, we can bring him to us. Until then, I will send you back the rukh. The wind will bear you to Qeshqer. I will have the woman brought there. You can send her on to me, and it's possible we'll have another opportunity at Re Temur soon. Qori Buqa cannot be permitted to win his war so easily. We do not have the armies to oppose generals who would rather fight us than each other."

Shahruz-in-Saadet nodded, his/her eyes revealing nothing but concentrated intensity. "For the Nameless," he said, his intonations making a woman's fair voice into a dark and knifelike thing.

"For the world," al-Sepehr answered.

 6

No one could have tended to so many dead. But that did not stop the mute monk from trying.

He should have raised scaffolds, lifted the dead into the air, where the carrion birds could come for them in convenience, unharried by the earthbound predators who squabbled and snarled all around. But there was not enough wood in the whole of the steppe for this many bodies, not if the monk could hew each tree that huddled in every river valley or climbed every sacred hill, where the dry and endless sea of grass could not choke the life from its seedlings, and enough deep water remained to feed deep roots.

So instead, the monk laid out each dead man—or boy, or in a few cases woman—anointed the eyes and mouth with a vulture's pinion soaked in sweet oil, and gestured a brief prayer. The first day it wasn't so bad, in the cold. By the second, the bodies were stiff with frost and age.

By the fifth, they were rotting.

That was the day on which the monk began to see the butterflies.

It was unseasonable for butterflies, and so he turned to watch the first one beating strongly into a headwind, its pale green-gold wings shimmering like a mare's hide in the sun. As he watched, the wind lashing his stringy hair about his face, it dipped down and lighted on the face of a corpse, a boy of no more than thirteen or fourteen who had fallen with a red-fletched arrow through his throat.

The monk had chosen silence, and he respected that vow even now, when there was no one to hear but the dead. He had *not* chosen to lose his sight, but it was failing him anyway. The dark irises of his eyes had a blue sheen in sunlight, and he saw the world—already—as if through dirty glass.

But he was not so blind yet that he could not see the color and motion as another butterfly flitted past—this one brilliant orange— then another, and another, and one more, until they filled the air with a tumult of wings so thick one could hear them whispering and smell their dusty scent. His fingertips crept to his lips and pressed there, as if to hold the exclamation in.

The butterflies swirled around him, shimmering changeable colors like rare jewels: blues and golds and greens and vermilions, pearl-whites, purples verging on blacks, reds like the heartsblood that twined slender vines up the steppe grass to wave above it, throwing its bright heads high into the ceaseless wind. He felt the brush of their wings. He breathed between his fingers so as not to inhale one.

If the monk had been able to see from the perspective of a falcon or one of the black birds to which he commended the dead, he would have known that each butterfly flitted into existence over the lips of a dead man or boy or occasional woman. That each one then beat wings to gain altitude and joined the general migration.

If the monk had seen from the perspective of a falcon, he could have seen that the butterflies numbered in the tens of thousands, and that all their myriad beating wings in myriad brilliant colors marked a general migration south.

He couldn't see that, but he could guess at it. It was the scarlet butterflies that gave it away.

Because all over the steppe, deep into the Rasan Empire, all across the lands of the Song, it was known that scarlet butterflies were the souls of witches. And it was said that they would whisper secrets and magic into your ears if you were silent and listened hard.

No one was more silent than the monk. But no matter how he strained his ears, the butterflies kept their peace, as silent to him as he was to them.

EDENE'S COUSINS LED TEMUR INTO THE CAMP, TO THE FIRE THAT HAD been allowed to die to embers overnight and was now being coaxed to flame for the boiling of tea. One of them—the one who'd all but lost her eye—kept bloody fingers pressed to the socket as swelling puffed the lid closed and pink-tinged fluid ran down her face. She *might* keep it. She might even keep some of the sight in it: Temur had seen worse healed, with time and good nursing, but he wouldn't care to wager a mare on it.

The other cousin—her sister, Temur thought, though he still had trouble keeping the Tsareg clan girl-cousins straight—pushed her down on a rolled hide and waved Temur to sit beside her. "You take care of Toragana. I'm going to fetch great-grandmother."

The swaddled babe on her back was visible as the girl disappeared between tents.

Toragana seemed not to require any extensive caretaking other than a prop to lean her shoulder against, so Temur did as the other girl had asked. He knew from hard experience that a wound that would not prove fatal by itself could put a chill in the bone that *would* bring down a wounded warrior—even before the wound could take heat and fester. He shrugged his coat off and threw it around Toragana's shoulders, adding an arm over it to keep her warm.

Around them, others were straggling to the fireside, some wounded or aiding wounded, some dragging the dead. Temur wanted to close his eyes against the faces of still more people he had known gone lifeless and empty.

Toragana, he thought, did. Or close the one eye that wasn't torn and swollen shut anyway. After a stiff moment, she leaned against him, burrowing her shoulder into his chest. She sighed, hard, then began to sob. "Edene..."

"I know," Temur said. "I'll get her back. Wherever they've taken her, I will ride after."

He said it with the force of a vow, and the vow filled him. *Yes*, he thought, suddenly certain. *I will go after her. To the Range of Ghosts and to Hell itself.*

Determination felt good in his mouth, like a round stone. Toragana took his hand; he squeezed.

When Temur told Tsareg Altantsetseg of his plan, she agreed that he must leave at once. The Tsareg clan, she said, would stay behind and sky-bury their dead. Temur would ride ahead. He would take Bansh and he would take Edene's rose-gray mare, Buldshak, as a remount—"and because Edene will need a horse, when you find her"—and the clan would give him food.

He insisted they keep their stores of salt in case the ghosts returned. Altantsetseg retaliated by handing him an *airag*-skin full not with mare's milk but with salted water.

As he threw a leg over Buldshak's back—Bansh snorting jealously by his knee—Temur found himself shaking his head at the ridiculousness of what he was about to undertake. Here he was, riding off to rescue a woman from ghosts as if it were as everyday a matter as stealing a kidnapped wife back from an enemy clan.

But they had taken her alive. Her and her only, when they had been killing everything else they touched. Surely if they had a reason to take her alive, they had a reason to keep her that way?

The remains of the Tsareg clan had assembled to see him off. He raised a hand to them; they waved as he made his mare bow. Altantsetseg called out, "May you ride comfortably and tirelessly on the road you travel!"

Gently, Temur reined the mares away.

He hadn't gone a *yart* at a canter when he realized that the shadow in the grass behind him was Sube, following at a ground-eating lope. He brought the rose-gray to a halt with his weight, letting a hand rest on her shoulder when she snorted and shook her slender neck. The dog stopped five paces off, tongue lolling, the felted shreds of his matted coat hanging about him like a coat of rags.

Temur's heart broke a little.

He understood the offer, and he was confident the dog understood it too: They were going raiding, to steal back what had been stolen from the clan. But what the dog didn't know—couldn't know—was that Temur had no idea where the trail would take him. To the Range of Ghosts, surely. And then what? How would he feed a dog? If he came to a place where he had to let the horses run wild, well, steppe ponies were half wild to begin with, and after sixty-odd days he had a good opinion of Bansh's good sense.

Sube would track. He would guard Temur and the mares from ghosts in the night. Temur had already seen that he would fight like a demon. He would be a companion by the fire, a sharp nose and sharper ears and fierce teeth. Temur longed to call him.

The clan needed him to guard their flocks—and their lives. And Temur was leading him into death if he took him.

"No, Sube," he said. He pointed back along the track, the faint trace of two mare's passage through the grass that already swished calf-high. "Go back."

Sube whined. He dropped his head and ears.

"No," Temur said. "Go back."

The big dog sat, obdurate.

Temur turned away. He urged the mare on.

Behind him, he was aware of the dog's eyes watching him out of sight.

IN THE MORNING, TEMUR GLIMPSED THE MOUNTAINS, JUST A DULL finger smudge on the horizon. It would only be the front range he could see so far, the smaller peaks called the Range of Ghosts.

Beyond them, reached by way of a perilous pass, lay a high plateau and the city of Qeshqer—with the even higher and more treacherous peaks of the Steles of the Sky at its back.

It was possible that Temur's path would lead him so far. But beyond that boundary lay the unconquered Rasan Empire, home of a people whose language he did not speak and whose customs he did not know.

Would he follow Edene there? Even assuming she still lived—he was taking a wild chance to suppose the ghosts had taken her to the storied (and purportedly haunted) mountains. But he had to do something.

And it was better than waiting for Qori Buqa's men to find him and kill him and probably kill the whole Tsareg clan for daring to shelter him, too.

For a long time, each day's passage seemed to bring that blue-smoke smudge at the horizon no closer. By the end of the first five-day, though, he could measure against his fingers that the mountains had grown. By then, Temur had outridden the refugee horde, burdened as they were with worldly goods. Another five-day and he could see each day that the Range of Ghosts stood closer, taller. In the third five-day water became more common, and the gazelles and antelope of the high steppe gave way to deer and hares. Temur still saw, occasionally, the broad angle of a vulture's wings circling overhead, but the bird never drifted close enough that he could tell which type it was.

As he chased the heights, he was leaving spring behind. Here among the gentle foothills, ice still lingered at the stony margins of streams and in the deep shade under evergreens. Temur supplemented his diet of rabbit and marmot with pale buds pinched from the ends of spruce boughs. He tucked these into his cheeks and sucked for their tangy flavor and power to prevent the winter sickness that sometimes made scalps bleed and teeth fall out. It was a good trick for the cold months when the milk of weaning mares dried up and that of the pregnant mares had not yet let down.

Buldshak had her season while they climbed; Bansh did not, and when Temur greased his hand with marmot fat and palpated her, he felt her womb as large and hard as a man's skull, buried deep in the muscle of her body. She twitched and stamped, but tolerated his indignities.

She was likely in foal, but it would be many months yet before the filly was born. Still, he felt a thrill of excitement; his luck in this mare was amazing. Here she was, the potential foundation of a herd that could be a new start for him—and she'd brought along a foal—if it came to term and all went well.

It struck him as a nakedly encouraging portent. For a few hours, as he rode the bay and led the rose-gray into wooded glades now, he allowed himself to dream that he would rescue Edene and make her his wife and that they would live to an untroubled old age with all their children and her cousins and her cousins' children.

It was a fantasy, and he knew it. But he was soldier enough to know that such fantasies were all that carried men through the supposed glory of war.

The mountains made their own weather. He knew these hills as well as he knew the steppe: They were the summer range of his folk. So he also knew how dangerous and unpredictable the springtime storms were. His rate of travel slowed, as one of the mares had to carry bundles of fuel—wood for fire here, where there were no casual piles of dry dung at every turning—and each night, he must seek out pasturage for them. The grass here was richer but found in meadows rather than vast sweeps of plain, and the mares needed time to crop and chew. Horses could not bolt their food like dogs or men.

Twice more, the ghosts found him, though not in such armies and vast numbers. Each time, Temur was wakened by the restlessness of the mares in time to cast a circle of salt water around them.

Each time, he spent the night uneasily alert, seated comfortably on Bansh's broad back with the salted arrows on his hip, his strung bow resting comfortably before him. Each time, the ghosts drifted around the borders of his secured circle, wailing soundlessly, displaying the gaping horrors of their bloodless wounds. Each time, they vanished with the mist, so Temur could almost convince himself in the exhausted blur of morning that he'd seen nothing at all.

Forest gave way to high alpine meadow, a lacework of harsh, hardy groundcover around tremendous scattered boulders. The green flanks of the mountains stretched up to stark, knife-blade granite, and Temur at last rejoined the road. There was only one pass through the mountains to Qeshqer. He would have to risk being recognized, if any of his uncle's men had come this far.

By the equinox, Temur was deep among the Range of Ghosts, their great shadows rendering the Eternal Sky finite. As if in mockery of his fears, the pass was deserted. He imagined caravans waited below for the warm days to come, his people forced early into their summer ranges and hoping there would be no late storm or snow.

Temur pushed on. For this, he'd been hoarding his dried rations, and the salt and sweets and grain for the mares. There was water aplenty at least. It tumbled down the mountainsides in streams so clear and cold his teeth ached just to look upon them. They would run north between the hills, and from there feed the sparse and necessary rivers of the steppe. The cold high air made his head spin, and for three days they climbed. The nights held clear, and the mares were eating from nose bags now, so by the light of thirteen moons they walked late into the night.

Thirteen moons. No less and no more, every night from rise to set. No matter how many times he allowed himself to count them.

Maybe somewhere, nine hundred *yart* behind him, the killing was over.

ONE DAY, TEMUR FIRST NOTICED THAT THE STREAMS WERE RUNNING south now, to eventually twine into the wild Tsarethi, thence to the ocean he'd heard described, but could not begin to imagine. That night, the killing ice came. The wind roused him from his cold bivouac between stones—the wind and the distress of the mares. He craned his head back in time to see the leading edge of the storm grope black and threatening across the scattered band of moons.

He cursed.

There were stones here, at least, great broken boulders leaned this way and that against each other as if they had tumbled from a great height. One rock slab slanted out from the cliff it had slid from, a narrow passage dark at its base.

There had been no fuel for a fire for days, but he still had some tallow and wicks in his pack. A hurried search found a hollow-surfaced stone that would do. Cold rain spit, freezing to a glaze where it struck, by the time he'd kindled a lamp with flint and steel. He cupped it in his left hand, leading the snorting and uncertain mares into the damp crevice with his right.

Though born under the watchful expanse of the Eternal Sky, the steppe horses were familiar with enclosed spaces. Clans regularly sheltered the most valuable livestock in their white-houses during the worst storms of winter, and the mares could smell the weather coming. So they were discontented and disconcerted, but not terrified. Still, it took time to coax them within, and by the time he had them under shelter, both mares and man were ice-coated and chilled to the bone. The frozen fur at Temur's collar scratched his throat.

Hastily, Temur set the lamp down and sidled back past the mares, squeezed hard against stone when Bansh shifted unexpectedly. He'd have to back the mares out when the storm ended; there was no way he was turning them in here. He hadn't retied their gear—just tossed the packs hastily across their withers for moving. Now he heaped the packs behind them, jamming a blanket into crevices to drape over the opening, weighting the bottom with saddlebags and stones. It didn't keep much wind out, but it was what he had.

The dull thump of icy rain against wool was soon replaced by the rattle of pellets on a frozen surface. Temur stood just within, breathing wearily, listening to it fall, until his makeshift lamp began to flicker and he had to sidle past the horses once more to tend it.

He stripped, bundled himself in a dry long wool shirt and counted on work to warm him while he rubbed the mares dry with scraps of blanket. They were steaming by the time he was done, and that was a good sign; they had not taken a chill.

A draft savaged him every time the wind shifted, and even padded with blankets the ground was stony and harsh, but the fragile warmth of the horses and the lamp soon sent tentative fingers through the confined space. Temur had not intended to doze; the lamp needed constant tending, and he worried for the mares. But the warmth and stillness and the endless hiss of ice entombing them within this crack in the mountainside lulled him, so eventually he bundled himself in fleeces and more blankets and slept.

IN HIS DREAM, TEMUR ROSE FROM HIS BODY. IT LAY ON THE GROUND, A shriveled, discarded thing. A rag. He wasn't dead; although the lamp had died he and the mares both seemed to cast a shallow, silvery light. In that, he could see how the pulse beat in the hollow of his throat and how the livid scar stood out on its pallor. Some self-consciousness made him shuffle his dream-feet clear of his crude mortal body. He stood astride himself, as if in stirrups, standing up in the saddle for a wider horizon.

The mares slept standing and did not stir as he walked past them—*through* them—and through the ice-shielded blanket that closed the door of the impromptu stable. Outside, it was day, by the light, but he could not tell if he stood embanked in a midday mountain fog or if this was the first cold light of morning. Every surface he saw—though he could not see far—was glazed with dull diamond.

The mists blew all around him, so he expected ghosts. But there was nothing—not even suggestive shapes in the fog.

Following an itch he did not fully understand, Temur stepped into the fog. Where his boots should have slipped on the glaze ice, he stood steady, and that too reminded him that he was dreaming. As did the sudden chirp and rise of birdsong—spring and meadow songbirds, not the great Berkut eagles, wolf-killers who haunted the high ranges. Piercing gold rays slanted through the fog, tattering it as swiftly as a sword blade run through silk. Temur raised a hand to shield dazzled eyes, and found himself looking a man in the face.

A man—or perhaps something more.

His moustache trailed black as ink across his chin to drape a scale coat of golden horse hooves, and from his shoulders billowed a cloak as blue as the lapis that had glazed the fountain bowls in Qarash's center square. He had one hand on the mountainside, one foot stepped up as if into a stirrup, and as Temur watched, he rose up and slung his other leg over the high saddle between peaks as if he straddled a mare.

The mountain seemed to agree with him, because he had no sooner settled himself than it snorted, shook itself loose of the earth, and climbed joyfully into the sky. It lifted its cliff-feet with frolicsome pleasure, kicking out once or twice for the sheer joy of it. Temur flinched, expecting a rockfall to follow, but the mountain-mare's step was light, and on her back the Eternal Sky gentled her with soft touches.

Of the sixty-four sacred colors of horses, she was the color they called storm, a smoked black with a streaked, sparse mane and tail the color of wind-pulled clouds lit from beneath by a rising sun. Her face was swathed broadly with white between the eyes and nostrils, and those eyes were kind and bright. Her ears pricked into a tall oval crown atop her head. She regarded Temur inquisitively from high above.

Perhaps the Eternal Sky saw her looking, because he turned and stared down at Temur.

"A mouse," he said. "A little steppe fox. Where did you come from, child?"

"I hid," Temur said. In his dream, it seemed perfectly reasonable to be speaking all the way up to the sky in a calm, low voice. "From the ice."

"Of course you did," the Eternal Sky said, and Temur was struck by how much he seemed like the Great Khagan, Temur's grandfather for whom he was named—or how the Great Khagan was remembered, anyway. Temur had been too young to know him when the old man had died. "Well, just a moment, then. I have a task to be about."

As Temur watched, the Eternal Sky reached into his coat of hooves and pulled out a long black veil. He wrapped it about his face in triple layers, all save the eyes, where he only drew one pass. Temur could still make out the brilliance of his black eyes behind. He thought the Eternal Sky winked at him.

Somehow, as the Eternal Sky wrapped his face, it seemed he wrapped the sky behind him as well, because with each pass of the cloth, that lapis color grayed and softened, became violet, became indigo. When the Eternal Sky tucked the ends of his scarf in, he became Mother Night.

Mother Night blew Temur a kiss.

"There," she said, and her voice was the same voice except it was sweet, a woman's. "That should do for now."

She began reaching into her pockets and saddlebags, drawing forth ornaments that chimed and clinked. The night was terribly dark now, without stars or moons, but Temur could see her outlined in the same pale silvery light he cast himself. He watched as she lit lamps with a taper and scattered them about the sky, hanging each one on an invisible hook before grasping the fabric of the night and giving it a pull, skating it along the sky. He watched her hang each lamp, but somehow there were thousands more in the sky every time he looked.

Then, the lanterns lit, she began to hang her sequins—a pendant of silver, a pendant of pearl, a pendant of horn, a pendant of costly pale shell all the way from the foreign seashore. A pendant of electrum, a pendant of diamond, a pendant of iron . . .

"You hung the moons," Temur said.

She smiled at him through her veil—or so he thought by the shape of the light behind it. "So I did, child. And this one is yours, is it not?"

"Yes," Temur said.

"Would you like to see it closer?" She extended her hand, her skin dusty gold, like pollen on a mirror-colored horse's hide.

Temur's mouth dried with nervousness. *Does that happen in a dream?*

He reached out his hand to Mother Night's, and felt her fingers, calloused and leather-damp, wrap his own. A strong pull, and he was behind her on the back of the storm-colored mare. The hot scent of horse surrounded him, and the musk of a woman hard at work.

"Hold on," Mother Night said, and pulled his hands around her waist as the storm-colored mare slapped her tail in delight and broke into a canter. All the sequins on Night's veil jingled. "We shall go and see it, then."

The moon was a tiny bangle hung on the fabric of the night. The moon was a sequin that sparkled by Temur's nose as he leaned over Night's shoulder. The moon was a great iron-colored disk swelling before them as the storm-colored mare bore them toward it at impossible speed. Her hooves made no sound in the sky; her mane whipped in scant threads as she tossed her head up to scent the wind. They flew as high as a vulture's gyre, and sooty wings beat all around them.

Then they were falling, curving down to the Iron Moon as if on the descent from a great leap, and the storm-colored mare reached out with her forelegs and caught them. Great puffs of iron-black and rust-red dust rose under her hooves.

Temur caught himself against Night's back, straightened, and turned to crane his neck each way. "Oh," he said.

In every direction, a rocky landscape in char-black and rust-red and streaks white as ash stretched away. The horizon curved down, and Temur felt curiously light, curiously free, as if he might float away from the storm-colored mare's back at any provocation. His fingers clutched on Night's belt. As the mare cantered, her muscular haunches working behind him, a silvery pall of air surrounded them, trailed them, leaving behind a confetti of minuscule bubbles.

It was broad day here, and the sun gleamed pale in a sky as black as new ice.

"Oh," he said again.

"Your moon, Temur Khanzadeh," said Mother Night.

"I'm no prince. . . ."

. . . AND HE AWOKE, COUGHING AND CHOKING, SHAKING WITH FEVER IN the dark and the cold, to hear the stamp of restive horses. The makeshift shelter was utterly dark, and the rattling plink of ice on ice no longer echoed through. Sweat-sour and shaking, Temur heaved himself onto his side. His arms felt like boiled dough; his body, a salt-stained rag. Another wracking cough rattled his lungs like hide dried stiff, filling his mouth with sick-sweet phlegm. In the dark, he groped for a corner to spit it in, doubled over, braced with both hands on rocks while his empty stomach spasmed.

He would have cursed, but he hadn't the energy. Instead, fortifying himself with shallow, cautious breaths, he straightened bit by bit. Head spinning in a darkness so complete that his eyes provided ghostly images of things that were not there, he managed to push himself upright against the chill, gritty stone. One of the mares whickered curiously—Bansh, by her voice, and close by.

He reached out to her, found her broad, warm shoulder. She was his prop as he edged back again along her side to her haunches until Buldshak's warm whiskery nose pushed at his cheek. At least the muzzles of horses were dry and satiny, unlike the slick snouts of cattle.

He ran his hand up Buldshak's forehead to the forelock. She leaned into him, and only the wall kept him from falling back. He was grateful for the darkness: Disorienting as it was, it also kept him from noticing how the world spun.

He edged past Buldshak's haunches, his boots slipping in half-frozen manure, until his groping hands found the rough, icy wool of the blanket he'd hung for shelter. He stood still for a moment, controlling his breath, waiting for his heart to stop racing from so slight an effort at this. He thought if he started coughing again, he would never stop.

When he pulled the packs aside, the blanket had frozen into the cracks where he'd wedged it, and the whole was saturated and sheathed in ice that rendered it as hard and heavy as an iron door.

Temur wrestled with it until his chest heaved and his legs trembled from exhaustion—a matter of a few moments only. The urge to cough was a fire in his lungs. He leaned against the rock slab, shuddering with cold even though he knew the exertion should have warmed him, and thought.

Hard and heavy as iron, yes. But ice was brittle.

He wished he'd had the foresight to pull Buldshak into the shelter first. Bansh was a warrior, and he did not know the rose-gray mare as well. But she was a steppe pony. Surely, she was trained?

He hated to risk her hooves, but they had to get out of here somehow, and he wasn't strong enough.

He wormed his way back up to her head, tracing the line of her neck to find her head. He'd left the mares bridled, only slipping their bits, and now he replaced the bit and took hold of the reins just under Buldshak's whiskery chin. He leaned in against her cheek. She snorted; he felt the heat of her breath across his shoulder.

"Kick," he said, and reined her back a step.

He felt her plant her forelegs on the rocky earth, felt the shiver of effort run through her. Her head came down, her rear came up, and both hind legs flew into the air. An enormous shattering filled the confined space as she jumped forward again, and only Temur's hand on her bridle kept her from charging up Bansh's backside. Buldshak danced, snorting, as light and icy air suddenly flooded their little nest, outlining the mares and the piles of gear in brittle morning brilliance.

The cold hit Temur a dizzying blow, but after two or three breaths his head settled and new strength braced him. When Buldshak settled under his hands, he staggered back. The fresh air was strength, even though it set him coughing again. These were shallower coughs, however, and he managed to stay on his feet.

She'd torn the blanket free at the top and broken much of the ice off it, though the bottom was still frozen to the ground. With effort, wheezing, Temur managed to push it back over itself until it lay more or less flat across the icy ground. He set about checking Buldshak's hooves and ankles for damage, then backed both mares out into the daylight.

They stepped cautiously on the glassy ground, ice creaking under their weight, ripped veils of steam following the movements of their heads. They stood steadily—Buldshak snorting and shifting her weight, Bansh calm and seemingly half asleep, mottled muzzle dipped toward her one white-splashed foreleg—while Temur ferried their gear out of the rockfall shelter in the largest bundles he could manage, barely avoiding the lake of piss the rose-gray unleashed as soon as he walked away from her head. He had to keep leaning on the wall or a mare's withers to rest, and when he bent to struggle the door blanket free of the ice, he set off another coughing fit that left him on his hands and knees before it subsided.

By the time he had the mares fed and tacked, their gear loaded, the morning was half gone and the sun had cleared the peaks. This proved a blessing and a nuisance, for the ice rotted almost as soon as the sun touched it—the ground underneath had still been too warm to freeze—but that made for water-slick ice interspersed with patches of mud.

Still, there was no choice but to go on. Temur was sickening, and the mares needed green fodder and clean water.

Buldshak had the smoother gait, but it was into Bansh's saddle that Temur struggled. The liver-bay was a rock, and she stood like one even though Temur mounted like a toddler, pulling on the saddle and her mane to drag himself across her back, bruising his thigh on the high cantle, thrashing grimly until he got himself seated. She knew he wasn't well, or so he fancied; normally she was light on the rein or the leg, soft as a cat. But now she ignored his crude attempts to direct her and simply stepped forward, one hoof after the other, in the most cautious of possible walks while Temur huddled in his coat and two wrapped blankets on her back.

Buldshak followed on like a patient pack mule, content with Bansh's lead. The day warmed. The ice melted into ankle-deep mud. Swarms of biting flies arrived with the heat, and Temur clung grimly to Bansh's saddle while she plodded on. The sun slid behind the peaks again. The long shadows of the mountains plunged the pass into shadow. Temur knew he should stop: The mares needed rest and food—though Bansh, in her wisdom, was stopping to water herself and Buldshak at every stream they passed. A few swallows only, then onward. He knew he should stop, but he couldn't lift his hands to draw the reins, and he thought if he slid out of the saddle he'd never make it back up again.

The heat was a blessing as he shook with chill. The stones on every side had soaked up the sun's warmth; now, in the drawing dark, they gave it back. Behind the mountains to the west, the sky blazed amber, crimson. To the east it grew as dusky as a bruise.

Temur roused himself from his fever-dream. There had been a man in golden armor, and a woman on a horse. She had taken him somewhere. . . .

He pushed back his cowl of blankets to see. They fell about his thighs; the cool evening air soothed his sweat-matted hair. A mist was rising, and Temur looked at it through the glaze of fever and shuddered. If the ghosts he sought came now, he and the mares stood no chance of survival.

He had to get to Qeshqer. There might be help there, treatment for his fever, and perhaps even someone he could ask for guidance on where to find the ghosts—and the woman he desperately hoped they still held captive.

Even as he thought this, something stirred the mist. Something flitting, sparkling even in the gloaming, like chips of mica on the wing. *Thousands* of somethings, smaller than the span of Temur's palm, their pale or dark wings largely robbed of color in the dusk.

Butterflies.

Thousands and thousands of butterflies.

Bansh stood stolidly as they swirled about her like windblown leaves. Buldshak snorted and shook out her tail, tossing her head when they landed between her eyes and crawled up her ears to take flight again. Their wings brushed Temur's skin like falling petals. The delicate prickers of their feet tickled his face when they lighted briefly, then took off again. The wind of their passing was comprised of a thousand shifting currents.

He sat Bansh's back and watched them pass until there was no light with which to watch them, and he merely heard and felt. There were so many he could smell them, a papery, dry-feather kind of smell he didn't exactly have a name for. When the sky grew silvery again in the east, Temur expected moonrise to reveal them as flitting shadows in the glow of thirteen orbs.

The glow did reveal them, but not as he expected. Or rather, the butterflies were exactly what he had thought to see—but the sky was not. One lone moon rose over the ragged silhouettes of the mountains, fat and copper-red shading to silver as it climbed.

One moon. Alone.

This was not the sky of the steppe. And it was not the sky of Rasa, either, or of Song. He had never seen this moon before, in all his travels, and he had not seen the constellations that shimmered behind it.

He had left the Qersnyk lands—and yet there were still miles to go to Qeshqer. Which could only mean that Qeshqer, too, had fallen and was no longer vassal to the Khaganate.

✳   ✳   ✳

TEMUR WOULD NEVER KNOW HOW ALL THREE OF THEM CAME ALIVE
from the Range of Ghosts, except that Bansh brought them safely
down. He had no memory of days or nights passing, just a jumble of
fever and pain and the patient lurching of the mare as she descended
the narrow switchback road step-by-step. There were moments of
clarity in the nightmare blue-and-white, some of them more night-
marish than the fever-dream itself. The mist coiled like serpents in
the mornings, and there were times when Temur was sure it blinked
enormous lambent eyes and brushed his face with salty tendrils.
There were supposed to be mist-dragons in Rasa, but if that was
what these were, they seemed content to let him pass.

Another time, he had the sense of something huge and silent pac-
ing him during the dark before sunrise, and when there was light to
see by, he made out pawprints in the sandy verge of the road, big as a
stallion's hoof and shaped something like a tiger paw and something
like the foot of a man. When the fever left him able, he searched the
dark for the shimmer of yellow eyes. When it did not, he dreamed
their existence and came back to himself clutching his knife in his
hand, as if that could protect him.

But the worst by far was the figure he glimpsed again and again
at the corner of his vision: a man, a strange leathery man naked as
a prisoner, his belly caved in and carved out until there was nothing below or behind the ribs, his back and his skull caved in and
scooped out like a polished wooden bowl, his buttocks and sex like
empty sacks, his thighs and arms hard and shiny as polished brown
twigs.

The man never came close. He never attacked. He never even
showed himself plainly but always appeared for an instant, perched
on a boulder, vanishing into mists, glimpsed as he strode between
outcroppings of rock. But in Temur's fever, he seemed the most terrible thing in the terrible mountains, and Temur greeted his appearance each time with wracking coughs and shuddering chills.

Finally, when he doubled over the belly-high pommel hacking,
clutching at the front-boards to keep himself from toppling sideways,

Bansh raised her head and craned back to regard him with one big brown eye.

"Foolish child," she said. "He doesn't exist. He can't hurt you unless you let him."

Temur's gasp of surprise set him coughing again. And when he could force himself to stop, there was nothing but a plain bay mare, thin and weary, plodding forward along a descending trail. He reached out to touch her shoulder, reassuring himself of her solidity, and the pressure of the pommel against his stomach sent him into a fit of coughing and a fever-dream once more.

7

WHATEVER SONGTSAN FEARED FROM THE QERSNYK, IN THE NEXT quarter-moons it took second place for Samarkar to her training in wizarding ways. As a novice, she had read from books and attended lectures. She had studied chemistry and natural history, surgery and healing. As a novice, she had tended the stinking saltpeter beds; there was no special status appended to her as a once-princess. As a novice, she had learned the blending of explosive compounds and those that produced brilliant fireworks and those that were useful to bringing the rains—and she had learned the meticulous care necessary in working with them.

Now she was expected to begin the manufacture of such rockets. But the primary focus of her training became physical and practical: Once she was healed from her surgery, the emphasis was on making her talent manifest.

If it was going to.

AS TSERING-LA LED HER THROUGH THE WARREN OF PASSAGES HEWN from the rock below the Citadel, Samarkar wondered if the failed wizard had been tasked with helping Samarkar find her magic

because she could serve as a warning of the price of failure or because she was an assurance that even if everything went wrong, there
would still be a place in the Citadel for Samarkar.

It wasn't such a bad place, Samarkar thought. Teaching, studying. Building fireworks. Tsering-la seemed content—not even merely
reconciled, but happy. Her stride was confident; her boots clicked
with purpose. And for the moment, she had it better than Samarkar:
Tsering was not lightheaded with fasting.

Samarkar, walking behind and bearing the lantern for both of
them, was drawn to the way the hems of Tsering-la's six-petaled wizard's coat of black brocade swished against the bloused black silk of
her trousers. Another might not be so sensitive to the sartorial details, and might find a wizard's costume timeless and interchange-
able with that of any other wizard. But Samarkar had grown up in
courts and among courtiers, and she was infinitely sensitive to the
nuances of style and construction.

Yongten-la wore the plainest coats of anyone: black cotton, fine-
milled, quilted for warmth with a layer of wool felt between facing
and lining. Their simplicity was a statement of such power as needed
to make no statement. Tsering's coat was costly silk brocade imported
from Song, and it bore a pattern of intertwined blossoms in silver,
steel gray, and glossy black on its matte-black ground. The six-petal
cut and collar meant it could never be mistaken for anything but wizard's weeds. Still, Samarkar wondered at the other woman's confidence, when she had no magic of her own, to wear anything other
than plain black.

Tsering stopped before an enormous double door of plain rough
wood and waited until Samarkar drew up beside her. Samarkar must
have given the train of her thoughts away when her right hand came
up to clutch the placket of her coat. Tsering reached out gently and
made a show of dusting off Samarkar's shoulders, her calloused,
short-nailed fingers whisking over Samarkar's more-sober Rasan
brocade decorated with neat rows of matte eternal knots on a glossy
ground. "Whatever happens, it will be well."

"Am I obvious?" Samarkar asked.

Tsering smiled, a quick flicker of her mouth corners. Samarkar was much taller, but the fact that Tsering had to tilt her head back to meet Samarkar's eyes did not seem to rob her of any authority. A serpent of silver coiled through the black river of her braid, and in the lantern light it matched the decorations of her coat.

"I remember," Tsering said. "Now give me your coat, Samarkar-la, and go and earn your power."

Go and earn your power.

Samarkar handed over the lantern, then put her chilled fingers to her knotted buttons. The sacrifice demanded of a wizard was one thing; barrenness merely paved the road for magic. The would-be wizard still had to walk down it.

She stripped off her coat, her blouse, her boots—hopping on each foot in turn for that last. She peeled off her felted socks and stood at last before Tsering in her quilted trousers, jeweled collar, and the black-bound scarlet wrap-vest that cinched her breasts. The cold air prickled gooseflesh up across her shoulders. Her feet curled, trying to minimize contact with the icy floor.

She reached up and pulled her collar open, the edges scraping the sides of her throat. She felt far more naked without it than without her coat, though she'd been wearing coats for so much longer. She handed it to Tsering fast, before she could weigh it in her hands. "Any words of advice?"

"Advice is the last thing you need." Tsering stood on tiptoe and kissed her forehead. "Go on, then," she said, having spoken the ritual words already.

Steeling herself with a deep, cooling breath, Samarkar heaved open the door. The chamber beyond was dark, lit only by the stray radiance of the single lantern, and it echoed with the sound of trickling water.

Samarkar trailed a hand along the wet wall as she entered. The floor, too, was moist and slick under bare feet. With groping steps she circled the perimeter until intermittent drops splashed her arm, her bare shoulder, the part of her hair. The water felt like the ice of the glaciers it melted from.

She folded her legs beneath her and sat.

"I am ready," she called to Tsering, just out of sight beyond the wall. *Please let this happen. Please let me show them.*

"Then commence, Samarkar-la!" Tsering said. And shut the door.

A thin vein of light flickered beneath the door edge for a moment, then receded with Tsering's hesitant footsteps until she rounded a corner, and light and sound died as one. Alone in the dark, dripping water trickling down her neck and plastering the silk of her breast-binding to her skin, Samarkar closed her eyes.

It made no difference to what she saw.

SAMARKAR KNEW THE THINGS THAT WIZARDS KNOW, THE THINGS THAT monks and ascetics have taught them. One of these things was how to live in cold.

Though by the standard of Yongten-la, she had barely begun her practices, she at least understood the theory—or understood it as much as one so insufficiently practiced could. The insufficient practice was part of the test; one must come to the understanding in the end that one was always insufficiently practiced, and yet one must sometimes act anyway. Practice itself was an act.

Samarkar sat in the cold darkness, the chill creeping into her muscles, then her bones. She folded her legs one atop the other and brought her hands before her groin, where the center of creation had once lived and lived no longer. There was the essence of wizardry. It was an act of creation; it was a pure delight in defiance of hunger, and thirst, and sorrow, and the inevitability of death and devouring. As she had sacrificed the power of creation with her body, so she gained the power of creation with her mind.

So it would be.

She was resolved. This thing for herself, who had given so much for others.

She emptied herself, emptied her mind. The thoughts came nevertheless: *I am cold. I am hungry. I am thirsty. I need to urinate.*

See the thought. Allow it. And then allow it to pass. Let the space behind be empty.

I WILL DO THIS THING.

No.

And no, too, was identity. She felt something flicker, briefly, gone like a fish in the cold savage water of the Tsarethi, but it was her that thought it. And that was enough to drive it away.

DRIFTING. WARMTH WITHIN, AS THERE WAS NONE WITHOUT. WARMTH filling a void, a void with no center. . . .

Some time passed.

Eyes opened. Or did they? All was darkness, darkness and the warmth of steaming skin. There was a space bounded by walls, and a space within the space, bounded by flesh. They were equivalent.

There was nothing.

More time, the space thought.

It considered the thought and let it pass.

EYES OPEN IN DARKNESS. WHAT WAS WARM GROWS COLD; WHAT WAS comfortable grows stiff and chill. Heart slows, breath rattles in time with plashing water.

Cooling like embers.

Eyes close in darkness.

AND ALL IS QUIET AND STILL.

ONE COULD BE CONTENT.

Content with this.

Content to die in the cold?

CONTENT IN A LIFE DEVOTED TO THE PURSUIT OF PERFECTION AND THE compassionate understanding that it is unattainable.

She was what she was and what she would be. She was imperfect and full of striving. And that would be all right.

Whatever she was would be enough. Or it would not. She had what she had to use, and she would use it to her best ability, and she would allow the silence within her to persist and inform. She had that much and no more.

You cannot fool the magic into entering you. You have to release control. You must let the world choose.

You must let the world choose. All the while understanding that this is not helplessness. It is choice. Openness to the stream of what is possible.

Openness to all the possibilities of the world, in the understanding that some of those possibilities are terrible. Openness to grace.

What is, let be.

Thus do victims become heroes, Samarkar.

Heroes?

Now, Samarkar. Now it is time to open your eyes. . . .

. . . ON A ROOM BATHED IN LIGHT.

The floor around her was dry; the water dripping from overhead evaporated before it touched her shoulders, her hair, the dry silk of her breast-wrap. Farther away than the reach of her arms, the walls of the small chamber glistened with wet and hoar; water drizzled from above.

She lifted her hands from her lap. Fingers still interlinked. Each one limned with a glacial fire.

She put a finger in her mouth and licked it.

Fire, still, though the inside of her mouth felt chill.

SAMARKAR-LA SAT ON THE COLD STONE FLOOR OF A DUNGEON AND BE-gan to laugh.

8

She came up out of the earth by the light of her own hands. She cast no shadow, but all shadows streamed away from her.

She found her coat and blouse and boots around the corner, where Tsering had left them. She clasped her collar around her throat. She saw by the lay of the light across her chest and shoulders how she shone through the translucent jade as if she were a sun and the collar were a window.

She had no concept of the hour of night or day. When she emerged, she half thought it would be midnight, and she would sulk back to her chamber and curl up in bed to sleep the sleep of the chilled and exhausted. But of course her people would not allow a ritual to pass without acknowledgment, and when she stepped blinking into the early morning light, a crowd waited in the courtyard at the top of the stairs to greet her.

Tsering was there, and Yongten-la, and every wizard who had passed initiation. They handed her from one to the next with hugs and cheers, a break in their formal reserve that left her blinking tears. A newish wizard with his long moustache draped over his ears to clear his mouth for drinking passed around cups of millet whiskey sweetened with mulberries. The *raktsi* tasted like fire going down, and her head spun and her ears rang and the world whirled about her until Yongten-la thrust a sweet red rice cake into her hands and said, "Eat. You need that more than whiskey."

She broke off a piece and put it in her mouth, surprised by the sudden growl of an awakened appetite. She would have crammed the whole cake into her mouth if he hadn't laid a finger on her wrist, beside the bone, and said, "Softly now. You need to start slowly."

Samarkar remembered hearing such parties before, during her own novitiate, and wondering what was occurring that she was not invited to. "Slowly?" she asked. And then she paused. "How long has it been?"

Yongten-la smiled, sweet and sudden, the creases around his eyes and mouth standing out like a landscape seen from a height. Samarkar was not sure she'd ever seen him smile like that before.

"Three nights," he said. "Not so long, as such things are reckoned."

The light that she had forgotten had wreathed her flickered and died, left her blinking as its blue glacial purity was replaced by the slowly warming grayness of morning. No wonder the *raktsi* made her head spin.

Slowly, she took a second bite of rice cake. Cardamom and coconut, spices from the faraway tropical coast. Someone had brought out instruments, and the first tentative sounds of improvised music trailed through the distant, habitual noise of the river. A round-faced wizard a few years younger than she but more advanced in his training—not the one with the pampered moustache—came by as she finished the rice cake. She wondered if Yongten-la had subtly waved him in; deviousness would be like the master wizard.

His name was Anil. He took her hand and asked her to dance, and when she would have demurred—she knew dances, but they were court dances, not these bawdy country things—he showed her the steps over and over, until laughing, her head spinning, she halfway got it.

She was the guest of honor today. She could do no wrong, and dancing drunkenly with a handsome child—unthinkable in her past life—was suddenly no disgrace. Freedom made her more giddy than the whiskey.

She should not have been so strong, so full of energy after three days sitting on a cold stone floor. She knew that, and she understood intellectually that there would be a price to pay later. But for now she let Anil swing her into a line of men and women holding hands, and let the wailing of voices and shawms and strings pick her up and carry her in a whirling of six-petal coats and joyous laughter.

She was alive. She was alive, and she had found her power—or it had found her.

Tomorrow's problems she'd take care of tomorrow.

EDENE KNEW SHE WAS NOT DEAD. NOT UNLESS DEATH MEANT STINK-ing (possible) and itching (unlikely) in a filthy shirt and trousers while a thin, icy wind cut her to the bone and burned her lungs with altitude. She didn't think ghosts suffered nausea or aching bones. She didn't think they quailed with terror at the unspeakable drop beneath the bars of the cage they huddled in. She didn't think they clung to those bars until their hands ached and their fingers locked in place.

Ergo, she must be alive.

She dangled below the hooked yellow talons of a bird with wings so wide she imagined it could have carried off an Indrik-zver. It certainly had no difficulty with her weight, iron cage and all. The wind of its wing beats buffeted her. Her tears did not quite freeze on her face, but it was a near thing.

She squinted through waterlogged lashes to see where the bird carried her. Below, the golden sweep of the steppe gave way to glaring white—sand or salt flats, she did not know—then the endless wrinkled blue that Edene knew must be the sea, though she had never seen it before. She had water in her cage, but no food, and her feet ached from balancing on the bars until she gave up and sat, whereupon her haunches ached instead. The sky overhead changed several times while the bird bore her—night and day, many moons and one, a sun that rose in the east and one that rose to the west—but she had a sense its direction had not changed.

"As the crow flies," she muttered, as the sea fell behind and a brown desert unscrolled below. If the bird were to carry her to the Eternal Sky, it was not doing a particularly good job. They were dropping now, and she could see some details of the land—the dry riverbeds, the sinuous ridges.

She saw stones standing high above the valleys, and one stone in particular—a stark rock upon which a castle of five mismatched towers perched. It must be their destination, because the great bird banked and came around to the tallest tower, landing into the wind.

Someone waited there, so tiny with distance that Edene at first saw only windswept robes and a veil of deepest indigo. Her cage scraped stone as the bird released it. She hastily made sure her toes and fingers were pulled within.

Sparks flew, metal bumping to a halt on stone. The great bird landed beyond, hopping to halt before it reached the battlements, and resettled itself facing inward with a flip of wings. The blue-veiled man tossed it meat—a leg of goat, she thought, that disappeared into the bird's great maw like a grape into a man's mouth. The bird gulped it like a crow gulping a locust and looked around for more.

When the man came to open her cage, she could barely stand. She pushed herself upright with her hands on her knees, her thighs and back screaming protest. She breathed out through her nose, fighting the cramps, telling herself they were no worse than the cramps of a day in the saddle.

It might be a lie, but it comforted her.

He thrust something into her hand—watered wine, she realized as she drank, and her head spun. There might be something else in it too—beef broth? She should cast it to the stones, but she needed it so badly, and was she not in his power anyway? If he wished her dead, all it would take was a knife.

The wine didn't settle her nausea—if anything, her stomach cramped more viciously—but it did lend her strength and numb her pains. She finished the draught and let the cup slip from her fingers.

The man in the rust-colored robes caught it before it touched the ground. She stood blinking, wondering if exhaustion and wine had blinded her.

Carefully, he set it down.

"Honored guest," he said in her own language, his words thick with a western inflection. "Welcome to the Rock. *Ala-Din* is its name in our language." He waved a hand to the massive bird that rocked from foot to foot behind him. "Some call it the Aerie, but they are wrong. I am Mukhtar ai-Idoj, called al-Sepehr of this place."

Edene blinked. She had fallen into a story, she thought, but that did not stop her from drawing herself up tall in her filthy, tattered sleepwear and squaring her shoulders before she spoke. "I've heard of you," she said. "You're the prince of some murder cult. You worship the Sorcerer-Prince."

"You may have heard of us," he said with quiet dignity. It bothered her that his face was hidden. "But it seems you have heard a great many lies. My God is the Scholar, and she speaks to us directly. As for Sepehr al-Rachīd ibn Sepehr"—she could not see the smile behind his veil, but she could imagine it by the way his eyes crinkled at the corners—"whom the ignorant call the Sorcerer-Prince, or the Carrion-King, or the Joy-of-Ravens . . . , while it is true he was the founder of my order, he is not a prophet. Nor do we worship him."

His words were calm enough—calmer than she would have expected for a man who had had her snatched by ghosts and flown for days across the world, dangling in the shadow of a bird as big as a caravan—but the set of his shoulders unnerved her. That, and the way he said the Sorcerer-Prince's name so lightly. With such comfort.

As if he did not fear to be overheard.

She would not take a step back. She folded her arms across her chest. "What do you want with me?" she asked.

He came no closer. "Oh," he said. "It's not you. But don't worry. You will be made quite comfortable."

LATER, SAMARKAR LEANED AGAINST A WHITE PILLAR OF THE CITADEL, the sun warming her collar, and let Anil press his cheek against her cheek. His arms were strong and slender, and he smelled of musk and sweet cinnamon, like something you should put in your mouth and suck. Maybe he had the same thought, because he turned and brushed his mouth over hers. She did not pull back; he looked in her eyes, as if seeking permission, and slowly drew her lower lip between his teeth, nibbling lightly.

A thrill ran up her spine, down her belly. She found herself hanging on him, pressing her thighs together. A heat burned her that was like the heat of magic, but lighter, tighter, more focused. . . .

She startled, jerked back, and found herself pinned between him and the pillar. He stepped back, giving her room. Though she felt the tug of disappointment when her hands fell away from the warm stone of his collar, she took the space he offered. "I—"

"You're one of us now," he said. "No harm can come of it."

Every novice knew that the elevated and the masters were not chaste. Samarkar, once-princess, wedded, widowed—had been too old and alien to giggle behind her hand with the rest of the novices, but she knew, just the same. There were advantages to what they lost besides the wizardry. A man gelded as an adult could set as straight a branch as any other; a neutered woman lost only the ability to bear.

But she had somehow never made the connection that the enforced—and policed—celibacy of the novitiate would come to an end for her as well.

She pressed her collar to her throat, feeling the reassuring cage of its stiffness. "This is fast. . . ."

He nodded, and let his hands hang by his sides. "You were widowed." He said it with sympathy, as if he did not know it was she who had called on her brothers to come avenge the slight to her family and wash it clean in her husband's blood.

She laughed, though. She turned away and pressed her hands to the pillar to support herself and laughed the harder, shaking her head like a horse shaking off flies—in irritation rather than denial. "He wouldn't have me," she said, bitterly. "Not once. Either he was afraid of women or he was afraid of getting an heir on me that Rasa might someday use to claim a part of Song. But either way, I went to my husband's pyre as virgin as I went to my marriage bed. So it's not that. . . ."

She couldn't look at him. She'd only once put this into words before, when she'd come to plead with Yongten-la for a place among his wizards, three years before, and begged him to consider her despite her age. She cringed, expecting to be reviled.

It was what her husband would have done. What he *had* done when she had tried to entice him to what should have been their marriage bed.

Anil put his hand on her shoulder. He sighed. He squeezed softly. "I do not care about him," he said. "When you don't care about him, either, you know where to find me."

And then he was gone, the energy of his presence replaced by an emptiness behind her.

Samarkar stood for a long time listening to the music filtering down the colonnaded walkway, the party in her honor carrying on in her absence. It was not so different, after all, from being a princess. Except now she could walk off alone, and there was no one to say otherwise.

The long gallery led to a stair, and the stair led down to the river. Its rush and hiss spoke to Samarkar. It summoned her as surely as a voice calling her name.

And so she descended, down to the river she had loved all her life. Here beneath the Citadel, it ran tight and fast, a boiling current that could dash an unwary swimmer against the boulders or suck her under in a boiling eddy. Samarkar had swum it—she had swum the whole length of the Tsarethi where it passed through Tsarepheth, and the calmer waters far downstream—and she knew just how easy it would be to die in its embrace.

She didn't strip off and dive in now. Strong as she felt, she also knew that strength was an illusion and could fail her at any moment. Instead, she climbed up amongst the jumbled boulders near the shore, skipping from one to another with well-timed leaps until she sat on a flat stone a body length from its closest neighbor in the midst of the churning water, the spray of its plunge dewing her cheek and jeweling her hair.

This boulder—and all the others that touched the water, and back from the water as high as the flood-waters rose—was carved all over with intricate sigils. Words. Prayers—prayers for luck and prosperity and good harvest and fertility and safety. Prayers for wellness and prayers for peace, all carved here in this hard gray granite so that the water might wash them downstream to Tsarepheth, to the fields that bounded it to the south, to the broad wide world below the Steles of the Sky, and eventually to the mythical sea beyond.

Samarkar stood there for a moment, hands fisted inside her black sleeves, and watched them go.

She imagined them shedding peace and grace on everything they touched—righting little evils, ameliorating great ones. She wasn't sure she believed in it.

But she wasn't sure she didn't, either, and the roar of the white water plunging past was cleaner than anything inside her head. Where had the peace and certainty she'd known in the dungeon gone?

"It's beautiful," Yongten-la said, beside her.

She never knew why his voice did not startle her back into the water, to plunge to her death.

"It is," she agreed. She glanced sideways. She was always surprised at what a compact man the master was; he was bigger inside her head. "I was going to come back."

"I know."

He waited; she waited too. Eventually, she imagined, the time would be right. Eventually, apparently, it was.

"I'm sending you and Tsering-la to Qeshqer the day after tomorrow."

"I'm sorry?" She turned, startled, sure she'd misheard. But he stood there comfortable, hands behind his back, boots comfortably apart on the wet stone.

"To Qeshqer," he said. "If there is war, they will need you. If there are refugees, they will need you. You have some power. . . ." He paused, considered, and shrugged, as if deciding to speak the whole truth. "You have *some* power. You may not be a mighty wizard, but you are patient and you study hard. You have the potential to become a crafty one. Which is in some ways better."

She nodded. It stung. Of course every novice dreamed of being revealed as another Tse-ten of the Five Eyes. But then, *every* novice dreamed it, and that meant that almost all of them would be disappointed. "Thank you, master."

"You have some power," he repeated, as if she had not spoken. "And Tsering has great craft and no power. She will continue to teach you. And you will stretch into your power better if you must use it for real."

She turned. He was not looking at her.

"This is a test," she said.

"Tests are games," he answered dismissively. Crouching, he trailed the tips of his left fingers in the water. "Lives will depend on what you do next. This is no test, Samarkar-la. This is your first assignment as a wizard of Tsarepheth."

PACKING WAS BOTH EASIER AND MORE COMPLICATED THAN SHE HAD anticipated. She had always had servants to handle such things for her—even when she packed up the few rags of clothes she had considered appropriate for her new station in life. (It had turned out she was wrong; the Citadel provided clothes for its novices. Only an elevated wizard bought her own coats and trousers, but the Citadel also employed tailors and seamstresses who knew well the cut of the ritual garments.)

But now she faced a journey of a moon or more, with only a single companion, and she had no idea what to bring. It would have to be light, of course, and durable. She would need a bedroll, and blankets were heavy, but this time of year a chill could still easily turn to storm. She would need water and travel rations; she could ask in the kitchens for that last, and the stables would have water for women and animals both. She would need extracts and herbs for a medical kit. She would need . . .

"Oh," she said tiredly, and sat on her bed, black clothing heaped on every side. Samarkar had long since stopped thinking of herself as a spoiled princess, but just this once, she had to admit that it would be easier if someone else would make the decisions. At least then, when inevitably something that later turned out to be critical was forgotten or dismissed, you had somebody other than yourself to blame.

She heaved a sigh and stood, trying to find the quiet within that had sustained her through the long cold vigil. But mostly now she was tired and ached in every bone from sitting so long in the cold. The wizardry could keep ill effects at bay while it held one's total focus, but there was always the hangover to deal with. And Samarkar suspected with ironic mirth that the majority of those who sat in the cold, waiting for their power to come, were considerably younger than she.

She was weighing underthings in her hands, deciding how many she really needed, when a diffident knock shivered the door. "Come," she called, turning to face the sound.

The door opened no more than a crack, and a nervous, splay-fingered novice stuck his head in. "Samarkar-la, there is someone here to see you."

He took a breath, stepped all the way through the door, and

bowed with stuck-out tongue. "It's your brother the second prince, *aphei*."

The young man trembled with excitement. His straight black hair was skinned back into a ponytail, and Samarkar could see the pale-brown tips of his ears flamed as red as if he'd been dipped in ink.

She took pity. "Thank you," she said, glancing around at the chaos of her small chamber with a prickling of dismay. She could not meet Tsansong here. Not that Tsansong would care about her house-keeping skills, but he would care that she seemed to be kept mewed up in a room no bigger than a monk's cell. And how could Samarkar admit to him that she found it cozy and admired the view? He would see only floors dished with many footsteps, velvet draperies that had been threadbare when the last occupant of this room died and that were probably already moldering a bit when she moved in, walls dark with centuries of fires.

"Which parlor would be best to receive him?"

The novice smiled. "Perhaps the Room of Butterflies?"

Samarkar nodded. "That would be perfect. And please bring him refreshment; I need to dress and clean myself up somewhat."

The novice vanished; Samarkar made the best toilette she could with a damp cloth and a pitcher of water. Her wardrobe was still limited—she'd only had three outfits made before she went for her surgery, as it seemed foolish to lay out too much money on cloth-ing she might not survive to wear—but she found a clean coat and trousers and pulled them on over her halter and loincloth. This coat was black silk, appliquéd with bright patterns in orange and tur-quoise, cut longer than the brocade one. She combed and dressed her hair—no time to wash it, but the coarseness of the strands would hide the oil and dirt as long as it was braided—and stomped into her boots.

Then she squared her shoulders and went downstairs to meet her brother.

Tsansong had taken his ease while awaiting her and sat cross-legged on—or rather, *in*—a large cushion, reading a small scroll in his lap. As Samarkar approached, he glanced at it to fix his place in his mind and slipped it into his sleeve, rustling only slightly. Then he rose, before Samarkar could gesture him back to his seat, and took her hand.

"I am glad you survived, sister dear," he said. "Both the surgery and the ritual. Although I am slightly peeved that when you came to the palace, you saw Songtsan and not me."

"It was a professional visit," she said, and kissed him on the cheek. "And I wanted to wait to see you until I knew if I would have magic or not."

He squeezed her hand and let go. "And?"

"What?" she said. "Your spies haven't told you every detail of my movements?"

"You mistake me for Songtsan." Impulsively, he hugged her tightly, then stepped back. "But I am me. And *I* know you wouldn't be teasing if you hadn't excelled. So out with it. Let me see!"

Silently, Samarkar held up her hand and willed the blue light into being. It washed the color from her skin, from Tsansong's overawed face, from the embroidered tapestries thick with the images of the room's eponymous butterflies. "Satisfied?"

"I knew you could do it!" With a glad sound, he hugged her once more, and she let the cold light die to hug him back. "So, about Songtsan? What was the business?"

Samarkar shrugged. She didn't know how close to his breast Songtsan was playing this, and it certainly wasn't her space to spill the news to Tsansong. Instead she crossed to the window and leaned out. "He's jealous of you."

"Jealous of our wives, you mean," Tsansong said. "Especially Payma, because she is closer to me than to him."

Samarkar might have nodded. Her head felt so heavy she was not sure.

"Hey," he said, coming up behind her. He put a hand on her shoulder. "I'm proud of you, you know."

"I ran away," she said.

He squeezed. "From here, it looks like running *to*."

TWO WOMEN IN WIZARD'S WEEDS AFOOT, LEADING A TRIO OF CAT-AGILE pack mules not much bigger than large dogs, could make good speed even through the mountains. As Yongten-la had promised, Samarkar's studies resumed, and the new learning was different. What had been theory became practice, and that which had been rote practicality clicked with slow precision into an elaborate set of theoretical scaffolds that began to take shape in Samarkar's head.

She learned to call forth that light and warmth that had flooded from her with consistency and refinement. She learned to do it while concentrating on her foot placement on a rocky trail at the edge of a cliff a hundred man-heights tall. She learned to finesse it to just warmth, to only light, then to focus both to cutting intensity using the lens of her will and also a lens of flawless rock crystal that Tsering gave her to hang upon a chain about her neck.

"Earth," Tsering said, "is the closest process to life, and so earth is the one of the five elemental processes that cannot be created by a wizard. And so it is the one we use to control the others—fire, air, water, and emptiness. We can *manipulate* earth. We can manipulate life. But we cannot create either."

"How do you manipulate earth?" Samarkar asked.

Tsering glanced from side to side. It was afternoon; they were in the midst of a plateau, and the long shadows were crawling across earth that blew with grass and flowers between bare rocky scrapes. There were no other travelers in sight.

"Here," she said, and moved the mules off the track, where they could graze in peace for a while. The mules, who had been snatching mouthfuls of roadside herbs at every opportunity, seemed contented with this solution.

She found a flat stone—not too much of a trick, as all Rasa abounded in them—and clambered up on it with a pack in her hand. "Here," she said. "Come. Sit."

Samarkar settled down cross-legged before her. She noticed the other end of the boulder housed a shrine to some traveler's god, and resolved to make him or her a gift of a pinch of salt and millet upon arising. A polite bribe to the local authorities had never hurt anyone.

Tsering-la set out soapstone bowls sized for pickles or relish in a line before herself and filled each one with powder from a different oiled leather pouch—sparkling white, sparkling yellow, silver-gray, dull black. She set a mortar and pestle out beside them and looked up at Samarkar with a familiar, challenging expression.

"Saltpeter," Samarkar said, touching the first bowl. "Sulfur, iodide of silver, charcoal. For a rocket to bring rain from a cloudy sky."

Tsering handed Samarkar the pestle. Samarkar accepted it with trepidation. It weighed heavy and cool in her hand—smooth on the haft, rough on the bulb. "And if I asked you to construct a rocket now?"

"Without a balance?" Samarkar hesitated. "I'd blow my hand off."

"A wise wizard keeps all her fingers," Tsering-la said with a smile. "But what if you *asked* the principles to combine? These are principles of earth, after all, but they combine to form principles of fire and water—"

"Ask them?" Samarkar frowned. "Just like that?"

Tsering-la held up the mortar. "It helps to put them into contact, first. First make the black powder, then add the silver."

Slowly, Samarkar emptied the sulfur into the mortar and ground it fine. She cleaned the mortar and repeated the process with the saltpeter and the charcoal. Sun warmed her shoulders and neck; when she pushed wispy locks off her sweaty forehead, the surface of her hair felt hot.

She glanced at Tsering for reassurance.

"Use your hands," Tsering said.

"A balance would be better."

"So it would," Tsering agreed. Her smile made little valleys up the sides of her nose.

"And once it is constructed, how am I to grind it fine enough to burn swiftly?"

"Are you a wizard or an alchemist?"

"Right." Samarkar ground the iodide of silver as well, just to have it done, and cleaned the mortar one last time. Slowly, pinch by pinch, trying to send her awareness into each particle, she began to build the black powder. *Combine,* she told it. *Three things make one. Three things make one.*

She thought she felt it happening. A creeping, prickling sensation, then that familiar warmth . . .

"No heat," Tsering said. "You must ask the fire to stay itself. Ask the heat to wait; bring in emptiness. Create the absence of fire."

"Emptiness," Samarkar mumbled.

"Emptiness," Tsering said.

She found the fire in the powder and coaxed it softly. Not to leave the powder, but merely to wait, to hold its warmth until a time of need. She stirred it with the pestle and realized that she did not need to grind it to powder; she could merely ask the flakes to pull themselves apart, smaller and smaller.

She lost herself in the process. When she looked up, she realized that the sun rode the shoulder of a mountain whose name she did not know, and the stuff she stirred in the pestle was fine as ash. "Good," Tsering said. "Now add the silver. And bear in mind, the silver carries the process of water, and you are adding it to a substance that carries the process of fire. If they are not kept separate, they will counteract one another."

"Right," Samarkar said. She looked up in surprise as Tsering stood, groaning a little with stiffness. "Where are you going?"

"To start a fire," said Tsering. "And heat some dinner."

"Don't forget to feed the shrine," Samarkar said, and turned back to her experiment.

SAMARKAR LEARNED TO CREATE OTHER THINGS AS WELL. WATER IN A bowl, though Tsering said that really they were just refining it from the moisture in the air, like dew or frost. She learned to create the semblance of solid objects from the force of her concentration—small ones: a key, a knife.

They practiced as they walked. For the first quarter-moons, when they set out in the mornings, they had kept their pockets stuffed with greasy rocks heated in the embers of the fires, for warming their fingers. But the road to Qeshqer led them down the back slope of the Steles of the Sky, and as summer advanced and they lost elevation, they needed water more than warmth. Fortunately, the streams were flush with glacial melt. The only problem was reaching them when so many ran deep in the bottoms of crudely bridged gullies. Tsering, though, proved able with a hide bucket and a length of rope.

The road between Tsarepheth and Qeshqer was not a graded thing wide enough for a cart—or, in places, two—like the Imperial Highway that led from Tsarepheth to Rasa. It was a trade route, a track worn over hills and through narrow passes by the hooves of innumerable mules and yaks and ponies and herds of wiry, wild-coated mountain sheep. Samarkar was grateful for the mules, who scrambled up hairy boulders without so much as leaving a hoof-scrape in their shrouds of moss and lichen and who seemed able to eat anything. She wasn't sure how she would have made it herself with a pack, but the mules were unfazed by anything, including bridges Samarkar hesitated to trust with her own weight.

It reminded her a little of her only other long journey—ignoring the ones to the winter palace in Rasa and back to Tsarepheth. But when she had gone to Song to be a bride, she had been borne in a horse litter, and when she had come back she had ridden astride behind her brothers, head held high and cheeks burning with wind or shame.

This was a very different passage. When they met other travelers,

Samarkar might have been nervous for her safety and that of Tsering, except without fail, traders and entertainers and priests alike treated the black-clad women with a deference bordering on terror. She had been accustomed to the obsequiousness of servants when she was a princess, and she had learned to efface herself and perform menial tasks without complaint during her novitiate, but this was alien. It was as if she moved in a bubble of silence, so conversations died away before her and resumed behind.

After the third or fourth time, Samarkar raised her eyebrows at Tsering, and Tsering answered with her usual sidelong smile. "It saves money on escorts," she said, with a shrug.

Samarkar laughed hard and heartily and went back to trying to open the small lock Tsering had given her to practice on while Tsering simmered rice over their small fire and sliced dried vegetables. She held it flat on her palm, letting the shape of the emptiness within tell her the shape of the pins and tumblers. It was a simple matter to fill that emptiness with strength, to focus her will within. Turning the key her mind constructed, though—*that* defeated her. Over and over again she strove, and over and over again the thing shredded itself when she imagined it twisting.

Finally, as Tsering sat back from the soup, Samarkar threw up her other hand and said, "What on earth am I doing wrong?"

"Here," Tsering said. She rose up, her hems whisking her calves, and came and sat beside Samarkar, all without touching the earth with her hands. She grasped Samarkar's wrist and pulled her palm out flat between them, the lock resting heavily on its arch. "What are you doing?"

"I can feel the lock. I can feel the key. But when I try to lift the pins—"

"That's the problem, then," Tsering said. "Don't lift the pins. Just be the key, and turn."

Be the key, and turn. Right.

Well, maybe. Because if the key was an extension of her will, not an object . . . She didn't think of turning her hand, did she, and how the muscles and tendons and bones made that happen? She just turned it.

Samarkar closed her eyes. She imagined the key; imagined it solid. Felt its surface fill the empty space in the lock.

Imagined it turning.

She heard a scrape, felt resistance. The key shredded in her awareness.

She would have cursed, but Tsering's hand was on her shoulder. "There," she said. "Much closer. Now do it another thousand times."

MAYBE NOT A THOUSAND, BUT SAMARKAR SAT AND PRACTICED UNTIL Tsering brought her soup and water. She opened the lock twice and made it scrape three or four more times. It was progress, she told herself, and she should not expect to perform perfectly without practice. *Perfection does not exist.*

Still, she was grateful to tuck the lock into one of her wizard's coat's many concealed pockets and take the bowl and spoon from her teacher's hands. Only after she had eaten a few bites—and expressed her appreciation—did she look up at Tsering and frown. "Forgive me—"

"How do I know so much about theory when I have no magic of my own?"

Samarkar looked down.

Tsering shrugged and bent over her bowl. "I still love wizardry," she said. "If, as a wizard, I am a technician and a teacher rather than a spellwright, then that is as fate ordains. We each serve given our ability."

"You are the best of teachers," Samarkar said. She tucked her chin in shame and wondered how long it had taken Tsering-la to achieve such peace and resolve, when Samarkar still felt a sting at Yongten-la's pronouncement that she would not be a great power.

WHEN SAMARKAR AND TSERING CAME OUT OF THE STELES OF THE SKY into the high cold plateau they must cross to reach Qeshqer—the city that had been called Kashe, before the Great Khagan Temusan the Terrible conquered it—the sky changed over them. Not as Samarkar had anticipated, not to the deep azure of the Qersnyk sky—but rather to a faded turquoise, framing a pale sun that moved from one corner to the other in alien directions.

So they knew something was wrong in Qeshqer long before they came within sight of the city. Then on the second day, they found themselves passed over and around by a seemingly endless swarm of butterflies, as if butterflies migrated like birds. It came upon them with the sunrise and did not flag until the moon was high in the sky. Samarkar lay awake in her bedroll, listening to the whisper of myriad papery wings, wondering what they portended.

They reached the waystones that marked a boundary three days out from Qeshqer, and from that point forward no further outbound caravans crossed paths with them. The road was well worn, the bridges maintained, but suddenly there were no other people along it. On the first day, this was unusual; by the third, it had become eerie.

By the time they passed the final set of waystones, Samarkar and Tsering were exchanging nervous glances and had stopped joking about the lack of people. "It should be just up this rise." Tsering traced the script on a stone.

Samarkar knew she should say something, but a silence so thick and ominous it felt like an effort to grunt agreement defeated her. She shifted a wet palm on the lead of the first mule and dug in, climbing.

Tsering fell in beside her.

This close to a city, they should have heard noise, smelled smoke. There was nothing—the scent of the sewers and midden heaps, the rustle of grasses and leaves. As they crested the rise of the foothill, Samarkar found herself looking down into a sweep of valley patchworked by lines of trees and broken into neat fields curved to fit the contours of the hills.

The road wound down between the fields, and the fields were empty. Not of crops—spring greens and the shoots of young grains poked through tilled soil, a translucent haze of green and peach and red seeming at this distance to hover above the earthy browns—but empty of the women and men and children who should have been engaged in weeding, transplanting, nurturing the crop.

Beyond the empty fields, the red-and-gold-roofed white buildings of Qeshqer heaped up one atop another among the roots of mountains that continued climbing behind them. Forested slopes gave way to stark peaks, and no haze of smoke obscured any detail. Tsering made a low noise and shifted from one foot to another, restive as the mules. Hand trembling, Samarkar drew her lens from her coat by its cord and raised it before her eye.

Across the intervening difference, through lucid air, Samarkar could see every window, every building whitewashed and framed by trees—rhododendron, mulberry, and cypress. Where the city mounted into the Range of Ghosts, she made out the metallic gleams off the clustered steel-and-silver trunks of lacebark pine and the darker colors of the Stele pine, with its conical habit and sweeping, open spiral of branches.

No sound carried across the valley, and nothing moved across Qeshqer's narrow plazas or along its stair-set roads. Through her lens, Samarkar could see the wind rippling oblong rhododendron leaves and hair-fine pine needles, but not a single animal crossed her field of view.

When she lowered the lens, Tsering must have read what she saw in her expression, because she didn't ask. She licked her lips and rocked back on her heels and said, "Not even refugees? How does that *happen*?"

"We don't go down into that valley," Samarkar said. She was already reining the mules back, considering how much food they were still carrying. It would be short rations back to Tsarepheth, even if they raced as fast as they could. She touched the collar at her throat for reassurance. "We have to get word back to Yongten-la and my brother."

She was tucking the lens back inside her coat for protection when she noticed Tsering staring over her shoulder.

"Samarkar—" the other wizard said. She pointed; Samarkar turned.

Somebody was moving along the road, just silhouetted now against the sky as he came through the high pass that flanked Qeshqer on its right side. Somebody? No. Something. Puffs of dust showed it was moving, and in a moment whatever it was had dropped below the ridge.

Samarkar clawed for her lens again.

Two horses, one pale and one dark, moved tiredly down the track. Their heads hung; their steps were plodding. And across the back of the darker one slumped an outlandishly dressed person, hands flopping at his thighs in a manner that indicated borderline consciousness at best. Behind and above them, as if it had followed them down from the pass, the black wings of a vulture drifted.

"Correction," Samarkar said dryly. "If that's a survivor, I guess *I'm* going down into the valley. Stay here with the mules?"

She saw Tsering consider arguing; Tsering was the senior wizard, after all. But Tsering, however knowledgeable, could not wield the magic she understood so well. Which left it up to Samarkar—dry-mouthed and cold-handed with fear as she was.

Tsering nodded. "Go on, Samarkar-la."

Samarkar divested herself of pack and goods and wizard's coat and collar. She stepped out of her boots, after considering, and stood barefoot and bare-armed in the wind. Whatever was down there, if it had silenced a city, she could not fight it. Her only chance was to be silent and swift.

And empty.

She let herself fall away, made herself nothing. Quick, light. A space in the air. No thought; no intention. Just action.

She was not aware of the decision to run. One moment she stood poised on the ridge with the cool dust between her toes. The next she was in motion, running on the balls of her feet, plunging forward wrapped in her veil of emptiness.

It was good to run. Good to feel the strength in her body, won back with such effort since her surgery. Good to feel the road vanishing between strides. It was a long run, and there was time to feel it—the whole width of the valley to cover, first in a downhill plunge, then the toil upward toward Qeshqer, which shortened her stride and burned her chest with the thin, dry air.

But she was Rasan born, and the air of Tsarepheth was thinner still. She breathed deeply, letting her body take what it needed of the process of air, imagining that energy spreading through her with each pump of her bellows chest. She dropped to a walk as she came up to the horses—mares, she could see now, the lanky light-boned steppe breed, thin and weary with travel. And the man on the bay one's back . . .

Samarkar would have extended her illusions to wrap horses and men, too, but as she came up she saw him lolling in the saddle, liver-red with fever and dewed with sharp sweat. She hesitated. By his clothes and the shape of his nose and eyes, she guessed him one of the Quersnyk plainsmen, though his complexion was very dark. Just the horses would have been sufficient evidence, in light of what Song-tsan had told her about the fall of Qarash and the likelihood of refugees.

Plague? A pestilence could have come in with the refugees, if refugees there were. . . .

But no. No plague could have silenced an entire city so quickly that no one fled it—and left no bodies lying in the fields. And Samarkar was wizard enough now to recognize the signs of influenza. A serious illness, one to fear—but one she was trained in caring for. She reached out to take the bay mare's sagging reins.

The plainsman lashed out—more at random than at her—sweeping with his knife. She jumped back, deflecting the blow with air, and watched him slide out of the saddle with slow inevitability. She would have tried to grab him, to cushion his fall or keep him from impaling himself, but even when she would have helped him, he warded her back with the knife.

He fell with a thump, boneless as a sack of wet laundry. The bay mare turned her head dully, swaying; the gray one managed a back step, a head shake, and a snort.

"Sir," Samarkar said in his language. "I am the wizard Samarkar of Rasa. You have come through the"—she searched for a moment for the Quersnyk words—"the Range of Ghosts. You are ill and your horses are exhausted. I wish to help."

She crouched, feeling the flex of bare toes, ready to spring away at any moment.

The plainsman drew his right hand to his chest, the knife pointed down along his sternum. It was the spasm of fever; as Samarkar watched, a great ague shook him. He mumbled something; the word she heard was *ghosts*.

"You've come through," she said. "You've come through the mountains. Let me help you."

Maybe her words reached him; maybe it was the concerned nosings of the bay mare. But the plainsman managed to relax his hand, and the curved horn hilt of his dagger slipped between his fingers.

"Good," Samarkar said. She glanced left and right, uphill and down, but there was no sign of anyone else. She was slightly stunned to realize how close she'd come to the outskirts of Qeshqer. She could smell the blossoms on the fruit trees in walled gardens, and the lowest tiers of buildings were no more than a stone's throw away.

"Can you stand? We have to hurry—"

He nodded. He found the knife again with groping fingers, this time managing to sheath it on the second try. "Temur," he said, which she thought was a name, because she couldn't imagine why he'd be calling for iron now. And half the men of his people in his age range must have been named for the Great Khagan. "Ride—"

Samarkar looked dubiously up at the bay mare, who was still *whuff*ing at the sick man's hair while the gray waited anxiously at the limit of her lead line. She couldn't drag this plainsman five *li* back up the hill to where Tsering waited. And while she could walk—or run—it was obvious he couldn't. It would have to be the ponies, then.

"I'll help," she said, and bent down to lift him to his feet.

He wasn't a big man, and she thanked her luck for that. And she thanked her ancestors that she *was* a big woman, broad-hipped and broad-shouldered, with strength in her arms and thighs. He was wasted with sickness and hard travel, as well, and so she managed to stand him up to where he could grab the bay mare's saddle, then help him heave himself back into it. The mare stood like a statue, her master slumped forward over the waist-high pommel, and Samarkar steeled herself to approach the nervy gray.

She stepped up to her gently, holding an aura of calm and still, and extended the palm of her hand. She wished she had a sweet or a piece of fruit. In her experience, horses bribed well.

But the mare watched, ears pricked rather than back, and let her approach. She might be cautious, then, rather than fearful. Samarkar could make friends with a cautious horse.

But could she do it with the blank windows of the empty city staring at her back? She knew by the hammering of her heart that her posture was not calm, and the idea that anything at all could come pouring down the hill from Qeshqer left her sweating cold and shaking.

Calm, she told herself. *You are a wizard of Tsarepheth. Where is your serenity?*

Here, at her core. With the warmth and the strength and the shadowless flame of her magic, bright and still. She must be calm for the horse. She must be loose and relaxed without being saggy.

She soothed herself, and in so doing, soothed the mare. The gray lipped her palm, let her smooth it along her cheek and down the high lean curve of her neck. Compared to the mountain ponies Samarkar knew so well, the steppe horses were almost naked of mane—but under the dust, the gray's coat glistered in the sun. "May I ride?" she asked.

The mare turned to observe as Samarkar walked down her side, maintaining contact, but did not object. Samarkar leaned lightly across a saddle so high to front and back it seemed you would have to work to fall out of it, and the mare did not step away. At least she wasn't tall, even if her saddle was.

Samarkar reached under her head to unhook the lead line, lowered the stirrups to where she could use them, and swung up into the saddle as lightly as possible. The mare was well trained; once Samarkar's weight hit the stirrup, she stood like a wall.

Samarkar found the other stirrup, lifted the reins, and sent the mare forward. The sway of a good horse under her was no different, and the ridiculous saddle made it easier to reach out and take the bay's reins as she went past. Not that she seemed to need to do so; the bay dropped in willingly on her right as soon as the gray came up even with her. Once they were walking—not fast, but every step taking them farther from the cursed, eerie silence that was Qeshqer— she fought the urge to glance over her shoulder constantly to see what might be coming up behind. She was superstitiously certain that whatever it was, as soon as she looked it would spring the ambush.

"Safe," Temur said, lifting his chin and opening glass-bright eyes. He turned to her, his hands flexing feebly on the saddle. He stretched a hand back toward the empty city. "*They* don't come until morning. I have to . . . have to go there. Please. Edene . . ."

Samarkar didn't know who *they* were. But she was afraid the dead city at her back held the answer, and whatever the sick man wanted would have to wait until she could afford to have it answered.

ALL THE LONG WALK BACK UP THE ROAD, SAMARKAR COULD SEE TSER-ing standing taut in the shade of a tall pine, one hand laid on the trunk as if for support. If their positions had been reversed, Samarkar knew she would have been leaning forward, breathless, as if she could urge the exhausted ponies faster with the rocking motion of her shoulders. Instead, they toiled up the hill at a snail's pace, and Samarkar kept her eyes fixed on Tsering.

She didn't know why she was so superstitiously convinced that the danger lay in the valley and safety on the ridge. Maybe it was the quiet of the unattended fields blowing softly in a low wind, the tender young vegetables curling in from lack of water, or the silence of the city at her back. But she could not shake the sense of malevolent eyes watching, and every creak of stirrup leather went through her like a blade of ice. The irons bit into her bare feet; the reins grew damp in her hand.

Finally, at the top of the ridge, she let herself relax and turn back over her shoulder. Nothing but the peaceful valley lay below, the mountains at its back.

Leaving the mules, Tsering hurried over. She showed the gray her hands and held her reins while Samarkar slid down, the saddle bumping across her belly. It took both of them to ease Temur down, especially as in his delirium he tended to cling to the saddle and fight them. At least he didn't draw his knife again, and eventually they managed to make him comfortable on the grass of the roadside.

"We'll have to rig a pony drag," Tsering said, while Samarkar slipped the mares' bits so they could crop the grass more comfortably. They didn't want to wait for her ministrations; Qeshqer was on the wet side of the mountain range, and Samarkar imagined that they'd had no fresh food in days. As soon as she had their mouths freed, they fell on the grass more like wolves than ponies.

Samarkar nodded. It was obvious Temur had ridden as far as he could. "The man's name is Temur, I think. These horses need water."

Silently, Tsering pulled the folding bucket from the mule pack and crouched over it with a water skin. It would take most of what they carried to water the mares once, and it was obvious from the stamping that the mules were envious. Samarkar could make more, though it would take time—and there was water in the valley below, if they dared it. And water back the way they had come.

Samarkar wanted to pull the gear from the two mares and check them for galls, but she didn't dare. If they had to move quickly . . .

Well, at least they seemed sound. She checked their feet and ankles for heat or swelling and found nothing. Neither one could be bothered to lift her head from her meal.

"We'll rig the drag," she said. "In case you have to run."

Tsering looked up, the fine wisps of dark brown hair that never seemed to stay in her braid, blowing about the oval of her face. She was pretty in the dappled shade, Samarkar realized, and wondered what exactly had driven this capable and charming woman to risk her life on wizardry.

"You're not going back down there."

Samarkar smiled. She rose from her squat beside the mares. "I need to see what's in the city, Tsering-la. Are we going to return to Tsarepheth only to tell Yongten-la and Songtsan-tsa that Qeshqer is fallen, and we—two wizards of the Citadel!—were too frightened to look within? And Temur said it was safe until morning." *How he knows, don't ask me.*

She made herself meet Tsering's eyes as Tsering stood. "I could order you to stay with me."

Samarkar pulled her coat from the back of the mule, where it was draped. It was amazing how secure the fall of the hem against her legs made her feel. "I sort of wish you would. Now, what did you do with my boots?"

Silently, Tsering pointed her to them.

In equal silence, Samarkar began to put them on. She could feel Tsering watching, but she was still stomping her left foot into the proper place in the boot when there came a sudden, exasperated sigh, and the gray mare shied slightly as Tsering threw her arms up. The grass was too much of an enticement, though, and she buried her nose again by the time Tsering said, "Fine, go on. I'll start back as soon as I can rig the pony drag. You can catch up if you live."

"I will," Samarkar said. "Hand me my collar while you're over by the mule."

"I'll hide a pack in the tree for you," Tsering said.

It takes a special kind of idiot to walk back into a dead city.

And yet here she was, dust rising from each stride, picking her way up from the road to the gardens that surrounded the lowest tier of buildings. She stepped at last onto cobblestones, but the dusty track had already glazed the black silk of her trousers beige.

It was cooler in the shade of the rhododendrons, which had been pruned to form an arching bower. The cobbled path mounting the hillside merged into stairs as the slope grew steeper. Samarkar found herself skirting the edge of the walk, as if to make way for downward traffic that never materialized.

These were beautiful streets—bounded on each side by the ranks of close white buildings with their scarlet roofs and pillars, over-hung with the graceful sweep of pine boughs. There were marks of plainsman conquest and occupation here and there, but not so many—the unfortified city had surrendered without a struggle, and so its people had been spared. It suffered a Qersnyk governor and men-at-arms and paid Qersnyk tribute. The plainsmen conquered for trade and tribute and open roads, not to spread their social or religious hegemony. In this, Samarkar preferred them to the Uthman Caliph-ate. Qeshqer, despite its name change, remained in many ways a Rasan town.

The houses had broad patios and gardens mulched with pine needles, which should have offered inviting refuge in the shade of many trees. But windows on each side were sealed as if against the night; doors bolted closed. She could tell the homes of tradesmen by their wide-shuttered shops, but all those shutters stood closed. There was no scent of fire anywhere—not even cold char. No dogs or hens scattered through the streets. No birds sang in low branches. No prayer bells rang, and where the low bridges of horizontal walk-ways crossed the stairs Samarkar climbed, no paper flags fluttered.

She reached up to touch a prayer-etched stone set below the railing on one of those bridges, expecting to feel the shiver of protective energy. She snatched her hand back as a chill shock jolted her, numbing her fingers to the knuckles. When she pulled her hand down, she was half surprised to see it hadn't frozen solid, but when she worked it, she saw it fist and extend normally. Pins and needles attended each gesture.

She stepped back, forcing herself to straighten up and examine the stones.

They were rounded, pulled from rivers, and small enough to rest neatly on the ledge below the railing—but there, any resemblance between them ended. Some were white and some were black, some earthy shades of russet or pink. A few were gray as the mountains, but mostly people chose unusual stones to hold their prayers. Some had been scratched with knives or pins, some etched with expertise and care. Some were merely scribed with charcoal or black or white paint.

Each of them, to Samarkar's trained senses, glistened with a film of sorcerous malevolence.

Like the rocks washed by the Tsarethi in the channel below the Citadel, these stones were prayers, meant to impart blessings and good intentions on all that came under their influence. Something had poisoned that, perverted it. And Samarkar had no idea what it might be.

Eyes still watering with pain, she reached into one of her many pockets and found a pair of black silk gloves. They were inside out from hasty removal, but that suited her purpose: carefully, she worked one over a small prayer stone and knotted it into an insulated bag. Through the protective silk, the stone felt air-temperature, neither warm nor cool, and no more or less weighty than it should be.

Uneasy nevertheless, Samarkar slipped it into her pocket.

She began again to climb. Now the silence in Qeshqer seemed even more oppressive, the emptiness more terrible. There should have been teeming streets, children at play, shaman-monks at prayer on street corners rattling their drums for offerings. Monkeys and birds should have filled the trees overhead, swinging down to filch food or scream at intruders. A storyteller should have shaken his ringed staff and cried aloud his wares. . . .

Instead, Samarkar walked through a tomb. A tomb without bodies, through which she mounted ever higher.

Finally, she paused before one particularly great house, so large it sat on three levels beside the street and reached four stories high. Like all the others, it was whitewashed stone. Its pillars and the tile roofs over its broad patios shone a red as wet as blood, and the gold leaf on the details of its eaves was real. It was spotlessly maintained— and completely dead.

Samarkar stood in the quiet for a moment, regarding its red-and-gold door, until she gathered herself and stepped onto the patio. She marched up to the door like a mendicant, back stiff, feeling the weight of jade at her throat, as if the collar could somehow support her courage or authority. *It isn't me doing this. It is the wizard Samarkar.*

Amazing how bold one could be in a uniform.

She raised a hand and thumped solidly on the barred door, proving only—by its lack of so much as a rattle—that it was soundly barricaded and locked as well. But she was the wizard Samarkar, and what was a lock to her?

She felt inside the lock for the pins and tumblers, imagined the shape of the empty space, and with greater ease than she would have imagined, opened the lock. It clicked, and the handle turned easily in her hand. Then there was only the bar to deal with. Samarkar reached through the door and felt it, the heavy, smooth outline of solid leadwood, ornate dog heads carved in gilded detail gracing each end. She felt the shape of it outlined in emptiness, and with the process of air and its quality of motion, she shifted it.

It was harder than pins and tumblers; a great *whoosh* rattled the door against the frame, and she almost jumped back. But the rush of air was followed by a sharp clatter, and the door swung in her hand.

The fallen bar scraped across the floor as she pushed the door open. Inside the house it was cool and dim. And silent—as silent as all the city so far. No babe in the crib, no children in the garden, no mother in the kitchen going over account books or supervising the servants while they worked the dough for noodles, no father hard at work treadling his lathe, spinning the fine wood for the finer furniture that paid for this great house.

And no sign of how they might have left, from foundation to rafters, or what might have become of them. Until she reached the stairs to the attic—even these were finely finished—and realized that the door at the top stood open and she could see the blue sky above and feel the cool wind from beyond.

Something had torn the center of the roof away. Samarkar, standing on the roof beams, careful not to step on the fragile ceiling between, craned her head back and reached up with both hands to touch the cracked and shattered tile and felt the same chill—although lesser, attenuated—she'd felt burning through the prayer stones.

She grasped the crumpled edge of the hole and, with a kick and a heave, hauled herself up. Her feet swung and her forearms burned with effort, but she slid an elbow across the tile—red dust smearing her coat—and crawled out onto the roof. Here, she stepped carefully. The tiles were slick, the roof greatly sloped, but she scrambled up to the ridgeline and made herself stand.

The house was one of the taller buildings in its neighborhood, and through the pines and cypresses she could see several streets up and a good way down across the sweep of the city below.

Every roof had a hole.

SHE CLIMBED THROUGH THE REST OF THE CITY TO BE SURE, NOT CERtain what she was looking for but remembering Temur, ill unto incoherence, asking for Edene. It sounded like a woman's name, she thought, and a painful memory of her widowhood drove her on—so, if nothing else, she could tell him she'd looked, and there was nothing else he could have done.

Assuming he lived long enough for her to tell him anything.

Assuming *she* got out of this cursed city alive.

It was on the highest plaza, before the temple to the Mother-God of Qeshqer, that she found her answer.

Somebody had polished all the bones clean of meat and sinew— so clean the marble plaza showed no stains beneath them—but six days was not enough to dry them. They had been sorted and mounded in the neatest piles imaginable—sightless skulls pink and air-dulled in a monstrous pyramid beside vertebrae like stacks of coin, femurs crusted red on the ends from the ooze of blood laid one atop the other like cordwood, knucklebones in baskets and barrows as if brought out for a market day. *Sucked clean,* Samarkar thought, and wished that particular phrase had not occurred to her.

She imagined herself staggering back, clutching at her face in horror, vomiting through the narrow confines of her sorcerer's collar. She imagined it, but it did not happen, though the bones smelled warmly of rancid marrow in the afternoon sun. Too many years of her father's instruction; too many years as a princess in a hostile realm; too many years as a novice wizard.

No. Samarkar paced the length of the pyramid and measured the height of five or six skulls with her palm. She counted the number of tiers and hunkered down on her heels to sketch numbers in her saliva on the white stone. She almost wished for the buzz of flies, the flocking of carrion birds.

She went through them three times before she believed them. Crude as her measurements were, that pile of skulls must represent every man, woman, serf, slave, herdsman, and child in Qeshqer. No human or natural force could have managed this, she thought, walking around the skulls again, careful to edge past the heaps of other bones. No wizard, no sorcerer—unless there were further limits to the powers of magic than she had ever heard of.

She needed to speak to Yongten-la, to tell him of this and see what he knew of the supernatural perils that might kill twenty-five thousand in a night.

She stood, regarding the pile of the dead, and made a deep obeisance.

She could not recite the Orison for the Dead twenty-five thousand times before nightfall. But she could say it for an hour, she thought, before the press of her other duties pulled her from this place and from the horrors left to bleach here in the sun.

AFTER A LONG RIDE, TEMUR REMEMBERED THE VEIL OF NIGHT returning for him, all in black and barefoot—but this time he saw her face, for she went about plainly and by day. Still, he knew her by her eyes, by the muscle in her arms, by the breadth of her shoulders, and by the bounty of her belly and her breasts. He knew her because she lifted him up and set him on Bansh's back when he could no longer cling there himself, and he knew her because she wore black cloth darker and softer than the night, and he knew her because after she had led him and the mares out of danger, she girded herself in her coat of night and her collar of stars and went back into the cold valley to seek Edene.

Her companion was another woman in black, and Temur did what he could to help her as she loaded him into a pony drag— drawn by sensible Bansh, not Buldshak—that she seemed to have made from tree limbs and blankets, and began hauling him away. She bound him in place with blankets wrapped tightly, and to his shame, he didn't have strength to prevent it.

It was not the most comfortable mode of travel. But when she brought Temur bitter water and bathed his cracked lips with oil, he did not complain. He asked for Edene, and he asked for the Veil of Night, but she did not seem to understand him. So he knew she wasn't a goddess, even though she accompanied one.

Sometime toward evening, his fever broke. Whether it was the astringent, musty-tasting mold-and-willow-bark tea the woman in black fed him, or the blankets she tucked around to warm him, or if the thing had just run its course, he could not have said. But his mind was clear for the first time in he knew not how long, though his body felt wasted and weak. The heat had gone out of his head and his wounds, and now when he coughed he brought up mouthfuls of musty-sweet phlegm.

He lay his head back in the travois and tried to rest, but he could not keep himself from noticing how the sun slid down the sky and the shadows grew long. And how the woman who had gone back for Edene had not yet returned.

SAMARKAR CAME DOWN OUT OF THE CITY AT SUNSET, LEAVING MARKS warning of plague on the walls behind her. The eastmost curve of the Range of Ghosts lay branded black against a red weal of dying light. Under a Qersnyk or a Rasan sky, Qeshqer would have lain in shadow already, shielded from the afternoon light by the mountains at its back. But this alien sun rose in the wrong part of the sky and set in the southeast over Rasa and Song, not west in the Uthman lands where any proper sun should come to rest.

So as Samarkar descended the tiers of Qeshqer, she walked from the gold light of evening to the blue gloom of twilight, passing through sunset along the way. When she reached the road again she hesitated, her hand on the buttons of her coat, and watched the red light slide up the white walls of the city.

She had lived under two skies, Rasan and Song, and passed through the lands ruled by Qersnyk skies on her road between. This one, she did not know. It unsettled her, as if its backwardness were somehow a personal transgression. *Whose sky is that, anyway? From what cradle has this evil sprung?*

Whose conquest is marked by this sun?

She readied herself for another run. The coat would be worse to carry than wear, she decided. But the boots—the boots would have to go.

She pulled them off, balancing on one foot then the other, and stuffed the felt liners back inside them. A bit of cord she found in one pocket made a sling with which to bind them to her back.

They'd thump, but not too badly, and the quilted fabric at least was soft, even if the soles were not.

She tested the road with her feet. The track was worn smooth by many hooves, and on the trail here, she had regained a lot of the callus she'd lost during her convalescence. Yes. By the light of her own wizardry, she could make this run.

She risked one more glance behind her. Now sunset dazzled on the last tips of the city. Soon it would glide up the mountains and fall into the sky and be gone. She remembered Temur saying they came with the morning. Whoever *they* were.

Samarkar lifted her gaze to the ridge where Tsering had waited for her just a few hours before. She drew one breath. Another.

She leaned forward into the sweep of the hill and began.

At first it was easy. Light lingered in the sky, one foot followed another, and she'd come along this road three times already. Before long, she crested that rise. Under the tree where Tsering had waited, she greeted the calls of insects and night birds with an immense and ragged relief. She found the water and food that Tsering had left for her. She found her stride, she found her breath. She found her light as the track faded into dim blueness before her, and one by one the unfamiliar stars and planets gleamed bright in the dark.

She ran. She breathed. She ran.

The chill of night fell around her. Her breath plumed in the air. Her bare feet left perfect outlines in the frost as she called warmth into her limbs. Her own summoned light was cooler and bluer than the clipped sliver of moon that rose late and set early and hardly drifted higher than the reach of the mountains. As she climbed, the fields she ran through gave way to trees then low scrub scattered with boulders as tall as a house.

Ten *li* in, the other set of footprints in the frost first crossed hers. Samarkar hurdled them on instinct and was three steps beyond when she realized it would be wise to investigate. She slowed, drop-ping momentum with floating steps, and turned back.

From a height, they might have been the marks of a man—a big man, barefoot—but when Samarkar crouched beside them she saw the four toes, the pinprick marks of retracted claws. Her own run-ning steps showed the ball of her foot, the spring of toes; this one was more like an animal's pad. But an animal's pad if the animal in question ran on two legs, like a man.

Still crouched, still bathed in her own cool light, Samarkar brought her awareness of the surrounding empty—or more precisely, air-filled—spaces to the fore. Outlines of scrub, rock, small moving things. Nothing of a size to leave a print like this—a print fresh since the frost settled.

"Hrr-tchee," she said under her breath, trying to force her human voice to make the snarl and chuff of the ancient warrior race's name for itself. Her people called them Cho-tse. She'd seen one once, in Song, when it came to treat with Prince Ryi's father. It was an enor-mous person, with the ruff and ears of a beast, a striped coat, lam-bent eyes, and a heavy lashing tail. She did not relish meeting another in the moonless night.

Samarkar rose to her feet. Could the carnage in Qeshqer be the result of Cho-tse action? *They come with morning.*

Surely, Cho-tse warriors would come not with dawn, but with the dark. . . .

In the darkness, something snarled. A purring rumble was fol-lowed by a series of chuffing booms, distant but loud enough that for long moments after, Samarkar listened to echoes ring from the surrounding cliffs and stones. She felt the coughs in her chest; they rattled her like the sounding chamber of a drum. Somewhere ahead of her Tsering had probably made camp for the night by now, and that cry in the dark wouldn't make the horses any easier to handle.

Samarkar began again to run.

The coughs chased her, sometimes close and sometimes far, and twice more she passed over Cho-tse footsteps on the trail. She had never been fleet of foot, but now she tried, aware as she did so that she had no idea how far she had yet to run, and that she risked exhausting herself. She knew also that the light she needed to see her path marked her for anything that cared to track her through the night, and yet running in darkness would be an advantage only to the Cho-tse—if it stalked her.

Song legend said that the first Cho-tse had been made by powerful spirits from the body of a tiger who fought an evil Song god. The Rasan people believed that Cho-tse were tigers so canny they had learned to walk upright, like men. What the Cho-tse thought of their own origins, however, Samarkar had never heard—though there might be a book or a scroll in the Citadel that could tell her. There was one thing of which she had no doubt, however.

Tiger eyes saw very well in the dark.

Still, she was glad to let the light lapse when the western sky began to gray, and a mist rose up around her. Her own breath streamed back into it, and there was brightness enough to see her path the few steps ahead she could see at all. Her legs and lungs burned; her feet ached with the impact of hard ground.

She heard the horses stamp, and one mare's welcoming—or questioning—neigh long before she caught sight of the camp. But they were close, very close, and when Samarkar called back to them, she heard Tsering's glad cry. And the voice of the plainsman, crying out in his own Qersnyk tongue: "Hurry, hurry!"

There was a glow through the mist overhead, the first rays of the crowning sun breaking across the western peaks behind Samarkar. She smelled fire and horse and soup, and saw a dark shape moving through the mist. A moment later, she burst into the small campsite amid the bodies of mules and the bay mare, who bugled a cry of challenge past Samarkar and laid her sharp ears back.

Tsering was crouched by an improvised pony drag, set up now between rocks as a cot, with the Quersnyk man lashed into it. She was restraining him, hands on his shoulders, while he half sat and struggled to release himself from the cloths that bound him down.

She glanced up as Samarkar appeared, making no attempt to disguise her expression of relief. "There's something out there—"

"Let him up," Samarkar said. He might be feverish and weak, but if a tiger-man came slaughtering his way into the camp, she wanted any hand that could wield a knife free to do so. "There's a Cho-tse out there, and I don't know what it wants."

Eyes wide, Tsering reached under the cot and yanked loose her knots, then stood.

"Temur," Samarkar said. She spoke in his language, aware as never before how flawed her accent was. "Do you know anything about the Cho-tse following us? Or following you?"

He extended his legs gingerly over the frame of the unsteady hammock, balancing on one of the rocks Tsering had wedged its poles against. Tsering retrieved his dagger from a mule pack and pressed it into his hand before leaning his bow and quiver against the rock beside him. He looked at her in patent relief. She nodded, her hair a shadow across her cheek in the indirect and growing light.

"It's not the cat you have to worry about," he said, pushing down on his knee with a palm to stand. He looked better—much better. Tsering's attentions had broken his fever, at least. *Willow-bark*, Samarkar thought with approval. "It's the blood ghosts."

It wasn't the mist that chilled Samarkar's cheeks; it was the blood draining from them. "Sweet mother mountain," she whispered. "Nobody tended the Qarashi dead?"

He licked his lips and lifted his chin, and for the first time she saw the raw, fresh scar across his throat and realized how he must have come by it. And that he would take what she had said as a personal judgment.

"There were a lot of dead," he said. "Do you have salt? We must salt the earth, the animals, ourselves. Our weapons—"

"Of course," she said, comprehending. And realizing that Tsering was watching them with a line of concentration drawn between her eyes, understanding not one word in ten. "We're from Tsarepheth.

Tsering, salt—salt everything. Temur says that there are blood ghosts on the loose, and maybe that's what destroyed Qeshqer."

Samarkar had hardly said the words *blood ghosts* when Tsering was moving, pulling a slab of salt from the same mule pack where she'd stowed Temur's knife, dragging her own knife from her sheath and scraping the rock—near-black in the gray light—into a pile of dust and chips on the surface of the nearest boulder. Temur grabbed it up by handfuls and dumped it in the leathern bucket. It must still have held some water, because his next action was to start pouring the stuff over the restive, calling mares and mules, splashing it all over himself in the process.

It seemed like a good idea. Samarkar threw a handful of salt in Tsering's hair, then started broadcasting it in all directions, sowing it more thickly than rice. In the morning damp, it stuck to the grass and her hands and the hides of the animals. She performed the work almost automatically, her every natural and wizardly sense straining out into the fog for any sign that danger approached them.

"When do they attack?" Samarkar gasped.

"Sunrise," Temur said, cupping up the last handful of salt sludge from the bottom of the bucket and smearing it into her hair. The touch jerked her attention home, and she found herself staring down into his eyes from a few handspans' distance. She pulled her attention away, cuffing salt water from her forehead before it could trickle into her eyes, a knotting but not unpleasant unease twisting in her belly.

Samarkar craned her head around. Just mist. Mist and lots of it. And a shadow cutting it as the sun finally crested the horizon and scraped across the land. A very black shadow, narrow and long.

And a great hollow grumbling *huff* of laughter.

She looked up across the muscled expanse of red-orange, fawn, and black-striped chest to meet the shadowed eyes of the figure that loomed nonchalantly out of the mist, arms folded, ears pricked, head cocked to one side like any curious cat. The gold rings in her

ear leather jingled with charms and pendant jewels; the ears themselves were ragged-edged with scars, as if older piercings had been
ripped out by violence. The horses and mules had stopped their bray-
ing and stamping and now stood stock-still, snorting deep breaths of
air, on the verge of panic and blind flight.

Samarkar realized with a shock that the Cho-tse she had met in
Song was, perhaps, not such a large example of his breed after all.

"Monkey-men," the she-tiger said, in a voice like sandy velvet.
"The mist will not kill you tonight. But you have other worries. I
am Hrahima; I have traveled from fabled Ctesifon to warn your
monkey-kinglet of a great evil."

9

"I'M SORRY," SAID THE LARGER OF THE TWO WOMEN. WIZARDS, TEMUR realized, now that his head was clearer. Her words were one of the phrases he knew in Rasan. Her politeness suggested to him that she was high ranking, indeed; he remembered the same excruciatingly gentle assurance of obedience in his father. "I did not see you there. Please . . ."

Whatever she said next was beyond him, but she gestured to the last coals of the fire, and Temur understood that she invited the tiger to sit. The tiger nodded. Temur remained somewhat overawed by her massive head, her shoulders like a bull's, the thick striped orange hide that covered the knitted sinew of her forearms. She wore only a satchel slung diagonally across her body and a tangle of beautifully cured leather straps with gold and amber fittings that supported three curved daggers.

Her rows of pale dugs—the color of skimmed milk—were how he knew she was female, because the shape of her body was not like a woman's and her female parts were tucked away behind fur and the thick diameter of her tail.

The bigger wizard-woman introduced them all; Temur must

have told them how he was called when he was delirious, because they shared it now. He learned that the bigger woman was Samarkar and the smaller was Tsering.

Meanwhile, the tiger—Hrahima—crouched before the fire, holding long fingers tipped with retractable claws out to the embers. The mules watched; the mares stamped and edged into one another. The muscle across Hrahima's thighs and haunches rippled. Her legs were curiously made—longer than a man's, with the knee higher on the leg and the heel levered up like a dog's hock, so she stood on only the ball and toe pads of feet Temur could not have spanned with his fingers stretched.

The structure of her lower leg reminded him of the design of a spear-thrower. She could probably leap like a tiger, too.

As he watched, Hrahima pulled a charred stick from the firepit and began to sketch on a nearby stone.

"You did not see me," she said carefully, "because I did not wish to be seen." She glanced about, frowning from Temur to Tsering to Samarkar, and switched to Temur's language. "Do all of you speak the same languages?"

"No," Tsering said. "I don't know Qersnyk."

"I know very little Rasan," Temur admitted.

The tiger sighed—a rumbling sound, which Temur only identified as a sigh because of the irritation with which her shoulders rose and fell. Her tail lashed like a granary cat's. "Then I shall say everything twice."

Her ears were large and mobile. The charms and rings in them jingled when she flicked them to and fro. Temur found himself staring into her textured, transparent golden eyes. He nodded.

She turned back to her sketching. Samarkar said, in Qersnyk, "When you say you bring news for the king—do you mean Songtsan-tse? He will be *bstangpo*—emperor—soon, but he is not yet."

"Him," Hrahima agreed, "or his regent. Are you a subject of this monkey-king?"

"After a fashion," Samarkar said. "I am his sister. But more importantly, right now, I am a wizard of the Citadel and tasked with discovering the fate of the city of Qeshqer." She repeated herself in her own language, glancing at the other wizard—Tsering—to make sure she understood.

"Ghosts," Hrahima said. "Ghosts summoned from among the dead of the steppe tribes by rotted sorcery, and by that same sorcery set upon the city."

Samarkar translated for Tsering. Tsering rubbed her eyes in exhaustion. Temur knew enough Rasan to follow when Tsering said, "So why Qeshqer? And how?"

Samarkar's hand slipped into a concealed pocket. "How, I may have an answer to."

She pulled out a glove, inside out and knotted, and began working it open with her teeth. When she upended it, a Rasan prayer stone rolled out into the trampled weeds. Temur would have reached for it, but Samarkar gestured him back. "It's cursed."

Tsering crouched beside it, pressing her cheek to the grass. "Roll it over."

Gingerly, using the glove to shield her hand, Samarkar turned the stone. A scraped-looking chalk mark smudged the back. She did not recognize the alphabet.

Tsering, however, made a small noise of dismay. "Rahazeen," she said. "And not just Rahazeen. The Nameless."

"Murderer's cult," the Cho-tse said. "It's one of their curse words. A Nameless sorcerer entered your city and twisted your priest's blessing into an invocation of the hungry dead."

Hrahima reached one hand out, fingers spread. Like any tiger, she had five digits on her hands and four on her feet. The bare skin on her palms was an inhuman shade of pink-white, mottled with irregularly sized and spaced round black dots. The claws that extended from her broad fingertips when she flexed them were as long as two joints of a man's finger, white with dark streaks like marble, translucent at the tips. She paused, her hand cupped as if cradling the stone but a span above it. Temur thought the expression that drew her whiskers back and lifted her flews from ivory-streaked canine teeth as big as tent pegs was a frown of concentration, but it could have been a snarl.

Whatever it meant, Temur found himself leaning back as if he could remove himself from her attention. Her arm could have taken the place of his leg for size and muscularity, but the delicacy with which she moved her fingers made him imagine she traced something tender and palpable with the needle points of her claws. Her nostrils flared, the long white whiskers slicked back against her cheeks, and she made a sound in her chest—*hrrh hrrh hrrrh*—that trembled his body like a drumhead.

"Oh, yes." Her mottled orange-and-tourmaline irises filled the whole aperture of her eyes; only when she looked up at him from a crouch could he see the rims of white sclera at the bottoms. Her pupils were round. "It's cursed all right. A prayer stone to deflect harm, suborned to draw it. Filthy magic."

Samarkar protested. Temur could imagine the meaning of her words, even if he didn't quite understand them: *Sorcery can't do that.*

He allowed himself to settle back on one of the rocks where his travois rested, trying to hide how exhaustion made the whole valley and all its stones and junipers and early wildflowers seem to spin. Tsering, coming from beside the fire, pushed something warm into his hand; he took it. A wooden cup, full of still more willow-bark tea. He drank it quickly, stoic before the acrid sourness, and thanked her in her own tongue. It might taste like mare's piss, but he knew he had it to thank for breaking his fever and leaving him even as clearheaded as he was.

"So," he said, across the bitterness, "either some Nameless assassin entered Qeshqer and altered the stones by night . . . How long would such a task have taken, Hrahima?"

"Quarter-moons," she said.

". . . Or," Temur continued, "an agent already within the city did it, and made it look Rahazeen."

"An agent who knows Rahazeen sorcery," Tsering said, cautioning, after Samarkar translated. "Or it could have been a long-term Rahazeen agent, of course, or—"

"It's curious," Temur said, "that this should happen so soon upon the fall of Qarash."

"And perhaps using the dead of that battle," Hrahima said.

Samarkar shifted uncomfortably, but when Temur looked at her, she shrugged. "My brother will have his quarter-century soon."

"Regime change." Temur's mouth dried unpleasantly.

Tsering moved away abruptly, thrusting odds and ends into saddlebags and piling each beside the appropriate mule. Samarkar spoke quickly in her own tongue, not pausing now to translate her words for Temur's sake.

Whatever else Samarkar said, Hrahima crouched and listened to the whole of it. She had a trick of stilling herself, whereby she could vanish like a stone among scrub. This despite the fact that she made more than three of Temur; she was easily two-thirds of Bansh's weight.

When Samarkar had finished, Hrahima glanced at Temur and said, "There is a man called Re Qori Buqa. 'Twenty bulls.' He is the chief living claimant to the Khaganate."

"I know him," Temur said, fingers knotting through fingers in his lap until his bones creaked with pain. "His army marched on Qarash as if it were a foreign city and not the seat of the Khagan himself. The defenders were the Great Khagan's grandson Qulan and his warriors. They rode out to meet Qori Buqa on the steppe a day's ride from Qarash."

Temur took a breath. No one interrupted. "But the army of Qori Buqa rolled over them and sacked the city, like they would sack any conquered western town. Only a few of the people escaped. Qori Buqa used the Great Khagan's tactics against the Great Khagan's own city. Some of the refugees said that he could not have made the sack of the town so complete without sorcery."

He hesitated, plunged ahead.

"But I have seen a city sacked, and it does not take any magic to destroy in hours what is built over centuries."

"I too have seen a city sacked." Samarkar said. "And what you say is true, Temur."

Tsering said something; whatever it was, Samarkar didn't bother to translate. It sounded like a question.

Hrahima laid down her stick. She covered her knees with her tremendous paws and seemed to hover in her powerful crouch. "Nevertheless, there is necromancy at work here. Because it is due to signs of necromancy that I came to warn your people before the worst happened. Alas that through the fault of long travel, I have arrived too late."

"Better a storm crow than a carrion bird," Temur said. Judging from the quizzical look Samarkar gave him, it was an idiom that didn't translate. He spread his hands. "Better to come in warning of crisis than scavenge the remains of disaster to survive?"

"Oh," Samarkar said. She pushed her braid behind her shoulder and straightened her back, moving back over to help Tsering finish packing the camp. "So Qeshqer was destroyed by the ghosts of a steppe war, and you've come from beyond the Uthman Caliphate to warn the people of Rasa, out of the goodness of your heart? Forgive me, Hrahima. I know your people have a reputation as tricksters to maintain."

But the Cho-tse did not lie. Even Temur knew that; it was in every story.

The tiger chuffed, a great hollow sound that made her throat swell like a bellows. Her ears flicked back and forth, and Samarkar could not shake the suspicion that she was forming an opinion. When she spoke again, it was as if she had decided to grant them candor.

"Hardly," she said. She opened her hands at shoulder level and raised them high, so they spread out as if describing the shape of a growing plant. "Do you see this sun above you?"

Temur tilted his head back. It was large and golden and indisputably in the wrong part of a strange, dusty, turquoise sky that had a look of blue cloth washed too often and left to dry in the light. The edges faded to a buff that was almost yellow; the center seemed shallow rather than deep. It was not the sky of his homeland—not the blue Eternal Sky his ancestors honored—and it seemed impossibly high and dry and far away.

"I see it," Samarkar said. "It is not the sky of Rasa."

"It is not the sky of the steppe," Temur said. "And since the Great Khagan claimed Qeshqer and the Qeshqerian plateau for his own, that is the sky that should cover it."

"It is the sky of Ctesifon," Hrahima said. "It is the sky of the Uthman Scholar-God, of which the Nameless cult of the Rahazeen sect is a part. And as your stone demonstrates, it is a rogue Rahazeen warlord-priest who has allied with your Re Qori Buqa, Temur. That is what I have come to warn your monkey-king of. The leader of the Nameless, ai-Idoj, what they call al-Sepehr, is working with your man who would be Khagan. In return for ai-Idoj's help, Re Qori Buqa has given the murder-cultist sovereignty over the city of Qeshqer, and the heap of skulls within is only the beginning."

Temur leaned forward, stomach churning with apprehension. He caught himself rubbing his chin left-handed and made himself stop, but the hand naturally strayed to the flaking skin along his scar. He stretched against it. When the constriction would have twisted his head to the left, he held his gaze straight. "Rahazeen?"

Temur knew who the Rahazeen were, of course. Too many of his family had fought them for their existence, to be a mystery. A sect from within the Ctesifonin lands—some lapping over into the Uthman Caliphate—they had for many years been engaged in a power struggle with the Falzeen, another sect of the same god.

Persecuted by more populous sects, a branch of the Rahazeen religion had withdrawn to mountain fastnesses that even the Great Khagan had sometimes chosen not to lay under siege. Temur had heard of the Nameless, too, as who had not? Within those holdfasts the Nameless had blossomed—a cult that worshipped the Uthman Scholar-God in her incarnation as Lady Death.

Not all, or even the majority, of Rahazeen were martial. But the martial ones—from among whom the Nameless were derived—were a contradiction. Like some Song monks, they swore themselves to peace and service. And like those self-same Song monks, they honored that service with an unrelenting study of the disciplines of combat.

Temur had met members of both Rahazeen and Falzeen sects in his uncle Mongke's court. He respected them as scholars and warriors but found their doctrinal differences an incomprehensible foundation for what amounted to a long-term, low-grade civil war within the Uthman Caliphate.

Still, it was the Qersnyk way not to question too much the customs of others but rather accept them as they found them—so long as they bent their heads to the Khagan. His people conquered for riches and knowledge, not to evangelize.

And if the Uthman Caliphate warred against itself, well, that made things all the better for the Qersnyk clans, didn't it? An enemy divided was easy prey. But now Temur's people had fallen into the same trap, and if the Cho-tse could be trusted, that division was being encouraged by equally predatory outsiders.

How long would a Rahazeen master allow Qori Buqa to rule unbowed? How long before the proud Qersnyk Empire became a vassal state to some western warlord?

The Great Khagan himself had started life as a simple herdsman. It was not unheard of for great empires to grow from humble beginnings. The Qersnyk tribes could find themselves a vassal state as easily as they had made vassals of other lands.

Samarkar turned her back to throw a set of packs across the withers of the nearest mule. It still wasn't happy about the proximity of the tiger, but it seemed to have decided that a predator making itself as small as possible all the way across the fire was not interested in mule flesh today, so the mule contented itself with wary staring. Buldshak was not so easily convinced, but she stayed on the far side of Bansh, and Bansh was so mild that if she were a cow, Temur would have expected her to be chewing cud.

Without looking around, Samarkar said, "Are you a wizard?"

Hrahima stifled a laugh before the horses could kick themselves free. "I am Hrr-tchee. We are not wizards. But I know necromancy when it freezes my flesh."

Casually, she dug her claws into the soil and raked dirt and vegetation over the defiled prayer stone. She stood, slowly, a controlled motion that revealed more power than jerking herself to her feet would have.

"Hrahima?" said Temur.

She turned to him, ears pricked, eyes glowing. Temur's tongue wanted to cleave to the roof of his mouth, but he ordered himself to speak on. "You have no wizards? No shamans?"

"We need them not." The skin across her neck and shoulders shuddered as if she flicked water from her hide.

"What do your people worship?"

Another chuffing laugh. "My people?" She paused, wiped her hands on the pillars of her thighs. "My *people* worship the Sun Within, and the Immanent Destiny."

"But not you?"

Samarkar was watching over the mule's back, attentive.

"I do not worship." Hrahima passed a palm over her ears. "I prefer the illusion of free will."

"Huh," Samarkar said. "And what is it that motivates a Cho-tse to involve herself in human affairs of empire?"

The tiger looked down, ears flat. Temur could not shake the impression that she was abashed, though what he knew of cats suggested they were as shameless as ravens.

"The Ctesifonin," she said, "have the same motivation anyone else does. They want to be out from under the Uthman yoke. And they do not care to replace it with a yoke of the Rahazeen." Her ears flicked again; the rings jangled again. "Or that of the plainsmen, or the Bey of Messaline."

She was looking directly at Temur. He found his fingertips pressed to his scar, ragged nails worrying it, and pulled them slowly away. "Empires grow or they collapse," he said. "Everything ends. You have not answered the wizard yet."

Tigers did not smile, but her ears flicked forward and her eyes went wide. "What do I gain in all this? Nothing, personally. Except the pay I claim for delivering the message. Even an exile must eat. And travel across the steppe is not so safe or speedy for you monkey-men as it once was, now that Mongke's children are devouring each other like queen bees hatched in the same hive."

Perhaps it was his own state, but Temur found himself fixating on the word *exile*. And on the scarred, rag-edged leather of her ears. He did not know the laws of Cho-tse society, but he knew the ways of cats, and no cat with ears like that stood very high in the hierar-chy of such creatures. Leaning forward when he wanted to lean back, he said, "And who is your employer, then? Who is the Ctesifonin who takes such interest in the fate of my people and of the royal family of Rasa?"

"Not a Ctesifonin," Hrahima said. "An Aezin noble in exile, who lives now in Ctesifon and who has ties to nobility in Asmaracanda—which still stands under the sky of the steppes, but I am sure the caliphate would welcome its return. This noble—his business lies along the Celadon Highway, and he is at pains to see peace restored. And as I said, the Uthman yoke can be onerous."

Samarkar snorted, sarcastic as a mare. "Especially when it in-volves the murder of whole cities. So your Aezin noble uses the politics of other nations to break the back of the caliphate, but not to set the Rahazeen in power, I take it?"

"I don't believe he cares who rules any of these cities—save Aezin, which I imagine he'd see made independent again. I can tell you he prefers to see peace the length of the Celadon Highway. And that necromancy is bad for business, especially when it involves the deaths of entire cities."

"Qeshqer won't be making good on any debts," Samarkar said. "That's truth. So his interest is less patriotic and more pecuniary?"

"War is bad for shopkeepers," Tsering said, speaking slowly enough that Temur followed her. "Even when they keep very large shops.

Who is this merchant-prince who wants to overthrow his conquerors, then?"

The Cho-tse folded her hands together, nails retracted, and
fluffed her whiskers smugly. Her shrug indicated she had no intention of answering. But Temur didn't need her to tell him.

"Ato Tesefahun," he blurted, naming his mother's father, and was
regarded by a slow, considering cat stare. "He is well known on the
steppe," Temur continued, desperately casual. "He had married his
daughter to an Asmaracandan noble. She came to the Great Khagan
as tribute when Asmaracanda fell and was married to Otgonbayar
Khanzadeh. She might have been Khatun, had her husband not been
murdered by his brother Mongke."

He met Hrahima's gaze. She held the look for long instants, then
blinked gently and looked down. "Of course."

"Hrahima. If you are going to Tsarepheth," Tsering said abruptly,
breaking the dragging, uncomfortable quiet, "you could come with
us. We're going that way."

Temur folded his own arms. In his rashness, he had already said
too much.

"Thank you," the tiger said, settling back on her haunches. "I
think I shall."

TEMUR WENT TO HELP THE WOMEN WITH THE HORSES AND MULES
while the big cat withdrew to a less-threatening distance. He felt
well enough to walk, and he thought it wise that they not burden
the mares while there was a chance for them to rest. Both Samarkar
and Tsering seemed content to walk as well. If he understood Tsering correctly, with his broken Rasan, she said that they had walked
here from Tsarepheth on their own two feet, an idea that Temur found
startling. Riding, certainly . . . but to *walk* here?

Eventually, he found himself standing beside Samarkar, impassive in her wizarding black, older than he and far more imposing.
He had been waiting for this moment, and now he screwed up his

second-son's courage to ask. He cleared his throat, and when she looked at him, he said, "You said . . . the destruction of Qeshqer. I had a friend . . ." he began. He swallowed. ". . . A friend who was stolen by the ghosts. I followed her here, hoping to bring her home again. Edene?"

"I'm sorry," Samarkar said, her dark eyes deepening with shadows as she dropped her chin. "Everyone in the city is dead."

Temur felt something harden within him, as if the iron of his name took a temper from the ice in her tone. "She's not dead," he said stubbornly, even as he doubted. "If she were dead, I would know it somehow. I would—"

Only when she laid her hand on his arm did he realize his voice had gone shrill. He breathed in, breathed out, and calmed himself. Trembling urgency filled him—the need to be *doing*. "I must ride back to Qeshqer," he said. "My people may seek shelter there. . . ."

Samarkar squeezed his bicep. "I left it warded with plague-sign," she said. "They will not enter. And if you truly believe your woman lives, you will not find her by returning to a city where the ghosts have already torn everyone limb from limb."

"And I'll find her in Tsarepheth?" he mocked. He regretted the sarcasm instantly, knowing it for the ineffectual, misdirected anger of a thwarted child.

"You'll find wizards in Tsarepheth," she said, continuing as if he had spoken in a much milder tone, which made him feel all the more shamed. "And if anyone can find a woman stolen by ghosts, it is my master Yongten-la. Besides, I have the poppy juice, and I have the extract of willow, and I have the blue-gray mold that saved your life this time—and if you sicken again when you are alone, I cannot guarantee that you will live through it. And you will be no good to your Edene dead of a fever."

He stared at her. She stared back.

Slowly, so she could not mistake his capitulation for agreement, he placed his hands palm to palm before his breast and bowed to the wizarding woman. He would have turned away, but she cleared her throat and said, "What are the horses called?"

He almost said, *horses.* But she was trying to mend a trespassed boundary, and it would be childish—and churlish—to stop her.

"Her name is Buldshak," he said, gesturing to the rose-gray. He pointed to the liver-bay with his chin. "And *her* name is Bansh."

"*Bansh?* It's not a word I know. What does that mean? Something like 'Fearless' or 'Sword of the Wind'?"

Temur looked down at his feet. "'Dumpling,'" he said. "It means 'Dumpling.'"

But Samarkar didn't laugh—or she didn't laugh cruelly. Instead she looked at the bone-thin mare and said, "She likes her dinner, I take it."

WITH TEMUR'S INFIRMITY AND THE TIME IT TOOK TO EXCHANGE NEWS with Hrahima, they weren't walking until the sun was a handspan into the sky. At first, Tsering led the mares and mules, and Samarkar walked ahead with Temur and Hrahima, out of the dust. But after they had been walking and filling the gaps between strained silences with even more strained conversation for some time, Samarkar dropped back beside Tsering. She held her hand out for the lead rope, forcing a smile.

"I talked to Temur," she said.

Tsering handed her the rope, stepping more quickly for a moment in order to pass in front of her and change places so she would not be between Samarkar and the bay mare. "What about?"

"I pointed out that one rider could move faster than four walkers and five animals. He's agreed to loan you the gray tomorrow, when she has had a night to rest, so that you can ride on ahead and warn Songtsan and Yongten-la of the danger." Samarkar looked down at her hands. "We agreed it should be you, because you are lighter than I am, and he is still weak and ill. He begs you, however, to care for the mare."

Tsering looked down at her hands in that way she had, hiding a smile. But when she glanced back up, her brow was quizzical. "He's a plainsman," she said. "What's in it for him? Why would he want to protect a Rasan city?"

Samarkar paused to consider what she would say next. "The ghosts are his people," she said. "Or so Hrahima thinks. And I think they attacked the refugees from Qarash, too, before they destroyed Qeshqer. They"—she lowered her voice—"took somebody from him. A wife? I'm not sure. Anyway, he's determined to find her. I convinced him that Yongten-la was his best resource, and who knows? Maybe it's true."

"I see." Tsering folded her arms before her for a stride or two, then let them swing at her sides to mark her pace. "You are right. Word must reach Yongten-la as soon as possible. And you are also right that I am the most able to carry it." She turned her head slightly. "What if the ghosts beat me there?"

From farther up the road, as if speaking to herself, Hrahima said, "The Steles of the Sky are underlaid by salt."

"Pardon me?" said Tsering.

Hrahima's ears flicked back to them. Samarkar wondered just how good her hearing was. "Under the Steles of the Sky, wizard. There is salt. Salt in great quantities. The ghosts will not pass through."

Tsering looked at Samarkar. Samarkar raised her eyebrows.

"Of course," Tsering said. "Still, I think some haste is called for."

ONCE TSERING LEFT THEM, THE DAYS OF THE JOURNEY BEGAN TO blend together mercilessly. Thanks to Hrahima, who spent most of the days ranging out away from the horses in order to keep herself awake, and who did not sleep well by night, they ate more meat in more varieties than Samarkar had ever considered possible, even as a princess of a royal house. This was a blessing, because she and Tsering had not brought food enough for a round trip, Temur's supplies were exhausted, and what little they *had* had, she had insisted Tsering take, for swift travel. But the rich diet did not sit well with her;

it bound her up and led to other troubles. Temur seemed to adapt to it well, though, so she chewed the meat and drank the broth and comforted herself that when they reached the Citadel, she would be able to fill her tea bowl not only with tea but with butter and noodles.

She amused herself with fantasies of food as she walked, between the time spent teaching Temur whatever Rasan she could. He was a quick study, at least—he told her that his father had had many wives, from many lands, taken in the wake of conquest. They had taught the sons of the house their tongues, that they would have someone to speak to in it. He knew the Uthman tongue, as did Samarkar, quite a lot of Song, and some Aezin.

Samarkar was fluent in several dialects of the Song language. But she did not know Aezin—had, in fact, heard almost nothing of that land except that it lay to the south of Ctesifon, of Messaline, of the Celadon Highway that connected them all, and that it was rich in gold and jewels, and the people who lived there had skins burned black by the fierce light of their desert sun.

She'd never credited that last, but she found herself studying Temur's face, finding elements of it familiar and others exotic. His color was dark, even for a Qersnyk, but the plainsmen had such a reputation for intermarrying with every nation they conquered that one could not exactly say that a steppe warrior looked like this or he looked like that. His eyes seemed wide open to her, his chin pointed and small, lips full and cheekbones high on either side of a nose tidy enough for even Rasan ideals of beauty. He wore his hair in a long plait, coiled up under his hat after the manner of his people, and as his health returned, he found the strength to unbraid, wash, oil, and comb it. When he did, she saw that it had a soft texture—more like fleece than her own hard, straight locks.

They practiced languages, conversing in Aezin when they did not speak in Rasan. The Rasan was not so different from Qersnyk or Song. The Aezin was more foreign, but Samarkar at least learned a little—and there was not much else to do besides walk.

On the fourth day of their journey, as they were ascending a switchback trail into the first of several high passes that would lead them eventually through the Steles of the Sky, Temur touched Samarkar's arm and, with a gesture for silence, drew her attention up the slope. Something moved among the stones there—a stocky, long-furred feline, ocher in color, its pelt marked with spots and its tail barred with rings. She slowed and stopped the bay mare and the mules, all of which she was leading single file.

"Manul cat," she said, giving him the Rasan word. The shadow of a circling vulture skipped down the stony slope at racing speed, passing between them.

"I wonder if Hrahima has seen it?"

Samarkar laughed. "I hope for its sake it's seen her, or it might wind up baked over coals tonight."

"The hide makes good hoods," Temur said. "But they're better to watch, living."

It was true, and so Samarkar smiled, nodding. She tilted her head back, enjoying the wind in her hair and the first sight of an honest Rasan sky in eight days. The blues were bluer, she thought. It made her think of something. In Rasan—for his practice—she said to Temur, "Your folk worship the sky, do they not?"

Temur scuffed a foot on stone, climbing. His hands chafed each other. "He is not merely the sky. He is the Eternal Sky. And I would not say we worship him. We send the dead back to him; we tell the ravens and the vultures their true names, and the sacred carrion birds carry them home. And then anyone who knows the name can call you back when they wish your counsel." He waved absently at the vulture that had just skimmed by overhead again in its hunting pattern of overlapping circles.

"A secret name," Samarkar said, considering. "But others know it?"

"Not secret," Temur said. "I mean, yes, secret. I do not know my true name, so the demons cannot use it to deceive me. But my family would know it. . . ."

He frowned abruptly and bent his efforts to faster climbing. Samarkar pretended she had to work to keep up, but at these heights, Temur's best effort was nothing she couldn't better.

His family is dead, she realized. *When he dies, there is no one to tell the birds his name.*

She wondered if that meant he, too, was doomed to walk the earth as a hungry ghost. Maybe it was time to change the subject. "Have you heard of the Carrion-King? Before I left, one of my brothers' wives was reading about him. A kind of demigod, supposedly a Qersnyk."

"Of course," Temur said, bracing a foot on a stone and standing up on it. "But he wasn't a Qersnyk; he was a sorcerer from Song or maybe one of the western horse clans. We call him the Sorcerer-Prince. In my homeland, they say he fought the Warrior-Gods of the Uthman Caliphate, and Song, and Rasa, and Messaline, and defeated them all. But they also say that the sky was hung much higher in those days. In the battles, the four ranges of mountains that supported the Eternal Sky's pavilion were damaged, so the Sky's roof sagged. And then the Sky came out to see what was the matter and put the Sorcerer-Prince in his place."

Struggling up the same rock, careful of the lead lines she was trailing, Samarkar said, "That's not how we tell it in Rasa."

Temur snorted like his mare and said complacently, "Of course not."

10

No party rode out from Tsarepheth to meet them. Once Tsering rode on ahead, Samarkar had expected to be greeted halfway by her brothers' men or by wizards. Instead, she fretted and worried the entire way that Hrahima had been wrong about the salt deposits offering protection and that they would come to Tsarepheth to find a city empty of life and heaped with bloody bones.

She and Temur crested the last rise in the pass above the city to find no one waiting for them except Hrahima, crouched on a ledge halfway up the cliff like a hunting snow leopard. Her red-orange, black, and ivory fur was no camouflage against lichen-spotted basalt. The Citadel spanned the pass ahead of them, wrapped in rainbow-raddled veils of steam and fog. Before it, the headwaters of the Tsarethi plunged from the glaciers of the Island-in-the-Mists to meet the hot upwelling of the Cold Fire's mineral waters. The moderate temperatures of the river, Samarkar knew, kept Tsarepheth extraordinarily mild in the brutal winters of the Steles.

The white wall behind those veils of mist could have been forged from them by sorcery. Prayer flags and banners in every bright color flapped from the battlements, and even at this distance Samarkar could see the black outlines of wizards against alabaster as they stood sentinel or scurried to and fro. There were too many of them overall, and too many of those were motionless, watching—awaiting war. If Tsering's warning had not reached them, some other portent had.

The city of Tsarepheth lay beyond.

Temur had stopped dead, transfixed. Samarkar came up beside him. Not without satisfaction, she whispered, "Tsarepheth."

He nodded. His breath came rapid and shallow; she could tell from his grayish color and the way he stood that the thin air pained him. It had slowed them, these last days, but at least he hadn't succumbed to headaches and vomiting.

"I see," he said, "why it has never been taken."

Hrahima descended from her aerie in three bounds, sensible enough to come to earth well away from the mules. Bansh seemed to have accepted her, but Samarkar had never met a mare as steady as the bay.

"I waited for you," Hrahima said. "The bridge is guarded."

"Always," Samarkar said. "It's called the Wreaking, by the way." She led them forward, her feet light for the first time in a moon of traveling, but her heart stone-cold with apprehension.

What Hrahima termed a bridge qualified in Temur's mind as a temple. Rivers on the steppe were forded. They ran broad and shallow over gravel when they ran at all. Many dried to trickles in the dry season, while in spring flood they were demons that no more could be bridged or forded or swum than a dragon could be chained. Now he stood on a white stone arch lost in mist, rainbows mounting one above another like jewels piled upon jewels, and listened to Samarkar coaxing the restive mules forward. He would go and help her in a moment, he thought. But just for this instant, he could not pull himself away from what he saw.

The bridge described an arc a hundred *ayl* long, graceful as a woman's white-clad arm, anchored only at the ends because there was nothing in the middle to which an architect could drop a pillar. It was so long in proportion to its width that it seemed frail and slender, even though it was wide enough for two carts to pass abreast. There were railings—stone balustrades to waist height— along the edges, and Temur found himself clutching reflexively at the hand rail.

He had seen waterfalls in the parts of Song that his grandfather and uncle had conquered. There was terrain there where the water melted the very stone from beneath the earth, so rivers vanished into yawning yellow-white pits draped at the edges with webs of roots; where measureless caverns made awful labyrinths under your feet; where alien towers of limestone netted with jungle-green thrust up from flat verdant fields. But he had never seen a waterfall like this.

The river Tsarethi plunged a distance he could not estimate—a hundred *ayl*, five hundred?—down a sheer granite cliff to a pool be- low, bouncing and splashing and scattering spray. In the tight canyon, the thunder was like the thunder of a thousand hooves when the herd was all around you. Louder—booming—so he could not hear Samarkar a few spans away calling to the mules.

The spray drifting against his face was cold as ice—so cold he could imagine it freezing *to* ice in his patchy, unshaven beard. But the mist that rose from below was warm as summer rain. Temur had to turn his shoulders to follow the water down. The stiffness of his scar made it hard to twist his neck away. He was fortunate the wound was on his left side. Otherwise, it would have interfered with drawing a bow.

Reluctantly, he pulled himself away from the view and went to help Samarkar chivy the mules forward. So many feet had worn the incline that you could see the dished places. As each person had leaned into any given depression to use it as a step, they had worn it deeper. Temur climbed them as if they were steps, and used them to slow his descent on spray-slick stone on the opposite side.

Hrahima waited with Bansh on the far side, flanked by four spear-armed guards in red and two in the same black coats and jade collars Tsering and Samarkar affected. These were men, though, and they wore long knives at their belts in addition to whatever wizarding weapons Temur could not see.

Samarkar's coat won them past the wizards. The red-coated men, however, were chilly until she shouted her name above the rumble that shook the stones on which they stood. Then frost melted to an excess of deference bordering on obsequiousness.

The mules were likely to prove more intransigent. But Temur was familiar with the minds of mules, and it did not take him long to bribe and cajole them into moving. Their unshod hooves echoed on the stone span as he and Samarkar led them forward. He leaned in to shout into her ear.

"Who built this?"

"Wizards." There was no mistaking the pride in the set of her shoulders.

He offered a mule another bit of leathery fruit to keep it moving, and watched Samarkar's straight back as she walked ahead. *Wizards.*

He thought about bones bleaching in an empty city. He thought about Edene. He thought about Qori Buqa, and he pressed one fist to his belly over a sudden, painful knot of emotion. He wanted revenge. Revenge for Edene, if she was dead—and no matter how he pretended to himself that she wasn't, some part of him knew it for a pretense.

Revenge. Wizards could help him get it.

Tsering did not meet them at the Citadel's northern gates, and the wizards at the Wreaking would or could tell Samarkar nothing of the results of her message—though she thought the extra bodies on the battlements an unsubtle hint. Someone else did, though. Anil, the wizard who had kissed her at the celebration of finding her powers, waited just within.

His face was furrowed with concern. He took no notice of Hrahima or Temur, and the first words he said were, "Yongten-la wishes to speak with you."

Samarkar looked to her traveling companions. "I need—"

"We'll see the animals cared for," Anil said, "and your friends accommodated. Go, run, Samarkar-la. He awaits."

The head of the wizards of the Citadel had never had a particular title or rank. Everyone knew who held the post; everyone knew under whose authority they lived. Once or twice in the history of the order, there had been internecine war, but most often the trouble was finding somebody who was willing to take on the burden of the job. Wizards tended to be more interested in their spells and chemicals than administration.

Samarkar paused long enough to explain to Hrahima and Temur that she was summoned by the master of her order and that they should accept whatever comfort the wizards could offer, then she took off—as Anil had suggested—at a run. The petal hem of her coat fluttered around her legs, fabric filthy and stiff with travel. The boots rubbed new raw places on her feet where the felt wrappings had worn thin.

Within two hundred heartbeats, she stood before the open door of Yongten-la's chamber. Light and the sound of falling water reached her through the windows. Two wizards and two novices waited in the hall, ready to attend any errand. Samarkar was taking a moment to compose herself when Yongten-la's voice emerged from within.

"Samarkar-la," he said. "You have returned. Come inside, and shut the door behind you."

The words chilled her innards. If he meant to chew her out for some infraction, he would not hesitate to do so in front of witnesses. Which meant he had some news to impart that he did not wish to become public knowledge just yet.

On raw feet, Samarkar stepped forward. She pulled the door closed after.

Yongten-la's chamber was spare and neat. His private workbenches, topped with slate and granite, lay to Samarkar's right, and all the equipment on them was clean and orderly. Even the chalk-scrawled notations on the surface of the slate beside the scale were precise enough to read from a distance, despite their economical size. His desk was before her, under the windows, raised on a little platform padded with rugs and cushions in deference to old bones. Yongten-la sat cross-legged behind it, bent over a sand tray from which he appeared to be transcribing notes to a wax tablet. When he was satisfied with them, Samarkar knew, the tablets would go to a scribe, who would transcribe them again, onto paper for binding and preservation in the archive.

He looked up and set his stylus aside. "Samarkar-la," he said, when she had bowed low. "Be seated. I have some unfortunate news for you."

Tsering, she thought, like a claw of ice. But she came up beside him and sat, pushing aside cushions so her head would be lower than his. Wizards did not stand on such ceremony, but court-bred Samarkar could not quite break the habit.

Seated, she bowed her head and waited for him to continue. He was kind and had the directness of age; he did not draw it out. "The Dowager Regent is dead. It is said she was poisoned, and Songtsan-tsa has arrested your younger brother for the crime. It seems likely Songtsan will burn Tsansong."

Samarkar put a hand out behind her for support, or she would have slumped backward against the cushions. "Tsansong is no killer."

Yongten's eyebrows rose. His hand moved idly on the rim of the sand tray. He smiled bitter approval. "If you believe so, then we are in agreement," he said. "And the new *bstangpo* is very clever in his timing. You will now produce no heirs to challenge his, and by removing his brother he removes also his only adult rival for the throne."

Samarkar nodded, feeling her head move as if on rods in another's hands. She remembered what Temur had said about the instability of regimes, and wondered. "Songtsan's ruthlessness is renowned."

The mildness of her own tone surprised her. She should know Songtsan's ruthlessness, having used it to remove the husband who would otherwise have set her aside. *Oh, Tsansong*, she thought. Whatever her face revealed, Yongten-la nodded in sympathy and sorrow. In the face of his kindness, she allowed herself to close her eyes. Briefly, just long enough to soothe the sting.

"Indeed," the old man said. "Now tell me in your own words what you discovered in Qeshqer. I have it from Tsering, but I would have it from you as well. And, when we are done here, from your traveling companions."

She took a breath. "The Cho-tse Hrahima has a message for you as well, Yongten-la. One that bodes ill for us all. She meant to deliver it to my brother, and I will go with her to do that—but I think you should hear it in her own words, too."

The lines in his face could not hide the hard sharpness of his eyes. "Thank you. Now. Tell me what you found in the north, Wizard Samarkar."

THE QERSNYK HARLOT PACED AND SWORE IN HER VELVET CAPTIVITY. Al-Sepehr caused drink to be brought to her, delicate ices against the heat. At first she hurled everything at the servants and raged. But al-Sepehr knew that any hawk can be gentled by hunger, and he persevered.

At last, driven by thirst, she drank a little tea with mint in it, and sugar. And having drunk, it was easier to eat the next time. And so he worked to tame her, bite by bite.

She had a delicate stomach, which frustrated him. He must dine with her to tame her, and so he made time in his schedule. But the foods she could tolerate—and keep inside her—were only the blandest offerings. Those ices, such fruits as were in season at the advent of summer's heat, plain yogurt, and pearls of wheat flour rolled small between the hands and steamed.

He heard reports of her behavior when he was not with her. She was watched at every moment: It was good practice for his young assassins to spy on her without her knowledge, and if she thought herself alone, she might let slip something useful. Al-Sepehr valued the harlot for what she contained, not what she was—and one of the things she contained was information. She was safe; she was immured in her cushioned mews until such time as al-Sepehr required her. It would serve.

He was the only visitor she was permitted, and that, too, wore at her. At last, in desperation, she spoke with him. Not at length and of no more than trivialities. Or what must seem to her trivialities, but there were chips and bits in what she said that al-Sepehr could put to use.

While he was not attending the woman, he spent a great deal of time on communication. Not with the stones in his pockets, for those were a finite resource and best reserved for emergencies. It was not as if virgin twins bloomed from the desert every time it rained, after all. Instead, al-Sepehr penned letters, coded and intentionally cryptic. These, he entrusted for delivery to the offspring of the rukh.

The young could fly in their first year but were not at that stage much larger than eagles. From a distance they could be mistaken for eagles, but eagles did not have snowy crests tipped blood-red. The immature rukh grew slowly. Even al-Sepehr did not know how long it would take them to reach the size of their mother, the adult that had carried the Qersnyk harlot to Ala-Din from the outermost east.

Or how long it would take to reach the size of even her smaller mate, which al-Sepehr kept mewed up like the girl. It was through the male's captivity that al-Sepehr assured the obedience of the female.

The rukh's children brought him letters in return, which was how he learned of the successful destruction of Qeshqer, and also the safe flight of that damned Qersnyk warlord's son to Tsarepheth in Rasa.

That last was not bad news, exactly. Al-Sepehr had agents in Rasa, and Qori Buqa would be easier to control if his attention was bent on a presumed enemy. And if the boy did turn out to be something special after all, well—al-Sepehr had his mate and unborn child to hand. What worked on a rukh would work on a man.

When a letter came to al-Sepehr by means of the same bird in whose talons he'd dispensed a deadly poison only a fortnight before, he thought long and carefully before he found paper and took up his pen to answer.

O most noble ally, he wrote.

News of your success reaches me through divers channels, and I rejoice to hear of it. You should find your path more clean going forward. A victory begets a victory. You must never underestimate the power of conquest to raise the morale of your folk. When Qeshqer is Kashe once again, you will be the most beloved of rulers.

Know then of a favor you can do me in return. I seek a Qersnyk man, not tall or especially well favored, got on an Aezin mother. He is a survivor of the fall of Qarash. It is likely that he will riding a bay mare of the steppe breed with one white-splashed foot and asking after a woman named Edene. He may be using the name Temur, which is hardly uncommon.

If you find him, do not harm him. I have uses for him.

> Yours,
>
> Mukhtar ai-Idoj, al-Sepehr

THE WALLS WERE TOO CLOSE, THE SKY TOO FAR AWAY. TEMUR COULD NOT smell the wind or sense the movement of the air—which was thin, and left him feeling as breathless as if kicked by a horse. The light he worked by came not from the golden sun, but from cold, pallid lanterns that burned on the walls without any smoke or flame.

But here inside the wizards' Citadel, he found at least one thing that smelled and felt of home. And so, once Samarkar and Hrahima had left him, he bent his back steadily to the business of finding Buldshak in her stall and locating the stable boy. Temur arranged in his broken Rasan to have Bansh quartered beside Buldshak, then going over each of his mares from one end to the other with eyes and hands and soft brushes made of pigs' bristle.

He was relieved to discover that the rose-gray had been well cared for and was sound—even beginning to hide her bones beneath a layer of flesh again. She had whickered when he led Bansh up; now, while he worked on the bay, the two mares spent their time communicating softly through the worked-stone filigree that separated their stalls.

The air was still, but not close, and it smelled comfortingly of animals. Temur was not sure from whence the ventilation came, but he suspected it had as much to do with Rasan wizardry as did those strange cold lights. In any case, the bedding was deep underfoot and the stalls clean enough that he could find no work to do with a pitchfork, so after one last pat—and communicating with that same stable boy in further pidgin to make sure Bansh would be fed small, frequent quantities at first and checked on often—he took his leave of her and Buldshak to find the mules and see to them as well.

By the time he arrived, though, they had been cared for and even curried gleaming, their pale muzzles and dark masks like glossy heartwood. He leaned on the wall of their pen with folded arms and watched them drink water and munch hay, wondering what should happen next. He was hungry himself, and filthy and tired; if Samarkar had spoken truly when she said he would be her guest, he should find some servant or slave to show him to a washbasin and a set of clean clothes.

He set out back to the mares, hoping serendipity would provide another stable hand along the way. What he found instead was a male wizard, leaning folded arms on the door of Buldshak's stall and watching her pull hay from the net. Temur paused a few steps back and cleared his throat.

The man turned, but not as if startled. He smiled. He was a bit older than Temur, with the roundness of cheek the Rasani thought handsome. His black satin coat was cut close to a narrow body, making him look as slender as a girl, and when he moved, Temur could see that it was lined in blood-red satin, the petals of its hem linked by golden chains.

He made a slight bow, however, and seemed to offer Temur every possible courtesy one could expect—more, in fact, if one were pretending to be a landless, exiled soldier of no family.

And some pretense it is. For which of those things does not describe you?

"I am Anil," the man said, in reasonably competent Qersnyk. "I had never seen a steppe pony, so I asked to be the one to come and find you. I hope you don't mind. . . ." He gestured at the horses diffidently, apparently unaware that Temur's regard was already won over by something as simple as curiosity about his mares.

"I am Temur, Anil-la," Temur said. "Please, can we speak in Rasan? I need the practice."

"Not as badly as I need to practice your tongue." Temur laughed. "You're here surrounded by it, and will be for at least a little while."

Temur forced a smile. That sounded like a sign that he might not be thrown summarily into a prison cell or across the nearest border. "You said I was summoned."

"Yes, of course." Anil gestured Temur to fall in beside him. Temur did so, trying not to mince on travel-sore feet. "First a bath and some clothes, I think, then Yongten-la will see you. I happen to know he has sent for food—or did, once he heard that you went straight to the stable with the animals and would not have even had a bowl of tea and noodles. Come on; wait until you see the bathing chambers."

Temur had expected to be led upward; instead, Anil brought him ever deeper into the bowels of the Citadel. The bathing pool was indeed unlike anything he'd ever imagined, even in his grandfather's famous and now-sacked provincial capital in Song, a city so full of wonders that poems had been composed in praise of its singing mechanical birds, its eternal gardens crafted of jewels and metal, its tame lions who lay about the court like cats in a granary, wearing jeweled collars.

The water was warm, the pool wide and deep enough to worry him about the danger of drowning. He stayed in waist-deep water and scrubbed the road filth from himself with handfuls of soap and scented sand and purple salts. Anil, he noted, stripped down and flung himself promptly into water so deep that he had to kick to stay upright, his head bobbing up and down above the surface as he spoke. Temur hid a flinch and tried not to watch. Was the silly fool trying to drown?

No, apparently he just swam like an otter. Temur had heard of such things in stories, but he had also heard of men flying in stories. Was he going to have to credit that now, too?

He turned his shoulder to the wizard and began to scrub the blood and sweat and filth from his hair. He knew the scar on his throat would have gone livid in the bath chamber's heat; he could feel its swelling by the softness when he touched it. It held his head rigidly, tilted a little to the left where it had contracted, but now the last flakes of dried skin and ancient scab came away from it, along with the itch he'd never quite been rid of since it started to granulate.

"That must have been quite a wound."

"I had it when Qarash fell," Temur said. He would not lie—his name might be lost and his soul with it, but that was no reason to stain his honor. "They left me for dead."

"I can see why." Anil stopped bobbing and walked forward through the water, coming up to where he could see better. "It was untreated?"

"I was alone," Temur said, reflexively touching the damned thing again. He could still feel the cramp in his fingers, the pain of pinching it closed and not daring to open his hand. "It saved my life. And it might have killed me anyway; there was heat in it when Samarkar rescued me, though I had thought it healed by then. But sometimes the heat takes a long time to kill."

"Sometimes it does," Anil agreed. And then he said, "Samarkar-*la*," with a heavy emphasis.

"I am sorry?" Temur turned, realizing that his modesty in hiding the scar was only drawing attention to it.

"You should use her title," Anil said. "She is Samarkar-la, the wizard Samarkar."

Temur resisted the urge to tell him that Samarkar had never corrected him. He hadn't Qulan's sense of politics, but he had enough of the common sort of sense to hold a wet finger up and feel which way the wind was blowing. "I know this thing."

"You may know it, but I doubt you understand." Anil ducked down, wetting his hair, and swam to a rack for soap with which to wash his hair. As he scrubbed, eyes closed, he said, "Do you know that she is also the Once-Princess Samarkar?"

"She said on the trail that the Emperor-in-Waiting is her brother," Temur admitted. "But did she not have to renounce rank and succession to become a wizard?"

Even on the steppe and in Song, there were stories of the wizards of Tsarepheth and what they sacrificed for their powers.

Anil snorted and ducked his head again to rinse it. When he came up, he said, "She is a new wizard. Does it strike you that she is a little older than the general run of novitiates?"

"I have not seen enough to know," Temur admitted. "So she came to it late? Is this the nunnery to which she was sent to get her out of the way, then?"

"No," Anil said. "It is the nunnery she chose in order to protect herself. You see, in her childhood, Samarkar was the only child of her father, and so was raised his heir. When she was seven years of age, though, her brother Songtsan was born, and she became just another princess to be dowered off for alliances."

"My people invented the practice," Temur said, allowing a tight smile. "Or at least, the practice of demanding princesses to wive as surety—and to give a conquered people a stake in the Qersnyk tribes."

"I had guessed," Anil said dryly, "that your mother was not born on the steppe."

"She will die there," Temur said with a shrug he could barely force across his shoulders. "If she has not already. That makes her a Qersnyk woman."

Anil nodded. "Samarkar-tsa, for that was her name then, was a true Rasan woman. At the age of fourteen, when her father the king died, she was sent to the court of Prince Ryi of Zhang Shung, a principality of Song. She was to be fostered there and raised as his bride, until such age as it was appropriate for her to marry. And in the fullness of time, marry her he did."

"So she is a widow? Or did he set her aside?"

"She is a widow," Anil said. "But not after the fashion you imagine. The prince, you see, refused to consummate the marriage. It was said that he feared offending Samarkar's brothers, so he married the woman, but he feared even more getting an heir on her and giving them a claim on his lands, so he would not cover her."

Temur rubbed at his cheeks, where the heat and itch had spread. He said nothing, gathering his thoughts, embarrassed to hear the proud, courageous woman he'd traveled with all the way from the Range of Ghosts spoken of as if she were a mare. "So what happened?"

Anil smiled crookedly. "She wrote to her brother the Emperor-in-Waiting and his mother the Dowager Regent and complained. And Songtsan took an army to bring her back, claiming the honor of his family was denigrated when Prince Ryi made no true wife of Samarkar at all. Samarkar said her loss of face could only be avenged in blood, and he came to take that for her."

Temur remembered something of this dimly now. He had been no more than a boy when it happened, but he'd heard of the bloody sack of Zhang Shung, and even then, the ferocity of the stories had impressed him. "She's supposed to have lit his funeral pyre," he said. "At least, that was the story we heard on the steppe."

"She lit it," Anil agreed. "There is some question as to whether Prince Ryi was entirely dead at the time. And Songtsan-tsa annexed Prince Ryi's kingdom, to clear away the insult to family honor." He reached out and grazed Temur's wet, naked shoulder with his fingertips. The bath chamber steamed with warmth, but the touch made him shiver.

"She is once-princess," Anil said kindly. "She is above you, even if she were not a wizard."

"I see," Temur said. He rubbed his hands together at the water's surface. As it happened, he was not entirely innocent of court politics himself. *Anil-la is jealous.*

Well, that might be useful to know, some day.

"Thank you for the warning," he said. "Is there anything else?"

Anil smiled. "We—the wizards of the Citadel, I mean—can help with that scar. There are unguents that will soften it and render it easier for you to move. If it is not too forward of me to suggest that."

"No," Temur said, forcing himself not to touch it again. "Not too forward at all."

WHEN SHE HAD BATHED, SAMARKAR SAT WITH BRUSH AND PAPER, CONsidering and discarding actions. The problem with childhood codes and family means was that anything Samarkar could do to get a message to Tsansong, Songtsan would be able to interrupt and understand.

At last she wrote, in plain calligraphy on plain paper, a single sentence: *If there is anything I can do, I shall do it.*

She left the note unsigned. She summoned a novice to act as a page. When the girl had gone, Samarkar leaned her elbows on the writing desk and her head against her fingertips, feeling how they dented the skin of her temples, her eyelids.

She did not exactly expect an answer, but that could not keep her from hoping.

AFTER TEMUR WAS CLEAN, NOVICES BROUGHT HIM FRESH CLOTHING and helped show him how to fasten it. The quilted trousers were simple enough, fastening with a wrap across the front that tied on one hip, but the ivory-colored linen jacket at first defeated him. It tied with a string that went around the waist and through a slit to knot with another string, and even when it was properly fixed, it gaped in a long triangle at the collar. Temur did not like having his chest so exposed, although he had to admit he did not feel cold, and he saw others in the Citadel—non-wizards, at least—wearing similar styles.

When he was dressed and put on slippers and his own clothes had been carried off to be laundered—or burned—he hung his knife from the wide cloth belt they also gave him. Anil led him through more seeming *yarts* of passage until they came up from the bowels of the Citadel into sunlit corridors.

There, Anil stood him before a door that was barely ajar, leaned in enough to say, "Remember: Yongten-*la*," and faded off to the left.

Temur squared his shoulders. *I am the grandson of Temusan Khagan. Nothing in this world can intimidate me.*

. . . And you claim you're not a liar.

Still, his chin was up as he entered the room.

He had known from the corridor that Hrahima was either just within the door or that she had left recently. He could smell the civety musk that surrounded her, and so he was not surprised to step within and find her looming over. "Hrahima," he said, and made a slight bow. "Yongten-la," he said also to the old man behind the desk, and this time his bow scraped the floor.

He hoped he'd remembered correctly that the Rasani expected to be greeted in ascending order of rank. What hadn't seemed so critical when he'd had rank of his own to fall back on was now a matter for attention and concern. If he'd failed some point of etiquette, at least the old man seemed unconcerned.

"Temur of the steppe," the old man said. "Please just push that door shut—thank you. Now. Hrahima and Samarkar-la tell me you come with news of grave import and that you wish to exchange it for a favor."

I do? But of course, Samarkar had covered for him and had found a way to tell him how to bargain. Perhaps she took her oblique promise to help him reclaim Edene as seriously as any Qersnyk.

Temur glanced at Hrahima. The Cho-tse folded her arms across her enormous chest, showing the musculature of her forearms. She looked down at him impassively. No help there, but at least no opposition, either.

He raised up his flagging courage and said, "If we are right, and Qeshqer was attacked by ghosts, then I know from my own experience that they are the ghosts of my people, and it is my duty to release them from their bonded state. Someone must stand for the dead. And more: On the steppe, they took someone who mattered to me, a woman named Edene. She was alive when I last saw her, being dragged into the sky, and I must either find her and win her back or know that she is dead."

Yongten-la leaned back against cushions, steepling his fingers. "Even if all you come to know is that you held her bloody bones in your hands?"

Hrahima made a huffing sound while Temur considered. Perhaps another man might have recoiled from the vividness of Yongten-la's image, but Temur had seen enough bloody bones in his young warrior's life to shrug away the memories, in full knowledge that he would pay for it later. These things had their own chilly logic. Right now, it was as if they had happened to someone else. Someone else had fought in those wars, lain among those dead.

"They say that what will be will be," Hrahima said. "I myself have little use for destinies."

"It would be an answer," Temur said, helplessly. "I would know she was not waiting for me."

"*Humph*," the old wizard said. "Very well. After you leave here, I will arrange for you to visit tomorrow with the wizards who study the natural history of ghosts. Hrahima, I will see whether Songtsan-tsa can be convinced to give you an audience"—he hesitated—"although I fear you have come at a bad time. In the meantime, though, you both come and have tea and noodles. And while you eat, you will tell me everything you remember of the ghosts, and of your journey, Temur."

Temur bowed. "Not much, I fear. But what I have, I will give you."

*   *   *

THAT NIGHT, HE DREAMED OF THE END OF THE WORLD—AND EDENE.

After an intricate round of questioning—during which Yongten eventually took pity on him and shifted to Qersnyk dialect much more accomplished than Temur's rudimentary Rasan—Yongten-la had arranged for Temur to be shown to a bedchamber. It was strange to lie down on a raised platform, trapped like a grub in a cyst between four walls, floor, and ceiling—but the bed rustled as if it were stuffed with dry husks, and it was softer than even grassy turf. There was a carved wooden pillow, padded along the inside of the arch with grass-stuffed leather, and the covers were warm. The hiss of falling water came attenuated through the window. Despite his discomfort at the enclosed space, Temur slept soon and hard.

Since his wound had turned hot, his dreams had become garish and strange. And memorable, which was unusual for Temur. This time he knew he was dreaming, whether it was the strangeness of the landscape underfoot or the fact that that landscape was roamed by vast herds of horses in vivid mineral colors mortal horses never approached—lavender, yellow, vermilion, indigo and sky blue. His eye was caught by a stallion the color of lapis lazuli, streaks of sparkling gold threading his haunches and withers like stars in a midnight sky, his mane and tail blown forward by a bitter wind.

"These are the sixty-four sacred colors of horses in their true incarnations," Edene said on his right. He had not heard her come up, and when he turned to face her, he could see the terrain behind her, as if she were made of the finest silk held up on a bright day.

And it was a bright day, a bright and beautiful day, with all the steppe stretching out before him, and the ragged mountains rising at the edge of the world to hold up a cerulean sky. The indigo stallion called; far away, another stallion answered him. *I am here with my mares, and a wise horse would avoid me.*

Perhaps both stallions were wise, because Temur saw no sign of another herd approaching. He opened his mouth and cupped his hands to his ears, hoping to hear the second one again and locate him, but there was only the rustle of the wind blowing through the long green stalks of new vegetation.

"Temur Khanzadeh," Edene said.

He turned to correct her—*I am not a prince*—only to find that she had become far more solid and real in his moment of inattention. Something was wrong with the bones of her face, though, and she seemed too tall, as if she had been stretched like leather for drying across a frame.

"Edene."

She turned away. He saw the thick black cord laddering her neck, the undersides of her arms. In his time, Temur had cooked enough cleaned and deboned marmots in pouches of their own skin to recognize the thick, whipped stitches for what they were.

He took a breath. Because it was a dream, he was calm and rational, rather than reaching already for his knife to plunge it through the monster's breast. "Who are you, to wear my woman's skin?"

The monster turned, and now he could see it was not Edene. The eyes were wrong, a luminous hazel brown flecked with gold. It laughed, showing teeth too large and sharp for the mouth that stretched to hold them. The skin at the corners of the lips and across the chin split; what blood trickled out was gelatinous, honey-thick, and slow.

Temur recoiled. This time, his hand did find his knife, and when he struck out he put his weight behind it.

It entered Edene's breast with no sense of pressure, as if he merely passed it through the smoke of a rising fire. But then it struck something hard and stuck as fast as if he had planted it in the heartwood of a tree.

The laughing monster stepped back, dragging the knife from horrified Temur's hand. It reached up, grabbing the hilt with a hand whose flesh split like a too-tight glove along the seams. Temur thought it would pull the knife free, but instead it seemed to anchor itself to the blade, to use it as a stable point and haul itself out of the stolen skin.

Temur didn't think leverage actually worked that way, but then, this was the world of dreams.

And then the thing stood before him, blood-slick as a newborn, and he recognized it—the hollow-bellied, sunken-eyed creature he'd seen in the Range of Ghosts and thought a fever dream.

It shook itself, and the rags that had been Edene fell around it.

"You," Temur said.

It tugged his knife from its chest, working the tip back and forth to free it as if it were an arrow stuck fast in bone or wood. The knife came loose with a pop; the monster weighed it in its hand and tossed it idly off to the side. "Very well, Temur Khanzadeh. You are not a prince. Then you have no hope of opposing one who is not ashamed to call himself one. Observe!"

The thing gestured—out across the steppe, the herds, the mountains. Temur saw a sweep of storm-shadow follow the sweep of its hand, boiling clouds mounting along the horizon and breaking over themselves to flood forward. Thunder rattled the earth so hard that Temur abruptly, unexpectedly, found himself sitting. Lightning flashed from a sky like a bruise, striking the earth in the midst of the herd. Terrified horses whinnied and were flung this way and that. Darkness followed, as complete as any moon-filled night. When the lightning flashed again, Temur imagined he could see the horses' very bones beneath their hides. Rain fell in drops as big as Temur's thumbnail, hammering his head, washing his hair across his eyes.

When it flashed a third time, he saw the vast crack that had opened up across the plains—a crack which was racing to meet him as he was swept forward to plunge into it, the steppe and the horses and the grass pouring into it like water draining from a tub. Ghosts rose from the chasm, arms outstretched, howling out loneliness and pain.

Something touched his chest.

He looked down and saw a hand, an arm draped in black veiling, a woman's black-clad body below a face draped with a sequined scarf.

She sat above him as if her storm-colored mare were a throne. "Temur Khanzadeh," she said. "Take my hand."

He started to reach up, to grasp the fingers that lay against his chest. But something stopped him. He hesitated.

She turned her hand over and caught his. "Be king or be carrion," she said. "The future is a monster either way."

He squeezed her hand, then tried to pull away. She held him tighter, and now the bones of her face looked wrong as well.

"Temur."

He yanked, but his arm felt numb, heavy. Paralyzed. Her grip was still brutally tight.

"Temur!"

She was pulling, still squeezing, until he thought she would drag him onto the horse. He didn't want to go with her. He twisted against her grip, but it was inexorable, and the paralysis was spreading now, numbing him from neck to feet.

"Temur!"

His eyes popped open, his body still foreign and numb with sleep. Samarkar had hold of his hand and was shaking him gently. Gold morning light filtered through the window, casting rainbows on the far wall, where it broke against the mist from the waterfall. He struggled to push himself upright as Samarkar let go of his wrist, but though he was clear-minded, his body remained alien and slow. At last, with effort, he managed to raise his head from the smooth wooden pillow.

"Wake up," she said. "We have an appointment with the naturalists. We're due to see Master Hong-la, and it's best not to keep wizards waiting."

"I was dreaming," he said. "I think I dreamed of the Sorcerer-Prince."

The urgency to be moving deserted her, replaced by another kind of urgency. She sat down on his bedside and said, "Tell me everything. Now, before it fades away."

He had no desire to elaborate on what he'd already said, but he realized the necessity of her request. Quickly, in as much detail as he could, he sketched the dream for her, feeling it already tattering out of recall. She listened solemnly, with folded arms, while he rose from his nest of blankets and began dressing in fresh clothes all but identical to those of the previous night. After more than a moon on the road, there was not much modesty lost between them anymore.

By the time he'd remembered how to tie the wraps on the jacket, he was finished recounting the dream. He did not tell her that the Veil of Night had called him *Khanzadeh*, and he did not repeat what she had said about king or carrion.

Samarkar rose, tugging her blousy trousers into place and smoothing the creases. "That's not reassuring. Have you been given to prophetic dreams?"

He shook his head. "But my grandfather was supposed to have the power. Are such things believed in, here?"

"Sometimes a tendency to dream true can indicate potential gifts as a wizard." She paused and snorted at some thought that seemed to bitterly amuse her. "I've never had the knack of it."

"Knack." It struck him funny, and he answered her huff with a chuckle. "Well, it's never happened to me before. Assuming this is a true dream. Which I'd rather it wasn't. But they're supposed to be allegorical, and this was certainly that."

She looked down at her hands, clasped before her. "Do you still think your woman is alive?"

He felt his lips thin, felt the muscles of his jaws tighten. "If she's not, can I leave her spirit captive to someone who will wield it as a weapon?"

She nodded—reluctant but resigned.

It seemed to Temur that Samarkar led him through corridors for the better part of the morning, but really it could not have been much more than the time it took the sun to move the width of two fingers across the sky. The length of the walk did more than the endless winding corridors to give him a sense of the scale. The place was practically a city unto itself.

He could tell when they were approaching the laboratories and quarters of the natural historians, because the corridor decor began to include a great many cabinets full of insects inexplicably mounted on pins and animal skins preserved whole with the heads.

"Your Master Hong-la," he asked, leaning close. "What is he like?"

"Shh," Samarkar said. She paused at a door framed on one side by the black-on-black rosette skin of a panther, on the other by a boulder that came to knee height. Its exterior looked like foundry clinker, melted and almost metallic. But some stonemason had cut into it and polished the cut smooth as a blade so that you could see the inside was composed of yellow-green crystals imbedded in an iron-black matrix.

Temur reached out hesitantly and stroked the cool surface. "I have never seen such a stone."

Samarkar paused in her knocking to glance sideways. "It's a sky-stone," she said. "Mostly iron. Some god hurled it to earth from the heavens. You should see the crater they pulled it out of."

Skystone. He remembered the storm-colored mare of his fever dream, the red-black dust of his moon under her running hooves. He wanted to ask her if she thought maybe the heavens were made of stone. If this was true, a chip could be knocked loose somehow.

Instead, he touched a translucent, glassy crystal and asked, "What's the green?"

"Olivine," she said, as the door swung open. "The piece that was removed to make the facet is now . . . now the *bstangpo*'s crown."

The *bstangpo*. Not "my brother."

So they were not close, then, the wizard Samarkar and her blood kin. Whatever else Temur might have asked would have to wait, though, because the open doorway was filled by a man of middle years, broad-shouldered and thick-necked. He had a square jaw and the fair, sand-colored complexion and dramatic, extremely willow-leaf-shaped eyes of the southern Song people. He was exceedingly tall, but he did not stoop, as tall men so often did. Instead, his shoulders were set like the planks of a great brassbound door.

"Hong-la," Samarkar said, bowing low. "Thank you for seeing us. This is Temur-tsa, an emissary of the plainsmen, who is seeking his wife."

Temur too bowed, remembering belatedly to thrust out his tongue in respect to the elder wizard.

"Your wife," he said.

"My woman," Temur said, unwilling to mislead this man. He met Hong-la's gaze. "I would have married her, in other times. . . ."

The wizard regarded him steadily, lips pursed, and seemed to come to some abrupt decision. Whatever it was, Hong-la stood aside, beckoning them into his chamber.

It could have been a workroom, sleeping quarters, or any combination of the two. There was a framed bed in one corner, the covers pulled taut and the wooden pillow tucked away underneath it so the surface could be used as a reading couch. This purpose was attested to by the small heap of scrolls at one end and a cup of tea cooling on the flat headrail.

The rest of the room had the long slate and granite tables that Temur was coming to expect of every room in the Citadel. These labored under the weight of minerals he could not begin to identify, a small fire-stained crucible, piles of shells from the far ocean, cruets and flat dishes of glass, metal, ceramic, stone. The floors were largely bare of rugs, except one small one sized for sitting or meditating. A low wooden table like Yongten-la's desk was pushed beneath the bed.

Temur presumed that was where Hong-la took his meals, when he did not eat in the dining hall which Samarkar had shown Temur the previous afternoon after the meeting with Yongten-la. The thought of supper reminded his stomach that it had yet to break its fast today, with predictable results: a sharp growl.

"Forgive me," Temur said, his ears burning. "I overslept."

Hong-la laughed and shut the door behind them. "Food can always be sent for," he said, and crossed the room to a small brass cover set flush with the stone wall. He opened it—it lifted on a cunning hinge—and leaned close to it to speak. Having finished, he set his ear to it. Temur could faintly hear a voice floating back, like an echo. He watched, entranced, as Hong-la put his mouth back to the aperture and said one short word: "Yes."

The wizard's black coat was unbuttoned, the sleeves rolled up past his elbows to show the linen shirt he wore beneath. His thick jet-black hair was cropped short as a slave's, and Temur tried to keep himself from staring at it.

Unsuccessfully, apparently. Because as Hong-la picked up the apron he must have flung over the edge of a table when he came to answer the door, he caught Temur's eye and rubbed a hand across his scalp self-consciously.

"Some of the substances I work with," he said, "are not things you'd want your hair trailing through."

"Of course," Temur said, acutely aware of his own locks flowing down his back unbraided, awkwardly flat in places from being slept on. "I take it Samarkar—Samarkar-*la*—or Yongten-la has told you what help I seek?"

Hong-la pulled the table out from under the bed and set it on the rug so that there was room for all three of them to sit around it. "The ghosts and the fate of Qeshqer are common knowledge now and have been almost since Tsering-la returned." He sighed. "We have not yet had much success in convincing the emperor-in-waiting that the situation requires his immediate attention, however."

"Ghosts don't respect frontiers," Temur said.

"Sit, please." Hong-la showed them places on the rug. Samarkar dropped into hers quickly. Temur found his with only slightly more trouble. "So what is it, specifically, that you want?"

Temur looked at Samarkar. Samarkar gestured him on with an exasperated head-tilt.

"I want to find a woman who was stolen by ghosts," he said.

Hong-la stared at him. He pulled a pair of lenses in a wire frame from his pocket and set them on his nose, then peered at Temur through them with furrowed brow. "Stolen alive?"

Temur said, "Yes."

"Hmm," Hong-la said, and bounced up off the rug with the energy of a much younger man. He crossed his chamber in five long strides, reached a rack of books and scrolls beside the door, and began searching through them, muttering under his breath. Temur glanced at Samarkar.

She had quite a vocabulary of those head gestures. He thought this one meant, "Go over there, you idiot."

So Temur, too, rose, and more hesitantly crossed the room. He was still a few steps from the door when a tapping came upon it.

"Come in," Hong-la barked irritably. A servant apparently well used to his moods carried in a covered tray and set it down on the small table without inquiring, then made himself vanish again.

Temur paused at the wizard's elbow, Samarkar a comforting presence at his back. "Can I help somehow?"

"Sit and eat," Hong-la said, without looking up from the armload of scrolls he was sorting. "You'll only be in my way here."

So he sat, and Samarkar also sat beside him. He thought he should serve the food in deference to her rank, but when he lifted the cover she was already there with spoon and tongs. There was the famous red mountain rice, steamed with some other hard grain he did not recognize and studded with bits of preserved lemons. Yak butter melted over the top. When she spooned it into a bowl over green leaves, she topped it with a generous portion of some flaky, snow-white meat he did not recognize. It was sweet and mild. Better tasting than snake, anyway.

It was farmer food, grains and greens with only a little meat beside, but it was filling and warm and tasted surprisingly good. He ate slowly, forcing himself to taste everything despite his body's desire to bolt it.

Samarkar, of course, ate like a princess. "There would be wine," she said. "But without the caravans . . ."

She shrugged.

Temur gestured to show he understood, but his mouth was too full of food to answer.

By the time they were done and had washed down the last lingering butteriness with mouthfuls of bitter tea, Hong-la came back with three scrolls and a book balanced between his chest and the crook of his left arm. He set them down on the rug and applied himself to his food with the concentration of someone who often forgets to eat. Between bites, without looking up, he asked, "Can you read?"

"Some," Temur said, setting his bowl down. "Song characters. My people did not have a written system until the Great Khagan adopted Uthman letters, but I can read and write my own language in those. I grew up with them."

Samarkar poured more steaming tea into Hong-la's bowl. He picked it up and blew across it. She set the teapot down without refilling her own cup, but something about the slight, expectant glance she gave Temur made him realize that there was a hierarchy at work here—younger to older, or apprentice to master? He wasn't sure.

He lifted the black clay pot and filled her cup and his own while Hong-la opened a scroll on the crumb-free end of the table and weighted it with dry, clean odds and ends. "Well," he said, "this is neither Qersnyk writing nor Song, but one of the ancient tribal languages of the people who would become the Uthman Caliphate. I will translate."

He did, slowly and with slight awkwardness, pausing once or twice to look up a word or a phrase in the lexicon he'd also carried over. "This is a history of the Carrion-King's war, which goes into detail about the dead armies of Sepehr al-Rachīd ibn Sepehr and the tactics he used to raise them. Now, this scroll is very old: It claims to be a copy of one written when the Carrion-King was still a living memory for a few of the most aged souls, which would make it—conservatively—better than five hundred years in age."

Temur looked at the thing with a fair reverence. One thing his grandfather had instilled in his sons, which had been passed down to Temur by way of Qulan, was a deep and abiding appreciation of art and craftsmanship. This scroll was both, and history, too—a thing of great beauty to Temur's eyes.

"It seems," Hong-la continued, "that al-Rachīd was most feared for his ability to send the dead of any conflict back into it, arrayed on his side."

"This al-Rachīd . . ." Temur hesitated until Hong-la nodded, granting him permission to continue. "Is that the same person as the Sorcerer-Prince?" He remembered his dream and the stalking corpse of the mountains. "You are suggesting that *he's* involved?"

"He is the same person. Al-Rachīd means 'the Brave.' Anyway"— Hong-la tapped the scroll—"this contains an account of the fall of fabled Erem, the city upon whose ruins Messaline was built and from which, it seems, it inherited the epithet City of Jackals. The anonymous historian"—he tapped again—"seems uncertain if it became known as such before or after it was overrun—but it was the *second* city named Erem. That much is sure. The first fell five hundred years before the second. In any case, the scroll recounts several stories of folk later witnessing attacks by their dead loved ones from Erem on other battlefields. Listen:

> 'The ghost of my father beckons
> But in his left hand conceals a bloody sword. . . .'

"Well, the scansion is better in the original, but you get the point. And *sword* might be *knife*, just as easily—"

"That's what I saw on the steppe. Ghosts that could mutilate humans at will, but only be hurt by salted weapons."

"And something broke through every roof in Qeshqer," Samarkar added.

"According to this," said Hong-la, "al-Rachīd was known to dress himself in the flesh and skin of his victims, and go out so disguised."

Temur's teacup rattled when he set it down. Samarkar was staring at him; quickly, as he noticed, she lowered her eyes.

"I saw that in a dream," Temur said around the ice in his heart. "It was terrible. But Hrahima said that one of the Rahazeen murder cults—al-Sepehr, she said, a leader of the Nameless—"

"They need another name," Hong-la said dryly. "They take that title, al-Sepehr, from the proper name of al-Rachīd."

Temur snorted. "Hrahima thinks the necromancy is *his* doing. She thinks, or her patron thinks, I suppose."

Hong-la contemplated his food for a moment before poking morsels into his mouth and chewing slowly and steadily, swallowing before he spoke again. "This al-Sepehr you mention is, as you say, the leader of an outlawed Rahazeen splinter group. One of the murder cults. One of the doctrines of the Nameless is that the Carrion-King was the true prophet of their Scholar-God, not Ysmat of the Beads or her Daughter. This is the same Scholar-God the Uthmans and the Aezin worship, though each tribe proclaims its own prophets. The Nameless believe that one day al-Rachīd will rise from the grave. As you can imagine, that doesn't make them . . . popular with less-radical sects."

A bit of the white meat found its way into Hong-la's mouth, followed by a sip of tea. Temur found himself spindling his fingers together, one over the other.

But it was Samarkar who answered. "I can't imagine why."

THIS TIME, IT WAS AL-SEPEHR WHO SUMMONED SAADET. THE YOUNG woman came at a run, her slippered feet scuffing on stone, the skirts of her robes trailing about her. She had been in the women's quarters, al-Sepehr thought, because she held an unpinned veil before her face in a hand still stained with turmeric.

Al-Sepehr still held a broken stone in his hand, rapidly cooling, the blood that linked it to its mate all but worn away. He slipped it into his pocket and regarded the young woman's eyes. "Your brother," he said, with less ceremony than he might have normally offered her.

"He can hear you," she said.

Not for the first time, he wondered what it was like—for two bodies, two minds, two *persons* to share one set of knowledge and sensations and memories. When he'd made them, he hadn't thought of Shahruz and Saadet as people. They had been infants, twins exposed in the desert because twins were unlucky. Especially fraternal twins: It was too easy to work magic through them, and the nomadic tribes wouldn't suffer them to live.

It wasn't much better in towns. Al-Sepehr never had much expense securing twins for his spell casting. Sometimes the greatest trouble was finding a set alive.

"I have spoken with my ally in Tsarepheth," al-Sepehr said. "Re Temur is there, in the company of a wizard. He is being kept at the Citadel."

Saadet exhaled softly and said in Shahruz's clipped tones, "Do you wish him dead?"

"I can bring his woman and unborn heir against Qori Buqa as easily," al-Sepehr said. "And Re Temur is . . . troublingly lucky. Yes. Be rid of him."

Saadet pressed a fist across her chest with warrior crispness. "It shall be as you command," she said.

 11

Samarkar watched Temur groping his way around the edges of his nightmare for the second time, and found it no easier than the first. Hong-la, however, watched intently, nodding encouragement now and again when Temur faltered. When the last faltering stretched into silence, Hong-la picked up the teacup that Samarkar had refilled yet again and cupped it before his face. He glanced at Samarkar, and Samarkar followed with a brief description of what Hrahima had told them about Qori Buqa and the tiger's patron, Ato Tesefahun—just to confirm that it jibed with what she'd revealed to the elder wizards.

The last name drew a blink, perhaps the most surprise she'd ever seen Hong-la register.

"Well," he said, "that makes things even more interesting. Master Tesefahun, as you may or may not know, is a wizard in his own right. A well-respected one. I have some of his works here. It would be interesting to speak with him in person regarding this issue, but if he has seen fit to warn us"—Hong-la sighed—"we must take that warning seriously.

"Especially when, based on the evidence of Qeshqer and Temur's experiences, we can only speculate that al-Sepehr has managed to reconstruct al-Rachīd's techniques for enslaving ghosts. If Temur-tsa's dream indeed proves prophetic, it suggests metaphorically that you may face an old enemy clad in new skin."

"Or literally," Samarkar said reluctantly.

Temur held very still, and she avoided looking at him.

Hong-la favored her with an encouraging grimace that smoothed away again in an instant. "Indeed," he said. "Still, it's early days to speculate on that. And it does not precisely answer your friend's question."

"What does answer the question?" Temur asked, leaning forward. Samarkar could see hope and fear at war in his face, but she did not pity him. Instead, she felt a strong new respect for his focus and determination.

"Well, if Idoj has her—which is speculation, too, because I know not what a Rahazeen warlord would want with a Qersnyk girl of no great alliances—then the thing Temur-tsa must do is find a way to get her back."

When he paused, as if waiting for an answer—or a protest, Samarkar thought—Temur held his tongue and nodded.

Gently, Samarkar asked, "Do you have any suggestions?"

Hong-la stood, gathering his scrolls. "The first thing you're going to need is an army."

"An army that can fight ghosts," Temur said. "That won't be easy to come by."

When Samarkar led him from Hong-la's chambers, Temur seemed to have turned inward, chewing over what Hong-la had said—or perhaps simply chewing himself to ribbons. She thought she should respect his silence, but she also thought it would be unkind to force him to interact when he was so deep in contemplation. They climbed steps, and he leaned on the rail heavily, chest heaving so he wheezed, but he seemed insensate. Or perhaps he was stubbornly ignoring his discomfort.

Samarkar touched his shoulder lightly, so lightly he barely startled, and said, "We have a range, if you want to practice your archery."

She watched his eyes focus, watched him decide to smile. "My bow won't love the wet here," he said. A moist climate could cause the laminated steppe bow to lose strength or even come apart entirely. He'd left it in his quarters, wrapped in oilskins and carefully cased. "I suppose I could borrow one?"

She nodded. As they crossed the plaza between the battlements, he stared away north—the direction of Qeshqer and the steppe. "I should leave in the morning," he said. "This will grow no easier for the waiting."

"This?"

"If it's an army I must raise, well, there is only one place to do that. In my own lands, with whatever small fame and face is mine. There is no help here, and I must do whatever it takes to save Edene. If I must ride to the Teeth of Ctesifon themselves."

He said it quietly, with a fatalism that Samarkar, accustomed to the portentous edicts of her brother, found chilling. He would, she thought. To the Teeth of Ctesifon—or to the seven gates of Hell.

"You are free to go," she said. "Your assistance in bringing word of the fall of Qeshqer to the *bstangpo* will not be forgotten."

He looked up. "Qeshqer was our city."

She let herself smile, but only one corner of her mouth would cooperate. "But our people."

He frowned, as if he'd never considered it quite that way before. He touched his lips, as if about to say something, and turned away. Samarkar stood rooted, wondering if she should let him walk off or follow. . . .

The shadow that fell over her came unheralded by any footsteps, and only the training of a once-princess kept her from flinching and crying out in surprise. It was Hrahima, of course, her black stripes glossy in the sun, her pale belly lustrous with grooming. Temur turned, his hand going to the hilt of his knife, and relaxed again when he saw who had come up on them. He stepped sideways, getting the sun to his back when he looked up at Hrahima, and Samarkar too stepped out of her shadow.

"You could try to make more noise," Samarkar said with a smile. "You might be greeted with less screaming."

Framed against a blue sky and snapping banners, the Cho-tse smoothed her whiskers back. "I have an audience with the *bstangpo* this afternoon. Perhaps you would come with me, Samarkar-la? To lend authority to my words?" She looked beyond Samarkar, to Temur, and spread her great hands. "And you, Temur? You have knowledge perhaps the monkey-king should hear as well."

Samarkar looked at Temur. He seemed to hesitate; she imagined he had spent much of his life effacing himself, in ways that reminded her of her younger brother Tsansong.

And there was a barbed arrow to the heart. There had been no answer to her note—but in reality, she expected none. What could she do? With one mountain-sick plainsman and a Cho-tse, mount an assault to free him? People did not escape the dungeons of the Black Palace.

"I will come," Samarkar said, setting herself forward, telling herself that the sense of portent that accompanied the words was nothing but her own overnurtured self-image. Though it was bitter in her mouth, she said, "There are ways I mollify him. Though they may do my dignity no good."

She made a point not to glance at Temur, not to make this about him. But she was unsurprised when his shadow nodded on the ground at her feet, and he said, "I too will come."

THE PALACE WAS AS IT ALWAYS WAS, BUT THIS TIME SAMARKAR WAS aware of her companions' reactions to its endless corridors and intricate stoneworks. As they trailed behind a doorman—not Baryan, this time, but a young man Samarkar did not know—she heard Hrahima's deep sniffs. The Cho-tse was memorizing and categorizing every scent. Samarkar was aware, too, of Temur glancing about—not as wide-eyed as she had anticipated, but rather considering, calculating.

Assessing the place as a warrior, Samarkar realized, with an eye to its frailties and strengths.

All men fancy themselves warriors, and all warriors are the same. Possibly that was not fair to men, but Samarkar had already worked herself into a lather of irritation at her brother, and it was spilling over to others.

Because it was Hrahima's audience, she followed closest behind the doorman, with Samarkar and Temur sweeping behind her like the wings of a cloak she was not wearing. The footman showed them into the antechamber that had been her father's privy closet. That was a good sign, as was the platter of tea and sweets set waiting.

She also knew that this room was replete with cunning hides and blinds where an emperor could have his closest advisors crouch behind the very stone walls and hear and see clearly what was said and done within. That suggested that Songtsan-tsa was taking his strange inhuman emissary seriously.

Whether he meant to give her a fair hearing, or whether he had already made up his mind what to do, was anybody's guess.

The doorman gestured them within the antechamber and shut the door. Into the ensuing silence, Hrahima muttered, "What now?"

"We wait the *bstangpo*'s pleasure," Samarkar said. "At least there is tea."

Hrahima's brow wrinkled. "What is the protocol?"

"We stand," Samarkar said, moving to the sideboard. "Until the Emperor-in-Waiting graces us with his presence. We stay on this carpet; the emperor will stand on that one." She gestured to where two carpets, one red and one white, lay separated by half the height of a man on the dark stone floor.

It turned out they had not long to wait. Samarkar had barely filled the cups when the door on the far side of the room opened, allowing her to smoothly fill a fourth and have it ready to present to her brother as he entered. She knelt at the edge of the white carpet, the cup upraised; he leaned out to take it, and touched her wrist with his other hand to bid her stand. Two guards who had entered with him set their backs against the wall beside the door and made of themselves statues, whose tassels could only be seen to flutter slightly when they breathed.

"You need not wait on me with your own hands, *aphei*," he said.

"I am here not as a wizard," Samarkar said, rising, "but as your sister, and so I do you what duty a family member may."

His eyebrows arched, but that was all, and as Samarkar passed out tea to the others present, he deigned to sip his. *At least he does not suspect I would poison him.* Or possibly he'd just resorted to philters. There was enough jewelry hung about his body that a wizarded pearl would go unnoticed, and Samarkar was not about to risk entering a trance state now to see if she could detect the presence of such an enchantment.

"You support the Cho-tse ambassador's story?" he said.

She nodded, glancing at Hrahima. But Hrahima held out a be-seeching hand—the one unburdened by tea—and said, "Your Magnificence must understand that I am not an ambassador of the Cho-tse. Rather, I come as an independent emissary of the wizard Ato Tesefahun of Ctesifon, on a matter of great concern to all nations."

"Proceed," Songtsan said, every inch the apparent emperor.

Samarkar cupped her own tea bowl and watched quietly while Hrahima recounted her story for Songtsan—a story in almost all respects similar to the one she had told Samarkar and Temur on the road. For Songtsan, she went into more detail about the Rahazeen fortifications, stressing how impressive they were, how mountain-fast, and that it would probably take siege machines or companies of wizards to breach them.

At this, Songtsan glanced at Temur. Temur nodded. "I have spoken with men who rode against the Rahazeen fortresses," he said. "Even the Great Khagan never managed to capture more than one or two of them, and at great cost for little gain. The Rahazeen put them in barren places by preference, and there is little won in the sack or conquest of such places."

"But they make excellent bases for war such as you monkey-men wage," Hrahima said. "Fastnesses are proof against all but the most resourceful and determined troops."

Songtsan tossed back the cold remains of his tea and set the bowl aside before Samarkar could move to refill it. It was a sign the interview was coming to an end, and Samarkar touched Hrahima's arm to be sure Hrahima knew it. Hrahima's great feet shifted at the edge of the white rug; the tips of her claws protruded. Samarkar saw her wrap one hand inside the other to hide the evidence of premature irritation.

Premature, or perhaps prescient. Because Songtsan looked up into the tiger's eyes and said, "There are benefits to allowing one's enemies to eat each other, when one is in position to pick up the pieces later. I do not think I will interfere in a war between the Rahazeen and the Qersnyk. It benefits me more than either of them."

Samarkar meant to bite her lip but could not. The memory of a pile of raw bones lay within her, forcing impassioned words from her mouth. "Honored Brother," she burst out, "are not the dead of Qeshqer our people? Is that not a sufficient act of war?"

"They are," he said. "And I have every intention of avenging them. Once the plainsmen and the assassins have thinned one another out."

Samarkar saw the muscle ripple in Temur's jaw as he clenched it against the words that wanted to fly loose. His hand trembled so the dregs of his tea wet his fingers. Carefully, he extended an arm and put the eggshell-thin porcelain bowl down before it could shatter.

He said nothing, even though Songtsan looked at him inquiringly for a moment. Samarkar also saw the curious gesture Hrahima made—arrested, half completed—and recognized it for something of arcane intent aborted before it was fully formed. *And yet she said her people did not have wizards.*

But that was a question for later, when they found themselves alone.

"Of course, Honored Brother," Samarkar said. She lowered her eyes, bent her body almost parallel to the floor with her arms at her sides. She held the pose, uncomfortable as it was, for a few dozen heartbeats before Songtsan deigned to notice her.

"Honored Sister," he said.

Everything she felt seemed to rise up at once, seizing her throat, banding her heart so tightly she felt each beat like a blow.

"I have heard," she began carefully, "that our brother is a prisoner."

Songtsan set himself back on his heels. "Our mother died of arsenic," he said. "Someone must go to the fire."

Her hands shook. She could not stop the heat of tears as they trickled down her cheeks, spotting the floor above which she held her face. Songtsan's voice seemed to come from all around her, and all she could see was the toes of his shoes. His voice was cold, a threat. A voice she had obeyed in almost all things, since it sent her away to be fostered then married at fourteen.

She found the ice of determination in her heart like a hook and hung her courage from it. "Must it be Tsansong?"

"Would you rather it were you?" Songtsan did not sound like a man who threatened, but merely like one who was tired. Of course, with his coronation looming, all the administrative tasks his mother had previously taken off his hands . . .

Somehow, she found the will to ask again. "Must it be our brother? Can he not . . . can he not come to the wizards, where he would be no threat to you?"

Songtsan stepped back. She knew him too well to think she had shamed him. More probably, she had bored him—but sometimes he would do things for the pleasure of seeing you plead again the next time.

"He is not dutiful," Songtsan said, and turned his back on her.

THIS TIME, WHEN AL-SEPEHR AROSE FROM HIS COPYIST'S PRAYER, IT WAS because he had come to the end of a chapter. He was not alone in the scriptorium this hour. Others of the Nameless toiled about him, heads bent as hands worked black ink into the ordained labyrinth of holy words across mottled, creamy vellum. Al-Sepehr left silently out of respect for them, his soft-shod feet making no noise on sanded stones.

The scriptorium's arched windows let in both breezes and the awning-filtered light of the sun. One did not do a copyist's work by lamplight—not for long, anyway, and not accurately. Because of this, the scholarly devotions of Rahazeen monks took place largely in daylight hours, while their more martial pursuits could be attended to in the morning or evening. Sorcery had its own times, the hours of the day being appropriate for different invocations depending upon their natures and energies.

Al-Sepehr tugged his veil across his face as he stepped into the brutal glare of the courtyard. The afternoon midway between noon and evenset was one such time. The hour of fire; the hour when the sun blazed hottest. The hour of Vajhir, a pagan god of Messaline who ruled over flames and the sun. But they were not in Messaline now, and this time was important to al-Sepehr's Scholar-God as well.

Unlike lesser deities, the Scholar-God was singular. She had no name because she needed none, being singular. The Nameless, too, were singular. It was the teaching of Sepehr al-Rachīd ibn Sepehr that there were no true prophets—not Ysmat of the Beads nor any other—and that only the naked word of the Scholar-God could be trusted.

It was an irony, al-Sepehr thought, that led some to treat al-Rachīd as a prophet himself, when the so-called Sorcerer-Prince had denied that any such existed. Al-Sepehr was not one of the ones who believed that al-Rachīd had been a prophet. Although he did acknowledge al-Rachīd's demidivinity—a different thing entirely.

And he, of the line of Sepehr himself, as the leader of the Nameless here in Ala-Din, had al-Rachīd's library at his disposal. It was to that library that he traveled now, past the courtyards dusty and empty in the sweltering sun, past the deep wells and cisterns with their heavy stone lids to hold the water within.

So little of sorcery was mystic circles scribed in blood and fuming censers. Oh, there was sacrifice, of course—al-Sepehr thought of the stones in his trouser pocket again—but most of his work was done bent over ancient tomes written in the crabbed handwriting of al-Rachīd or al-Rachīd's heirs.

Al-Sepehr knew the name he wanted; he knew the book that name resided in. But it harmed nothing to be extra careful when one was dealing with djinn.

He took the book from the shelf, its bound pages heavy in their limp leather covering. It fell open to the page he wanted; the parchment was stained with strange chemicals and—perhaps—tea around the margins.

He knew better than to summon a spirit of fire and wind to a library, and so he copied the name he needed onto a scrap of eastern paper, taking pains over the vowels. He blew it dry and folded it into his sleeve before putting the volume away. Then he climbed the seventy steps from that white-pillared room to the tower's flat roof.

Al-Sepehr kept a brazier here, for convenience. As he kindled it, he turned the name over and over in his mind, considering stresses and how he would use his breath.

At last there was flame. Al-Sepehr stood over it, the scrap of paper in his hand, and cast the djinn's name into the fire an instant before he pronounced it, all seventeen syllables in a fluid roll like the lines of a poem.

And then he raised up his arms and said, "Come."

It was an unnecessary bit of theater, and there was no one to observe it, but he felt the sorcery deserved a little pomp. And indeed, by the time he lowered his hands again, he had an audience. A flash of heat stung al-Sepehr's face where the veil did not cover it. A hot wind fluttered his loose garments like banners.

Sparks rose about the djinn's sinewy feet where they rested on the brazier's deep cherry coals. It was smaller than al-Sepehr had expected, having taken the form of a slight man with indigo hair and lapis lazuli skin that caught flashes of gold in the sun. Its eyes blazed in their sockets like orange-yellow embers, though its hands were thrust insouciantly into the pockets of white pantaloons. It wore nothing else.

It lifted its chin, straightening from a curve-backed slouch, and pulled its shoulders back. "So you're the new al-Sepehr."

"These twenty years gone by," al-Sepehr said, conscious, as he was usually not, of the gray streaks in his hair and beard. He tugged his veil down to show his face. "I suppose that might be *new* to a djinn."

"Barely born," the djinn said. It drew hands overlarge for its frame from its pockets, spreading them as if for balance as it stepped down from the brazier. Its feet left soot smudges. Pressing its palms together, it performed the mockery of a bow. "Shall we dispense with the pleasantries and get right down to the haggling, then?"

"I did not call you because I wanted to haggle," al-Sepehr said.

The djinn looked around, craning its neck this way and that. The stone smoked under its feet. "Well, I don't see a binding circle, and there's a distinct lack of bottles and lamps. So you don't intend to imprison me. I don't hand out wishes to just anybody who can say my name. That leaves haggling."

It smiled and spread outsized hands again. The face it wore was youthful, diamond-shaped, crooked-nosed, under curly hair that swept up into the kind of appealing tousle one might expect in an indulged bed-slave. The eyes might even have looked sultry if they had not blazed like fire opals. Al-Sepehr wondered from whom the djinn had borrowed the face.

Al-Sepehr smiled back and bowed low. "What could I offer one so great as yourself, O djinn? For surely, your mastery of fire and air, your powers of transformation and your cunning are so immense that I—a small one, a mere mortal, all of whose ability has amounted only to the leadership of one small, all-but-forgotten sect—have nothing you could want. Moreover, there is nothing I could obtain that you would want, O great power of the desert wind and sun. For is not the very desert itself in essence that wind and sun? You are eternal, O djinn. Whereas I am only a man, a brief thing that will flicker out before you even notice my existence."

The djinn looked at him, one eyebrow rising, head cocked to the side. It had folded its arms in irritation when al-Sepehr began speaking, but now they swung relaxed.

"It is true," the djinn said. "That I am powerful."

"You are powerful!" al-Sepehr said. "Truly I believe there is almost no task you could not complete, you are so great."

The djinn scowled, and sparks flew from the corners of its eyes. "Almost none?"

"I should not ask you to wrestle gods," al-Sepehr said. "For that would be blasphemy. But short of that—"

"Gods?" the djinn said. Now it smiled, seeming to believe he had misstepped, and pressed its advantage. "I believed your religion admitted of but one, and that one omnipotent."

"It is so," al-Sepehr said. "But I believe you could do almost anything else."

"*Almost,*" the djinn said, mocking. It moved in a slow circle around him, considering. He turned to follow it. "*Almost.* You and that *almost!* Set me a task then, mortal man, and I will show you your *almost.*"

Al-Sepehr clapped his hands together, unable to restrain himself, and saw the expression of chagrin cross the djinn's face a moment too late.

"Damn," it said. "You're good at this. All right then, mortal, let's hear your task."

"Bring me the Green Ring of Erem, once borne by Danupati of the Dragon Banner—the ring that can command scorpions and storms and lets a man speak in the language of Ghuls. And bring me the skull of that same Danupati."

The djinn stopped its circling. It folded its arms again across its narrow, muscled chest. Al-Sepehr saw the fingers of its right hand tapping gently against the bulge of its left bicep. He thought it might be sucking its teeth.

It smiled a gloating smile, and he saw fangs.

"As you wish," it said, and vanished in a curl of smoke and a wind so hot he felt his face redden as if from the sun.

He did not fear the source of the djinn's cold smirk. He knew what he had asked for. And he knew the price with which those things came.

He was counting on it.

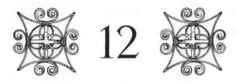

12

Edene prayed as befitted a Qersnyk woman: standing straight, her arms at her sides, her eyes open and raised to the sky above. But it was not the Eternal Sky; it was the featureless sky of the Scholar-God, all textureless shallows and pale, flat sun.

She did not know if the Eternal Sky heard her.

Al-Sepehr—the man who came, the only person she spoke to or saw—had brought her clothes in the Ctesifonin style, and she wore those now because they were clean and soft. And enveloping, protective—wool the buff color of the desert sheep, as light as a veil, woven so fine the breeze passed through it but not the sun. She missed the freedom of her coat and trousers and did not like the way these clothes left her breasts and slowly mounding belly free to sway.

She was standing at her window praying to the alien sky on the day that everything changed.

First, her meal was not brought to her by al-Sepehr, but by a woman veiled in the buff and cream veils that Edene let fall about her neck like scarves when she bothered to wear them at all. Only the veiled woman's startling hazel eyes set in nut-brown skin showed to show her attention or emotions. There was a dot as black as a spot of ink in the left iris, so dark Edene wanted to touch it and see if it was really a hole.

Fortunately, captivity had not yet driven her so mad that she jabbed the other woman in the eye. Instead, she stepped forward as the new visitor set the tray down, and said—in Qersnyk, it being the only tongue in which she was fluent—"Hello. I am Edene."

She pointed to her chest as she said her name, in case the other woman did not speak her language. And that might have been the case, because the woman simply stared at her, furrows forming in the slip of forehead Edene could see.

"Edene," Edene said again, tapping her breastbone again.

"Ah," the woman said. She touched herself. "Saadet." She pointed to the food then and said a word that must mean "eat."

So Edene ate, because food was strength, and she had every intention of someday leaving this place, whether her captors willed it or no. When she had eaten, Saadet touched her arm and tugged her veil up to cover her hair and mouth. Edene would have hooked her fingers behind the cloth and pulled it back down again, but Saadet touched Edene's wrist and shook her head.

With a sigh, Edene nodded.

Leaving the tray lying on the table, Saadet led Edene to the door and knocked. To Edene's surprise and amazement—even a little fear—the door swung open. There were two large men beyond, both wearing scimitars, but they averted their eyes as Saadet and Edene moved past. Edene tried to copy Saadet's way of moving— almost a scurry, with quick short footsteps and head ducked down, watching the corridor before her. Edene would have strode tall, turning her head to take in the architecture and peer out windows, but if this was the way they did things here, Edene did not wish to attract attention. She wasn't sure if this was an escape or something else—but whatever it was, it was better than sitting in her small room five stories above the clifftop, watching shadows trail across the inhospitable desert below.

Saadet led her through pillared halls and across a wide courtyard to a wall that even Edene could tell must be the exterior curtain of this mountain fastness. They climbed steps then, and guards did not stop them. An acrid, unidentifiable scent reached Edene on the sweltering wind. Evening encroached, the harsh direct light of the sun cut by the walls, and the plaza below began to fill with men wielding swords and staves, ready to practice battle.

They attained the battlements, and that moderately unpleasant scent grew eye-watering, ammoniac. Edene pressed her veil across her mouth and nose, grateful suddenly for its faint scent of sandalwood and cedar.

Below her, on a ledge beside the castle, was an enormous nest—trees bigger than the span of her arms piled like twigs, woven together with enormous feathers and scraps of cloth.

Edene recognized the great bird crouched within. It had carried her here, or one like it had. Another, she thought, for this one's great, brassy wings were clipped. She could see the bright ends of its primaries where they were cut short. She wondered what hand could complete such a task. Smaller birds surrounded it, similar in coloring and outline but no larger than the great eagles of the steppe. Some flew in groups from the cliff, circling like flocks of vultures on the rising heat of the desert below.

The large bird had a long neck—longer than an eagle's, in proportion—and its savagely hooked beak projected below a snow-white crest as red at the tips as if it had been steeped in blood.

Any one of those crest feathers, Edene thought, was as tall as she.

When it saw her and Saadet on the wall above, it made a piercing noise, sweet and sharp as a falcon's cry and strong enough to shiver dust in the joins between the stones Edene stood upon. It could have snapped her up in a bite, but instead it stood, unsteadily, and Edene saw the waist-thick chain that ran from its ankle to an enormous bolt in the stone.

"Poor thing," she said aloud, and was surprised almost to tumbling from the wall by the deep chuckle of someone beside her. She spun, but there was no one there.

And then just as suddenly there was. Her eyes widened as al-Sepehr seemed to appear not an *ayl* away, his form revealed as if cloaking dust fell from it to pool at his feet, then was swept away by a gust of wind.

"Sorcerer!"

"Just a simple priest," he said, and inclined his head. Today, his veils were pushed back, and she could see the neat gray-streaked beard he wore shaved at both sides, as if he were vain about his strong jawline—and perhaps hiding a weak chin. Once upon a time, she judged, it had been black as ink. His hands were clasped together as if he hid something behind the right one. As he drew them apart, she saw something flash between his fingers. Green-gold, like the most ancient of Messaline coins, then gone.

A ring, she thought, as he slipped the right hand into his pocket and drew it out again, empty. A ring that had hidden him from her view.

A ring that he kept in his pocket.

She swallowed and pretended she had seen nothing of the kind. "Your god grants you great abilities, then."

"She provides," he agreed with a pleasant nod. He put his hand into his pocket again, as if casually, and pursed his lips in a sweet, birdy whistle. Once, twice, piping softly. Something appeared among the stones, then—a scorpion, scuttling on many legs, glossy brown in the brilliant sun. Edene stepped back cautiously.

Al-Sepehr thrust out his left hand, resting a crooked finger on the wall, and whistled again. The scorpion crawled to him and ran up his finger, its heavy barb swaying over its back like ripe fruit on the vine.

He lifted it to eye level, while Edene turned her face away and pretended not to watch. When he chirruped, it raised its claws and lowered its head, seeming to curtsy. Al-Sepehr nodded in return and set it down. Quickly, it scuttled away.

Out of the corner of her eye, she studied him—the long rectangular face, the long rectangular hands laced with tattoos or henna the color of dried blood on the palms and sooty ink across the backs. He looked weathered and capable, with broad shoulders under his desert robes.

He said, "How do you like my pretty?"

She followed his gaze back to the bird. "They're more beautiful in flight," she said.

It had terrified and frozen her. She had vomited until she had nothing left to bring up except her own intestines and her just-kindled babe. And yet she felt a peculiar loyalty to the terrible bird, especially now that she knew its mate lay chained and crippled under al-Sepehr's care. She too would do what he wanted, she thought, if he had such a hold over her.

With an effort, she managed not to press her hands to her belly. It was possible he did not yet know she was with child. She must escape while she could still run. And before she gave him something he could use to control her as easily as he controlled his giant birds.

"It's called the rukh," he said. "I will have you trained to take over its care. It is time you made yourself useful. Do you understand how little chance you have of surviving an attempt to escape?"

He gestured to the sheer walls of the cliff below, the rumpled desert beyond, the frame of stark brown mountains that limited the horizon. You could not walk out of that; not without knowledge and supplies.

Edene nodded. Even if she had not believed him, she would have nodded.

"If you wear your veil where men can see you," al-Sepehr said, "you may have the freedom of the keep. The archers know to shoot you down if they see you fleeing."

"I understand," she said.

He gestured to the bird. The rukh. Against the pale sky, Edene saw the dark wings of its mate outlined and approaching. Some massive dead thing hung limply from her enormous claws. A camel, perhaps; the outline was correct.

Al-Sepehr said, "You say they are more beautiful in flight. They are," he said. "But they are more useful to me here."

Edene nodded as if she understood him. But all she could think was *A ring. A ring in his pocket that makes you move in silence, without being seen.*

THE EMPEROR (NO LONGER IN-WAITING) WAS SO GRACIOUS AS TO DISmiss them before he withdrew, flanked again by his two guards. Hrahima managed to hold her silence until the little group was outside the royal precinct and well away from any eavesdropping ear. And then her ears flattened and her tail lashed and she spat a Cho-tse word or phrase in tones that indicated it would be best for everyone if nobody asked what it meant. It echoed from the stone walls of the corridor. Samarkar imagined the force of it trembled the tears that still clung to her face.

She would not break down entirely. She would not give Songtsan that much. But it was hard.

Samarkar waited another ten steps or so, forcing herself to breathe by focusing on the pressure of her collar against her throat. Finally, as mildly as she could and in the lowest audible tones, she asked, "Were you about to cast a spell against his magnificence?"

That brought Hrahima's ears up; in their ignominious retreat, they had outpaced the footman, and a few moments remained before he would catch up. "My people do not practice wizardry," she said, but Samarkar heard the elision.

"But the legends of your people are full of stories of sorcery—"

"It's not sorcery. And those are not my people's legends." Hrahima extended her stride.

With a glance backward at Temur, Samarkar broke into a trot to keep up. Her head came only to the Cho-tse's bicep; a fast walk for Hrahima was very nearly a run for Samarkar.

"But the hypnotic gaze of your eyes—"

Samarkar choked off when Hrahima pinned her on just such a look, the irises of her eyes green and orange and shot through with fracture lines like the eyes of some tortoiseshell cats. Samarkar almost stumbled, and kept her balance only through deep concentration.

Hrahima hissed, but her hand snaked out to steady Samarkar, so Samarkar guessed the Cho-tse was not truly angry. "It is not sorcery," she insisted. And then she, too, glanced over her shoulder—where bandy-legged Temur and the doorman were catching up—and muttered, "I spoke of the Immanent Destiny and the Sun Within."

"You did."

"The faith of my people demands surrender to these things. And in return, we are granted certain abilities." Her shrug was a thing out of legend, shoulders rising and settling like the shaking of a mountain. "I have broken with the faith. Apparently my destiny was not something I could make myself surrender to."

"And the abilities?"

"Oh," Hrahima said. "*Those* remain. And *our* legends are full to brimming with stories of those who used them with insufficient humility. Imagine, if you will, what such a creature could wreak, unrestrained by the Bond of Service."

"A Cho-tse Carrion-King."

"At the least."

"And you were tempted?" She knew the answer. But Hrahima's anger was an opportunity to establish trust, and Samarkar was too many years a politician to allow that to slip through her hands.

Hrahima snorted, slowing at last. "Every day."

Whatever Samarkar might have said in reply was interrupted by the hushing patter of feet running in silk slippers, echoing down one of the cross-corridors up ahead. Hrahima held up her hand, but Samarkar was already moving forward, calling on the patterns of protection worked into her collar. The light that blazed around her was green as jade this time, filtered through the energies of the translucent stones, painting the black stone walls with a viridian sheen. Now Hrahima extended her stride to keep up with Samarkar, and Temur and the footman, too, broke into a trot. But the running woman came into sight before either of them had taken more than a few steps.

It was Payma, dressed all in trailing robes of white and apricot silk, sliding, stumbling as she rounded the corner, righting herself against the far wall and charging on. The oiled tower of her hair fell in disarray from jeweled combs; her hands were bare of rings. Tears or sweat streaked the careful maquillage on her cheeks, the shadows that made her eyes seem as huge and dazzling as stars. She plunged forward, tripping on uneven stones, and Samarkar closed the distance between them in order to catch Payma before she could fall and bloody her knees and her palms.

The girl in Samarkar's arms felt like a caterpillar's twiggy tent, but as she fell against Samarkar's side, Samarkar felt the firm, ripe curve of her belly and fought down a sharp moment of envy. *It's not a sacrifice if it doesn't mean anything to you.*

"Payma," Samarkar said, pulling her into the shelter of Samarkar's green and airy light. The effect was as if Payma stood in the verdant tunnel beneath trees in a garden, her skin smoothed by flattering green shade. "Honored Sister-in-Law. What's wrong?"

The girl—the *child*, in all honesty—might be in hysterics, but she was still a force. With one hand on Samarkar's arm as a prop, she pushed herself upright, and erect as a queen she held up the other imperious hand.

"You," Payma said to the footman, "you must go elsewhere."

"Highness," the footman said without question, and faded back down the hall. His evident relief told Samarkar that there was no question but that the chamberlain—then, perforce, Songtsan—would be informed of these events in mere moments.

Payma sagged, as if that had been her last strength. Samarkar slid a supporting arm around Payma's shoulders, bending her knees to hold the princess upright. Hrahima bounded past, reaching the intersection Payma had just run through in a single leap. She scanned the side corridors with her tail lashing, her knees bent to a half crouch.

"Nothing," she said, but Samarkar knew it was only a matter of time before some pursuit materialized. Princesses were not left to wander the palace corridors unescorted, in tears and in dishabille.

"You have to help me," Payma said. She raised a hand to Samarkar's cheek. She smelled of tears and snot and sandalwood and the tinted grease on her cheeks. "My husbands are going to . . . I mean . . ."— she gulped in a breath and seemed to draw strength from it, for the quaver dropped out of her voice and she spoke with strained dignity—"Songtsan is going to kill Tsansong. And I know I am not meant to have favorites between my husbands, but there is no doubt that the babe I carry is Tsansong's child."

Samarkar needed no help with the pitiless equations of politics. Songtsan had a boy child born; he had finally dispensed with his hated mother. What would stop him from removing his brother, his rival, and that rival's unborn son?

She was a wizard of Tsarepheth. She was under the authority of the *bstangpo.* She had chosen that role in part so that her sons could never prove rivals to Songtsan's lineage, because she knew precisely what her brother was capable of—and in part because it was the best measure of freedom from his machinations that she could buy.

"That's treason," she said, with a glance at Temur. *I'm willing,* she said with her eyes, praying he would understand. It had to be his choice.

He swallowed, one hand on his knife, and said only, "Do we try to rescue your brother?"

Samarkar wanted to close her eyes, but she would not. If she would condemn Tsansong to the flames, she would do it while meeting his lover's gaze. "If we had an army, it might be possible."

Payma wiped the runnels of makeup off her cheeks, smearing the apricot sleeve of her gown. She lifted her chin and put her free hand on the belly that Samarkar could not yet see beneath her robes. "I will save his scion," she said, and Samarkar heard the ice in it—and how thin that ice was over the pain.

"If we can." Hrahima, of course, had heard it all. Now she came striding back, her feet soundless as the wind through her fur. "Sa- markar-la, this was your home. Tell us how to proceed."

There were secret ways, of course—the palace at Tsarepheth was no different from any other palace in this regard. And while Samarkar was confident she knew them all, Songtsan was by no means more ignorant. Still, the first thing they must do was get Payma out of the corridor and start moving. And they could not take her out a guarded door, not unless they were prepared to fight.

The good news was that the Black Palace of Tsarepheth was like all fortresses; it was designed to keep enemies out, not in, and if one would keep certain ways within its walls secret, that meant they must also be kept secret from the majority of the men at arms.

Heart pounding against her collar, showing in the hollows of her wrists, Samarkar dimmed the green light of her wards and led her party quickly, by devious routes, into a lamplit servant's hall and from there to a concealed stair. In the stair there was a wall that seemed solid until one touched a particular block and muttered an incantation consisting of the lineage of the Rasan imperial household for eight generations. The wall angled in, silently, and silently Samarkar brought her companions through. She sealed the wall behind them and drew one free breath, scented with the tallow smoke from the lamps that had seeped into everyone's hair and clothes.

The light of Samarkar's wards revealed a corridor wide enough for two to walk abreast, low enough that it brushed Temur's hair, while Samarkar had to walk hunched and Hrahima just dropped down to all fours and scuttled like a frog crossed with a tiger.

"We need to keep moving," Payma said. She minced on slippered feet as if they pained her, but made no complaint.

Samarkar took her hand. "We are."

"This could not smell more empty," Hrahima said. "There is not even dust."

"That is why we must hurry," Samarkar said. "There is no ventilation in these corridors. If we stood and waited, we would breathe all the air and suffocate."

Temur reached out to put one hand on the wall, his face dewed in sweat although the passage was chill as a grave. He set off in ad-

vance, moving quietly, supporting himself as if the presence of the
walls and ceiling were a weight he carried, which made him stagger.
Of course: No steppe horse-lord would love this place.

But their only path out was through.

THE WEIGHT OF THE PALACE ITSELF SEEMED TO PRESS DOWN ON TEMUR'S
chest, shortening his breathing and closing his vision to a tunnel.
His people believed it ill luck to spill blood at an execution, and so
they sewed criminals into leather bags and heaped stones upon them
until they died. He knew this was not the same—not even remotely
the same—but for the moment he imagined that each breath grew
shallower than the last, his lungs exhausted with pushing out against
all that stone.

The space was not silent. It should, he thought, be as close as it
was still, but every breath and every footstep rang around them until the sound fell in tiers, like thunder echoing from distant mountains.

It is only a corridor. And Samarkar knows where you are going.

She walked behind him, her green light casting forward so he
could see to place his feet and see his own shadow stretching out
front. The princess in the silken robes shuffled beside her, and each
breath came with a squeak. Someone was as terrified here as Temur.
The cat was as silent as mist, but she, too, breathed more quickly
than was her wont, and the long tunnel took up the echoes of her
breath and made it seem like a whole tribe of tigers panting.

Temur heard Samarkar take a quick breath, make a small noise
of assessing, and start to speak.

He thought at first she was asking a question, but before long,
the rhythm of her words lulled him, and he realized she was telling
a story. A children's tale, the sort of thing you soothed a babe with.

"Long ago," Samarkar began, "there was a woman of the borderlands, a princess who was the daughter of a Dowager Queen. Their
demesne lay at the foot of the Steles of the Sky, and it would have

been a poor land, except that by good fortune it was inhabited by a race of great stone beings called *talus,* who mined for the people there and produced metals and jewels.

"Now like many others, this land had been conquered by the Great Khagan, and the people owed him tribute. . . ."

She told a story, Temur realized with a smile, that he almost knew—and knew as history. In listening to it, he forgot for a little the cold fear that wanted to creep in and numb his limbs. The woman she described, who through trickery had saved her land from a bandit prince and her mother's machinations towards rebellion, was Temur's kin, for she had married his uncle Toghrul, and with Toghrul defended the borders of the Khaganate with great success. If his memory served him, her name was Nilufer, and unless news had missed him, she was still alive somewhere to the west in her holdfast called Stone Steading, in the foothills of the Steles, where she had reigned since long before Temur was born.

The wall under his hand had been smoothed by many hands before. The light was good, and even if they had had no light at all, there would be no great difficulty in walking; the floor was polished smooth—to ease finding one's way in the dark, Temur thought, should one, in fleeing for one's life, neglect a torch or lantern.

Eventually, Samarkar finished her story. Everyone—even the Cho-tse—breathed more easily. *Wizard,* Temur thought, with a fondness it would have been foolish to express openly. They were allies of convenience, he knew, and she of as royal and devious a line as he. They could never truly be friends when their houses were at war.

Could they?

After the story, they walked in calm quiet for a little while longer, until the tunnel began to slope up. Payma said, quietly, so Temur knew it had been gnawing at her for a good while, "Where will I go from here?"

"To the Citadel, first," Samarkar said. She must have been thinking on the same lines, because the answer came naturally. "But we will not be able to linger there. Yongten-la will not allow even the

bstangpo to drag a wizard from the Citadel, but if we are so unfortunate as to be trapped there . . . we will never leave."

Temur bit his lip. This was where he should speak. The secret of
his birth weighed on him suddenly, when before, keeping it to himself
had only been a matter of modeling the life he intended to adopt.
He had never felt Qulan's passion to become Khagan, or even Khan.

"I will return to the west," Hrahima said, and Temur's courage
failed him. "You may accompany me. Whether your monkey-king
will fight or no, I assure you, there are those who will not turn away
able assistance in the coming war."

"Into exile," Samarkar said bitterly. Her voice held so much experience that Temur understood instantly that this would not be
her first such journey. "Well, better that than burning."

"Don't say it," Payma begged. Temur felt a spike of pity for her,
and by extension for every woman murdered in games of power where
she was awarded no control. But perhaps that wasn't fair to the
women: His mother might have been traded away as a spoil of war,
but she had risen high in his father's councils and consideration, and
certainly the Great Khagan had never scrupled to ask *his* mother's
advice.

And Nilufer, as Samarkar had so aptly reminded him—she had
taken on bandits, rebels, and her *own* mother to make a safe haven
for herself. No, women were as capable—and as dangerous—as any
man. Sometimes more so.

And a good thing, too, since you are stuck in the dark with three of them. If
Hrahima could be reckoned as a woman, in this accounting.

He stopped, so abruptly that Payma almost walked up his heels.
He turned to face them—Samarkar stooped, Payma leaning on her
for support anyway, Hrahima crouched behind.

"Temur?" Samarkar asked.

He said, with as much conviction as he could muster, "Nilufer—
the woman you just told the story about—her name is Nilufer. Her
estate is called Stone Steading. She is still alive, or if she has died,
she died recently."

Samarkar watched him patiently. "I see."

"She's my relative. She married my uncle, Toghrul Khanzadeh. My father was Otgonbayar Khanzadeh, son of the Great Khagan."

Payma's hands tightened on Samarkar's arm, rumpling the fabric of the wizard's coat, which took on an emerald gleam under the light that surrounded her. "You're the Great Khagan's grandson?"

"One of." Temur snorted. "There were hundreds. Qori Buqa has been killing his way through every one of us that he can find. But I am the one he should not have hammered on the anvil until I was forged into an enemy."

He took a breath. The words that were coming out of him had the ring of portent, the air of a gathering storm. But he had not rehearsed them, and he did not know from what reservoir within him they sprang. "I am Re Temur. I will help you fight your Rahazeen warlord, Hrahima. And I will take back from him in turn what he first took from me. And then I will come back and see Qori Buqa put out of the place that was rightfully my brother's."

Something poured out from him as he spoke. He saw Samarkar's light react to it. It sped from him like the shadow of a ripple on the sandy bottom of a river's ebb. He saw the movement of Samarkar's collar as she swallowed; he saw Hrahima's whiskers come forward and her tired ears perk up. He saw Payma's left hand fall to her side and squeeze her robes against her thigh.

"That's what I'm going to do," Temur said lamely, aware that something of significance had happened and yet unable to express it. "I will take you all with me, if you want."

"That was a blood-vow," Samarkar said, in the curious tones that Temur had already learned to associate with a wizard confronted with some new mystery. "There's never been one observed from the beginning. I wouldn't miss it for the world."

SHAHRUZ AND HIS MERCENARIES HAD BEEN LOOTING THE REMAINS OF a small caravan along the Celadon Highway, making it look like the

work of bandits, when his sister's summons to the presence of al-
Sepehr came. He had greeted the command to move on to Tsarepheth
with more pleasure than he would show his leader. "Re Temur—
capture him alive if you can," al-Sepehr said. "If not, make a martyr
of him. We have his unborn child; that will serve as enough of a
rallying banner to his brother's faction. I shall send you a journeyman to assist. Brother Aban. He will come with the wind and meet
you on the road. You need not wait for him: I will send Saadet with
the rukh, so it may easily find you."

"Thank you." Shahruz studied his leader's face through his sister's
eyes. Al-Sepehr had allowed his veil to drape low, revealing his face,
and Shahruz could see too clearly the purple shadows that smudged
the sockets of his eyes, the gaunt hollows below the bones of his
cheeks. Al-Sepehr was worn thin, and Shahruz was not surprised
that he had not risen from his divan to greet Saadet.

Saadet's worry was there, too, a gnawing presence in the pit of
Shahruz's stomach. He knew from Saadet's memories that since
he brought down the heathen ghosts upon Qeshqer, al-Sepehr had
been keeping to his private chambers as much as possible, appearing
in public only to make his prayers and retreating again as soon as
the ink was dry upon the page. The magic took a heavy toll, and al-
Sepehr would allow very few of his followers to realize that.

A rush of warmth and affection filled Shahruz and Saadet, to be
so included in their leader's private world. It came coupled with
gratitude: Shahruz understood that the Nameless were a small group,
without force of arms, and that they must fight—for now—by convincing their enemies to make war on each other.

But hunting a fugitive prince was far more satisfying than robbing
and slaughtering caravanners. Shahruz understood that the deaths
were necessary, in order to discourage trade and set the petty princes
of the Celadon Highway even more at each others' throats in the
absence of a strong Khagan to enforce the peace. But he loathed
the spilling of innocent blood: These men were neither warriors nor

warlords who had chosen a life and a death by the sword. They were simply men who must trade to eat.

Much better was to chase down some Qersnyk princeling. Shah-ruz rode hard and made sure his rented men rode hard behind him.

13

TEMUR AND THE WOMEN CAME OUT OF THE EARTH AFTER NIGHTFALL, close to moonrise. The gate was unobserved, and Samarkar let her wards drop before they walked from the shelter of the corridor. Temur missed the light, with its implication of watchful protection; it seemed to him like a shaman's talismans. But he had to admit the prudence of moving in darkness, with adapted vision, rather than setting a beacon for anyone to find them by.

The passage led them out high on the slope of the Island-in-the-Mist, above the Citadel, under the light of a scatter of early stars. Temur watched the single moon of Rasa rise as they descended the mountain's rocky flank, still unsettled by its waning crescent shape—like a bow, like a horn. He'd seen it fade and return since he came to these alien lands, but he was not sure he would ever become used to it.

The moons, in his heart, should always be those of his Eternal Sky, like a scatter of coins across a merchant's cloth, not like a fingernail paring.

Hrahima, who saw more clearly in the dark than in the day, led the way. Her stripes made her part of the moon shadows, but she moved slowly so the night-blind man and women could follow. As they came down to the Citadel, Temur saw the guards at the base of every stair. Not Citadel guards, but Songtsan's soldiers, fully armored, standing at careful arms-span from the stones of the Citadel. Samarkar had been right; her brother was not quite ready to personally challenge the authority of the wizards, even given his recent elevation in rank.

But he could try to prevent his fugitive wife and sister—and their entourage—from gaining the safety of the Citadel. Hrahima had halted, crouched low among boulders and stunted trees; Temur came up beside her on his belly, crawling as if on a horse raid.

"It would be easy to kill three or four," Hrahima said. Her hands flexed against the stony earth, pale claws drawing parallel lines.

"Easy," Samarkar said from her other side. "But they are only men doing their lawful lord's bidding. They and their fathers have served my family for generations. I will not have their blood spent cheaply—or, if I can prevent it, at all."

"*Hruh*," the Cho-tse said. She glanced back over her shoulder, to where Princess Payma still huddled in the shadow of a boulder, her apricot gown gleaming in the moonlight like the wings of a white owl.

Temur could read Hrahima's thoughts quite clearly. To Samarkar, he said, "Do you have a spell to get us past them, then?"

"I could wrap us in darkness," she said. "But that would fail when we came within their lights."

Hrahima's eyes seemed to gather that light and reflect it. When she closed them, Temur imagined the night grew a little dimmer—or perhaps it was not his imagination at all. She rubbed a hand down her face in a gesture he would have called tired resignation had a man performed it, and muttered something in Cho-tse.

"What was that?" Samarkar asked.

"I should not be tempted," the Cho-tse answered. "To be tempted, and to justify that temptation, is the path to evil. You wait here; you will know the time to move."

"Hrahima—"

But even as Temur reached out for her, she charged. Her thick pelt brushed his fingertips. He had just time enough to marvel at the texture before she was gone, bounding down the slope, her voice a guttural snarl that rose to a terrible wail. She sprang down the mountain in two great leaps, hurtled in among the nearest group of guards, and slashed about herself. From this height, looking from darkness into light, he could see how far her claws were from ever touching skin, but he imagined if you were faced with her, it would feel like blind luck only that she had not torn your throat out. And then she was away, bounding toward the next group of guards at the foot of the next stair, and the ones she had first confronted charged in pursuit.

Temur scrambled back up the slope as Samarkar rose to her feet. He found Payma in the darkness of the standing stone and grasped her arm, reminded by her shocked intake of breath that he was manhandling a princess. Well, it seemed his head was already forfeit for rescuing one; what was one more affront against her regal dignity?

He could not carry her in his arms, not and run in the moonlight. Nor could she run herself, in the thin slippers and on tender feet already worn bloody by the night's walking. Instead he pulled her up onto his back. She got the idea quickly enough, clutching his shoulders rather than across his throat, her legs locked tight around his waist. Samarkar certainly knew how to handle a horse; now, judging by the strength of Payma-tsa's thighs, Temur guessed all Rasan princesses rode.

Even pregnant, she was no great burden for his strength. He slithered down the slope half-sideways, Samarkar beside him and to the right, steadying him with a hand on his arm. He hopped from stone to stone, feeling the shock of each jump in ankles and hips, a scatter of small stones building to a minor landslide before him.

Samarkar and he—still bearing Payma—cascaded to the level place where the stair had landed. He swung Payma to the ground so she could run. Samarkar caught her other hand, and together they plunged for the narrow white steps. Payma whimpered between her teeth with each jarring step. She did not slow them.

A shout told Temur that one of the imperial guards had seen them, no matter how involved those guards might be in trying to pin Hrahima against the wall. The Cho-tse, he saw at a hurried glance, was still evading them with ease, leaping in and out of the skirmish like a cat playing tag with her kittens. She sprang ahead to cut off the ones who broke away to pursue Temur, Samarkar, and Payma. Temur heard one scream in undignified terror as she reared up and showed her claws, arms spread wide.

"Come on," he urged Payma, who ran grimly as he and Samarkar dragged her along, trying to take as much of her weight as they could. Each stride of her feet left wet darkness on the stones, but she made no complaint.

Now all the guards were coming. The thing in Temur's chest— the battle rage, the instinct that told him that flight was useless, that the only option was to stand and hew until he was in turn hewn down—flared bright. He clamped his jaw, tooth gritting on tooth, and forced himself to pick his feet up, to fall forward. To *run*.

The rattle of the Rasan soldiers' armor echoed off the great curved wall of the Citadel. They streamed around Hrahima wherever she leaped to try and slow them. Temur could feel the ground shake under their running feet: There must have been fifteen or twenty now, drawn from every neighboring stair.

Samarkar pushed Payma forward, and the momentum pulled him an extra step. The stair was there, less than an *ayl* ahead. He slung Payma in front of him and pushed her bodily up the steps— two, then four—while the stark jade light of Samarkar's wards washed their shadows black and bottomless on white stone. Her voice boomed, rattling dust from the crevices between blocks of stone: "You will not lay hands on me!"

Above, Temur saw wizards gathering, a stream of black coats lining the battlements, trickling down the stairs, rushing to meet them. He could not leave Samarkar undefended at his back. He gave Payma one more push toward the wizards and turned around, his knife in his hand, not sure what he would do, afoot, against a score of armed and armored men.

Stand until he fell, he thought, because once the battle was joined, he knew he would not be able to force himself to back down.

But no—he would do nothing, it turned out, because the soldiers had stopped at the edge of the glare that burned from Samarkar. She backed away, hands outstretched, and they followed, still at the perimeter of her light. Temur had a sense that they were waiting for a signal, some command from a leader that had not yet materialized.

Samarkar's foot touched the lowest stair. She turned and fled toward Temur; Temur, who was blocking her path, spun about and climbed as fast as he could. Above, wizards were lifting the princess off her feet, carrying her upward and out of harm's way.

"Hrahima!" Samarkar cried.

As if her name had summoned her, like a djinn, the tiger landed whisper-soft on the stair before Temur. She was scratched and bleeding from a dozen superficial wounds, and her eyes glared green as jewels in the light of Samarkar's magic. Her tail lashed, but she spun feather-light on the pads of her feet and bounded up the stairs to the descending wizards. One or two cowered from her—more from instinct than personal fear, Temur thought—then she crouched and leaped over them, gaining the battlements in an impossible bound.

"Hrahima is fine," he said, and reached behind himself to offer Samarkar a hand.

YONGTEN-LA MET THEM AT THE TOP OF THE STAIRS AND PROMPTLY swept them down the other side again. Samarkar struggled to keep up with him. Payma was simply bundled into a litter and carried, while a wizard trotted alongside tending her feet. Temur and Hrahima followed as if bobbing in the eddies of a wake.

"You must leave tonight," Yongten-la said. "Before he can move troops around the mountains to intercept you. We will clear the

Wreaking that you may pass in safety. I have had your luggage pre-pared, and Temur-tsa's horses stand ready. We have taken the lib-erty of saddling a gelding for the princess."

"I am grateful. But how did you—"

He interrupted with a smile that made Samarkar want to smite her own forehead. Of course he knew. She said, "The *bstangpo* will not be pleased."

Yongten-la snorted. "I've crossed worse emperors than he. On with you, wizard."

He tapped her shoulder affectionately, like a father. Samarkar felt the sting all the way down her chest to her belly.

"Where will we go?" she asked. She glanced over her shoulder and lowered her voice. "We cannot take Payma all the way to Ctesi-fon. Even if she and the babe survived it, she would come to term on the road."

"Nilufer," Temur said.

She turned, feeling the surprise blank her face. "Your aunt?"

"You mentioned her," Temur said, spreading his hands. He'd resheathed his knife. "What better portent than the uttering of a wizard? Her husband Toghrul was my father's brother, and she no doubt still holds influence over her children. We honor our mothers and grandmothers among the Qersnyk, for who can know what man fathered him? I can claim some kinright with her. And if she or her sons have fallen in with Qori Buqa, well . . ." He waved a hand. "Better to find out, I guess."

"So be it," Samarkar said with a smile, and lowered her voice to add, "Your highness."

Temur glanced down. "Come on. There's no time to waste."

EVEN AS HER HANDS CARRIED OUT NECESSARY TASKS, AS HER FEET carried her through the familiar halls of the Citadel, Samarkar felt unreal, as if she had become someone out of a story. She might have been mist, blown through the corridors as on a gale. She might have been one of Temur's enslaved blood-ghosts, flying on the wings of the dead. Later, she could never remember how she came to be in the stables, faced with three horses—Temur's two leggy mares and a stoic, shaggy, thick-necked Rasan gelding in an unexceptional pale-nosed dun—and three mealy-colored, pack-laden mules. Temur—*Temur Khanzadeh*, and in truth Samarkar could not say she hadn't suspected something of the sort—stood at her left hand.

The same mules from her and Tsering's earlier trip, she was delighted to realize. Including the stubborn one, but better in flight to have animals whose foibles she knew than have to establish relationships anew.

Tsering was there, to hug her and shove medical bags and one full of paper rockets into her hands. Hong-la was there, sliding flat slabs of purple salt into the bulging saddlebags of the largest mule. He handed Temur something else, as well—a small bag of undyed chamois wrapped around something that clinked thickly as Temur slid it inside his fleece-lined vest. The wizard clapped the plainsman's arm; the plainsman bowed in answer.

He's the Great Khagan's grandson. That, too, was unreal—part of the storybook. Like the princess being led back to meet them. Payma seemed smaller, clad now not in billowing court robes but in a cara-vanner's chamois trousers and tough boots, her hair dressed in a plain braid down her back, the tight, high mound of her belly poking a gap in her vest. *Five months,* Samarkar estimated. If Temur could find his aunt's small kingdom, somewhere to the west, they should have time to get Payma there in safety.

Hong-la and Tsering helped them lead the horses and mules from the stable. Hrahima followed, well away from the horses, and skirted the wall to move out to the edge of the torchlight. She would lead them on foot. Tsering, eyes bright in the moonlight, held Samarkar's stirrup when Temur lead Buldshak over for her to mount. Temur and Samarkar didn't speak; there was nothing left to say.

Samarkar leaned down from the high-cantled steppe saddle and touched Tsering's hair. "Guard yourself."

Tsering touched her hand. "May all the little gods of the roads smooth your way."

Payma had mounted with fair ease; now Temur floated into Bansh's saddle. The liver-bay flicked her tail against her own flanks with a slap that echoed, as if to say *At last, you're back where you belong*. Samarkar watched with tenderness that surprised her as Temur leaned forward to stroke the crest of the mare's long neck. Bansh turned one ear back to him, shifting her weight, and stretched her dished nose forward.

Toward the gates, toward the night beyond.

"Go," Temur said, and eased the reins to send her forward. Samarkar and Payma fell into line behind him, each leading a snorting, long-eared mule.

They crossed the Wreaking by its own light—Temur, who had seen it only by day, made a mumble of surprise at its blue-white moonstone glow, caught and refracted by its veils of mist. Yongten-la had been as good as his word; wizards and imperial guards were likewise absent. Hrahima crossed before them. Samarkar glimpsed her as a shadow against the whiteness, stooped and moving fast, before she vanished again against the stones of the other side.

The sound of falling water drowned out the ringing of shod and unshod hooves on the long white span. Temur might have called something or he might not; Samarkar couldn't hear him over the falls. Possibly, he just turned over his shoulder to look at her and his lips moved. . . .

She glanced back at Payma—riding grimly forward, her cheeks bare of paint and streaked with tears, the hastily scoured shadows of kohl still blackening her eyes. Good enough. She'd keep up.

They came down the far side of the span damp with drifting spray. Samarkar let herself sigh in relief, then touched Buldshak with her heels to send her forward. The road here was broad enough for two riders abreast, and she wanted to keep Hrahima in sight if it was at all possible.

It wasn't. The Cho-tse vanished in the night as if she were a part of it. For a long while, they walked the horses by starlight and moonlight, accompanied only by the creak of leather, the soft jingle of the tack. The night curled around them, chill and dark, dew making stones slick and wet. They came through the narrowest part of the pass before moonset, and Samarkar began to breathe easier as the stars faded slowly into a lightening sky.

THEY RODE THROUGH THE DAY THAT FOLLOWED, TEMUR UNABLE TO shake an itch between his shoulder blades as if, at any moment, an arrow could sprout from his back. As the sun briefly made itself visible through the narrow gap of the pass overhead, he asked Samarkar if she worried about pursuit.

"Assured of it, rather," she said, with a glance over her shoulder. "But the Citadel will slow them; if Yongten-la says he will help us, he will. They won't come through the pass behind us. They'll have to come around the Island-in-the-Mists, which will add a couple of hundred *li* to their journey. I'm not worried about them catching us unless we are delayed somehow."

"But you are worried?"

She bit her lip and glanced at Payma, who sat huddled in bright cloaks on the back of the gelding. Payma lifted her head, pain and exhaustion graying her skin, but her expression was nothing but quiet determination. Samarkar said, "Songtsan will send pigeons ahead to the garrison at the bottom of the pass, and they will be coming for us from the front. Pigeons may fail to arrive, of course. And these mountains are full of predators. But we'll need to leave the road as soon as we can.

"He'll know we're not taking the Kashe Road," Samarkar said. "We'll go west at the first opportunity. There are more trails open in summer. We can lose my brother's men among the mountains." She looked at Temur. "We *can* lose my brother's men among the mountains?"

"Get us to the hills," he said, a pang of determination sharp in his chest, "and I will get us to the steppe."

"Ride," Payma said. "And hope the mountain hawks are hungry."

SAMARKAR AND THE OTHERS RODE THROUGH THE DAY AND INTO THE long twilight of the mountains, stopping to rest and water the horses briefly in the darkness after sunset. When their eyes had adjusted to the starlit brightness of the night, they mounted again—Temur lifting Payma into her saddle over her protests, when he saw that she could barely stand on her bloodied feet—and let the horses choose their way among the stones of the narrow, treacherous road.

Samarkar was exquisitely aware that each of their lives depended on the sure hooves and good instincts of their mounts. Fortunately, it seemed their forced trust was warranted. Even Buldshak, prone as she was to snorting and staring at nothing, dropped her head close to the trail and descended step-by-step with meticulous surefootedness.

And so they proceeded, exhausted but moving, barely refreshed by the little sleep they'd snatched, until the sky paled once more and a little more light filtered around the black shapes of unfamiliar mountains.

"Tonight we have to sleep," Samarkar said, as they came to a sharp switchback curve. "Or we *will* die of stupidity before morning."

Temur tugged his sleeves down as if to cover cold hands. "I know—"

A stone clattered down the slope behind them. Temur reined his bay mare to the inside of the road, away from a steep drop. In the shadow of several large boulders, he turned. Samarkar heard him hiss, "Go! Run!"

She gave Buldshak her head, and the mare broke into a canter, sharp and sure. It was faster than Samarkar would have traveled on the narrow road, but then these were not her feet beneath them, and the steppe ponies were nimble and strong. Behind, the mule fought the lead line for a moment before falling in, and Samarkar heard the tattoo of Payma's mount's hooves accelerating.

She was glad of Buldshak's speed when the first arrow shattered on the rock beside her. Samarkar crouched in the saddle, head ducked, curled in as if to make herself part of the mare's neck. Her first thought was to fling up a shield, a wall of dazzling light and hot wind that would deflect the arrows as they fell. But the dim light and speed were her allies—surely it would take an archer of incredible abilities to strike her by anything other than luck in this light while firing at a downward angle.

More arrows fell around her—volleys of three or four, rather than a steady rain. One brushed her thigh and left a burning line of wetness and pain. *If it hurts so quickly, it isn't serious.* But she fought the urge to clap her hand to it, to probe it with her fingers. She needed her hands for the reins.

Behind her, Temur cried out, urging Bansh forward, and by the sound of hooves, the bay mare responded. Payma's chunky gelding found another notch of speed when Bansh drove the mule up on his backside, and Buldshak, too, put her head down and ran. Stones showered behind them, rattled down the cliff on Samarkar's right to vanish into empty space, falling until she could not hear them strike. Samarkar hunched herself over her horse's withers and clung, gulping great breaths of fear, trying not to make any move that would throw the mare off balance.

A line of five figures in black crossed the road ahead, two mounted men behind them. The five raised bows, nocked arrows; Samarkar's heart clenched in her chest. She yanked the mule's lead line from the saddle and cast it away so it would not foul Buldshak's feet, knowing the others would do the same behind her. The mules should follow. If they didn't, and Samarkar and the others lived, they could come back and get the animals. If she and Temur and Payma died, they wouldn't need the supplies.

A line of fire sprang across the narrow road, burning the intense violet of sorcery—or chemicals.

Now would be the time for sorcery. For a moment, Samarkar wished her wizardry was the magic of stories, to bring down lightning from a blue sky, or that she held a captive eagle's soul in bond and could call it screaming into battle. If she had time, she could have kindled the rockets in her saddlebags and sent them to scatter the enemy, but for now, all she could do was urge her horse on and hope Buldshak had the strength to break the line—and the courage to cross fire.

The rose-gray mare was game. She might be cautious of anything that cast a shadow, but having decided to run, she ran with all her heart and concentration. She stretched out long, galloping in earnest now, and Samarkar got herself as deep into the saddle as she could and called on the heat that came from within. With a sharp scent like lightning, the green aura flared before her, quick and sharp, a gust of hot wind that deflected the arrows and pushed back the violet fire. It flickered and trembled, guttering with each thump of Buldshak's hooves, but it held until the first flight of arrows spun wide. When it shivered out, Samarkar grasped after it—and found nothing.

Samarkar gasped, lightheaded, mocked from within by Yongten-la's voice saying *You will never be a powerful wizard.* This was the first real test of her powers. Was all she was good for calling light, gusts of air? The toys of apprentices? The world spun around her, and it took all her strength to cling to the saddle and ride Buldshak's rolling gait.

An arrow sizzled past her from behind, invisible in the gloaming, and a few more pattered like sharp rain all around. The one Temur must have loosed would have slain the veiled horseman on the right, but like a storybook hero, he caught it in his hand. *Nameless,* she thought, and wondered if it was he who had called the fire. And even more, she wondered where they had come from. Had they pursued Hrahima this far, or was there something still more subtle going on?

But another arrow followed, and this one took the horseman through the throat. He rose up in the saddle, toppling back, hauling on the reins, and the horse beneath him reared in confusion and fear. It stepped wide, the road-edge crumbling under its hoof, and

Samarkar wished she dared close her eyes as it tottered, toppled, and fell.

The dying man fell silently. The horse screamed all the way down. The line of fire—burned on.

Where in the ten thousand hells was Hrahima?

When Samarkar glanced back over her shoulder, she saw Bansh at a run and gaining on Buldshak, having passed Payma's gelding somewhere along the way. Temur stood sideways *atop* the saddle, a third arrow on his bowstring, the nock pulled back to his ear.

Hair blown free of Samarkar's braid lashed her face, stinging the corners of her eyes. Temur loosed; his arrow flew toward the second horseman, and this one did not trouble himself to catch it. He batted it from the air negligently, without seeming to turn his eyes. He sat straight in the saddle of a dark, elegant mare of evident Asitaneh bloodlines. When he lowered his right hand again, Samarkar saw the flash of a small blade. He shouted something in a fluid, quicksilver tongue she did not know.

The five archers still standing crouched to lay down their bows and—as one—stood again with heavy spears couched against the road behind.

No horse would charge against that, not without the weight of a hundred others pushing it from behind, especially when coupled with the fire. Buldshak broke stride and whirled, her haunches nearly touching the road, turning in twice her own length, as another flight of arrows from above spent itself harmlessly against the road where she would have been. Samarkar was thrown hard against the pommel and the left stirrup, losing the reins as she scrabbled at wood. Her fingers strained, and something in the palm of her right hand popped with a sharp, lancing ache. She caught a squeak of pain between her teeth and swallowed it just in time to see Bansh and her rider loom out of the dim light.

There was just room for two horses to pass. Not at a gallop, and not when one rider was balanced on the saddle as if it were the branch of a tree, half crouched, swaying, reaching into the quiver for his fourth arrow. Temur heard the hooves, looked up, and Samarkar saw his gaze lock on hers in the instant before the horses drew abreast.

Buldshak was on the inside of the road. Bansh came up over her forefeet, her own trim forehooves clattering on the crumbling edge of the road. Stones rattled; the mare wobbled. Samarkar reflexively reached out with her left hand even as she knew there was nothing—*nothing*—she could do to keep horse and rider from the long emptiness below.

But Temur did not fall, though his feet skipped on the saddle leather. He lost the arrow. His right hand caught the tall cantle, and he swung beside Bansh's haunches for a moment while Samarkar frantically clawed after her own reins. Down the pass, riding hard on her stockier mount, Payma was coming, standing crouched over her stirrups, braid bouncing against her shoulders with each stride. More arrows from above feathered the road around her and her gelding, but through some grace none seemed to strike home.

"Come on, girl, come on," Samarkar whispered, leather cutting her hands. She drew back slowly, fearful for her own mare's balance, dreading that at any moment she would hear the sound of Temur and Bansh plummeting to their deaths.

But she got Buldshak quieted before Payma drew abreast—in no small part because Payma saw her coming, and the wall of spears behind her, and reined the gelding in.

There were cries of fear and wonder from the spearmen. When Samarkar risked a glance back, she couldn't believe what she saw: Temur had regained the saddle, and he and Bansh were beyond the line and had turned to flank the mounted man, his bow once more drawn. The man whirled his dark mare in place. She was a dancer, one dainty hoof falling where another had rested a moment before, and now Samarkar saw that the man on her back held not a blade, but a mirror. He raised it high just as Temur loosed. Though Samarkar could not see where the arrow struck, she could see that he did not manage to knock this one away.

The veiled man sagged sideways in the saddle. His horse bolted past Bansh and, in a thunder of hoofbeats, was gone.

Now, at last, the violet flames guttered and died, leaving the ozone stink of sorcery behind.

The spearmen struggled to reverse their unwieldy weapons, hindered by the cramped space that had protected them a moment before. Samarkar could not understand how Temur had passed them, unless Bansh could run on air.

The air was growing brighter as the sun crawled up the sky behind the caging mountains. Another flight of arrows whistled around her as she turned Buldshak back to the fight, one piercing the meat of her left arm. There was a sharp and sudden shock; it knocked her forward, bruising her belly against the pommel yet again, but she felt no pain. She trembled, yes, but it was with weariness and fear.

Calm.

If she could walk into the belly of the earth in her underthings, she could face an assassination attempt on the highway. She had the strength within herself. Or if not the strength, she had the stamina. She had the craft.

She touched the protruding arrowhead with her fingers. Even that light touch sent nauseating agony through her. But she gritted her teeth and stayed upright. She stayed in the saddle, and she did not scream.

She was Samarkar-la, and she was far from finished yet.

She reached down within herself and found the spark, the quiet, the flame in the darkness, and the darkness at the heart of the flame, paradoxically where the fire burned hottest. Payma drew up beside her, face grimly stoic, her gelding favoring a rear leg. Samarkar reached out and put her hand on Payma's thigh, feeling rough wool. Samarkar's wards flickered into tattered brilliance again, thin and worn in places, moth-eaten, threadbare—but there. If more arrows fell, Samarkar never saw them.

"We should charge them from behind," Payma said. "If your mare will fight."

"She's a steppe horse," Samarkar said. "Have you ever heard of one that wouldn't?"

The princess nodded, her lips bitten thin. She touched her gelding's neck. He snorted, mincing. When Samarkar turned her head, she could see the dark wetness that streaked his flank.

"Go," Payma said, both hands on the reins, and touched her gelding forward as Temur loosed the first of three arrows shot in such quick succession Samarkar barely saw his hand move.

It was only a half hundred strides or so to the spearmen. They had learned already tonight that Buldshak was faster over a distance, but the dun gelding had sharp speed in his chunky rump. In three leaps, during which his body bunched and extended like that of a frightened hare, he drew ahead, blood streaking his wounded haunch. Buldshak, irritated to be shown his hindquarters, shook her head and stretched out to compete, nibbling at his lead.

He was still ahead when they swept into the disorganized spearmen, snorting and kicking out. Buldshak bulled into one of the men who was still standing, knocking him aside. He clutched at Samarkar's wounded leg, trying to drag her from the saddle. She kicked him hard in the chest with the edge of the stirrup; Buldshak struck out with a hoof in passing; he let go and sat down.

Something fell past her from above, a russet blur in the morning gloom, silent as the grave. She heard the thud as it struck the man she'd knocked aside, and no other sound but the tearing of flesh.

This time, when she brought the mare around, no one remained to fight. Hrahima, her arms red halfway up the forearm, bleeding from new wounds, stood over one downed man.

Temur was rising from the side of another, his knife dripping in his hand. In the wash of green from Samarkar's wards, she saw his face twisted into a grimace, saw the way he moved without seeming to see.

He came straight toward her.

"Payma," she said. "Stay back."

She'd read of this before, men caught up in war rage, and she knew only one answer. Flexing her left arm sent showers of agony through her, and moving cloth against the arrow shaft was worse. Still she fumbled her jacket open, wincing through tears. Buldshak backed away as Temur came closer, as unnerved by him as was Samarkar. There was no time to unlace her halter; she simply grasped the lower hem in her right hand and yanked it up over her breasts. Fabric cut across her spine, burned her hooked fingers.

"Look at me, Temur," she called. "I am no warrior."

He faltered, staggering to a stop as his hind foot caught up to the fore. The knife lowered, and lines formed in his brow as he considered her. The light of intelligence flickered across his visage once more.

"Samarkar—" he said. And then, steadier, "Samarkar-la."

She nodded. He turned his gaze aside. Samarkar tugged her halter down, bruising the tops of her breasts this time. It was as much a need to busy herself as modesty. She felt waxen with pain. She swayed in circles over the saddle while Temur, chest still heaving, wiped his knife on a scrap of black cloth.

He had parted company with Bansh, and she stood three span away, square and stubborn as the mules.

"Archers?" he said, his voice rough and unsteady. The edge of the sun crept beyond the side of a mountain whose name Samarkar did not know. She squinted into the dazzle, shuddering, her nervous reaction or the smell of blood making Buldshak dance.

"Handled." Hrahima shrugged. "There were only three. I didn't manage the Nameless assassin, however." She touched a gash across her chest with more irritation than dismay. "He looked like he had an arrow in him, but it didn't slow him down much."

She snarled in distaste at the sticky fur of her arms, and tore a rag from a dead man's shirt to mop the worst of the blood away. Samarkar suspected she did not lick the fur clean mostly out of respect for the sensibilities of weak-stomached humans.

Payma had swung down from her mount and was examining the gelding's injuries. The harsh morning sun cast everything in stark shadows. Temur shaded his eyes. Payma made an irritated sound and said, "He took an arrow. We'll have to cut it out."

Temur looked at his knife. Samarkar said hastily, "I have a scalpel."

"You're wounded," Temur said, gesturing.

She glanced down; the tails of her coat hid the wound on her leg, but the wetness soaked her trousers to the knee, and the wound where the arrow had passed through her arm was finally starting to hurt as her heart slowed and her breathing came less like a bellows. She curled the arm up carefully and relaxed it, feeling sting and strain and a sharp throbbing. Trying to close her hand brought a worse gasp of pain.

"I won't be able to use the arm tomorrow," she said. "But it missed the bone and the artery. If I can keep the heat out of it, it won't kill me."

Gingerly, she moved to dismount. Hrahima was crouching to examine the clothing and implements of the dead men; Temur came forward to hold Buldshak steady while she got the foot on her injured leg out of the stirrup.

When she was grounded, she gently pinched the arrow shaft that pierced her arm below the fletching and thought of fire. Heat gathered in her fingertips, a slow process, measured in hundreds of heartbeats. But when she released it, it charred the width of the shaft to coals in a breath, and the fletching tumbled away.

"Temur," she said.

Understanding, he came forward and grasped the arrow by the head. "Ready?"

She nodded, and before the motion was complete, he pulled. The shaft was smooth, at least; it moved without snagging, and so she managed to scream between her teeth, muffled against her knuckles.

When she drew a breath in again, the morning wheeled around her. She put a hand out, and Temur steadied her.

"I've seen generals who didn't handle that so well," he said. "Now what?"

"I'll let this bleed for a little. The gelding next, unless—Payma, are you hurt?"

The princess shook her head. "Scratched," she said. "I'll go see if I can catch the mules."

"Take Bansh," Temur said, shaking his head. "She's not hurt. And she's sure-footed as a goat. I thought for sure we were going over the edge, but she must have glue on her hooves."

Samarkar showed the flat of her hand to the gelding. He snuffed her, and she stroked his velvet, porridge-colored nose, cupping his warm breath in her palm. "What's his name?"

Payma, turning away, stopped and laughed lightly. "I never asked," she said. "I guess we'll have to ask him what he wants to be called."

She nodded to Hrahima as she passed, and kept going. Samarkar trailed her hand along the gelding's shoulder as she walked back to the broken arrow jutting from his haunch. It had struck deep in the muscle, and blood still welled from around it. He favored the leg, holding it awkwardly off the ground. Samarkar didn't touch the wound, but she leaned close to it.

Payma was right; the arrowhead was barbed and would have to be cut free. But she could smear the cut with poppy to numb it. That would help.

She didn't relish doing the surgery here, on the edge of a cliff, surrounded by dead men—but asking the horse to move on with the arrow still imbedded in the wound was asking him to continue shredding his muscle. "Come hold his head?"

Temur did as she asked. A span or so away, Hrahima stood. She held up a crumpled scrap of rice paper, stained with red where she had touched the edges. There, sketched in confident, even flattering brush strokes, was a portrait of Temur.

"I think Qori Buqa knows you're alive," she said. "These dead men are not Nameless. They are mercenaries dressed as Nameless. But the one who fell or the one who fled—they might have been the real thing."

"How do you know?" Payma asked.

"The Nameless tattoo their hands," she said. "These have no marks."

Temur's face did a number of interesting things before he thought to press it against the gelding's neck. He took a breath, and when he turned back to them his voice was steady. "A good thing they didn't know I was traveling with a trio of warrior women. I wouldn't have stood a chance alone."

THE MERCENARY DEAD—WHEN TEMUR HAD A CHANCE TO EXAMINE them after helping Samarkar with her horse doctoring—did not resemble men of the east. They might not be Nameless, but like the Rahazeen he had met in his uncle Mongke's court, they were taller and of a leggier build, and when he unwrapped the black gauze veils that covered their heads and faces, their skin was a warmer shade of brown. They wore bronze helms under the veils, and leather armor under their flowing tunics.

The veils too were a hint that they were imposters, being black and not true indigo.

They had high-bridged noses and high-arched cheekbones, and their staring eyes were brown as tea. Tea going milky, as death began to cloud them.

They stank like any dead man, of urine and voided bowels. Their bows were of a different manufacture than his own, longer than the span of his arms, and so he could not use their arrows. Of the ones he'd fired, he could reclaim none. Two had been spent for nothing, one was gone with a bolted horse, and the other had plunged over the cliff. He'd lost a fifth himself when he nearly fell, and he mourned it bitterly. There would be no new arrows unless he made them.

Thoughtfully, he examined the western fletchings. There was nothing *wrong* with the shafts or the heads—or even the fletchings, which were the undyed feathers of some bird Temur had never seen. His own people fletched arrows with the feathers of vultures, the birds that carried souls to rest. But there was no reason he could not rework these. . . .

He gathered as many as he could, bundling them up and hanging them from the packs of one of the mules when Payma returned with them—two of them, anyway; she had been unable to find the third, and Temur hoped for all their sakes that the wizards had overpacked.

They threw the bodies off the road, first searching them for unspoiled food and other useful objects. While they worked, all five animals crunched grain in nose bags. The gelding wore an awkward bandage on his hip, but the poppy seemed to have eased his pain.

Samarkar sat on a rock nearby, darning her trousers where the arrow had cut them, having already packed her wounds with a bluish powder and wrapped them tightly in white cotton gauze. It shone against the sturdy curve of her thigh, and Temur had to keep reminding himself not to stare. She winced as she pinched the needle, leading him to wonder if she had hurt her right hand, too. Payma slumped against a rock, snatching a few moments of sleep, and Hrahima stood sentry at the outside curve of the road, where she could see a distance in both directions.

Finally, Samarkar heaved herself up, struggled into the trousers, and stood painfully. She'd tied a sling for her injured arm but was not using it now. He knew that her wounds—especially the deep puncture in her arm—would stiffen overnight, the insulted muscles knotting hard as wood around them. Tomorrow, moving her leg or arm would be an agony. He'd have to massage the gelding's leg tonight, if he was going to be able to walk tomorrow. Temur did not fancy leading a lame horse through more mountain roads, but they'd need the gelding if he healed. In the meantime, Payma could double up on Bansh or Buldshak, but that would wear the mares out faster, and they did not have remounts so the horses could rest on alternate days.

They were—unavoidably—going to do some walking. And Payma's feet would not stand up to much of that until they healed, then hardened.

It would have been a hard enough journey with all of them sound and hale. Starting the trip exhausted and injured . . .

Temur shook his head. He was making things worse, not better. He gave Samarkar a small smile of encouragement and said, "Come on. Let's put some more ground under us before sunset."

Samarkar nodded. But she touched his hand and drew him toward Bansh's saddlebags. "All right. But you have to eat something while we ride."

Her palm was cold; her fingers trembled. "I will if you will," he said.

14

In the days that followed, they never found the other rider or his horse, and Temur was forced to assume—despite the arrow, despite the Cho-tse—that he had survived. But neither did they encounter any more Rahazeen assassins—real or feigning—nor Rasan men-at-arms, and under Samarkar's care their various wounds healed rapidly. There was something to be said for wizards.

They followed a road through passes that lead more west than north until the mountains flattened enough that they could pick their way across forested foothills, and then they followed the sun—the Rasan sun, and then the sun of the Eternal Sky. They came out of the Steles of the Sky into the western reaches of the steppe, rather than passing through the Range of Ghosts. They descended the last foothill of the mountains at midday, as summer was sweeping the plains. The smell of sweetgrass was a balm to Temur. The Eternal Sky above shone a blue like the turquoise beads adorning the eight blue knots on a shaman-rememberer's saddle. Other than birds, the first steppe wildlife they saw was a herd of ten or so Indrik-zver. These were long-necked, dust-colored beasts so massive a mounted man could ride under their rotund bellies. They took no notice of the people or the equines, even when the party's route brought them within four or five *ayls*, though one great female with a cow-sized newborn gamboling about her feet turned to watch Hrahima pass. She made a sound of alarm or threat, a deep-chested huffing rumble combined with a hollow boom, which brought the ears of all the mules and horses up and had them scanning the horizon for predators.

The mules and horses had grown accustomed to Hrahima, apparently deciding that she did not eat horses, and in return she was careful to stay away from them when she came back from a hunt bearing fresh meat. The steppe ponies were used enough to dead animals, but it seemed wise not to force them to deal with a *bloody* tiger.

Temur could tell from Payma and Samarkar's wide eyes and the way they turned to stare that the women had never seen an Indrik-zver.

"What is that?" Payma asked.

Temur was glad to explain. "They only live along the edge of the steppe, where they can retreat among the hills when the rivers dry up. They're named for a magic beast of the far west," Temur said, "where the mushroom people live."

"'Mushroom people'?" Payma pointed to the ground.

Temur shook his head. "Their faces are pale, like mushrooms, and they burn in the sun, as if you held them beside a fire. They call themselves Russhi or sometimes Kyivvin, as if anybody could get a tongue around that."

Samarkar snorted laughter. Temur let himself meet her eyes and smile.

He said, "My grandfather conquered them before I was born. They have a beast of legend called the Indrik, which is like those"—he pointed with his chin—"but it has a horn on its nose. It dwells in a sacred mountain where no other foot may tread, and when it moves, the whole earth trembles. I knew a mushroom person in Qarash, an old man whom my grandfather took as tribute when he was young. He was a goldsmith. He told me about the Indrik."

"Huh," Samarkar said. The set of her shoulders was uncomfortable, hunched up to her ears, but Temur did not think she was upset with him. "We say the earth moves when the Dragon Mother stirs inside the Cold Fire."

"Different skies. Different gods," Temur said, repeating the wisdom of his mother. Now that they were under Quersnyk skies again, he still checked the moons every nightfall, and every nightfall they remained the same. And every morning, he arose before the sun and guarded the others against ghosts—but they, too, did not come.

In some ways the lack of change was worse; it was both a hammer over his head and a peace that might lull him into complacence.

He waited until Samarkar nodded before he looked away.

"Anyway," she said, "we should pick up some of their dung for burning."

Temur breathed easier to find himself no longer hemmed in by mountains, foothills, and forests. Here in his homeland, you could see an enemy coming as clearly as you could see the vultures that circled overhead until the sun set and the sky darkened. The grass crushed under horse hooves smelled of sage, and there were herbs to boil for tea growing among it.

Where they stopped for the evening, the pale disks of datura blossoms shone through the dusk like small moons, nodding on vines that bound and bowed the long grasses. He made sure to hobble the horses well away from the poisonous plant. When that was done and they were all rubbed down and eating lazily, he made his way back to the fire circle. The women had prepared it by yanking up turf so the grass could not catch fire in the roots and set the whole steppe ablaze. Now Payma was sorting their supplies. Samarkar was piling dry Indrik-zver dung up with air spaces between the clods, so a fire could catch easily. Hrahima had slipped into the dusk to seek prey.

Temur hunkered down beside Samarkar. He drew his flint and steel from inside his vest and began kindling a spark on a flat stone she'd heaped with dry grass. Her shoulders were still hunched protectively, her chin dropped.

As the flint scraped down the file, shedding sparks, he said, "You're as stiff as butter in a cold house. Is something wrong?"

The tinder caught immediately, and Temur muttered a thanks to the spirit of the fire while Samarkar considered his question. "It's hard for me to leave the mountains," she said at last, quietly. "The sky is too big."

And he could appreciate what Anil-la had left unsaid, to know that she had not enjoyed her last sojourn away from Tsarepheth. He nodded to direct her attention to Payma, who had paused in assembling dinner preparations to lift her face to the wind and take deep breaths of the wide space spread all around them, except to the south where the mountains loomed still.

"She enjoys it," Temur said. "But I understand—sort of—how you feel. In the mountains everything was too thick and close, and the sky was heavy overhead."

"Yes," she said. "It's higher out here, too."

The tinder was burning merrily as Temur slid the flat stone carefully into the air space under the dung. He watched flames bathe the underside of Samarkar's pyramid, igniting glowing embers, and hunkered forward to blow gently across the fire.

When it caught solidly, he leaned back, satisfied, and rubbed his hands together. "If you think this is bad, wait until we reach the Salt Desert."

WHEN SAADET APPEARED AT THE DOOR OF THE SCRIPTORIUM DURING al-Sepehr's prayers, al-Sepehr knew the news was ill. Through twisting apprehension, he forced himself to remain calm. To copy to the bottom of the page before he stood and left the scriptorium. Saadet turned and walked beside him, matching his pace with a man's stride.

"We failed," Saadet said crisply, in her brother's tones. No excuses. "Re Temur fled Tsarepheth before we made it. He is traveling in the company of a Cho-tse and a Rasan witch. And a runaway princess, who carries the dead prince's child. I imagine there is a bird en route from your Rasan ally—"

"Too slow by half," al-Sepehr said, doubling his fists inside his sleeves. He forced his hands to open. He paused before the balustrade surrounding the courtyard and laid his hands on white stone, forcing himself to focus on the words of scripture written black across their backs. "Aban?"

"Dead," said Saadet for her brother. "I saved his hands."

"His family will be grateful." A wave of exhaustion blurred al-Sepehr's vision: He could summon the ghosts, but could he survive the summoning? *Not so soon after Qeshqer*, he thought. They were hungry things, and though they did not draw so much from their summoner as from their prey, to raise ten thousand of them had cost more than he'd anticipated. "Follow," he said. "If he's traveling with a gravid woman, he will be slowed. Overtake him. I will send the birds to find him, and Saadet will show your path. That is all."

"Thank you, al-Sepehr." Saadet bowed like a man and arose with a woman's grace. She looked up at al-Sepehr from behind her veil. "Have you further need of me?"

He waved her away so she would not see him leaning heavily on the rail. Once she was gone, he drew a breath or two and made sure his veil was neat across his face. Then he turned his back to a featureless wall, so as to afford Qori Buqa as little intelligence about Ala-Din as possible, and pulled the appropriate stone from his pocket.

He held it up and concentrated on it while the dried blood flaked onto his fingers. A moment later, the ghostly visage of the Qersnyk usurper swam before him, wavering like rising smoke.

In spare words, al-Sepehr sketched the situation. "My man is in pursuit of Re Temur. I believe we will have him soon."

Qori Buqa sighed like a tired horse. "There are rumors everywhere that Otgonbayar's brat means to raise an army against me. I cannot raise my banner while he lives and can be seen to oppose me. The clans will not gather if I call them now, and I will lose any chance of ever uniting them. I cannot be Khagan while Re Temur lives, unless he bends to me. So send your ghosts, al-Sepehr! I am tired of waiting!"

"It's not that simple," al-Sepehr said. "You must trust me to deal with him my way. Have I not earned that?"

Qori Buqa clasped long hands before his mouth, then let them drop out of sight. "You have," he said. He glanced away, as if looking over his shoulder. "But I beg you, al-Sepehr. Make haste. Make haste, or there will be no Khagan."

FOR MANY DAYS THEY TRAVELED WITHOUT TROUBLE, AND SAMARKAR felt the terror of that night ride through the mountains start to ebb. If she had ever been about to forget that they were running before a devil, though, Temur's weariness, worry, and the way he checked the sky each moonrise would have kept it present in her mind.

He only spoke of it once, though, at dawn on their fourth day, when he came to her with bloody, seared meat—Hrahima's kill—and hunkered beside her while she tore at it with knife and teeth. Payma had finished loading the mules, and only eating remained before they set out once more.

"Before my uncle Mongke died," he said softly, "A rider could go from the Song border to Asitaneh in six weeks, with remounts and rest at the Khagan's outposts along the way. But the roads are unmaintained, and the outposts emptied by the war."

Hot juice ran down Samarkar's throat as she chewed. She licked blood from the back of her hand. There was nothing she could say to address the loss in his voice, so she touched his hand and changed the subject. "We'll reach the Celadon Highway in another quartermoon or so." She glanced at the skies, at the thirteen unchanging moons. "I mean, in a little more than a hand of days."

If her failing manners made her less the once-princess in his eyes, it never showed in his courtesy. "Until we leave it for Nilufer's Stone Steading. It might be better to move cross-country, where there is less chance of being overtaken by Songtsan's men."

"Or headed by al-Sepehr's," Hrahima said, from where she lay among long grasses, her broad hands propped on the meat-distended mound of her belly. The Cho-tse did not dine every night, but when she did, she dined in quantity. They would move more slowly today, in deference to Hrahima's sluggishness, but they would make it up on the morrow.

The four of them were developing a sort of language of their own, a pidgin of Temur's milk tongue and that of Samarkar and Payma, with Cho-tse words thrown in as Hrahima acquainted them with a few. But as the days wore on, Temur began insisting that they all practice Qersnyk, which was the language of Nilufer Khatun's principality. Samarkar knew this was for Payma's benefit, because Hrahima seemed to pick up human languages—"monkey-tongues," as she called them—with ridiculous ease, and Samarkar already knew enough Qersnyk to get by.

But when Payma was elsewhere, Temur rode close to Samarkar and made her help him practice the Uthman tongue, dialects of which were spoken from Asmaracanda as far west as Ctesifon.

For the first hand of days, the mist-wreathed mountains still loomed so huge behind them it seemed Samarkar could just walk over there in an afternoon. Bit by bit, the haze of distance began to cut them off from their feet. Then they seemed to float over the earth, and Samarkar had to force herself to train her eyes on the blank and endless waves of grass crawling under the wind before her. Looking back was like pulling the stitches from an unhealed wound, too much like the view from her tower window in Prince Ryi's palace.

On the tenth day they came to and crossed one river that had dropped from flood but was yet too deep to ford, though the horses could just about tiptoe across. Payma and Samarkar stripped and plunged into the water, which still ran cold from the snowpack that spawned it, though days of sun crossing the steppe had taken the worst of the edge off. Hrahima swam too, with apparent unconcern for how it plastered her fur to her body and twisted her ruff to dripping spikes. Temur, however, stood on Bansh's saddle, keeping the water out of his boots, and held the women's clothes above the flood.

The current was still fast enough to push them a *li* downstream in the time it took to cross, but fortunately there were gravel beaches along both sides of the ford. Samarkar stood up out of the water, dripping, gasping with cold, slapping her arms and thighs to feel anything in them. Payma was red all over her body, cradling her belly with one arm and wiping water from her face with the other, fingertips and toetips dusky with chill.

That was as far as they got that day, because having crossed, they camped on the far bank to build fires, spread their bodies and belongings in the afternoon sun, and fill their bottles against the next long dry stretch of steppe.

The river flowed northwest, and Samarkar wondered aloud if they could follow it to the inland sea whose trade fed the great port cities of Asmaracanda—once Uthman, now Qersnyk—and Asitaneh—which was Uthman still.

"Probably," Temur said. He'd just finished rubbing the horses and mules dry with rough cloth and was giving them sweets mixed with mutton fat, for warmth and energy. "It's the Red Stone River, unless I miss my guess." He waved at the round rocks and jumbled boulders that filled its bed; they were indeed mostly of a dark pinkish granite. Then, as if what he'd said disturbed him, he turned away with some excuse about finding more driftwood for a fire.

Samarkar watched him go, frowning until she felt more than heard Hrahima come up beside her. The Cho-tse watched him go, and huffed. "Will you come with him to Asitaneh?" she asked. "Or will you stay with Payma and her son?"

Samarkar glanced at Payma. The princess's hair was bleached to a reddish black by the sun, her face burnished as bronze as any Qersnyk girl's. She was unselfconsciously laying wet clothes across clumps of grass to dry, like a peasant woman, her belly and breasts and back bare to the warmth of the sun. The dark wings of vultures drifted lazily overhead in the heat of the day, and Samarkar—reluctant though she was to succumb to it—felt a still peace steal over her.

"Asitaneh?" she said. "I thought once we found safety for Payma, he was raising a Qersnyk army to oust his uncle and wrest his woman away from your necromancer priest." *And make himself Khan or Khagan, as the case may be.*

Hrahima laughed, a *ch-ch-ch* with a rumble that seemed to come from deep in her chest. Samarkar remembered from legend that the Cho-tse could not lie; it was why they were so often paid as messengers. She wondered if that had something to do with the religion Hrahima claimed she had abandoned.

The Cho-tse said, "Do you recollect what he said about Ato Tesefahun?"

"Your patron? That his daughter married a horse-lord—"

Hrahima made a left-handed brushing gesture, as if dismissing the word *patron*. But she said, "Ato Tesefahun is Temur's grandfather. Why do you think he has you teaching him the Uthman tongue? He means to go on to Asitaneh, to cross the White Sea and the Uthman Narrows and present himself to his grandfather."

She paused. Samarkar was learning to distinguish that motion of Hrahima's ears and whiskers as the Cho-tse equivalent of a smile. The tigers only curled their lips to snarl.

"I thought Ato Tesefahun was in Ctesifon."

"He was," Hrahima said. "But I am to meet him in Asitaneh." She gestured to Temur's back. "His grandfather will likely welcome him," she said, confidingly. "Especially if he brings news of his mother."

Samarkar pressed her hands together. "Don't you think it strange—coincidental—that you met him, and me, as you did?"

Hrahima shrugged. Her tail lashed. "My people would say there is no strangeness. No coincidence in destiny."

"But you don't believe in destiny. Even when it presents itself at your door?"

The Cho-tse bent, picked up a flat stone, and skipped it across the rushing river. The smile left her ears. "Ah," she said. "You remembered."

Whatever Samarkar might have said next, she lost it in the shriek of a bird of prey. Something big beat blue-gray wings against the sky, mobbed by vultures behaving as Samarkar had never seen vultures behave. The larger bird side-slipped below the carrion fowl, as in turn they folded wings and dive-bombed it like angry hawks. Samarkar heard the impacts clearly, each time it failed to dodge the assaults. She winced as one last vulture struck the larger bird, knocking it in a tumble of limp plumage from the sky.

Instantly, Hrahima was off in pursuit, leaping through tall grass. A moment later, she returned, carrying some crested raptor that Samarkar did not recognize by its long, broken neck.

"What's that?"

Hrahima shrugged.

Temur had somehow appeared beside them. "I've never seen anything like that before," he said. "Vultures attacking a—what is that?"

Hrahima held it up, pulling a wing wide to display the span. "Food?"

IN HER NEW FREEDOM—IF YOU COULD CALL VEILED ANONYMITY IN such an inescapable fastness as Ala-Din "freedom"—Edene toiled with all her will. It was better than thinking, and Saadet's company was pleasant. Because they did not share a language, Saadet had to first show Edene every task and how it was done. But Edene learned quickly, and in short order they began exchanging a few words. They developed their own shorthand language, and through it, Edene began to learn a little of the Uthman tongue.

At least there was enough sky, stretched out on all sides, even if it was the wrong color. And at least she had the filthy, exhausting, but ultimately rewarding work of caring for the mewed birds to distract her. She had always enjoyed caring for animals over other work. Now she lost herself in it, scrubbing and carrying as her belly swelled, and tried not to remember that she toiled as a slave.

She particularly enjoyed working with the male rukh. She felt a bond to him, in the clipped wings and chains he wore physically and she in her heart.

Though she worked almost ceaselessly, like any Qersnyk woman bearing, she still found time to explore the bastion of the Nameless—

and to learn what she could of the group. They brought her to services, where she knelt with the other women, divided from the men by filigreed barriers. She heard al-Sepehr's prayers in Uthman and learned a few more words, but not enough to understand the sense of the thing. His charisma moved her, though, and she noticed he still made time to dine with her a few times in a hand of days.

So it was not too unexpected when on one sunny day he came to her—rather than sending Saadet or a servant—and said, "Come and dine in my quarters today."

Edene, who had just come in from bringing water to the rukh—which she did from beneath a metal grate, lest he decide to snatch up one of his attendants and make a meal of her—looked from al-Sepehr to her own sweat-soaked robes. She had sweated into her veil until it stuck against her face, but she knew better than to pick it away. She could not quite keep herself from covering the small rise of her belly with her hand, however. Qersnyk women knew about being raided away, willing or no, by men of other tribes. Edene's own mother had been brought to the Tsareg clan by a husband who had cut her and her cart out of a traveling band.

If he kept that ring in the pocket of his robe, this might be her best chance to get it.

"When I have cleaned myself," she said. And an hour later, she met him in his own austere chamber.

She knew not all the monks were celibate; some practiced with each other, some upon the women of the stronghold. To her surprise, however, al-Sepehr offered her no attentions beyond conversation and spiced lamb over some pearls of flour and water—dumplings the size of grains of sand. He made polite conversation, poured her tea, and averted his eyes from her face when she lowered her veil to place morsels of food in her mouth.

At one point, when he rose to fetch water, she took a moment to glance around his chamber. Spare, as she had noticed. Far plainer than her own. There was a low pallet, barely padded over stone. There was a chest at its foot.

And on the chest in a wooden tray lay a few personal articles, including a plain beaten band of green gold.

Edene might just have been about to touch it—her fingers trembling, twisted together behind her back, like those of a child who knows she's not supposed to steal a preemptive bite of supper—when al-Sepehr returned with a tray of ices.

"I remembered you liked these," he said, as she stepped away from the bed, grateful for the veil that hid her expression. "And it's so hot out."

She went back to her room frowning and contemplative. Her feet ached and her back ached, but her nausea was ebbing. If she was going to escape, she must do so now while she could still move and, no matter how uncomfortably, still run.

All the monks of the place spent their time each day in copying when they were not in the practice yard fighting. She began to get a sense of the rhythms of the place, the hours when things happened, the hours when things changed.

Until one day the pattern changed.

Edene awoke when dawn crept through the arched window of her room, painting the whitewashed stone window-ledge in rose and gold. Later in the day, the awnings would keep the afternoon sun from doing the same, but for now she had the glow. With it came unaccustomed raucous sounds from the courts below.

When she went to the window, veiling her face first, and leaned out, she witnessed a familiar kind of chaos. Everywhere, men bustled. They strapped on swords and piled goods into packs. They strode about with apparent ferocity of purpose, though Edene had no idea where they were going, and sometimes she saw the same one cross a courtyard repeatedly, seemingly at random.

These were monks and not Qersnyk, but an army preparing to march to battle looked the same at Ala-Din as it did among the white-houses of Qarash.

This, Edene thought. *This is my chance.*

✳   ✳   ✳

Beyond the river, the steppe continued. It receded until it merged with the sky, gold and green, stretching out until Samarkar felt herself lost in the heart of something so vast and boundless that she took refuge in that emptiness she'd discovered in the dark under the Citadel. If she was nothing, then no vastness could make her small.

In that there was peace, as in the endless ripples of wind across tossing grasses racing to meet them, the endless bands of white clouds scudding across a windowpane sky. Her hair tangled in the ceaseless breezes; it blew from its braid and trailed across her eyes. They saw animals again—more Indrik-zver, antelope, wild horses with their dirty-black manes and dust-colored hides, the omnipresent vultures, and a steppe eagle with wings so broad Samarkar mistook it for a vulture, until Temur pointed out how its wings made the shape of a bow, not a triangle. Songbirds and crows harried at it as it flew, dwarfed by the spread of its wings.

Five hands and a day after leaving the mountains, they intersected the great road that led from Song to Messaline.

The Celadon Highway was named not for any quality of its own, but for the color of the rare and valuable pottery brought along it from the east.

It looked, Temur had to admit, somewhat unprepossessing—two ruts through the long grass, running to the east and west—until you stared at it long enough to realize that the ruts faded into blue distance in either direction without showing a bend or a curve.

Samarkar stood up in her stirrups, craning along the length of the road. "Surely they don't use . . . wagons?"

"Carts," Temur said. "The clans use this road as well as traders. And our women's carts can go anywhere on the steppe. Some of the caravans use carts as well. Some use beasts of burden."

Payma said, "The ruts are overgrown."

Temur nodded. "No caravans without the peace of the Khagan."

The princess reached down and scratched the ear of the mule

nosing along her saddle. Temur, too, was growing fond of the mules—
they were sturdy and steadfast and smarter than most horses. *Besides Bansh,* he corrected himself.

The mare snorted as if she could hear him thinking. He would not have been particularly surprised. "Come on," he said. "Let's ride."

"Wait a minute," Payma said, swinging her awkward belly over the saddle to dismount. "While we're stopped, I have to pee."

AFTER THE FIRST STORM, THERE WERE NO OTHERS, CALMING TEMUR'S fears. As the nights warmed, they made cold camps except when there was meat to cook, and so they covered ground faster than he had dared hope despite the need to rest and graze the horses. Payma's belly swelled like a puffball mushroom, and her ankles swelled like sausages. She had to be suffering, but she made no complaint over long days in the saddle, confirming Temur's ever-more-favorable opinion of Rasan royal women.

She did let him and Samarkar take over more of the work of setting camp as days went by. Twice they were awakened in the night by the territorial cough of the great steppe lion. Twice Hrahima replied, then they heard nothing more. The grass faded to ashy gold as the summer's true heat manifested. The little party refilled their water at stagnant shallow lakes gone jewel-green, straining it through folds of cloth to remove the algae and the threat of cholera. Sometimes they went so long between water sources that Samarkar had to pull it from the air. In providing for three people, the Cho-tse, and five equines, she exhausted herself, and Temur worried what they would do when they reached the desert.

They met no caravans bound for Qarash—a sign Temur welcomed, for it hinted that Qori Buqa was having trouble consolidating his rule. No sensible caravan master would lead his train into the teeth of war or banditry. Indeed, Temur and the others did find the charred remains of one cart train led by a rash or desperate master, thus proving the wisdom of the others.

Safe roads had been another gift of the Great Khagan's peace.

Temur found himself half satisfied that Qori Buqa had not yet made himself Khagan in fact as well as name, and half sorrowful to see his grandfather's achievement crumble within the lifetime of his sons.

Perfect flatness gave way to rolling countryside, brown and treeless, and the westernmost horn of the Steles of the Sky edged up over the horizon.

"We turn south here," Temur said, trying to hold a half-remembered map before his mind's eye while imagining how it would look seen as a landscape. "Nilufer's stronghold is somewhere among the roots of that range."

"Good," Samarkar said.

Payma only sighed. Relief, he thought, and Temur could in no way fault her for it.

When they noticed the first *talus*, they knew they could not be far from Nilufer's Stone Steading. Payma and Samarkar had been scanning the steepening hillsides with focused attention, alert to the legendary living boulders—as well as their legendary bandit tribes, which were probably growing larger and more dangerous again with the death of Mongke Khagan and the civil war among his relatives.

But it was Hrahima who spotted one first.

It resembled nothing so much as a shaggy, lichen-coated slab, moving as slowly as the sun, so its progress was impossible to track unless you glanced at it repeatedly and noticed it shifting against the background. But there was a trail in the rock behind it, and if Samarkar listened very intently, she could hear the grinding noise as its mouth parts wore away the stone.

It was not as large as she had imagined. In her head, the *talus* were more like small hills than boulders. But this one was perhaps ten paces long and two men tall—gigantic for a living thing, but not too big as rocks went.

Temur swung down from the saddle when they drew abreast of it and led Bansh over. Samarkar would have imitated him, but Buldshak being what she was, she handed the reins to Payma before she followed. She might have felt bad about it, but Payma evinced no interest in going close to the beast. Which was probably more sensible than Samarkar's combination of audacity and curiosity.

When she came up on him, Temur was walking speculatively around the great, placid living stone. Samarkar heard the grinding from within it. She had read that the *talus* were docile. Now she extended her hand to touch its flank, testing the theory.

It paid her no heed. The rough gray skin was as hard as the stone it resembled. It did not dent like flesh under her touch, and it was the temperature you'd expect of sun-warmed rock.

"This is a wild *talus*," Temur said, having completed his circuit.

"How do you know?" Samarkar stepped back to save her toes as it inched forward, chewing away.

He gestured to its flanks. "No marks. The herdsmen file symbols into the skin so they can identify their beasts."

Men cultivated—could you say domesticated?—the *talus* to use for mining. They consumed stone, excreting the metal, and their guts tended to be full of hard jewels—diamonds, sapphires, rubies—that they swallowed, much as a chicken pecks up gravel.

"Still," Samarkar said. "We must be close."

"Yes. And finding this one so close to the track unmolested tells me the bandit armies have not yet returned to claim these lands. Which is very good news."

"Indeed."

Samarkar knew from his discourses on the subject that the Great Khagan had first driven the bandit tribes from these lands. These mountains had long been a holdfast for lawless men who preyed upon the caravans of the Celadon Highway and upon the *talus* for their precious bellyfuls of jewels.

As the Great Khagan aged, those lawless men had tried to reclaim supremacy, but his son and daughter-in-law had driven them out, though the skirmishing had cost the life of Nilufer's mother, the Dowager Khatun. Samarkar might have initially thought Temur a simple barbarian, but she was starting to realize that his head was as much an encyclopedia of sophisticated family politics as her own.

"What gods do these people observe?" she asked, as they made their way back to the horses. "Surely Nilufer is no Qersnyk name."

"It's Messaline, I think. Before your ancestors pushed them back and made a crack for the Uthman Caliphate to expand into, their empire reached this far." Temur shrugged. "My grandfather had no interest in forcing conversions. He conquered for wealth and to gain scholars and artisans. All faiths are equal under the Eternal Sky."

Samarkar hid a smile. *All faiths are equal, under mine.* Not such an uncommon sentiment.

It wasn't actually the differences between tribes that caused wars. It was the ways in which all people were alike.

She said, "This is the borderlands."

He said, "It was also Uthman once, but the Great Salt Desert lies between Stone Steading and the Uthman cities. And the Steles of the Sky fence it away from the steppe and from your people. If it weren't for the *talus,* no one would live here at all. But as it stands, though this is a small kingdom and isolated, it is wealthy."

"And friendly."

He smiled. "We hope."

When they finally came within sight of Stone Steading, Samarkar was surprised at how much it looked like home. By the richness of the air, she could tell they were far lower than any Rasan city except perhaps the southern capital itself—but what she *saw* as they rode down into it was a broad valley surrounded on three sides by mountainous foothills terraced for agriculture. The fields there were green with summer rice; Samarkar suspected the paddies were fed by qanats bringing water from the glaciers above. The rice fields could then be drained and the water used a second time—to irrigate the apricot and almond trees below.

Little crofts and stands of trees scattered the dished valley floor, surrounded by fields of wheat and cotton and hedged pastures flocked with fat-tailed sheep. She saw the glint of water in irrigation ditches, and the cackle of hens rose up on the dry air, carrying who knew how far. People went about in clothes dyed homespun colors, hauling fat bundles or driving oxcarts.

Beyond this richness, closer to the mountain, stood a pillared stronghold with a pair of tall white towers and a hall between, capped with an onion-shaped dome such as Samarkar had seen only in paintings. The dome glinted in the afternoon sun, reflecting sparks of crimson and cobalt like light shining through a diamond. Samarkar could tell even from here that it was decorated with glass tile, though she could not make out the pattern.

Buldshak huffed around her bit, scenting water.

"Well," Payma said. "We're here."

They had only begun their descent into the valley when a group of ten riders broke from the stronghold's gates, coming along the high road at a brisk canter. Ten was a good number, Samarkar thought. Enough—and responding quickly enough—to make a point, not so many as to startle a peaceable group into flight. Peasants came out along the road to watch Samarkar's party ride in, which also felt familiar, but these folks did not wear the lined vests and flap-fronted shirts that Samarkar's folk preferred. Their faces were more angular, the eyes rounder, the noses higher bridged. She could see the evidence of Rasan and Qersnyk blood in some faces, and western heritage—Uthman, Messaline—in most.

When the riders came closer, she could see that their armor, too, was in a western style—conical helms and studded leather cuirasses— and their swords were scimitars. But what made Samarkar blink and turn with raised brows to Temur was that two of them were women.

And one of those women was the leader.

She dressed unlike the others, in a breastplate over monkish robes dyed orange-red with madder and with barberry. She was not young, but she carried herself with a straight back. She seemed like the curved blade at her hip: The hilt was worn, and Samarkar imagined the blade would show scrapes of honing along the edge, but she would not care to fence with the woman who carried it.

She glanced from left to right and saw Temur and Payma both hanging back. Hrahima stood at the rear of the group, so still your eye could skip over her.

Isn't this supposed to be Temur's family?

Samarkar sighed and raised her hands, showing them empty except for the reins. "I am Samarkar-la, a wizard of the Citadel of Tsarepheth. With me are my brother's wife Payma, the Cho-tse Hrahima, and Re Temur. We seek sanctuary and your mistress's indulgence, by way of Temur's kinship to her."

She stood aside so Temur could come forward. He moved Bansh up without visibly shifting his weight or moving his hands, as if the bay were an extension of his body. She halted shoulder-to-shoulder with Buldshak, shying a half step as the gray nipped air near her neck.

Temur controlled her without seeming to notice that she'd shifted. "I am Re Temur," he said. "What Samarkar-la says is true. Nilufer Khatun, the Dowager Regent, was married to my uncle Re Toghrul. I wish to throw myself upon her mercy."

The monkish warrior woman looked them up and down. Her hair had once been black as a bay horse's mane. Her piercing eyes were still sharply contemplative. She considered the rise of Payma's belly, the bulky shoulders of the Cho-tse. Samarkar could almost see her adding columns of benefits and disadvantages behind the impassive mask of her eyes.

"Ride ahead," she said at last. "We will follow. The way should be obvious."

And of course it was.

THEY ENTERED THE STRONGHOLD THROUGH THE MAIN GATE, AFTER A trio of grooms came to relieve them of their mules and horses. Temur was reluctant to let the animals and baggage out of his sight, and even more so his bow. He kept his knife, and he imagined if worse came to worst he could relieve one of the guards of his or her weapon.

The local bows were different. They were longer, of a pale amber-white wood rather than laminate, and he could see from the position of the arrow rest that they were meant to be shot with a tab or fingertips rather than a horn thumb-ring. But Temur was confident he could get inside one if necessary and make it sing.

Now the four of them crossed the packed-earth yard to the main doors. These were tall edifices of polished wood, peaked at the tops in order to fit snugly in the arched doorway. One stood open, and people came and went through it in great profusion. They gave way for the guards escorting the small party.

Inside, a wide corridor led across mosaic tiles to the arched and echoing space below the dome. It was decorated inside as well as out, the colors resolving into bright geometric patterns.

The height and the weight of all that stone lofted overhead made Temur dizzy. He glanced down again in time to keep himself from tripping as they passed from small bright inlaid tiles to larger flag-stones. It seemed the dome was just for show, a kind of grand entry-way, because no one was at work there except the guards standing at attention beside each set of doors. Just as well, Temur thought. He'd hate to spend too much time under those bizarrely suspended stones, waiting for the sky to fall.

They moved through a series of corridors—nothing like those in the Citadel or the Great Khagan's winter palace in the territories that had once been northern Song, but sufficiently imposing (and en-closing) after spending most of a season between the empty hori-zons. Temur was also amused to see that once they were beyond the glittering white marble facade, these inner corridors were hewn from prosaic—and harder-wearing—granite. Perhaps this was an old stronghold, wrapped by the sparkling modern facade. Or per-haps the wealth of such a small principality only stretched so far, even with the taxes levied upon the *talus* herders.

Finally, however, the guards led them to a small chamber and left them there. One monkish woman warrior remained. The room was furnished in the Song style but with broad windows open on a courtyard garden. Sunlight trickled through green leaves and honey-scented blossoms. Rice-paper screens had been pushed back to allow the air and light to move unimpeded, and the floor was thick with cushions, rugs, and low tables of just the height to take a bite out of an incautious man's ankle. Everything was embroidered—gold flowers and dragons on silk, windmills and elegant trees. A fine celadon vase sat on a table in the corner, dripping a profusion of midsummer blooms—peonies, poppies, and some Temur could not identify.

Temur had to glance out the window to remind himself that he was not in Song. They did not build this way there, and nothing in that far kingdom matched the shadow of the Steles mounting above the garden walls.

The far door opened, and a woman younger than Temur had anticipated stepped within. Not young, of course, but perhaps only ten years or so beyond Samarkar's age, with white strands brushed from her temples into the elaborate coils of her hair. Perhaps she was a sister or a servant, he thought. He would have been expected to be relieved of his knife before he met the Dowager Khatun herself.

But no, this woman wore an ivory gown of Song silk, brocaded with a motif of tiny dragons in gold and green. It was fit for a queen, and this woman carried herself like one.

She was tall and broad-hipped, well proportioned to Temur's eye, built more like a Qersnyk woman than the willowy western princesses he recollected from Qarash. She had a face that showed some Rasan or Qersnyk descent—almond eyes with smooth eyelids, oval cheeks—but her skin was the pale olive-wood color of the southern Song—or, Temur supposed, the Uthman mountain people.

She carried herself straight as a wand. The top seams of her sleeves had been left open, so graceful swags of fabric swung from shoulder to wrist and left her arms largely bare, showing the strong cables of tendons in her forearms, the firm curve of her upper arms. Qersnyk women who hunted had arms like that, and the delicate scar that curved like a lash around her left wrist was the mark of a bowstring snapped under pressure.

Temur bowed from the waist, not quite willing to prostrate himself. He was aware of Samarkar at his side, also bowing so the sweep of her travel-worn coat fell about her legs, and of Payma and Hrahima making their obeisances behind, though Hrahima's was little more than a shallow bow.

He said, "Nilufer Khatun. I am Re Temur. I have come from Qarash and Tsarepheth with grave news of our family, and to beg a boon of you."

Nilufer gestured to the cushions and the low tables. "Sit, please," she said, her eyes on Payma, who rocked from one swollen foot to the other as subtly as she could. "I'll send for tea."

She did not seem to issue any such command, just seating herself at one of the low tables and leaving her guests to sort themselves as they saw fit. But by the time Temur had seen to Payma's comfort and Hrahima reclined against a bolster, there was tea and some small dry cakes and a bowl of peeled boiled eggs cooked in spiced tea. He took a cake and an egg, to be polite, and passed the bowl to Hrahima. She sniffed the eggs dubiously but took one.

Temur tasted the cake—sweet and sharp with honey and spices— and washed it down with tea that smelled of roses. "Perhaps you have heard," he began, "that the Khaganate is at war with itself? It seems the unrest is spreading. . . ."

Awkwardly, he spoke for almost an hour—with occasional interruptions for clarification from the others or questions from Nilufer. When he was done, he sat back and cradled a fresh bowl of tea. His mouth ached.

"So this woman, Payma—you, dear—bears an heir to the Rasan throne?"

"I do," Payma said. "And it's worth my life and the babe's if I go back there."

"I believe you," Nilufer said. She passed a plump hand across the low table, gesturing Payma to eat. "I know you probably have no appetite, but you need to eat. Eat and move and stay strong, so you have stamina for the birthing."

"I feel like I can't get a breath," Payma admitted, the first complaint Temur had heard her utter. "Let alone eat a bite of food."

"You're full up with babe," Nilufer said. Jade bracelets clinked on her wrist as she gestured. "It's only to be expected. Is this your first?"

Payma picked up a cake and soaked it in her tea while she nodded. Nilufer smiled, but it did not touch her eyes.

"You're safe here," she said. "Unless they come with an army. This is still the Khagan's land."

"For what that's worth," Temur said, half numb as the words pressed his lips apart. "What has the Khagan ever done for you?"

Nilufer's smile was mysterious. Intentionally so, he thought. "He let me reign in peace," she said. "Sent me a fine husband. Gave me the strength of arms to defend my land from bandits and mercenaries, and never demanded more in tribute than I could pay. He was a decent lord."

"Every lord who offers a modicum of safety in exchange for the bribe money he extracts is a decent lord. If you can make the peasant believe it matters who collects his taxes," Temur said with a shrug, "then you have all but won the war."

Her smile widened. "And you have no intention to make yourself Khan of Khans, Re Temur, Khanzadeh?"

It stung. She meant it to, and he deserved it. "I'm not in it for the riches."

"Of course not," she said. "More tea?"

As THEY WERE LEAVING THE ROOM, NILUFER CAUGHT SAMARKAR'S arm and pulled her aside. Samarkar had not expected to be manhandled by a Dowager Khatun; she stood as still as if frozen. But the woman treated her like a long-lost confidante, and that seeming openness had its charms. Even if Samarkar was sure it was entirely feigned. "She's young for childbearing."

"She is," Samarkar said. "And I would stay with her until she was delivered, but——"

"——More is at stake," Nilufer said. "Yes, I gathered. Never fear. I have a witch, and if the girl or the babe can be saved, she will save them. You may go on without guilt."

"Unlikely," Samarkar said, feeling a real smile split her face in the first time for spans of days.

Nilufer released Samarkar's arm and spread her hands. "Still worth trying. You know, you are not the first travelers seeking refuge to arrive here from the east this month. There is a monk, who by his habit and the condition of his feet could have walked all the way from Song."

"What news?"

Nilufer shrugged. "He is either mute or he's taken a vow of silence. I gave him some of the Song watercolor ink in solid bars, though that is not what we use, and some brushes he seemed to find acceptable. But I cannot read his writing. I thought perhaps one of you——"

"I can read Song script," Samarkar said. "And Temur can, a little."

Nilufer made a beckoning gesture, languid and graceful, that spoke volumes to Samarkar of the training in deportment and bearing that Samarkar, too, had suffered through.

"By all means," the Dowager Khatun said. "Come with me."

As they walked, Samarkar made polite conversation, allowing Temur and Payma and Hrahima to trail behind in what she hoped was comfortable silence. When she stole a glance backward, Payma and Temur both looked relaxed, and who could really read a Chotse's expressions, unless the tiger were making an effort to be intelligible?

"You have children?" Samarkar asked, casting about for a subject.

Nilufer nodded. "Three," she said. "The eldest is a daughter; the others, sons. The girl is married out to the son of one of Mongke

Khagan's generals, north near the city of Kyiv. My elder son has little use for politics, and so I am left to rule while he hunts bandits in the hills."

"And the younger son?"

"Chatagai is his name. Away to war," Nilufer said. "He was born before the Great Khagan's death, and so I can check the sky each night for his moon and know he lives."

For a moment, her trained facade cracked, and Samarkar saw the woman beneath. It was easy for a peasant to forget that queens and kings were merely mortal, nothing more—especially when the queens and kings in question were trained from birth to hold themselves apart. Some of ruling was creating your legend, enforcing your authority.

But that was a lonely place to stand.

As lonely as being a wizard, perhaps.

"I will pray he comes home safely," Samarkar said. "Who does he fight for?" Now Temur was listening—listening, and trying not to look as if he listened.

"He fought for Mongke Khagan," Nilufer said. "I do not know who he fights for now. If, as you say, two cities have fallen—"

"Aye, indeed," Temur put in. "If he was with Mongke's army, he may not even be in the fighting, unless some loyalty constrained him to join my brother's ranks or those of Qori Buqa. I did not know every man who fought for Qulan, but I knew when cousins joined us. He could be in Song, or he could be just about anywhere. But if his moon still shines, he is alive. And that is the best we can hope for in these times."

He sounded so young, so naïve, that Samarkar hid a smile. Nilufer saw it, though, and hid her own in return. "Through here," she said, gesturing them to a side passage.

Nobility in the borderlands was not like nobility in Rasa. Samarkar tried to imagine her brother leading guests through the palace by himself, but wound up shaking her head.

They came at last to an airy stone room, bright with sunlight

from the courtyard, in which two equally outlandish folks awaited.
One was a bald man, barrel-chested and fit, perhaps Samarkar's age,
who wore the onion-dyed robes of a Song monk kilted up to reveal
his legs and sandals. The other was an old woman who hunched
under layers of tattered rugs, as if she wore the mossy carapace of a
talus on her own back. The man, who had been idly staring out the
window, turned and stood as they entered. The woman did not. She
did not even look up from the beads and buttons she was sorting.

"Witch," Nilufer said.

The old woman grunted. The movement of her arm as she reached
for a bit of carnelian set swinging a row of charms stitched to the
lumpy breast of her cloak. But she did look up. The monk, meanwhile, bowed, and Nilufer met him with a nod that Samarkar copied.

He seemed calmly accepting of the ragged Rasan princess, the
bowlegged Qersnyk warrior, and the towering Cho-tse, but his focus was definitely on Samarkar. He bowed low.

In the speech of northern Song, she said, "I am Samarkar-la, a
wizard of Tsarepheth. I am here to serve as your voice. You have ink
and paper?"

He backed away, gesturing her to the table. He moved with a
fluidity of balance, reassuring Samarkar that he was exactly what he
appeared to be. The martial discipline showed in his straight spine,
the set of his head, the watchful eyes.

He was a round man: round of head, under the stubble of his
shaven hair; round of feature; round of shoulder; and round of belly.
She could see the muscular bulge of his thick arms and legs under
the fall of his robe, the calf muscles like knots in sheets as he moved.
He found paper and a brush and settled cobbler-fashion on the floor,
leaning over the small bare area that the witch's sorting did not
cover.

Despite his relative youth, his eyes were clouding blue around
the iris edges. Samarkar frowned; she knew what that meant, and she
knew as well that even the wizards of the Citadel had no cure for it.
No permanent cure, anyway. She knew there was a surgery that could

drain the fluid from the eye and give a few days of clear sight—but then the eyeball collapsed, and the blindness became total.

He wet the brush in a water glass and stroked it against the block of ink. Then quickly, with a practiced hand, he wrote.

Like Nilufer's tongue, the written language of Song was a kind of incantation in itself. Samarkar knew that these border peoples had once ruled great empires of their own. The word-picture spells and blessings of those ancient days still adorned some of Rasa's oldest temples, a memorial of when the sky that stretched over Rasa— and over Stone Steading—had been a sky no one had seen for hundreds of years.

But the Song language did not rely on word-pictures. Instead, it was constructed of sound-glyphs, each word built by layering the glyphs of its consonants one over the next in a harmonious shape. It was written from the bottom of the page to the top—from foundation to heavens, as buildings are constructed. In the hands of a scholar, the act of writing was a sort of performance—an ephemeral art that produced a permanent record.

But the monk was not performing. He wrote with a spare efficiency, a speed that was in itself beautiful, his head bent close to the paper so he could read his own work through clouded eyes. Samarkar read the columns of words aloud as fast as he could construct them, sounding out a few unfamiliar words.

His name (he wrote) was Hsiung. He was a mendicant, a journeyman monk who went forth from his order for a period of twenty-one years to learn and to be of service in the world.

Samarkar had walked into the room to read over Hsiung's shoulder. But as she read his words aloud, Temur stirred in his place beside the door.

"You are from the Red Forest," Temur said, more fluent in Song than Samarkar would have expected, though he spoke a more northeastern dialect. Of course, his grandfather had conquered a great deal of the kingdom that called itself the Heart of the World. Temur had probably fought there.

Samarkar thought Rasa, barricaded deep in the Steles of the Sky, had more to recommend it as the Heart of the World. But no one in Song had ever asked her. And the ones she might have expressed that opinion to, full of scorn, were all dead now.

Meanwhile, Brother Hsiung was still writing. *Yes. You have been there?*

"I served the Khagan," Temur said. "When there was a Khagan to serve."

Then you know of the fall of Qarash.

"We do. And also the destruction of Qeshqer."

He paused. Samarkar saw his hand tremble, a droplet of ink shivering at the tip of the brush. *I did not know Qeshqer had fallen.*

"Blood ghosts," she said, as softly as she could. She *felt* more than saw Nilufer stiffen. There was a rustle of filthy silk as Payma pressed her hand to her mouth.

One quick tear rounded the plump curve of the monk's cheek. Then another. He leaned back to keep them from splashing the page. Samarkar saw him squint against his clouded vision. Writing at arm's length, he scribed: *I myself saw flights of butterflies, some of them red. I traveled with a caravan and heard from the caravanners that in the east, many were dying of*—his hand hesitated, then he wrote hastily, as if to get by the words as fast as possible—*the black bloat.*

Samarkar tasted bile and disbelief. She'd read histories of the plague years, accounts by survivors, wizards, physicians, historians. She knew that it could sweep from Song to Messaline along the Celadon Highway, that it would keep going beyond the borders of the known world and into strange realms, where it would kill stranger people. That when it came, whole tribes died. That villages starved, everyone too ill to harvest. That in cities too decimated to bury their dead, piled corpses rotted in market squares. But there had not been an outbreak of the bloat in her lifetime.

"You're sure?" she asked, aware it was stupid, but needing reassurance in her horror.

I have read, Hsiung wrote, *the writings of the Joy-of-Vultures. I am certain.*

It was the Song name for the Carrion-King, the one the Uthmans and Qersnyk called the Sorcerer-Prince. Samarkar fearfully swallowed saliva and leaned forward to see what else he wrote.

They had heard, too, that a great bird, large as an Indrik-zver, hunts the plains.

"A terror bird?" They were not unheard of, deadly, flightless things whose shoulders stood as high as a man, which could stalk human children as a hen stalked grubs.

No. One that flew. He laid the brush down beside the block of ink and spread his hands, illustrating a vast wingspread.

Samarkar stepped back. She glanced at Hrahima and saw the Cho-tse's ears laid flat. "Rukh," Hrahima said.

Beside her, Payma hugged her arms to herself. "A what?"

"A kind of western devil-bird," Samarkar said. "Supposedly, it can carry off an elephant. To feed its young."

"It can," Hrahima said.

Samarkar almost asked, but this didn't seem the time for a digression. She looked back at Brother Hsiung. He had picked up his brush again and appeared to be waiting.

Nilufer asked. "So, what is an Uthman monster doing on the steppe?"

Samarkar had to wet her lips before she spoke. "It's said they can be tamed," she offered. "And used in war. If you can find one."

Temur's chest rose and fell once or twice, as if he fought to control his breath. His hands were clasped. Samarkar wondered if it was to control the shaking. She'd pulled her own into the sleeves of her coat, as if she felt a draft, though the room was warm. The witch rattled beads, and when Samarkar looked up, she saw that the old woman had cast them across the table and was studying the way they fell.

She grunted. When she stood, everyone in the room turned to her, and Brother Hsiung started up. She ignored them all, though, stumping to the doorway with her mossy cloak sweeping the floor by her ankles, shedding raveled threads.

She must have found a servant when she opened the door and

leaned out, because Samarkar heard her ask for tea in tones of surprising normalcy.

It was curious to watch, everyone else standing around the room artlessly, twisting their hands, waiting for some instruction or direction. The old woman settled herself again and set about sweeping together the beads she'd cast.

"What do you see?" said Nilufer.

The witch looked up. "I see red," she said. "Come and sit. All of you."

Peremptorily, she waved Brother Hsiung back to his place. He folded himself up and set his hands on his knees, assuming an attitude of waiting.

Samarkar sat beside him. Three beads remained before her place—crazed glass, moonstone, and a nugget of copper. She brushed them lightly with a fingertip and felt a tingle.

"Give those here," the witch said.

Samarkar obeyed, and around the table the others helped sweep together bright jackdaw baubles and pass them to the witch. By the time the tea arrived, the surface was clear.

Samarkar watched carefully, unsure of the etiquette. The servant placed the tray before the witch, and the witch poured tea into tall-sided bowls and passed them around. Samarkar took hers from Brother Hsiung after first passing one to her right, to Payma. The thick clay was ridged where fingers had shaped it, glazed softly in browns and grays. She realized her hands were aching only as the heat eased them.

"Drink your tea," the witch said. She demonstrated, downing the steaming fluid almost to the dregs. She swirled those in the cup, then quickly inverted it.

Nilufer did the same, and so Samarkar and the others copied her, some with more grace and some with less. The witch gestured for the upturned cups, and all were returned to her.

One by one, she righted them, and studied what lay inside.

She looked at Payma first. "It is a girl," she told the woman. "And healthy. You will stay here, of course."

"Of course," Nilufer echoed, with a raised eyebrow that Samarkar interpreted easily: *Am I not mistress in my own house?*

The old did what they would.

Payma looked down, nodding. "Thank you," she said.

The witch frowned at Samarkar. "You will need all your strength, Once-Princess and Wizard," she said. "It is upon you that the outcome rests."

"What outcome?" she asked, unable to stop herself.

"The outcome of the war." The witch looked at Temur. "You cannot be Khan without a sworn band. You will not find them in the west, but it is to the west you must go. You are hunted."

"I had gathered," Temur said. He softened it with a smile.

The witch smiled, too, showing sunken gums. "When it comes time, remember to seek the dragon. In the early part of your journey, you will meet a warrior woman, with tens of chariots and tens of consorts. Ask after her ancestors; it may help you find something you need to know. And watch for the black birds. The eaters of carrion are your allies, you who will feed them so well in time to come."

Temur frowned at her. But he was obviously wise to the ways of soothsayers, because he said nothing.

The witch gestured to Brother Hsiung. He leaned forward on his elbows, listening. "You," she said. "Your path lies west as well."

He nodded. Samarkar wondered, as the monk sat back, what questions he harbored and would not ask. Samarkar rubbed absently at the palm of her right hand, where a dull ache still sometimes lingered. She was healing, but healing took time. At least it took her mind off the itching in her arrow-shot arm.

But the witch had already turned to Hrahima. The Cho-tse looked ... defensive. Arms crossed over her chest, whiskers slicked back.

Steadily, the witch regarded her.

"You are a tangle," she said. "But I suppose you know that. So many threads lead in, and none out."

"I do not subscribe," Hrahima said, "to this ideal of destiny."

"I had gathered," the witch said, a dry mockery of Temur's earlier tone, which made Samarkar bite her lip to keep the smirk in.

That was the end of it, it seemed, because Nilufer stood and moved away from the table, obliging everyone else to follow. Samarkar was surprised when the witch caught her at the end of the line and pulled her arm to bend her down so she could speak in her ear. "She may not survive the childbirth," the witch whispered. "She is young and small. And I cannot see her future, one way or the other."

Samarkar swallowed. She'd harbored that fear all along. "If I send Temur on ahead with Hrahima—"

The witch huffed. "You are new to your skill. I have brought more babies into this world than you have years. What can you do for her that I cannot? Your place is in the war, Wizard."

Samarkar stared at her, then pulled away. But in her ears she heard Hrahima's voice—*I do not subscribe to this ideal of destiny*—and wondered.

THE BEDS HERE WERE VERY HIGH, STUFFED WITH STRAW AND FEATHERS and dressed with layers of bedclothes and hung about with tapestries to keep the draft off. Climbing the steps to the bed he'd been given to sleep in, Temur thought how like it was to a frame for a sky-burial. If he were being left for the vultures, though, no one would have given him such soft blankets.

He lay his head on a pillow that must have been filled with wool or down. Under the pressure of his head, it breathed forth a delicate scent of mint. What would it be like, he wondered, to sleep in this softness each night, to awaken to the silhouettes of the mountains against the dawn?

They hemmed him. Through the wide windows of the white tower in which he slept, he could see how their bulks shadowed the bright night sky. He could see how the snowy mountains gathered starlight, how it glimmered blue, flattened distance and made each facet of the peaks seem like a small close thing he could reach out and brush with his hand.

In the softness, he could not sleep. Despite the exhaustion of travel, despite a bellyful of Nilufer's peculiar food, despite being scrubbed clean in an entire tub of hot water, his thoughts refused to silence themselves. His heart hummed with worry and questions, and they were enough to keep the ache of weariness that weighed his limbs from pulling him into slumber.

And so he lay and watched the stars cross the sky, measuring their stately progress against the window frame. He imagined his death and what it would be like to lie motionless and watch the stars wheel over him as he lay naked on a cold frame.

It would be easier than this, he imagined.

It was with almost a sense of relief that he saw the shadow rise above the window frame and lean in. One leg, dark clad, crept across the threshold. The intruder was only a silhouette, but Temur saw him plainly until he dropped below the level of the sill and was hidden by the edge of the ridiculous bed.

He made no sound, but Temur knew he was creeping closer. And Temur's knife was with his kit, on the chest at the foot of the bed.

Once he moved, Temur knew the fight would be on. And perhaps death might be easier, but he found he was not ready to lie down just yet.

He gathered himself and rolled into a crouch, moving before he entirely had his balance under him. The soft bed shifted, ropes supporting the mattress creaking. The featherbed grabbed at his ankles. But he managed to jump, lunging toward the foot of the bed, and clawed the things heaped atop the chest into a clattering pile on the floor.

The room was dark, but his eyes were adapted. He saw the glitter of the partially sheathed blade against a knotted wool rug as the assassin came around the corner of the bed, no longer bothering with stealth. The knife that flashed in *his* hand was not sheathed.

Temur rolled aside as the assassin lunged for him. Stones beneath thick wool bruised his shoulder. Scar tissue binding his neck and chest pulled as he tucked and let the roll carry him out of the way.

He lashed out left-handed and felt the cool hilt of his knife. Ridges on the grip dug into his palm as he got a foot down and stood, dancing back almost immediately to avoid the glittering sweep of a blade.

He dodged the knife but not the boot that followed. The kick knocked him sharply to the wall. Something behind him clattered as it fell. He wheezed, lungs spasming, and barely drew a breath.

Temur's knife was longer, but the other man had more reach. And there was always the threat that the blade might be poisoned.

In songs, they sang always of the red tide of war fury rising. Temur had never experienced it so. Instead, he found himself detached and aloof, as if he floated above his body while it calmly made decisions and moved to kill or be killed.

The assassin's dark shape was more a blur of motion than the outline of a man. Temur's body darted forward, reaching with the knife. The assassin moved aside as effortlessly as if he had never been there. Temur let the lunge turn to a roll and came back to his feet, but not before the assassin's blade touched him. The force of the blow rocked him, but he felt no pain.

He'd felt no pain from the blow that could have severed his head, either. A thick streamer of wetness crossed his right hand, slicking his grip on the knife. But now the assassin was between Temur and the window and clearly silhouetted.

Not too big of a man, though taller than Temur. Temur thought he might be stronger than the assassin. The other man did not look broad across the shoulders.

He kicked out for the knee, a feint, ready to follow with a knife thrust if the assassin moved the way Temur wanted. But instead he stepped inside the arc of the blow, and Temur's shin bounced harmlessly off the other man's thigh. The assassin closed, pressing his advantage. Temur lashed out with his blade, trying for the assassin's knife arm. Something dragged; perhaps he had just caught cloth, but the assassin's breath changed—a grunt and a hiss. The knife scored Temur's shoulder instead of plunging into his chest.

They broke apart, breathing hard. Temur had managed to keep his back to the wall. The silhouette helped, but not enough.

Unless he managed something quickly, he was going to lose this fight. The battle-ready animal in charge of his body now did not know it. But Temur, above and behind himself, understood. He knew his chest heaved; he knew his heart thundered. But it was as if the body that knowledge encompassed belonged to someone else.

He watched himself gather to charge the knife again, and would have drawn a breath to shout if he'd had lungs to draw it with.

The door of his sleeping chamber burst open, and a blaze of brilliance flooded the room. He saw his own stark shadow, the assassin's hazel eyes lit through as if by the sun. He saw the indigo of the assassin's veil and the fluidity with which he threw himself back into a handspring and was gone out the fourth-story window as if he had never been.

"I heard the fight. You're bleeding," Samarkar said from the doorway, as Temur fell back into himself.

Suddenly there was pain, sharp, drawn in lines across his arm and shoulder. Pain and the stickiness of blood.

"I've been cut," he said, and put out his empty hand to the wall as he swayed.

 16

NILUFER KHATUN TURNED OUT HER GARRISON, BUT THEY FOUND NO trace of the assassin. Temur thought it was the same man they'd fought in the pass, though it was hard to tell in the dark. Still, something about the way he moved was familiar.

It was some days before they were well and rested enough to travel on. In that time Nilufer saw to it that they had new boots, provisions, and enveloping robes to protect them against the glare of the desert sun.

For Temur, the hardest part was leaving the mares behind: for Samarkar it was Payma. But neither mares nor princess could come with them across the Great Salt Desert, and so eventually they made their farewells, shouldered their packs, and joined Hrahima and Brother Hsiung on the road below.

When they walked away from Stone Steading, it was all Temur could do to keep himself from looking back over his shoulder every few strides. By the stiffness of her own spine, Samarkar felt no different.

The desert lay five days' march beyond, according to the map with which Nilufer had provided them. By the fourth day, it was desert enough to meet Temur's not terribly exacting standards; scrub struggled through hardpan baked to cracking, and their footprints left no lingering trace.

They used their food sparingly, and Samarkar took time in the evening before sleep to supplement their water with what she called out of the air, seemingly from nothing. They were coming into the heat of summer, when caravans avoided crossing the desert at all. Temur had a sense that they all feared the crossing. The days were passed in trudging forward, discussing their worries in low tones. The nights were passed staring awake on watches or sleeping hard, as they did in shifts. Even Hrahima must sleep sometime, and Temur was not an experienced walker, though he was slowly adapting.

But as they came up to the range of low hills where they planned to spend the night—preferably by the shores of a seep oasis, if they could find one of the ones the map suggested should be there—Temur's measured step faltered. Because he saw green ahead, yes, a patch of grass and huddled trees, and from behind them he caught the glint and the scent of water.

But in the grass by that water stood something impossible: a liver-bay mare, head down, cropping the grass in the shade of a bush burdened with unripe pomegranates.

"I'm imagining things," he said.

He would have rubbed his eyes to clear them, but Samarkar touched his wrist and said, "If you are, I'm imagining them too. That's Bansh."

She started forward, about to break into a jog despite the lingering ache in her thigh, but Brother Hsiung threw his arm in front of her. She checked sharply. When she glanced up at him, he shook his head.

She blinked and nodded. "If Bansh is here, it's because someone rode her here. And that person is waiting for us."

"And possibly does not have our best intentions at heart." Hrahima crouched, bringing her face close to the earth, and sniffed. She stepped a little sideways, a movement that should have seemed crab-like but was instead powerful, and sniffed again. "Nothing," she said, standing. "The wind blows over the hills, from the east. The curve of the bluff could be holding the scent in a pocket of dead air, I suppose. But I can smell the mare."

Temur drew his knife. "Carefully, then."

As a group, they advanced, Brother Hsiung and Temur to the front—Temur holding his knife, Hsiung barehanded. Hrahima ranged out to the side, and Samarkar followed them, every sense straining.

But no matter how they searched, they found nothing. Nothing except Bansh, curried to a shine like afternoon sunlight, her tack hung neatly on the branches of a nearby pomegranate tree.

"Somebody brought you your horse," Hrahima said, at last, tail lashing. "And I cannot smell on her—or her furniture—who."

Temur had already come up to her and was rubbing her velvet nose, feeding her chips of dried fruit that he'd been intending to eat himself. Overhead, a drifting vulture circled.

A gift of the Eternal Sky, before we leave his lands entirely?

"Well," Temur said. "I guess we work with it."

In the morning, they topped the bluffs and looked out over the salt pan of a dead ancient sea. Temur wondered how he had thought the cracked lands behind them a desert, when all to the horizon this one stretched off-white, featureless, infinite.

Beside him, the others too stood and stared.

Bansh now carried most of their gear. What had been heavy packs for four humans and a Cho-tse was a moderate load for the mare. Temur was worried about water—how much, realistically, could Samarkar create?—but if all went well, they should be out of the desert in a hand of days and a little more. The mare could live on very limited food for that long, if Samarkar could keep her watered.

If all went well.

It was a faster route than rejoining the Celadon Highway, and Temur thought they'd have less chance of meeting up with assassins or Qori Buqa's men. The attempt in Stone Steading left no doubt the killers were seeking Temur in particular. And of course, the blood ghosts could not cross the salt flats. They hoped.

The glare was eye-splintering, and salt dust rose up from their footsteps to coat their faces and mouths. After the first half day, they sheltered under canvas from late morning until evening, and walked by moon and starlight through the night. The hard-baked salt reflected even the sparsest starlight, giving them light to walk by. At least the pale hot sun crossed the sky in the proper direction. These were Uthman skies and not Rahazeen.

EVERY EVENING WHEN SHE AWOKE AND DRAGGED HERSELF FROM HER hard bed, Samarkar found Temur leaning close to the bay mare, singing into her ears and stroking her mane. Well away from him, the barrel-bodied monk, stripped to his trews, was practicing the forms of his martial art in the still warmth and waning light.

The first thing Samarkar did was create water. With practice, she'd gained dexterity. Now she looked back at her fumbling first attempts with a kind of awe for how far she'd come in a few moons.

The deeper they traveled into the Salt Desert, however, the harder it became to summon water. Her eyes dried and her lips cracked, despite all the balm of fat and herbs she could muster from the contents of her medical bag. There was just too little moisture in the air to make a difference.

At least Samarkar's wizarding disciplines could be used to keep her from baking in the unforgiving sun. Hrahima, who did not sweat, suffered more. She did not complain, but Samarkar did not need an interpreter to read the slouched posture, the open-mouthed pant. On one particular afternoon, as Hrahima lay flat in the shade, Samarkar came and crouched beside her with a bowl of water brimming in her hands.

Hrahima cracked an eye.

"I might be able to help," Samarkar said, as the Cho-tse reached out for the water. "There's a meditation against the heat—"

"I know one," Hrahima said. She pushed herself up on one elbow and took the bowl gratefully. Though Samarkar had diminished the process of fire within it until it almost smoked with cold, the air here was so dry that no moisture beaded on the outside. Hrahima cupped both broad hands against it, savoring the chill.

"And you will not use it," Samarkar said.

A tiger's sigh was a mighty thing. Her chest rose and fell; her whiskers blew forward. "Have you heard of 'soldier's heart'?"

Guiltily, Samarkar's eyes crept to Temur. But what she said was, "I have it a little myself, I think."

Hrahima drank deeply. When she looked up, transparent droplets shivered on her whiskers. "War begets fear. Fear begets rage. Rage propagates hate. Hate draws rage. The Sun Within abhors hate; hate is inharmonious. Hate is the weapon of entropy."

"The Sun Within." Samarkar fought her smile, but she wasn't any better at keeping it inside than Temur. "That god you don't believe in."

The Cho-tse huff of amusement was becoming as familiar to her as a sister's sigh. "Yes, well. He drops by once in a while and we hash it over. It's never going to be resolved, but we're still friends." She spread her hands. "It is what it is."

Samarkar thought about that, thought about this idea that one could . . . disagree philosophically with a force of nature. With a deity.

If you could disagree with kings, were gods so far above?

She said, "You're a warrior. So how do you kill without rage?"

"In compassion. Because of necessity." Hrahima set the empty bowl back in Samarkar's hands. "The same way you carry water."

DAY FELL INTO DAY, NIGHT TO NIGHT. THE SILVER EARTH BLED INTO the silver sky so Temur could scarcely find a horizon, and the pale sun seared down through the haze. In the dark, the salt below seemed brighter than the heavens. The wind was ceaseless, blowing delicate rills of salt in winding bands, like the first snows of autumn.

Temur sang to his mare, the milk-letting songs and the soft-muscle songs. His own muscles hardened in new ways. His feet broke into the new boots, or possibly the other way around.

The sun did not kill them.

They walked on.

AFTER THREE DAYS IN THE DESERT, BANSH'S MILK LET DOWN. IT WAS an art of the Qersnyk to coax their mares to lactate so early in the pregnancy, he explained, when Samarkar expressed surprise that she was bearing.

Temur showed her how to make *airag* and explained to her that the mare's milk was too strong for humans until it fermented. "It will make your bowels loose," he said. "Which would kill you, here. But in three days, it is good food."

Samarkar looked at the mare, standing patiently while Temur crouched before her hind legs, streams of milk jetting into the leather pail of white froth by his feet.

"She'll need more water, then," Samarkar said. "We can get some of ours from the milk, when in turn we drink it."

If his hands hadn't been milk-covered and busy, Temur would have put an arm around her then.

ON THE FIFTH DAY OF THE DESERT, SAMARKAR JOINED THE MUTE MONK in his forms.

She did not excel. Her body felt bulky, awkward, badly shaped for what was expected of it. But he was patient with her.

At dawn on the sixth day, when they had been walking all night, they found themselves climbing out of the salt basin, blistered and exhausted.

Samarkar would have hugged the first scrubby tree she saw, if it had not been so thorny.

THAT AFTERNOON WHILE THE MEN AND HRAHIMA SLEPT AND SAMARKAR kept watch, Temur dreamed again. She'd become used to his nightmares by now. Some might be prophesy, though he had not spoken of such since Tsarepheth, and the rest were likely "soldier's heart," as Hrahima diagnosed. He regularly mewled and kicked in his sleep, scrabbling at something Samarkar could not see and that she knew he would never explain.

This time, though, she got up and moved over beside him, laying his head against her thigh. She thought he'd awaken fighting. She was prepared for it.

Instead he curled up to her, made one last noise, and sighed into relaxation.

That evening, when Temur uncased his bow and strung it, she saw that the meat he'd also packed in its case for moisture had dried to leather.

THE SUN THAT ROSE IN THE MORNING WAS AN UTHMAN SUN. AS THEY approached the sea, they found themselves in sparse grasslands again—a rocky sort of terrain fit for goats but not cattle. When the first band of riders approached, heralded by much whickering from Bansh, Samarkar turned over her shoulder and glanced at Temur, who was leading Bansh along in the rear of the group. Her face showed concern and chagrin. He nodded.

"Score a point for the witch," he said, as six mounted men circled them. They had arrows nocked, but the bows were not drawn. Temur noticed that the design of the bows was different from either the long Song bows or the back-curved Qersnyk variety, though he thought they were—like his—of laminated construction.

The men wore armor coats made of scales cut from horse hooves. The coats covered them to their knees. Beneath, they wore baggy pantaloons in bright colors. Their horses were grays, except for one black and one sorrel; they were dish-nosed and short-backed like the famed Asitaneh bloodlines. They were beautiful—bright-coated, bright-eyed, with deep nostrils and luxurious manes—and the rugs they wore under their saddles were all the bright, clear colors of jewels and fruits.

The men on their backs carried lances as well as their bows, banners snapping bright with crimson dragons. The leader, on the palest and tallest of the grays, put his horse a step forward. Their saddles were low, by Temur's standards, and he noticed with a start that they had no stirrups. The men rode by balance and the grasp of their legs.

That is why they go to war in chariots, he thought, remembering the words of the witch.

"You are off the road," the leader said in broken Qersnyk. "But you do not look like bandits. What is your intention in our lands?"

He spoke to Temur, and as he glanced from side to side, Temur understood that they would consider him the leader of this group. Just as Temur himself tended to look to Samarkar to fill that role.

"To pass through," he said. "We are bound for the White Sea. I am Temur; this is Samarkar, Brother Hsiung, and the Cho-tse is Hrahima." As he said them, it occurred to him that perhaps he should have given feigned names—but lying was a good way to attract unfavorable spirits, Hrahima would never support it, and a lie of names could not disguise the unmistakable composition of their group.

If Qori Buqa were seeking him through Nameless assassins, there was no way to conceal the news of his travel other than to avoid everyone.

One of the other men said something to the leader in a tongue Temur did not know. The leader held up a hand, which meant *Wait your turn* in any language. He said, "Do you have news of the east?"

"We do," Temur said. "A great deal of it. And we need food and supplies, for which we wish to trade."

A hesitant smile creased the man's wind-tanned face. "You will come with us," he said. "The Queen Dragon will wish to receive you."

"Queen Dragon," Samarkar whispered, leaning close. "These are the lizard-folk!"

They did not look like lizards, but Temur, too, had heard of the tribes to the west who rode under the banners of dragons and wore their hide as armor. These men's mail was horse-hoof scale, and he saw no sign of the forked tongues attributed to the lizard-people by folklore. But he also knew that stories of faraway people grew stranger in the telling.

"If they are the lizard-folk," he answered, "then we are indeed nearly to the sea."

THREE OF THE MEN PULLED TEMUR, SAMARKAR, AND HSIUNG ONTO their mares, to ride pillion behind the saddle. One of the riders ponied Bansh behind his horse, which made Temur nervous. But he dried his hands on his thighs and held his tongue, mindful of what the witch had said over the tea leaves. Hrahima paced alongside, keeping up easily and apparently unconcerned.

At least the land they rode through was comfortingly familiar, after so many cities of farmers. The horses moved through grass that waved shoulder-high, its heads swaying with unripe grain. He spotted round white-houses with felted walls that differed in their decoration from the white-houses of home, but not in their construction. Sheep, cattle, and goats moved in flocks tended by boys and girls on horseback and guarded by curly-tailed yellow dogs. The details of dress were unfamiliar, the construction of the saddles— but the bold outlines were home. At the horizon, gold-green steppe lay like a razor's edge against that pale Uthman sky.

Its smoothness was broken here and there by conical earth mounds girded and surmounted by standing stones. As they passed between the mounds, Temur saw that the stelae were carved with crude reliefs, representations of men and women with their hands folded before them or holding cups or weapons.

Hsiung, of course, rode with his partner in silence. Off to his left, Samarkar was holding a conversation in low tones with her guide, but Temur could not pick out more than the occasional word. He tried Qersnyk and Uthman greetings on the man he rode behind, getting a nod and a grunt on the second.

"What are these?" he asked, gesturing to the mounds. He suspected he knew, but—

"Kurgans." The man craned over his shoulder to see if Temur understood. When Temur frowned and shook his head, the man's brow furrowed. "Graves," he said. "Spirit houses. The dead live in there."

"I see," Temur said. He hoped he hid his shudder.

BEFORE LONG, THEY CAME UP ON A STOCKADE OF HEAVY TREE BOLES set in the earth and lashed together, their tips axe-hewn to sharp points. Temur imagined the logs hauled from a forested slope or river valley, the labor to set them in place. It would not stand long against a concerted Qersnyk army or even a raiding band—but it was proof against most bandits, and the fact that it stood and was so well maintained proved without a doubt that they needed it.

The borders of the Uthman Caliphate suffered the same neglect as the hinterlands of any empire.

There was a conversation at the gates when the patrol approached. Temur would not have been surprised if he and his companions were bound before they were brought inside. But after a brief conference, they were led within, with the horses. Temur moved to take charge of Bansh; the patrol leader intercepted him with the same gesture of warning he'd made to his own man earlier.

"The mare will stay here. I don't suppose she's one of the things you are interested in trading? She looks to have good blood behind her."

"Steppe ponies are not for sale," Temur said, careful to keep the insult from his voice. These people could know no better, and his years with the army had taught him that not all peoples were as cosmopolitan—or as open to the beliefs and cultures of others—as the Qersnyk were.

It was the difference between an empire and a village, he supposed. He changed the subject. "I am Temur," he said again. "If it is not impolite to ask, I would know what you are called?"

The man blinked at him. Temur was struck by his leathery appearance: skin so similar to a Qersnyk's, but western features, with a high-bridged nose and bright, light eyes like an eagle's almost buried in his squint.

"My name is Saura," he said, as if Temur had honored him with the request.

Then he nodded and folded his hands over his horse-hoof breastplate. Close up, the armor did look as smooth and flexible as the scales of a snake, and Temur could see the care that had gone into arranging it in patterns of dark and light.

Idly—professionally—rather than with belligerence, he wondered how it would stand up to an arrow.

"Come," Saura said, pulling his helm from a gray-streaked mane of hair. "It is not wise to keep the Queen Dragon waiting."

Temur felt his companions closing around him as they marched into the hall—Samarkar on his right, Hsiung behind. On the ground, now, he realized that these westerners were tall. Not by the towering standards of the moon-white Kyivvin traders who sometimes came to Qarash, but most of them had half a head on him, if a bit less on Samarkar.

"They are very polite," Samarkar said, in Rasan. "Should that worry me?"

"Guests are treasured on the steppe," Temur answered, in the same language—so much more easily now, after months of practice, than before. "Perhaps by these people as much as by mine."

She made a noise of discontent, until Hrahima leaned between them. "Rudeness is a weak person's imitation of strength. If we are in their power, what need have they to be rude?"

Samarkar subsided, seeming somehow more comforted by Hrahima's statement than worried. Given the politics of the court she must have grown up in, Temur tried not to be surprised.

If the white-houses on the steppe outside had seemed cozy and familiar, this structure was like nothing he had experienced. It was a great wooden hall, big as a temple in Song, with a sod roof pierced at intervals by covered apertures to allow smoke to escape. The doors were in the middle of the long side, which—judging by the unpainted planks of the wall—was the height of three tall trees taken together.

It would have sounded terribly plain had Temur tried to describe it to one of his own folk, but standing before it he could see the care and craftsmanship with which every plank dovetailed the next and how they had been sanded and oiled until they gleamed like a mirror-colored horse's hide.

And they were carved in relief like the stelae guarding the barrows outside. Which he could see now was not crude at all, but when the rain and snow of countless winters had not weathered it, instead consisted of intricate stylized depictions of men and women, warriors and horses that intertwined in elaborate knotworks.

The moving shadow of more dragon banners fell across Temur's face. He paused and glanced from Samarkar to Hsiung to see if they noticed what he did. Brother Hsiung was a master of subtle communication, and his eyebrows spoke volumes now.

"I have seen carvings like this," Temur said, "in Song. But they were of jade, not wood."

"Well, of course," Saura said. "You are Qersnyk—"

"I have that honor."

"—And so you know the Khagan's empire stretches from the rising to the setting of the sun."

"That is how I came to be in Song."

Saura smiled. "Five hundred years ago, the empire that reached the ocean to the east and the sea to the west was ours; all the known earth was the realm of the Dragon Peoples. But men are weak; empires fall. The Dragon Peoples are subjects of the caliph, now."

Temur felt the flash of heat through his body as he considered all his grandfather had built, as he thought of what the Nameless might plan for Uthman and Qersnyk alike, and the fate of all these little kingdoms, should they crumble back into lawless borderlands.

"You speak nothing but truth," he said, though the words were painful.

Saura nodded. "I will need your weapons," he said.

That was actually quite funny, as Temur divested himself of his sheath knife, and the other three showed their empty hands. The fact that each of them was more than capable of dealing death, messy or precise, with those hands went unremarked. Possibly Saura did not quite realize it, although he would have been hard-pressed to misunderstand the capabilities of the Cho-tse.

Saura stepped forward, and a pair of servants in yellow cotton coats bowed low and opened wide the bravely carved doors.

"Her name is King Tzitzik," Saura said kindly, and pushed Temur forward into the gloom.

He did not stumble, because the floor inside was wide wooden boards smoothed and joined with every bit as much attention and care as the cladding on the walls. But his feet did scuff a little.

By the time he righted himself, Samarkar and Hsiung were beside him. Samarkar snaked a hand out and gave his wrist a squeeze, the touch gone before he knew it, but—he offered her a smile— appreciated.

And then his eyes adjusted and he gained some sense of the place in which he stood.

Wooden trusses bore the weight of the roof, supported by pillars in columns midway along each side of the hall. The long middle span was left clear, a corridor twice as wide as Temur was tall, vaulted high enough that a man on horseback could have ridden down it with no fear for lance or his plumes. Into this torchlit space Temur strode, turned toward the greatest concentration of noise and light, and made his way forward.

There was music. A woman sang, and in addition to the torches, indirect daylight trickled through the gaps where the roof overhung but did not touch the tops of the walls, which Temur had not noticed from outside.

He knew they were expected—and which of Saura's men had ducked inside to bring the word?—because the singer did not falter. Instead, her melody ended naturally, hauntingly, on a held note, as Temur approached the table that sat athwart the end of the hall, below a dais on which rested an elaborate wooden chair.

Saura's strange phrase at the end became plain to him. This was not a queen, Temur realized as he saw her seated there, trousered and dressed in boots, with her hair cut short beneath the hammered copper filet that marked her rank. No queen, but a woman-king— western sword on her hip, books piled on the table before her, her face as weathered by the sun as any of her riders.

She rose from the midst of her advisors as Temur approached. They all followed suit an instant later. As for Temur, he stopped several strides short and bowed as low as his road-weary body would allow. She was bare-chested, as were half her male advisors—and many of the women carven on the stelae. Her fingertips were elongated with elaborate, taloned finger-stalls which mimicked the claws of a dragon.

She was not a young woman. Her body was leathery, lean, muscular, feathery about the hips with lines of childbirth. Her arms were crossed with white scars and inked with tattoos of intertwined beasts, like those that adorned the carven walls and doors. Her trousers hissed like silk as she came forward. Her booted feet clicked softly.

A man walked with her, three steps behind.

"Speak," he said, in the Qersnyk tongue.

"King Tzitzik," Temur said, without raising his eyes. "I am called Temur; my companions are Samarkar-la, Hrahima, and Brother Hsiung. We have come to you as travelers passing, with news and in the hope you will trade with us."

The man who had spoken said something—a string of liquid syllables Temur could only assume was the local language. The woman-king answered with a wave of her hand that ended—thankfully—far from her well-polished sword hilt.

The man translated. "What do you have to trade?"

"Salt," Temur said. "Purple salt from Rasa. And Samarkar-la is a healer. We have her skills, as well."

"And the news you bring. Is it news of great doings?"

"It's what news there is," Temur said.

There was a pause, longer than the pause for translation. "Rise," she said through her advisor. "You will be brought water and clean clothing, if you need it. You will dine with us, and we will share . . . what news there is."

THE FOOD AT THE WOMAN-KING'S TABLE WAS HORSE MEAT, STEWED long with onions, and flat, chewy cakes of baked dough. The people had not heard of the ruin of Qeshqer, although news of the Qersnyk war had reached them. Try as he might, Temur never quite found a way to ask the woman-king about her ancestors. *The witch will be disappointed in you,* he thought.

The Celadon Highway was north; it was not too far to reach, they said, but if Temur and his people were traveling to Asitaneh, it would be more direct to follow the river the Dragon Peoples called the Hard Drinker to the seacoast.

"Two days ride," they said. And, "You will have to build a signal fire. A ship will put in, and if you can pay, they will carry you across the Strait to Asitaneh."

They stressed the expense of travel in and near the cities. Temur, having lived in cities in Song as well as Qarash itself, could imagine. And the woman-king herself seemed very taken with him. He sat beside her on one side, Samarkar on the other—the position of honored guests—but she spent more attention on him. She brushed morsels from her plate to his, and once or twice fed him directly from her gold-armored fingers.

Temur found himself uncomfortable with the attention. Or perhaps with Samarkar's evident amusement, because every time he looked around King Tzitzik, there was the wizard, smirking at him from over the collar of her borrowed coat, her jade and pearls still hidden away in the bottom of a saddlebag. Their own clothing, while not quite worn to rags, was definitely in need of laundering somewhere where it could be boiled with soap.

They were sent to sleep, not along the walls of the hall, as Temur had half expected, but in smaller white-houses scattered within the walls of the stockade.

TEMUR AWAKENED IN THE DARK, FIGHTING TOO MANY HANDS TO count.

He would have shouted, but a black hood covered his face, and someone larger and stronger twisted his arms behind him. The hood was filled with some muffling fabric. His shout sounded flat and close, even to his own ears. He could tell it had not carried.

They did not drag him but carried him out and slung him over the back of a horse. His head bounced against its hay-smelling ribs, and though he fought and the horse spooked and sidestepped, there were enough hands to hold him in place until the ropes made it impossible to flop himself free. Hemp burned his wrists, his bare ankles. He wore only a breechclout and the hood, but the night was not too cold. The horse's rough hair pricked his skin.

Someone mounted: He heard the hooves beside his own unwitting steed. Someone jerked the horse into motion from the front, and they were running. His ribs bruised and burned with every bounce. His abdomen was scoured. The horse was unhappy, fighting the lead, fighting the unbalanced weight across its back.

Temur finally gave up struggling. He had to concentrate on his breath and on not giving voice to the whimpers that wanted to bubble from his lips. Crying would only make it worse.

After a long time, they jounced to a stop.

The trot was worse than the gallop, but it was over sooner. Temur lay in wait, feigning docility, until they came and unknotted the ropes that bound him to the horse. He thrashed, fishtailing his feet, and caught someone in the chest hard enough to knock him over. When he toppled backward, though, Temur suffered—the fall from the horse's back was more severe than whatever he'd dished out to his assailant.

He gasped a mouthful of cloth trying to regain his breath and almost vomited. *That would surely improve things.*

But he got his knees up, rolled on to them. Would have hopped himself upright with the same move you'd use to leap to the saddle of a running horse, but someone struck him across the chest—it felt like a kick—and he went down. Choking on fabric, light-headed, thinking *After everything, this is a pathetic way to die.*

They dragged him. He couldn't have walked anyway. That long grass whipped his legs and ankles at first, but fell away. And somewhere in the dragging, the texture of the air changed.

It became cool, moist. Earthy. A smell he half-remembered through fever dreams, from when he and the horses had cowered behind stones while the ice rained down.

They're burying me, Temur thought, and could not keep this wail of fury and terror within. To rot inside the earth, forever out of the sight of the Eternal Sky—if there was a fate worse than becoming a blood ghost, this was it.

Someone whispered in his ear, rough Uthman words, an accent worse than Saura's. "This is the grave of Danupati," he snarled. "His curse should keep you busy."

Something heavy groaned. Temur struck a clay floor and lay still.

The footsteps receded.

There was the sound of a door shutting, with weight behind. He barely heard it over the thunder of his heart, the ragged rasp of his terrified, panting breaths. He had to calm himself, slow his breath. He had to get control.

He counted breaths in the darkness. He counted heartbeats. He closed his eyes so he could imagine he controlled the absence of light.

Slowly, he calmed himself. He listened, lying perfectly still.

Silence followed.

Then the sound of something wet and heavy slipping over stone.

*   *   *

THE BLINDFOLDING SACK WAS NOT SO HARD TO SCRAPE OFF AGAINST the stone floor. It still dragged from the ropes at his throat, but he could worry about that later. Even with it off, Temur found he could not see.

Wherever he was (*buried alive*), there was no trace of light. It was not just the darkness of night that surrounded him. It was a blackness so absolute that he imagined he saw motion where there was none.

But something scraped in the darkness, and it was not the villains who had dragged him here wedging the doors.

His hands were still bound behind him. But that was a small problem. He stretched his arms around his hips, wincing as rope wore into flesh that was already torn and burned, and pulled his feet through the hoop of his arms.

Now the ropes at his ankles. But his fingers were already slick with blood, and the knots had pulled tight from his struggles. It took only a few moments work to convince him that this was futile.

If this were a barrow, though—what had Saura called it? A kurgan?—then there would be grave goods. There would be knives, perhaps.

Temur felt his breath quicken, and forced the terror back with reason. He had heard of this Danupati. A great king, a conqueror like the Great Khagan Temusan. He had ruled a realm that swept, as Saura had intimated, from the White Sea to the Eastern ocean . . . a thousand years before. Farther, even: For it was he who had conquered the first Erem, long before the Sorcerer-Prince razed the second one stone from stone for daring to stand against him.

There was said to be a curse upon his tomb, such that should his bones be stolen, war would rage unceasing across every land he had called his own until the damage was put right. Whatever obligation of hospitality the woman-king Tzitzik felt to Temur, it was obvious that her men had no intention of allowing him to leave this place.

His bound hands held before his body, Temur groped forward a few inches at a time, in a hop that was also a shuffle. It was painstakingly, maddeningly slow progress, made worse when, between his own scuffling movements, he heard that scraping again.

When the darkness seemed to lessen incrementally, at first he thought his eyes were still fooling him. But then he realized that he could make out the hulked shapes of biers—one higher than the other—and the shadows of ranks of lances leaned against the earthen walls. *Those.*

The pale light had a moonlit quality, and it was so faint that if he had not just been in pitch blackness, he would have hesitated to call it light at all. But there it was, faint but slowly brightening.

And there among the crumbled remains of the others was a lance with an obsidian point, chipped glass sharp and ready no matter how many years it had lain below the earth. Now that he could see where his feet landed, Temur cast aside caution and hopped frantically to the wall.

The shaft had been wood, and it was fungus-eaten and crumbling. The glass head of the lance, though—that drew blood when he brushed his fingers across it. He clutched his prize.

He bent to reach his ankles and overbalanced, toppling to one side. He groaned; his head spun with the stink of sorcery or lightning. Sharp agony numbed his left hip and left arm.

One more scrape, one more rustle. And the source of the moonish light crept into view.

It was a fat worm, a grub big as a man, dull red in color and surrounded by a crackling blue light. It humped forward, damp and horrible, dragging its fat abdomen with three pairs of short, pointed legs. A trail of moisture glistened on the stone behind it.

Temur's throat closed on his breath.

"Gut-worm," he whispered soundlessly. *Gut-worm,* because it looked like an enormous intestine spilled on the floor. At least until it reared up on its viscous-looking rear end and clicked its sharp-tipped legs together.

A chill of terror numbed Temur's limbs. It was one thing to face an armed man or a hungry beast of prey. Another to face a beast whose touch could melt flesh, that was reputed to carry the spark of lightning in its skin.

You do not die this way, he thought, and tightened his fingers around the shard of obsidian. Blood flowed fresh again, and the worm's head—black, glossy, ridiculously tiny on the bloated shape of its body—swung too and fro. *You do not die this way.*

Hadn't Nilufer's witch said that Tzitzik's ancestors had something to teach him?

No. He would not die here.

He lacerated his fingers again turning the lance-head, and did worse sawing away at the ropes. Each strand parted easily, but there were multiple wraps to cut through.

And as soon as he started sawing, the gut-worm stopped swaying side to side like a casting dog and humped its bloated body toward him. It did not move quickly. Each jerk of its form took two motions—the lunge forward of the upper parts, then the heave up of the hindquarters. Slap, then scrape.

As a method of locomotion, it would have been hideously fascinating if Temur had not been experiencing it from eye level and the perspective of a target. His hands free, he gathered himself. They could spit acid, it was said, as well as hurl miniature lightning. He would have to move fast.

And his ankles were still bound, but no time for that now.

It reared up one last time, towering an arm span over the floor where Temur lay. He saw its body swell.

He heaved himself up and dove behind the nearest bier, trying to roll as he fell, trying to keep his grip on the dull end of the lance head. A pool of glowing yellow bile splattered where he had lain, smoking on the stone floor. A brief sharp crack, thunder's little brother, followed.

Clay pots rocked and shattered as Temur kicked through them. He slashed his ankles free—an easier task than the hands. The stench of the gut-worm's poison vomit brought water to his eyes and stung his skin. More tamed lightning crackled around it. He could not get close to that thing. And yet here he was without bow, without arrows, in a tomb full of crumbling weapons and dead men's bones.

Meanwhile, the gut-worm turned to seek him again. It dropped down and dragged its front another span. Temur stole a glimpse across the top of the bier and cursed as the thing spit again. Acid splashed against the crumbling armor of the warrior laid out there, eating into what remained of his bones.

Can't touch it, Temur thought. *Can't let it see me. Have to kill it somehow.*

There was the lance head, but no shaft. There was the scrap of sacking still stuck in the ropes around his neck.

There were the stoppered clay pots of grave goods he crouched among.

He tucked the lance head into his loincloth and hefted a pot the size of his head. Heavy. Heavy and full of something that rattled. The clay stopper was sealed in with pitch.

He stood fluidly, sidearmed the pot, and hurled. The worm clicked furiously and whipped its upper body aside, but Temur had been aiming for the fat, half-fluid body it dragged behind. The pot shattered, spilling coins that might have been gold this way and that. The worm shrieked, its body splashing away from the point of impact in visible waves.

Temur winced and ducked again. That had hurt it, but not enough. How many pots of coins were available?

Not, he suspected, enough.

There had to be a better way. He slung another coin pot and dodged from the closer bier behind the farther, taller one, nearly knocking himself prone on a support column along the way.

Support column. Carefully, he peered over the edge of the bier, hoping the worm's eyesight was not good enough to notice eyes peeking through a headless dead man's dusty ribcage. And yes, there were more columns, scattered here and there throughout the room. Which had to be maintained, because if the wood of the lance shafts had crumbled to dust, would not the wooden columns that bore the very weight of the earth piled overhead do the same?

The only problem with his plan was that he'd have to close with the worm to put it into practice.

There were more coin pots here. He snatched one up and hurled it, sidestepping as he did. This time he did not throw it at the worm, but rather at the wall behind the worm.

As he had hoped, the worm jerked at his motion. Then it whipped around, wasting its venom on the empty space where the jar had shattered. Temur vaulted the bier, scattering dry bones, and dodged around luminescent venom. He ran not *for* the worm but past it, closer to the wall where the sealed-up entrance lay, and struck the wooden column there with all the strength of his shoulder.

It creaked and slipped halfway from its footing.

The gut-worm was turning back, seeking. Temur thought it took a few moments to work itself up to spitting. Its body swelled now as it had before. Temur threw his arms around the pillar and heaved. Once, twice—the worm's head reared up—and Temur hurled himself backward, his whole weight against the pole. It slid from its footing and hit the floor with a crack as Temur flew from his feet and tumbled hard against the wall beside the door.

He was pushing himself up on his elbows in the sudden darkness when the roof fell in.

Temur ducked, shielding his head with his arms, but he was in the shelter of the wall and no timbers struck him. Instead he huddled in a triangular gap like a lean-to. The crypt was plunged in darkness. Temur did not know if he'd crushed the worm, or merely brought timbers and earth down between them. Dust and particles of earth coated his skin and made him wheeze. But it was no longer trying to eat him, and that was enough for now.

He tested the door and could not move it. Cleaner air flowed through the gap beneath; he would die of thirst before he suffocated. It was not a cheering thought.

He did not know how long he crouched there—not pinned, but constrained—before he heard the hollow ring of footsteps and saw the flicker of torchlight below the great stone door. At first he feared it was the scrape and glow of another gut-worm, but it was too rhythmic and too bright. The crisp, smoky sharpness of burning pitch reached him, and he stood up behind the door and began to pound against it with his fists.

Someone shouted back. A muffled voice, but one he knew. A woman's voice. *Samarkar.*

"Blessings on a wizard," he muttered, as the old door gritted on stone. It pulled away from him, and he all but fell through it into her arms. She was strong; she caught him. The first thing she did after that was lean him against the wall and put a skin of water in his hands.

While he drank, she checked his injuries and he told her about the gut-worm and the desecrated corpse of a dead conqueror. "Somebody took his skull. At least, I assume it was his skull. The other skeleton was wearing women's garb—"

"Huh," she said. "There's supposed to be a curse—"

"I know."

Only then, when she was satisfied that he could walk, did she lead him outside. A liver-bay mare with one white sock waited there. To his chagrin, Temur found himself hugging the mare with all the fervid affection he suddenly could not show for Samarkar. But the mare was warm and solid, and she blew softly against his hair while he clung to her neck.

Until, when Samarkar came up and touched him on the shoulder, he could turn to her without collapsing and say, "Thank you."

It was the gray part of morning before dawn, and he was shocked that so little time had passed. At first he asked her if he'd been trapped a day or more, but she shook her head. "One night only. I can imagine it seemed like more." She paused. "Which ones did this to you?"

"I'd know their voices." He shrugged then paused. "How did you know I was missing?"

"I . . . came to find you. And did not. Bansh led me to you."

There was a space in what she said. He thought he would come back to it. Maybe when his head wasn't spinning so much, his body aching. "Bansh?"

"She was waiting outside. She seemed to know where she was going."

"You should have brought Hsiung and Hrahima," he said. "What if there had been a fight?"

"I . . ." She looked down. "I didn't think of it."

In the gray morning, he sought her gaze. She seemed to fill herself with a resolute breath and turn her eyes deliberately upward. There was not so much space between them. Bansh stamped a hoof. It echoed in the cool dawn air. Some birds that Temur did not know were singing.

She leaned over and kissed Temur on the mouth. He kissed back, ignoring all the wisdom in his head about what a bad idea this was. He forgot, for a moment, the pain of bumps and bruises and a night spent hunched in the cold, the grit of grave dirt on his skin.

They pulled a little apart, but not fully.

"What an odd custom that is."

Her breath brushed his face. "Do you dislike it?"

"I don't know," he said. "Let's try it again."

17

By the time Samarkar and Temur had worked out to their satisfaction that however odd a custom kissing might seem, Temur was willing to experiment with it, the sun was lifting with slow dignity above the horizon, its pale rays trickling between the wind-tossed stems of grass. The whole steppe seemed to roll out before them, endless and vast. Temur leaned an aching hand on Bansh's flank and soaked in the warmth of the sun.

He might be filthy, nearly naked, and bruised black in all his limbs. But he had a purpose and he had a goal.

When the sun had lifted its belly clear of the grasses, he turned back to the west to see where they must go.

He must have gasped aloud, because Samarkar turned at once, a hand on his naked shoulder. She reeled back against Bansh's side as if struck. Without tearing his eyes from the western sky, Temur cast a muddy, bloody hand out to her.

She grasped his and held it.

A trail of gray-brown wood smoke crossed the turquoise sky. Temur knew with a plainsman's instincts that it came from the direction of Tzitzik's wooden hall. Before he knew what he was doing, he had a double handful of Bansh's sparse mane and was slithering across her bare back, belly down like a serpent until he could swing his left leg over and sit upright. She snorted and stamped a hoof with a sound like a wooden clog. Temur turned and offered a hand to Samarkar.

She needed it. Between them, they hauled her onto Bansh's back. Once she was settled she rode bareback well enough.

Temur let his hands rest, open, on the mare's shoulders. He knew she felt the shift of his weight, the pressure of a thigh as he urged her around. She broke into a trot, then a smoother canter, moving in a great easy circle until she faced the rising pall.

Samarkar said, as if begging him to disagree with her, "We caused that."

Temur said, "I know. Hold on."

Her hands tightened on his waist. He leaned forward, and the bay mare broke from a canter into a flat-necked run.

IF SAMARKAR HAD EXPERIENCED DOUBT DURING THEIR WILD FLIGHT back to the lizard-folk's hall that she and Temur were responsible for bringing disaster upon these people, she lost that reservation when they passed the gates of the burning hall and found the indigo-veiled body just within. One blue-veiled body, only one. And half a dozen of the woman-king's warriors, some gutted, some beheaded, one split like a boiled egg from bottom to top.

All around them, chaos reigned. The hall was burning. Men and women ran around it, screaming—some in combat, some weeping, some clutching children or valuables. Horses screamed in the stables, a sound so horrible Samarkar wished herself deaf. There were grooms; someone, surely, was trying to rescue the animals. Bansh stared in that direction, ears flat, eyes rolling white. Steady as she was, battle-hardened, she danced a step or two. The sweat that soaked Samarkar's trousers crotch to boot was not entirely the result of exertion.

"A bow," Temur said, looking over his shoulder. "A blade. Any-thing."

She slid down, realizing suddenly that he was all but naked on his equally naked mare, brown legs paler than Bansh's glossy brown barrel, his stocky body streaked with her sweat and the clinging dust of the dead emperor's tomb. But there were bows and arrows here, blades and bucklers. She threw him a helm, a pair of quivers. The bow and short sword she handed up.

He took them without looking at her, scanning the sack of the hall, watching skirmishing lizard-folk and assassins charge from place to place. His fingers brushed hers. He neither looked at her nor made a comment but pressed his hand to his mouth before raising the bow.

"I will see you again," he said to her, a soft promise. "In the Eternal Sky if not under it."

"We'll be reborn twinned stones," she answered, and saw him glance and smile. Then he lifted the bow and nocked an arrow, and Samarkar watched him kick his mare into the thick of battle.

She called up the sharp light of magic, aware that she was marking herself as a target. Clad in her borrowed brown coat, she moved toward a knot of men in indigo veils who were assailing the barricaded doors of a structure she did not know the purpose of.

TEMUR HAD NO TAB OR THUMB-RING, AND THE BOWSTRING CUT HIS fingers. The draw was unfamiliar, and the weapon itself overlong to use from the saddle—if he had even had a saddle to use it from. But it was a bow, and there was no bow made he could not kill with.

Into the storm of battle he rode his bay mare, aware that he was risking her, risking himself. That they were in no way prepared to fight. And aware also that this was his battle, and he could not leave the woman-king's people to fight it without him.

So he rode Bansh bareback by leg-grip and balance, laying down arrows on every side where men fought under the dragon banner. He saw Saura beset, back to the wall of the burning hall, and put an arrow through one of his attackers and into the other. He saw the woman-king herself—in a breastplate and wielding a lance from the deck of a chariot, shouting orders as her fighters regrouped around her. Hrahima fought beside her, hurling human bodies through the air as a man might hurl kittens, her arms red wet to the shoulders, her face a tiger-demon's mask of concentration.

And Temur saw the hordes of assassins, who must have attacked at dawnlight, swarming over the walls on ropes that still dangled there. These he killed at every turn, mostly with arrows. Bansh with her hooves and teeth shredded every one that came within striking distance of her, and Temur shot down those that would strike from afar.

His stolen quivers ran dry of arrows. He was groping for the hilt of the short sword when the mare turned and swung another quiver into his hands, the strap gripped between her teeth.

In surprise, Temur caught it. His surprise was not enough, though, to keep him from drawing an arrow from the quiver, nocking it, drawing, and loosing.

And again. And again.

SOME OF THE RAIDERS CAME ON HORSEBACK. FINE ASITANEH HORSES, like the ones the two mounted men in the pass below Tsarepheth had ridden, stormed past in clusters of two or three, the men on their backs raining fiery arrows. So much burned, everywhere the arrows fell. More than should have, Samarkar thought. The flames seemed . . . virulent.

Sorcerous or not, flame was something she could cope with. She strode through the courtyard, the heat and winds of her wards gusting about her, and into those wards she pulled the properties of fire when she passed close to it. Heat, tumult, and the need to consume. No arrow that flew toward her survived, and in the burning dwellings she passed, the flames guttered and died.

Samarkar felt more than heard the cries. A white-house stood in flames; outside it, someone restrained a young girl who wept and whose arms waved wildly. An assassin whose indigo veil had slipped in the struggle was attempting to drag her away, while others waited with bows to shoot anyone who ran from the blazing building. Samarkar did not need an interpreter to tell her what *Mami!* meant.

Samarkar ran between scorched piles of once-homes and heaped and bloodied bodies. She pulled a burning stick from a fallen house as she passed, and advanced upon the men.

Suddenly, someone was there beside her, just beyond the wards. From the corner of her eye, she recognized the chunky form and barrel body of Brother Hsiung. Whether he had come for her or because of the child's screaming she did not know. But as the assassin lifted the girl-child up and began to swing her around, Brother Hsiung entered the field like a stalking wolf and suddenly, effortlessly, took her from him.

The assassin sprawled on the ground, stunned for half a moment before he rocked up and rolled to his feet. In that moment, Samarkar hit him across the back of the head with her flaming club. She hit him twice more, for good measure. When she looked up again, she was surrounded by four dead or incapacitated assassins, and Brother Hsiung was thrusting the girl at her.

She tuned her wards so they would not burn the child, and grabbed her. A little thing, maybe eight summers, and some of them lean. Samarkar propped her on a hip and turned back to Hsiung.

He was running toward the burning house.

Samarkar cursed like a priest and ran after him, carrying the child, groping outward with all her strength to find the fire and draw it down.

THEY WERE WINNING, THAT WAS THE HELL OF IT. THE ASSASSINS WERE each worth several of Tzitzik's men, but there were not so many of them. And Temur, on Bansh's back, was winning through to Hrahima and Tzitzik when the vast, unspeakable shadow passed over.

The mare froze like a rabbit; Temur would have sworn he felt her very hide chill. He cowered unintentionally, dropping an arrow, and twisted to look up.

Its wings blotted out the sky.

"Rukh," he said, remembering. He could not see the end of it; it came and seemed to keep coming, and the wind of its passing swirled garbage from the packed earth, guttered flame, and blew his hair straight forward across his face. *How can we fight that?*

From the look on her feline face as she tipped her head back, Hrahima was thinking the same.

Tzitzik did not pause to think. She drew her strong hand back and hurled her silver-headed lance high, higher, so it should have glinted in the morning sun had not the rukh's shadow eclipsed it. It peaked, though, and began to fall back, and Temur checked frantically to make sure he would not be under it.

Arrows.

He fumbled the bow, lifted it, and with his right hand checked the quiver. Three arrows left, and it would be like shooting cactus needles at a water buffalo. Like trying to shoot down a dragon. He drew one from the quiver anyway and fitted it to the string.

His good mare shivered under him. He drew his knees up, came to his feet on her broad back. He stood, arched his head back, and lifted the bow.

Not an impossible shot, not with his *own* bow. Just a horribly unlikely one. Here, with this alien weapon—who could say?

Temur drew the string back to his jaw and found his anchor point. At that moment, the rukh's yellow eye looked straight at him. He saw clearly the indigo-veiled man it bore skyward, straddling its neck like the barrel of a mare.

The rukh folded wings too broad for comprehending and stooped into a dive.

When the rukh passed over, Samarkar was helping Hsiung drag a seared but living woman from the deadly shelter of her ravaged home. The child clutched to her bosom was entirely unharmed, and Samarkar thought that the woman would be scarred, but might live. If there were only one small triumph in this butcher's morning, she would take it.

And then the shadow fell across her face and she almost dropped to her knees in despair. She looked up; she saw the wings dark against the morning sky.

How did you fight something like that?

With wind, Wizard Samarkar.

She looked down at her hands. With wind.

She knew a little of wind.

She gathered it up, what she could. Pulled it into her hands. Coaxed it, coached it. For a moment, she remembered bitterly and too well that she was not Tse-ten of the Five Eyes. And then she closed her fingers tight to make fists and did it anyway.

The gust of wind struck the rukh just as it was folding its wings tight to stoop.

TEMUR SAW THE BIRD DIVE, AND HE SAW IT SLEW SIDEWAYS AS IF SOMEthing equally massive had struck it from the flank. The rukh's feather's gusted and flattened from the blow, and the veiled man on its back rocked side to side and clutched what must have been the harness, though distance and angle made it difficult to see.

Him, Temur thought, and felt the bow grow around him like the limbs of an ancient tree. He felt his breath; he felt himself fall into it. *That man, there.* That one who flew above the battlefield, so cowardly.

He was the man Temur needed to kill. For Edene and for everyone.

His fingers relaxed on the string. The arrow snapped forward.

Before it left the bow, someone struck him—and Bansh—from the side.

THE GREAT BIRD TUMBLED. SAMARKAR HIT IT AGAIN AND AGAIN. SHE watched its laborious wingbeats as it righted itself. She watched it catch the wind properly and become the master of the air again. *Not enough,* she thought, as the yellow eye found her, as the bird came about into the wind.

"Get back," she yelled, knowing she did not have enough time to run for cover. "Get back! Everybody get away from me!"

TEMUR ROLLED SIDEWAYS, THE MARE STAGGERING AS ANOTHER HORSE charged into her side. If he'd had a saddle, he might have stayed on his mount; as it was, he slipped sideways from his perch atop her back and fell.

Fortunately, he had a good deal of experience falling off of horses. He hit the ground and rolled, one hand scrabbling for his borrowed short sword.

All the breath left him, and the pain of old bruises awakened. Someone landed atop him. He heard the squeals as Bansh fought back against the horse that had attacked her. He would have levered himself up and gone to cripple the beast, but whoever straddled his chest hit him sharply across the face.

Temur hit back. Once and again, punching with his empty hand and with the hand clenched on the hilt of the sword. He should have drawn it and used it properly, but there was no opportunity. The enemy was too close. He hit, was all. He hit and hit again.

The man fell back, and Temur clung to his collar and let him pull them both together as they rolled. He lost the sword and struck barehanded, only half cognizant of the blows that landed on his own body and face. He had the assassin's collar in both hands when he realized he recognized the other man's eyes: hazel, dark-ringed, bright-centered.

His grip must have softened, because the assassin was atop him. A sharp blow knocked Temur prone; dizzy, he fought to focus his eyes. Horses squealed nearby; the thud of hooves on flesh. Mares fighting.

The assassin pulled something from his belt—a pistol, an un-reliable but destructive western weapon that used black powder to hurl a lead ball at the target with shattering force. In the struggle, the Nameless one's indigo veil had pulled free. Temur found him-self looking into the face of the man he'd fought three times now, making an effort to focus past the black pit of the barrel to see, finally, the features of his enemy.

It was a bland, ordinary Uthman face, except for those extraordinary eyes.

"We would have kept you alive," the Nameless said, in Qersnyk, "if you hadn't proven so difficult. But your woman will serve as well. Better, if she's biddable."

Temur lay sprawled under the gun, the Nameless kneeling over him. "My woman," he said, the knowledge that Edene was alive and captive a numbing shock. *"Edene?"*

The Nameless smiled. He swung his pistol up, to sight between Temur's eyes. "Die with it," he said—

Bansh kicked the assassin's skull in from the side.

ALL THE HEAT AND ALL THE WIND SAMARKAR HAD PULLED INTO HERself, she unleashed it now. The rukh screamed. She saw its great bronze-colored feathers shriveling like flower petals before the heat. She saw it ignore the pain and beat its wings hard to align itself above her, when her winds would have pushed it away.

She saw the flock upon flock upon flock of birds that suddenly surrounded it, mobbing it like songbirds mob an eagle, pestering and pulling and diving at its head. One bold one even pulled the plumage of its crest.

They were vultures and ravens, carrion beasts, and Samarkar had never been so glad to see them in her life. The rukh swatted at them, snapped and snatched—but it could catch none, and before long they had it running.

THE SOUND OF THE GUNSHOT SHATTERED TEMUR'S MIND. HE LAY stunned, certain he was shot, as the assassin slumped atop him, his temple caved in, blood and gray jelly oozing across the ruin of his face. Bansh was there, then, pushing her pink-spotted nose against Temur's cheek, *whuff*ing sharply. She might have whickered. Temur felt a vibration but did not hear her. He lay still, panting, as she shoved her muzzle under the dead assassin and pushed him off Temur.

Only then did Temur find the strength to sit up, to draw in a breath that hurt enough to convince him that he was not dead. He knelt; the mare dropped her neck beside him. He threw an arm across it, behind her ears, and clung while she lifted him to his feet. She was filthy and wet with blood and sweat, scraped and battered; he leaned against her and tried to turn so he could watch for anyone that might approach to hurt them.

Smoke drifted on the sky; people—lizard-folk, not Nameless—stood here and there, turning slowly, looking at one another as if expecting an enemy. Temur shook his head; through the ringing, he faintly began to hear the sound of the wind, of the fire, of people talking.

Samarkar came up behind him and spoke softly, said his name, summoned him back from the place he had drifted to. He turned to her, the blood and soot on his body streaked with sweat, eyes aching with smoke and unshed tears.

The wizard put a hand on his shoulder. He slumped against Bansh and closed his eyes. Samarkar was scratched and exhausted, smoke-stained, her hands blistered as if she had been handling naked fire. Who knew? Maybe she had been.

"Come back, Temur," she said. "We've lived through it."

18

Tzitzik feasted them again, but this time it was a somber affair. There were too many dead and too much to consider for anything to be otherwise.

They ate under the setting sun and the open sky, gathered around campfires, because the ancient hall had burned and many of Tzitzik's sworn band had burned along with it.

The few who remained—among them Saura, for a mercy—no longer seemed inclined to take offense at anything the easterners did or said or any attention they received. Nothing, though, could alleviate the sorrow of the woman-king over her losses. And to Temur's distaste, it became his task to further burden her.

"The kurgan of Danupati," he said, "has been desecrated."

Saura translated, and Tzitzik turned to Temur with eyes afire with rage. Quickly and down the bare bones, he outlined what had been done to him and what he had discovered—the warlord's skeleton with its missing head, the infestation of gut-worms. He did not ask what would be done to those who had tried to murder him, but he noticed a significant glance from Samarkar when he brushed past the topic.

"Someone came here to sow war," Tzitzik said, finally, through Saura. Her chin rested on her fingers. A wooden trencher lay on the grass before her, food untouched. "To sow war all across our ancient domain. Someone incurred the curse, intentionally."

Hrahima snorted. "You know I have my theories."

The woman-king pushed a morsel of baked grain around with the point of her knife. "Do you know how Danupati died?"

Temur glanced at Samarkar, who shook her head. "I think not."

Tzitzik looked about herself. Her sworn band sat close, and Temur knew some of them were probably those who had tried out of jealousy to kill him. But that had been before the battle, in a time that might as well be the width of the world away. He set aside his anger.

She spoke, and Saura translated. "He died not in battle, but of an illness. The Black Bloat, some say, but the truth is no one knows. Except that when he took ill, he mounted up his best mare and rode her into the desert, where he died in the saddle. The mare brought his body back."

"That is a sad story," Temur said.

"After a fashion," Tzitzik said. "Some say he could not sing his death song, being too weak, and so the mare sang it for him. But of course, who could have witnessed such a thing?"

"That would be some mare."

The woman-king smiled. "They say she was a liver-bay with one white hoof," she said. "You tell me."

Their gazes locked. A peculiar shiver ran up Temur's spine. He sat back, suddenly no more interested in his dinner than Tzitzik was.

She could have asked him where he would go, what he would do. But she knew the answer: He would go and get Edene and bring her home again. He would hunt down the man on the rukh, and if that man was not the master of the Nameless, he would use him to find whoever was.

The woman-king looked back at her neglected plate and said,

"When you are done with that bird rider, Qersnyk, I want his skull to wash my hands in. You can count on my help in making it so."

Temur said, "It will be yours."

In the morning, Samarkar, Temur, Hrahima, Bansh, and Brother Hsiung made for the coast. Two days' fast ride, Tzitzik said. It would have been five, if they went easy for their own sake and the battered mare's, as they should have. As they could not, when they were hunted. Despite the chaos of her household, Tzitzik pushed supplies upon the travelers—camel fat, measures of grain for Bansh, a little of the local beer.

Samarkar knew they should have traveled by night. But she also knew that there was no easy way to avoid the rukh and its rider if it returned, and sleeping out by day in these endless grasslands would not hide them much better than walking.

They would rely on speed, instead, and resting as little as possible. They would walk by moonlight and the light of the sun. Although, she thought with irony as they staggered through darkness that night, it was possible that rukhs, like owls, could fly by night.

At least what Tzitzik had told them about the Hard Drinker emptying into the White Sea was no exaggeration. Samarkar had known they must be drawing closer, because the trees that lined the Hard Drinker's banks grew more squat and twisted. Samarkar had heard that seas were salty, and she wondered if that was the cause of it—or if it was the increasingly poor and sandy soil.

In any case, nothing could prepare her for the sight of the White Sea itself.

They'd been forced farther and farther from the channel of the Hard Drinker as she flattened and broadened into a swampy delta. Samarkar had already been expecting water for half a day when they crested a little rise among stunted conifers. The branches were swept to the east by the same ceaseless wind that lifted Samarkar's unbraided hair and—despite the summer's heat—cooled her face. That wind smelled of nothing she'd ever experienced before: tangy, rotten, sweet and salty both at once, strong and bitter. She sneezed, and Bansh flattened her long neck, tossed her head, and sneezed as well.

When Samarkar opened her eyes, the blue stretched to the horizon. It moved, too—she'd heard of waves, of course, but reading of them or studying Song prints could not prepare her for that vast, white-capped expanse, or the way the sun glittered off it.

"Mother," Temur said. Hrahima laughed behind her whiskers.

Samarkar could barely see a smudge at the horizon that might be land. Thirty *li* at least—and this was supposed to be the narrows, the place where a natural dam separated the White Sea from an arm of the Western Ocean.

"Tzitzik said to light a signal fire." Samarkar could see a rocky promontory from here, and the soot-stained fire ring at its tip. "And a ship would put in eventually."

She wondered exactly what a ship looked like, if this was an ocean. At least there was wood enough in the stunted forest behind.

But on her left, Brother Hsiung made a throat-cutting gesture and rolled his eyes. When Samarkar glanced at him inquiringly, he pointed to the skies.

Of course. A fire would summon enemies as well as allies. Samarkar bit her lip and comforted herself that she'd have thought of that before calling down the devil on their heads.

Temur said, "We cannot walk around. I suppose we could follow the shore northeast, until we come to a village."

He sounded dubious. Hrahima shook her head. "Or Asmaracanda," she said. "That could take a moon or more."

"And Asmaracanda is under Qersnyk control, unless it, too, has fallen. Do you want to risk your uncle's men, Temur?"

"No," he said.

Samarkar took a deep breath. Calmly, she stretched up on tiptoe, measuring the distances against her hand. Of course it was hard to do, but if she could *see* land at all, and what lay on the other side was not mountainous . . .

She dropped to the ground and began stripping off her boots.

Temur frowned down at her, needing no explanation. "You'll never make it."

The set of his mouth warmed her. They hadn't spoken alone or touched except in passing since the morning when they kissed, but she felt his regard in his concern. Still, she was the only one who could do this.

"Of course I will," she scoffed, tugging her heel free. "I'm Samarkar. I've been swimming in the Tsarethi since before I could walk. Just because *you* can't swim . . ."

TEMUR WANTED TO REACH OUT AND GRAB HER STRONG ARM ABOVE the elbow, where the flesh dimpled in to show the bone and the scars of the Nameless arrow lingered. Instead he stayed his hand and made a fist of it, hiding it in the folds of the robe he'd been wearing off and on since Nilufer gave it to him for protection in crossing the desert.

He said, "Bansh can swim it."

Samarkar snorted. "With you on her back? Both of you still injured from your fights? Don't think I haven't seen the cuts and bruises. You'll kill your pony in the sea, man."

Not to mention yourself. But she wouldn't say that.

She lifted her chin as the sea air lifted her hair, rough streamers draping her shoulders and trailing as if the tide already washed them. He had a vision of her drowned.

But her eyes were trained on the western shore. "I can see across," she said. "What I can see, I can swim to."

Temur looked to Brother Hsiung for support, but the monk shrugged and folded his arms across his chest. He wasn't about to get in the way of a wizard of Tsarepheth. And Hrahima had wandered off down the shore, where she was turning over driftwood and prospecting among the weeds tossed on the shore—whether out of curiosity or after something edible, Temur had no idea.

Samarkar stripped off her clothing with rough efficiency, handing each piece to Brother Hsiung to fold and store in Bansh's saddle-bags. Brother Hsiung averted his eyes after her coat came off, merely holding out one hand behind him. She gave him her jeweled collar as well, to be padded and packed reverentially. Even her loincloth she pushed down her hips and seemed about to discard, but at the last moment she paused, twisting travel-stained linen between her hands.

Her breasts were full, slightly pendulous. Temur winced to see the scars of her neutering and how they marred the round moon of her belly. Travel had slackened her flesh, shrunken her ripe hips.

If she stayed with him, he could offer her nothing different. Not for a long time.

"I'll need the gold," she said, as Brother Hsiung made himself scarce by walking down the beach toward Hrahima. "To hire a boat to come and fetch you. Also, the grease for the lamp."

Silently, he handed her what she asked for. While Samarkar coated her body liberally with the oil from the camel fat, he milked the mare and exchanged the fermented milk in her saddle-skin for fresh. While Samarkar twisted her loincloth into a kind of harness and sewed the gold inside, Temur sharpened his knife on a stone. When the edge was a razor, he sheathed it and stood. Taking up the bowl of *airag*, Temur went to stand by Bansh's fine-boned dark head. He touched her soft nose, admiring how the sunlight filled her hide with gleams of red and white-gold.

"Bring me clean water," he said to the naked woman, and realized only when she returned with the leathern pail brimming and cold with the salty seawater, that he'd addressed a princess and a wizard as if she were a serving girl. She merely arched an eyebrow as she handed it over, but he looked down, abashed.

He took a rag and washed the mare's neck. Not until he drew the honed knife from his pocket and felt for the heat and pressure of the vein behind delicate skin did Samarkar lay her fingertips on his hand. "Temur," she said.

"You will have this," he said, and nicked the mare's neck with the sharpest bit of blade.

The trickle that ran from the cut was deep red, flowing freely but not too strong. He reached out his hand; Samarkar put the bowl into it, and Temur pressed it into place to catch the flow of blood. Red ran into white, a puddle then a spiral as Temur swirled the cup to mix it. He handed the cup to Samarkar and picked up the salt-water-soaked rag once more.

"Drink it while it's warm." His good mare didn't snort once, until he pressed the rag to her wound, staunching the flow. She stamped and leaned away but did not move off.

When he turned back, though, Samarkar was still staring at him over the wooden rim. He raised his brows; silently she toasted him and downed the draught.

"Take the camel fat, too." He pressed harder against Bansh's neck, though the bleeding had stopped. "You can suck on it while you swim. And take my knife in case you have to fight something."

THE SEA WAS WARM AT THE SURFACE, COLD IF SHE LET HER LEGS DIP below that top layer. It was challenging at first; the waves approaching the beach had strong currents and eddies. But even they did not rival the currents of the Tsarethi. And once she was out past the breakers into the swells, she found it was easy to time them, and she let them lift her on their backs like a mother dandling a child. The water seemed thicker than water she had known before, bearing her up more easily, and Samarkar's wizard mind wondered if that was a result of the salt she could taste in it. Salt could make an egg float; why not a woman?

After the first few *li*, Samarkar found her rhythm. She stroked long and evenly, working for endurance rather than speed. There was a long way to go, and she did not want to exhaust herself. It was hard to pace herself, though, and her only opportunities to rest would come while treading water. Hard to remember that her left arm was still weaker than it should be and might fail her or cramp disastrously.

She could rest, though, and that was a way in which this sea was different from the mountain rivers she had learned in. There, to rest was to risk being dashed into rocks or swept out of the safe parts of the river. Here, it just meant losing time while you floated.

Losing time—and losing ground, she soon realized. Because there was a current here, something she had not anticipated. She'd been thinking of this sea as a big lake, static water. But she could see the land on the far side slipping past.

The White Sea, she remembered, flowed through the Strait of Asitaneh into the Western Ocean. It drained all the north- and west-flowing rivers on this side of the Steles.

Of course it had a current. She should have started off a good way upstream. But she was committed now; there was no option except to keep going or turn back and admit defeat.

Samarkar cursed herself for an idiot and kept swimming, nibbling pieces of Temur's camel fat from time to time for strength and trying not to swallow too much seawater while she did so. The sun might bake her, the salt water parch her skin. She was the wizard Samarkar. She was not going to quietly drown.

NIGHT FELL, A BLESSED RELIEF FROM THE BATTERING SUN. A SINGLE moon rose, a cupped sliver guiding her with its light.

She was tired. She ached in every limb. Hunger cramped her stomach; exhaustion cramped her muscles. She called upon wizarding disciplines now and hoped that would be enough to give her strength.

She had sat unmoving in a hole in the cold darkness for three days and walked out a magician. What was swimming a sea to that?

Samarkar looked into herself and found the quiet. The quiet sustained her. She swam on.

THE SUNSET. IT SPILLED THROUGH THE HALLS OF ALA-DIN THROUGH each high window, its angle low enough now to make the shades and awnings useless. Because Ala-Din stood on a high place, the sun dipped below it before it dipped below the rim of the world. Edene followed its light as it rose through the bastion, sweeping up walls and across ceilings.

She stole down passages, a tray in her hands, anonymous in her veil among other women scurrying with short steps and hunched shoulders. The stronghold was still empty, curiously so—the monks had not returned yet from whatever excursion took most of them away. Several of the old masters remained behind, too infirm for hard travel, and a half dozen of the youngest novices, who were beardless boys still.

That tray was her safe conduct, and she carried it before her like a shield until she came to al-Sepehr's rooms. They were not locked— what need had al-Sepehr to lock his own rooms at the very heart of his power?—and Edene slipped inside with little trouble.

She set the tray on a stool beside the door and closed the door softly. The latch clicked; she pulled in the cord that made it easy to open from the outside. Anyone who wanted to come in now would have to break the door open.

She did not think she would need very much time.

He might have taken the ring with him, and a terrible unease filled Edene when she realized it no longer sat so carelessly in the teakwood tray on his chest. Forcing herself to move calmly, she crouched, her belly pressing her thighs wide, and opened the lid.

It was heavy and plain, lined with cedar, from the smell. Sturdy brass hinges operated without a squeak.

Edene lifted the first layer of woven cotton and found a small silk pouch embroidered in Song style just below. It lay flat, as if empty or nearly so. When she lifted it, she could feel a smooth, hard round within, so heavy it startled her.

Now her hands trembled as the tugged at the drawstrings. They shook so much when she tried to reach inside the pouch that she gave in and upended the contents into her palm.

A ring.

Plain and stark as the room she squatted in, crudely hammered so it barely shone, its only beauty was in the metal. She'd never seen metal quite this color; not green and also *not* not-green, exactly, but more the color a leaf would be if a plant grew gold.

She held it in her palm. It was cold. She lifted it to her eye. When her breath blew across it, the metal misted. It was made of one continuous piece that must have been cast that way, or pierced and stretched. There was no inscription within or without, no symbols etched into the band. Just hammer marks.

It weighed more, she thought, than even gold should weigh.

She stood up, aware as always of late how her balance had shifted from the day before, aware of how the life inside her changed her body. Trembling still, she slipped the ring onto her finger.

Her hand vanished before her eyes, as if a layer of soft dust blew across it.

IT WAS NOT LAND SAMARKAR FOUND AT LAST, BUT A SHIP. A SHIP FULL of men very surprised to pull a naked woman from the sea. But they wrapped her in blankets and gave her boiled coffee on the brazier, so sugared she would normally have found it undrinkable. She hadn't had coffee since she lived in Song, and the burnt astringency and syrupy sweetness seared through her fast and hard. It stopped her shivering, though, and gave her empty stomach something to cramp around.

The deck of the ship pitched beneath her, all its instability feeling peculiarly solid after so long in the sea. The crew clustered around her until one—the captain?—yelled at them to get back to work. Samarkar watched the bustle in awe. It seemed to require a lot of constant effort to keep the square sails doing what they should.

The presumptive captain alone approached her. "Do you speak human?" he asked in Uthman.

She blinked, only then realizing that the whole time they hauled her from the sea, she had not spoken a word. "I do," she said, her voice creaky with disuse. She coughed and sipped more syrupy coffee. "I need your help. I want to pay you to carry some passengers from the far shore to Asitaneh."

"Pay us?" he laughed. "With what?"

Silently, she untied the sling from around her waist and began counting out heavy, hammer-struck coins of Rasan gold. "There's more on the far shore," she said. "And Rasan salt. And Ato Tesafa-hun will no doubt reward you for our rescue as well."

The name, as she had hoped, was one to conjure with. She spoke it, and suddenly men moved to wrap her in still more dry blankets and replace her empty cup with one filled with a gruel of beef and grain.

TEMUR FOUND TO HIS SURPRISE THAT THE BOAT SUITED HIM WELL. It was like a mare of the sea. Brother Hsiung did not enjoy the rock-ing motion, however, and Samarkar was kept busy treating him for nausea.

Samarkar: Temur would never forget how she had looked, wav-ing to him from the prow of a longboat in sailors' borrowed clothes. The way his heart had leaped up to see her.

After all their adventures, it seemed a little ridiculous how easy it was to reach Temur's grandfather. The hardest part was getting Bansh on and off the ship, and the crew had slings and tackle they seemed accustomed to using for just such a process. Samarkar swam out with the mare and dove under her belly to secure the sling, while Temur waited unsettled for her on the deck and called down en-couragement and praise.

Temur was grateful that it was Bansh who had to be so treated, and not Buldshak.

The passage was quick and uneventful. After less than a day, Asitaneh came into view—the fabled city of red stone and onion-topped towers that guarded the strait. The ship docked, its captain and men much the richer. They led Bansh down the gangplank, Temur first having muffled her hooves in sacking so the hollow ring of the wood underfoot would not frighten her. Deep in his heart, he suspected that it was more to comfort him than because she needed the reassurance. And Hrahima—after sending a runner ahead with a message to expect them—simply brought them through the crowded, bustling streets as if it were of no more consequence than bringing the flock in for shearing.

Temur had seen cities before, of course—but nothing quite like Asitaneh. Its streets were *paved*, with the same red stone of which its walls were built, and some of its towers were six stories or more. The streets crawled with people—a living carpet of them—the majority of the women veiled and cloaked, the men wearing shawls draped over their heads and filleted in place against the sun. People stared openly at Samarkar, who had resumed her worn black coat and jade collar, and who wore her long hair combed shining over her shoulders.

They saw the caliph's men on their dish-nosed geldings and mares, sunlight glittering off tassled saddles as adorned with bullion and silk as an emperor's chair. They saw beggars and cripples and half-naked slaves hustling along barefoot, bearing heavy baskets. They passed water sellers and concealed nobility in palanquins.

The city had more than one market—they passed three, and Hrahima told Samarkar that none of these was even the main one. In one, there were camels lined up, unharnessed except for plain halters, and a stern-looking man in black walked along the line, scowling at each one.

"Are they for sale?" Temur asked.

"It's a show," Hrahima said, as one of the camels stamped its big soft foot. "A sort of . . . beauty contest."

"Oh," Temur said, reaching out to touch the shoulder of his mare. She was warm, reassuringly solid. Here was a people that sent their women about under blankets and showed off their camels. Well, he was Qersnyk; it was not for him to question the ways of others.

He tripped on the edge of a paving stone but did not fall. When he looked up from his stumble there was music—cymbals, drums, the wild ululations of women. The crowd parted as if before a procession. . . .

Actually, that was not far from the truth. Women, a dozen of them, were arranged in two lines of four, with four in the middle. They wore gauzy veils that displayed only their eyes and the high piles of their glossy hair, which chimed and shone with gold. Tenspan skirts in teal and vermilion swirled around their switching hips; halters and tiers of necklaces covered their bosoms. Their midriffs were bare, navels shining with jewels, and the stone walls rang with their cries. The four in the middle—by their black hair and firm bodies, younger—danced. The ones on either side—by *their* graying hair and the slackness of their bellies, older—drummed and sang. Coins rained down among them from passersby, and the dancing women swooped and bowed to collect them.

"Hasitani," Hrahima said, when Samarkar stopped to stare.

"Sacred whores?" she asked softly.

"Mendicant scientists," Hrahima said. "You would like them."

"Huh." They passed, but Samarkar turned to watch them, and Temur saw her reach into her pouch and hurl a shower of small silver to the road among their horny, naked feet.

There was not too much farther to walk after that encounter. Hrahima led them until they reached the house of Ato Tesafahun. She presented herself at the wrought-iron gate and spoke through it to a servant. There was a brief pause—probably, Temur thought, for consultation—and then he returned and admitted them.

IT WAS EVENING WHEN THEY ENTERED THE GARDEN OF ATO TESEFAhun. Great walls held the city and the desert out; they were of red clay smoothed over red stone. A bubbling fountain played amidst a stone patio, and gracious trees gave shade all around the edges. Except for datura and moonwise, Temur could not even name the flowers. There was one like clusters of tiny paper lanterns in brilliant shades of pink and orange, its vines draping through the trees. There was another that grew at their feet and was green and lush and covered with four-pointed pale blue blossoms like stars.

As the sky dimmed, the glow they twinkled in was cast by candles, fixed in glass jars to the shells of ambling tortoises, so as the sun set, the whole of the garden was filled with a moving light. Birds sang themselves to sleep in the tree branches, and the twilight made a canopy overhead.

Ato Tesefahun waited for them in his garden, on a bench before a table set with a meal of strange foods: bread and cured olives with garlic and salt, sliced fruits, sweet wine with lemon slices floating in it. He stood when Temur, Hrahima, Brother Hsiung, and Samarkar entered, setting aside the small bound book he had been cupping in the palm of his hand.

He was not a tall man, nor was he young. But his hair hovered in a white cloud all around his lined, mole-sprinkled face, and his long age-gaunt brown hands were deft. "Welcome to my home," he said. "I am Tesefahun."

"Grandfather," Temur said, through the portcullis of emotion that bid fair to close his throat. "It is a joy to meet you, finally."

THE RUKH FURLED HER WINGS AND DROPPED LIKE A STONE THROUGH the sky. Al-Sepehr knew she wished she could kill him, shake him from her back and then dive to catch him in her talons and crush him where she fell. And he knew also that she never would, that the lives of her mate and offspring were surety for her obedience.

It amused him.

She snapped her wings at the last possible moment, an impact with the air as ferocious as striking a mountainside. He had been expecting it, yet his head still snapped forward painfully. Someday she was going to break his neck.

Well, she would pay the price if she did.

Al-Sepehr waited while she back-winged and settled atop the highest tower, half its width from the veiled woman who waited there. As he swung off her neck, the woman bowed low, hiding even her eyes.

It didn't matter. He knew them. "Saadet," he said. "I am sorry to tell you your brother is dead."

She nodded, eyes still downcast. "I remember. What he was persists. And I still serve you."

It should not have reassured him, but it did. And even eased the lance of grief in his own gut. Shahruz had, perhaps, been the closest thing al-Sepehr could count as a friend.

"I must inform you that the prisoner has escaped, al-Sepehr."

"Good. She found the ring then?"

Saadet nodded, using the motion as an excuse to steal a glance at his face.

Al-Sepehr felt in his empty pocket and smiled. "She will bring our war to the Qersnyk, then. Your brother will be avenged."

THAT NIGHT, IN TEMUR'S GRANDFATHER'S HOUSE, IN YET ANOTHER alien bed, Samarkar came to Temur in darkness. There was a whir of fabric as she dropped her robe. And then she slipped under the covers beside him and took him in her arms.

The ghost of the sea lingered between her breasts like yesterday's perfume.

TSAREG EDENE WALKED EAST, AWAY FROM ALA-DIN.

She did not know how long she had been walking. A long time, sunrise and sunset, across the barren land. She had not drunk the water she brought with her. She had not been thirsty. She had not worn the cloak she carried. She had not been cold. She had little food, but she was not hungry.

A carpet of scorpions ringed her, scuttling on every side, and she had no trouble from serpents or any other predator.

She cast no shadow on the stones below her, not by moonlight or by sunlight. She could not see her own foot, her own hand. It was as if nothing could affect her. Except the babe in her belly, which grew heavier with every passing day.

Once, the shadow of a great bird passed over. She turned to

watch it go, and felt no fear. No horror. The bird could not harm her. The ring burned cold and heavy on her hand. Such a comforting weight, like a lover's arm.

She was in the world but not of it. When she came to the sea, she though she might just walk across.

When I am Khatun, she thought, *I will see to it that women are not stolen from their families. I will see that wars do not rage over who will be king of what and where and when.*

Edene had to press her hand against her mouth to keep from bursting out laughing. The scorpions kept pace easily. They made a dry sound over the desert stones.

A loving voice echoed her silently. *Yes. Edene. That is how it shall be. When you are Queen.*

✳

To be continued in
THE SHATTERED PILLARS

✳